Praise for Jodi Thomas

"Jodi Thomas is a masterful storyteller. She grabs your attention on the first page, captures your heart, and then makes you sad when it's time to bid her wonderful characters farewell. You can count on Jodi Thomas to give you a satisfying and memorable read."
—Catherine Anderson, *New York Times* bestselling author

"Thomas sketches a slow, sweet surrender."
—*Publishers Weekly*

"Compelling and beautifully written, it is exactly the kind of heart-wrenching, emotional story one has come to expect from Jodi Thomas."
—Debbie Macomber, #1 *New York Times* bestselling author

"Tender, realistic, and insightful."
—*Library Journal*

"Once I started [*Ransom Canyon*], I quickly found myself unable to put down this book."
—*Night Owl Reviews*

"This book is like once again visiting old friends while making new ones and will leave readers eager for the next visit. A pure joy to read."
—*RT Book Reviews*

"This is terrific reading from page one to the end. Jodi Thomas is a passionate writer who puts real feelings into her characters."
—*Fresh Fiction*

Also available from Jodi Thomas

RANSOM CANYON

ebook novella
WINTER'S CAMP

Don't miss LONE HEART PASS and the rest of the books
in the Ransom Canyon series!

JODI
THOMAS

RUSTLER'S
MOON

ISBN-13: 978-0-373-78980-1

Rustler's Moon

For questions and comments about the quality of this book, please contact us at CustomerService@Harlequin.com.

www.HQNBooks.com

Printed in U.S.A.

RUSTLER'S
MOON

PROLOGUE

Anna Marie Island, Florida
September

Angela Harold sat in her father's cluttered office, still wearing the black dress she'd worn to his funeral. She stared at the framed picture on his desk. The one she'd given him when she was seven. Their first fishing trip. He was smiling, the sun shining off his glasses. She stood by his side holding up a fish half her length.

A memory saved forever in the heart. For Angela, this one photo had come to signify the time before the fall. Before Florida. Before her mother's illness. Before her father started withering inside. Before she'd felt trapped in her life.

Only now the bars that held her here were crumbling like columns of sugar in the rain. She should feel free, but all Angela felt was fear. A trapped bird staring at an open cage door. Afraid to fly. Afraid to stay.

The police had explained to her the night they'd found his body that he'd been mugged as he left his office. Neither the blows he'd suffered nor the gash on his head when he'd fallen had killed him. But his heart hadn't been strong enough to survive the attack. Benjamin Harold's heart may have stopped three days ago, but he'd stopped living years ago, one unfulfilled dream at a time.

"Who robs the bookkeeper on a Sunday night?" Angela whispered to the smiling man in the picture. The antiques store had been closed that day. Her father had said he was going in to straighten out the books. Whoever attacked him couldn't have gotten more than a few hundred dollars from his wallet. They couldn't have known about his weak heart.

Out of curiosity, she flipped open her father's ledger book. He'd kept the books for his brother's business since they first moved to Florida when she was seven. Her uncle Anthony owned the multimillion-dollar antiques business and he trusted no one with the books but her father. After all, Anthony might be the head of the company, but his brother had loaned him the money to get started. The last entry was a transfer from the store's account to a numbered bank account.

She stared at the logbook and recalled the family story. Her father had loaned his younger brother, Anthony, fifty thousand dollars and the priceless necklace that was his inheritance for display once the store was built. The necklace was an heirloom and had been in the family for generations: an ancient Greek coin set in a cradle of gold and diamonds. Her grandparents' will had stipulated the necklace go to the oldest son and never be sold off for profit.

In those early days, it was the one draw to an antiques store full of otherwise questionable treasures.

In exchange for the loan and letting the store display the necklace, Anthony agreed that her father would always be the bookkeeper. He'd have a job as long as he lived. Her father, who'd lost half a dozen jobs in his thirties and been injured at his last employment site, saw the offer as too good to turn down, even though he and Anthony had never been close.

Only, her father had grown tired of his brother's questionable practices, even though the company flourished, opening stores all along the East Coast. Her father wanted no part of the profits and took only his salary as Uncle Anthony grew rich selling early colonial antiques that came on a boat from China.

Angela knew her father would have quit years ago if her mother hadn't been ill. A slow-moving cancer had eaten away at her body. At first they fought with operations and treatments between short periods of remission, until she was finally too weak to fight any more. Angela stayed with her, missing proms and dating and sleepovers through her teen years.

For a few hours each day, the tiny office became her father's refuge from the constant reality of his wife's illness. Once out of college, Angela got a job at a local museum and moved in with her parents to help. By then, her mother needed constant care and Angela and her father managed the night shift.

When her mother passed peacefully in her sleep at home, Angela felt as if she lost her father, too. Within weeks, he was working six, sometimes seven, days a week in his office, usually late into the night. At first, she'd thought he was simply *catching up*, but finally she understood he was hiding away, living a little less each day.

"Something's not right," he'd sometimes mutter when he came home late. He mentioned more than once his concern over the company's accounting.

She asked if he'd talked to Anthony about it and her father had simply smiled and told her not to worry, that his brother didn't want to hear about problems.

Angela picked up the fishing picture as his worry over the accounts seemed to echo in her memory. She wished she could have helped him. "I love you, Dad," she whispered to his picture.

Absently, she flipped over the frame to see if the note she had put in the back saying how she loved him to the moon and back was still there.

She opened the frame and a small piece of paper fell out. She recognized her writing and the hearts drawn all around the edges.

Smiling, she pulled it out and noticed, in deep pen marks, someone had scribbled something on the back of her note. The note was addressed "To my Angel" and dated three days ago. *The day he died.*

"You have to get away from here," the note read. Three words were printed in all capitals. "RUN DISAPPEAR VANISH. Your life depends on it. Trust no…"

He hadn't finished. Something must have stopped him. Maybe a noise in the alley that interrupted his thoughts. She imagined him hastily returning the unfinished note to the frame, then going to investigate.

For a while she looked from the picture to the note, to the ledger. Florida was her home. Why would he tell her to run?

He must have known he was in danger. The police said the phone line to his office had been cut, but the muggers couldn't have known he'd left his cell at home that night, as usual. And even if he knew he was in danger, why would he tell her to run or disappear?

A chill slid along her spine. Her father had hidden the note. He'd been afraid someone would find it. Someone besides her.

Bits of conversation they'd had over the past few weeks circled in her mind. He'd suggested she apply for a curator job in Texas he'd seen online, even posted the job opening on the note board in the kitchen to remind her. He'd told her it would be good to get away. He'd brought home a little trailer he'd picked up at a yard sale and tucked it away in a garage full of other useless junk. He'd transferred all his stocks to her name, claiming he no longer had time to keep up with them.

Maybe he never guessed he would be mugged, but suspected his heart might give out. Or had he feared violence might be coming his direction? Now, looking back, she wondered if he had wanted her to leave Florida so he could do the same. But why? He had a job for life. Even if Uncle Anthony was shady in his dealings, Benjamin would never have turned in his own brother.

She'd thought all his changes were part of the grieving for her mother, but now she reconsidered. Her forever-organized father must have had a plan, but what?

Slowly, she saw the answer. Not in the picture, or the note he'd written, but in the ledger. The numbered account where he'd transferred the money was hers, and the amount was exactly what he'd loaned his brother years ago. He didn't even calculate the interest he was entitled to.

Her father might not have ever been able to leave Florida, but he was telling her to and making sure she had the funds to do it.

No, not telling, demanding. Even from the grave.

Angela stood, put the note back behind the picture, stuffed the frame and the ledger into her purse, and walked out of her father's office.

How could she disappear? Everyone she knew lived in Florida, which admittedly wasn't too many. She'd had a few jobs in college, but she'd always worked alone in the back of a museum. She had no real friends she could call on, and all the family she had left belonged to her uncle Anthony. Even at the funeral they'd treated her as if they thought she might try to claim part of the Harold Antiques Company now that her father was dead.

She needed answers and couldn't think of leaving before she had them. Tomorrow she'd begin. She might be a mouse of a warrior, but at dawn she'd begin her quest. Once she had answers to why her father had left such a strange note, she'd take his advice. She'd vanish. There was nothing left for her here. Her relatives wouldn't miss her. Her job had dwindled to part-time. She hadn't had the time to develop even one friendship since she'd returned from college.

As she crawled into bed in the tiny room that had been hers most of her life, she didn't stop the tears. She could almost see her father standing in the doorway whispering to her. "Good night, dear one. May the angels watch over you this night."

He may never have talked to her about anything more serious than what they planned to have for dinner, but she never doubted his love. Even the day he died, he'd been thinking of her.

"Good night," she whispered as if his shadow were still lingering in the doorway.

A little after sunrise, Angela emerged from her room. As she entered the kitchen of her parents' beach house, she found her aunt sitting at the dining table as if waiting for her to join her. A half-empty cup of coffee was near her elbow. She'd opened three days' worth of mail and scattered it across the table like trash.

Crystal Harold was Uncle Anthony's third wife, so Angela thought of her as her aunt-trice-removed. Never helpful. Never friendly. Never caring. If Crystal was on Anna Marie Island, it was because Uncle Anthony had sent her.

Of course she had a key, even though she rarely visited. The house and the car her father drove were all part of Harold Antiques' holdings. Just one more way Anthony kept her father tied to the business.

"Where have you been, dear?" her aunt said in her cold voice. "I thought you'd come straight home after the funeral yesterday. I waited here until after dark."

"I just drove around," Angela said carefully, remembering the note. *Trust no one.*

"Well, I came by to tell you that you can stay here as long as you like. The house belongs to the company, as does most of the furniture, but your uncle and I want you to know that no matter what you are still family. Of course, after a month you'll need to start paying rent and your father's car has already been picked up. I'm sure with your degree in museum studies you'll find work *somewhere*. Maybe not at a museum like you planned…" She looked Angela up and down and added, "Although running a museum gift shop would suit you. Those kind of people wouldn't care about how you dress or that you're shy as a crab.

Museum-goers probably expect the staff in those places to be a little quirky or odd."

Crystal's dragon fingernails tapped against her cup. "I never have seen the point of museums or art galleries for that matter. Who wants to look at something you can't buy? Anthony must have told your father a dozen times to make you get a degree you could use, like accounting. Then you could step into your father's role with us." She made a sound as if half coughing to disguise a laugh. "Well, not today. Someone broke the windows to the accounting office early this morning. Wet papers scattered everywhere. If I believed in ghosts, I might think your father went back one more time."

Angela shook her head. She didn't believe in ghosts and even if she had, Angela guessed the last place her father would return to would be the office.

"You could get married, Angela." Crystal's mind bounced again. "You're pretty enough in a plain kind of way."

"Gee, thanks," Angela managed, already knowing that she didn't fit Crystal's ideal look for marriage material—tall, tan and blonde. Her aunt had even mentioned once that she should consider cutting her strawberry-colored curly hair and wearing a wig. She'd bought Angela a year's worth of spray tans saying that "any little bit might help."

Crystal had always behaved as though she felt sorry for her. "It's not your *fault*, Angela. Not everyone can be blessed with beauty. You're smart, though. There's bound to be one man in Florida into that kind of thing." Crystal downed the rest of her coffee as if waiting to be thanked.

"I need to be alone if you don't mind." Angela wasn't really up for a makeover right now. "My world seems to be spinning."

"Of course, dear." Her aunt breezed by without offering any comfort. "We'll talk in a few days." Angela noticed her parents' cat rubbing against Crystal's black pant leg.

Her aunt quickly stepped away and glared down at it. "Now that your parents are gone, you'll be getting rid of that ugly cat,

I assume. I told your father that the thing could damage the furniture, but he didn't seem to care."

"Of course," Angela answered. "I'll pack Doc Holliday off to the pound tomorrow."

Her aunt nodded once as if having won the first of many arguments. "Dumb name for a cat, Angela, but then I've never understood your side of the Harold family. Your father and Anthony were ten years apart, but I swear it always seemed like the only thing they ever had in common was a last name."

"It's not a side of the family anymore. It's me," she said. "Just me."

As soon as Crystal walked out, Angela closed the door on what had been her life.

It crossed her mind that Anthony and Crystal knew her father worked late at night. They'd known about his bad heart. They'd even known he never took his cell phone with him when he worked late after his wife died.

Angela shook her head. She was being ridiculous. Maybe her father had left the note simply to save her sanity, knowing Crystal and Anthony would drive her mad.

Only in hindsight, she knew she'd seen other signs of his preparing to leave. Empty boxes stacked in the pantry. A dozen hundred-dollar bills tucked in the bathroom cabinet behind her mother's medicine bottles.

She began sorting through the mail scattered across the dining table when a map buried among the mess of papers caught her eye. A route heading west from Florida had been outlined with a red pen, and a town in West Texas circled. She understood then what her father had been planning. It was the same town that was looking to hire a curator for their local museum.

Closing her eyes, she could almost hear him talking to her. *Might be just the place for you, Angie. You know how you've always loved Texas history. Looks like the perfect place to start over.*

Clutching the map, she drove out to the cemetery. Her father's grave still covered with flowers.

If she could talk to him one more time… If he would answer why to what he'd said and written on the note… If he'd just hold her once more so she could feel safe…

But the world was silent, making her feel more alone than she had been in her entire life. A shy girl, an only child, a solitary person who liked to work by herself. And now she was utterly and probably forever alone.

She looked down at her father's grave. "Good night, dear one. May the angels watch over you. Goodbye, Dad."

Walking away, she knew she'd never return to this garden of stone and dying flowers. Her father wasn't here. He was with her mother now.

The sun was low when she finally drove back to her parents' little house near the water. All the lights were on and for a second she thought her father was home.

Slowly, she walked to the front door. Maybe her aunt had come back?

Glass crunched beneath Angela's shoes. The door's small window had been shattered.

Her heart hammering in her chest, she pulled out her cell phone, dialed 911, then backed away to her car and locked the doors until the police arrived. Room by room they searched the small house. Drawers were open. Contents scattered on the floor. Cabinets were all swept clean, the floor a mess of broken dishes.

The search revealed nothing had been taken, not even the cash hidden in the bathroom cabinet or her laptop.

The police told her it was likely just kids, but Angela knew it was something more.

She locked the house up and tried to relax enough to sleep, but the words from the note and the events of recent days haunted her. Her father's office vandalized…a break-in at her home, so soon after her father's mugging…it couldn't be a coincidence. Somehow, her father had been in danger. Angela knew then what she had to do. She had to run.

★ ★ ★

Early the next morning, she made a trip to the bank and cashed out her account, bought cat food and plastic boxes. By midnight, she was packed. Her mother's quilts, her father's fishing equipment, her grandmother's pots and one very ugly cat named Doc Holliday.

Run. Vanish. Disappear. The words kept beating through her brain in a steady rhythm.

She still had far more questions than answers, but the break-in had convinced her that her father was right. Something was wrong. Maybe she was letting her imagination run away with her to think that her father's death might not have been simply a heart attack brought on by a random mugging, but she believed in her core that she was in danger, and that she had to take action.

With a letter describing a job at a small museum in Texas tucked away in her black raincoat and fifty thousand dollars in cash, Angela Harold walked away from what she'd always thought of as her home.

It was time to take her father's advice. She would disappear.

CHAPTER ONE

Crossroads, Texas
October
Angela

Dried weeds scratched against Angela Harold's bare legs as she walked the neglected grounds behind the Ransom Canyon Museum near Crossroads, Texas. Rumbling gray clouds spotted the sky above. Wind raged as though trying to push her back to the East Coast. She decided any rain might blow all the way to Oklahoma before it could land on Texas soil. But the weather didn't matter. She had made it here. She'd done exactly what her father told her. She'd vanished.

Angela had meant to stop long enough to clean up before she took her first look at the museum, but she could not wait. So, in sandals, shorts and a tank top, she explored the land behind the boarded-up building on the edge of Ransom Canyon.

When she'd talked to the board president, Staten Kirkland, five days ago, he'd sounded excited. They'd had to close the museum when the last curator left and in six months she'd been the only one to call about the job opening. Before the phone call ended Kirkland offered her a three-month trial if she could answer one question.

Angela thought it would be about her experience or her education, but it was pure Texas folk history.

"What or who was the Yellow Rose of Texas?" the man on the phone asked in his pure Texas twang.

She laughed. "The woman who entertained Santa Anna before the Battle of San Jacinto. The battle that won Texas independence." She'd always loved that story, which often got left out of history books.

"We'll be waiting for you, Mrs. Jones."

He hung up before she had time to tell him that her name wasn't Jones. In a moment of paranoia, she'd used a false name when she'd bought a laptop and phone. Then again on the application, figuring she'd be just one of hundreds who applied. Now, if he checked her transcripts or references, she'd have to make up another lie. That would be easier than finding some guy named Jones, marrying him and dragging him along to Texas with her.

Angela had driven a hundred miles before she decided she would tell Kirkland that she used Jones because she had been engaged but he left her at the altar. Kirkland would feel sorry for her, but that was better than killing off her imaginary husband.

She'd straighten it all out Monday. She'd even practice just how she'd say it.

Monday, she'd dress in a suit and accept the position as curator for the three-month trial period, but today simply exploring the place would be enough. After days in the car she needed to stretch her legs and breathe in the clean air. She'd dreamed of being in Texas for years. A wild country—untamed, open, free. Something she'd never felt before, but she planned to now. For the first time, she was free to make her own future.

The grounds behind the museum had been left natural, just as it must have looked a hundred and fifty years ago when settlers came to this top square of Texas.

Since the day she'd read there was an opening here for a curator, Angela learned everything she could about this area. The
history was interesting, but the people who founded this frontier
town fascinated her. They were hearty. Stubborn. Independent.
Honest. All things she'd never been. But the first settlers were
also broken, desperate and lost. Somehow they'd managed to
work together to build, not just ranches and a town, but a future.

Now she had to do the same with no family or friends to
help her.

She didn't know if she belonged here. She fainted at the sight
of blood. Gave in at the first sign of disagreement.

That left honest. She didn't want to even think about how
dishonest she was. She'd lied to get the job as curator of this
closed museum.

Standing near the edge of a canyon that dropped a hundred
feet straight down, she let the sun's dying rays warm her face.
Everything about her had to change. She had to make it so. She
had to start over.

Somewhere along the road between Florida and here, she'd
come to the conclusion that her father's death wasn't an accident.
Maybe he knew something about the company or his brother.
Maybe he'd overheard trouble moving in. Why else would he
have told her to run? If her life weren't in danger, why would
it be so important that she vanish?

Maybe he'd been planning to disappear with her, only time
ran out for him. But he had left her prepared. He'd put money
in her account. He'd even suggested that she tell no one about
this job in Texas.

The old trailer he bought and hid in the garage fit into the
plan. Last month, he'd had her car fit with the hitch. She'd told
him she had no need to pull a trailer, but he'd said that if he
ever needed the trailer, he didn't want to use it on the company
car he drove. Only, she'd been the one who needed the trailer.
She'd done what he'd told her to do in the note and now she
had to somehow blend in here in Texas.

Taking the curator job was the first step. This time her title didn't have "assistant" attached to it. She would be the boss. This time she would have no aunt to criticize every move she made.

Angela smiled. Her aunt had probably dropped by the beach house to have that talk with her by now. After all, it had been a week. She'd find the key in the mailbox. No note. No forwarding address. No friends notified. Any mail concerning her life on Anna Marie Island would be trashed.

Angela had even cancelled her cell phone service and tossed the phone off the Bradenton Bridge when she crossed onto the mainland.

Disappear, her father's note had said. She'd seen enough spy movies to know what that meant.

She touched the necklace she wore. A replica of the Greek coin on display at her uncle's store. She'd thought of tossing it into the ocean with her phone, but decided it would always remind her of her father. The real one had caused many an argument between the brothers. Her father saw it as a family treasure. Uncle Anthony saw it as something to be sold to the highest bidder. They'd compromised and made copies to sell for a few hundred dollars each.

Glancing toward the sound of crunching gravel, she watched a white-and-blue sheriff's car pull into the museum's parking lot. Her heart stopped.

Trouble had found her halfway across the country. Somehow her uncle had tracked her. But how? She'd parked her old car in a twenty-four-hour Walmart lot in Orlando and walked across the street to rent a pickup with a hitch for her trailer. Then she'd turned the pickup in before she crossed the Florida state line. She'd bought a junker of a car with cash but it wasn't powerful enough to pull the trailer, giving her nothing but trouble for two hundred miles. Two days later in Georgia she'd traded in the junker and her old two-wheel trailer to a mechanic for a van in a town too small to have a stop sign. The guy said he'd mail the title to the van, but she had given him a fake name and address.

What if the van had been stolen? The law could be about to arrest her, and she had no proof she bought the van.

Angela stared at the patrol car as it pulled in beside her van. Her freedom had lasted less then a week. Maybe her uncle had put out a missing person alert? That wouldn't surprise her. Her aunt probably told everyone Angela was so lost in grief she wasn't to be left alone.

A man in a uniform unfolded out of his car. She expected him to pull his gun as he walked toward her. After all, she'd run away from home at twenty-seven. Something all her relatives would swear quiet Angela would never do.

"Pardon me, miss," the man said as he neared. "This place has been closed for months. We got a no-trespassing sign at the turnoff, but you must have missed it."

In her shorts, no makeup and her strawberry-blond hair in a day-old ponytail, she must look more girl than woman. The echo of her mother's familiar speech about how Angela was too chubby, too squat to wear shorts, circled through her tired mind.

"I'm sorry. I didn't notice the sign." She straightened, trying to look at least five foot five, though she knew she missed her goal by two inches.

She moved toward the lawman trying her best to look like a professional. "I'm Angela—"

Hesitating, she tried to remember the last name she'd used on the application. It slipped her mind completely. "Smith." Angela mentally shook her tired brain awake. *"Jones." Of course. How hard could that be to remember?*

There, she'd gotten it out. After not talking for three days, words didn't want to form in her brain.

She stared at his name tag. Sheriff Brigman looked as if he easily read the lie that lay in her mind like oil slush. He pulled off his Stetson stalling for time, but she didn't miss the way he looked her up and down from ponytail to sandals.

"Welcome to town, Mrs. Jones. Kirkland told me you were coming."

A hint of a smile lifted the corner of his mouth. He reminded her of a sheriff from the Wild West days. Well built, a touch of gray in his sideburns and stone-cold eyes that said he'd finish the job, no matter what it took, whether it was catching the outlaw or satisfying his woman.

She mentally slapped herself. No time to flirt or daydream. Angela had to think of what to say. Was it too early to ask for a lawyer? Should she start confessing? But to what? She wasn't even sure what crimes she'd committed. Running away at her age didn't seem to be illegal, and she'd read somewhere that you can go by an alias if you were not doing anything wrong.

When she didn't offer any comment, the cop in the Stetson added, "My guess is you couldn't wait to see the inside of this place. Did you just get to town?"

She nodded, thankful he didn't add "Dressed like a fifteen-year-old." With luck, he hadn't noticed she couldn't remember her own name. Maybe he thought she had early onset Alzheimer's.

"Yes, sorry, I've been driving for twelve hours, so I'm a bit scattered. I wanted a quick look at the canyon before dark. It's beautiful out here near the edge."

Brigman nodded as he watched the last bit of sunlight running over the canyon walls turn the rocks gold. "I like to check on the museum this time of day. It kind of reminds me of a great painting. No matter what kind of day I've had, all is calm out here."

"I can see that." She'd feared she would miss the ocean and the beautiful sunsets at Anna Marie Island, but Ransom Canyon had its own kind of wonder. She had a feeling the canyon would grow on her.

"You know, Mrs. Jones, your office has a great view." He pointed to a huge window on the second floor of the big barn of a building.

Angela smiled. "No one told me that, or I might have driven all night."

They both started walking toward the parking lot.

"Your husband driving the moving van in?" Sheriff Brigman had an easy way of asking questions as if he were just being friendly.

"I'm not married," she said, then remembered the application listing her new name as Jones.

"When I interviewed over the phone with Mr. Kirkland, I was two days away from being married." She did her best to look brokenhearted, but it wasn't easy, since she'd never once given her heart away. "The night before the wedding, we called it off."

The sheriff studied her as if planning to wait for more information.

"We didn't work out. My fiancé didn't want to move." She shrugged as if fighting back tears. "When we broke up, I thought a clean getaway would be best, so I went ahead and came to Texas." Since *fiancé* Jones never existed, it wasn't really very painful to walk out on him. "I'd already changed my email and accounts over to Jones."

Brigman raised an eyebrow. "Are you planning to keep his name?"

Angela fought down a nervous giggle. "I'm sentimental about names. Turns out his name was the only thing I liked about the man. As soon as I settle, I'll change everything back. Of course, my driver's license is still in my maiden name." This whole thing was getting mixed up in her brain. At this point any way she could climb out of this little lie was probably going to end up making her look like an idiot.

Thank goodness they had reached her van. A few more lies and the sheriff would probably figure out she was on the run and have her arrested or committed.

"Have you been by your new house yet?" he asked as he opened her car door.

"Do you know where it is?" Mr. Kirkland had mentioned that he'd email her some information, but she'd forgotten to look.

"Sure." He grinned, looking younger. "This is a small town, Mrs. Jones, I mean..."

He waited for her to fill in the blank.

"Harold," she answered.

The sheriff nodded once. "Kirkland said you wanted to rent a two-bedroom furnished place that allowed cats. Half the Chamber of Commerce started looking for something special. We don't get many professional curators around here. I could show you the one we picked for you and the runner-up, Miss Harold. I've got keys to both."

"Please call me Angela, Sheriff."

He touched two fingers to the brim of his Stetson in a salute. "All right, Angela. Why don't you call me Dan. Which do you want to see first, a nice little house between the two churches in town or a cabin house on the lake? The church house has more room, but the lake house backs into the shoreline."

"I'll take the lake house," she said immediately. She almost hugged him. *Water.* She'd be near water.

"Follow me, then."

"I don't want to be any trouble," she said. "If you'll give me the key, I can probably find it."

"No trouble. You have to pass my house at the lake to get to yours. Showing you the place isn't out of my way home at all."

As the sheriff's car led her through the small town of Crossroads, Angela fought down another wave of panic that seemed to be coming over her as often as hiccups. This open country where anyone could see for miles in every direction didn't seem like a very wise place to hide. Probably half the people in town would know where she lived. How could she have ever thought she'd be safe here?

What if Anthony came after her? If he found her? If he or one of his associates had killed her father and made it look like a robbery, maybe they'd kill her, too. They might think her father had told her more than just that the books didn't balance. Maybe they thought she had something that belonged to Uncle Anthony. After all, someone had turned her parents' home upside down looking for something.

Of course, if they came for her, she'd swear she didn't know anything. But would they believe her if her father had already confronted them with some illegal activity he knew about? Whatever her father overheard or found in the books must have been bad. A secret worth murdering for?

She was letting her imagination run away with her again. The police said her father's mugging was just one of a half dozen in the area that weekend. Probably drug related. The investigator hadn't given her much hope that the killer would ever be found. Dark alley. No witnesses. He even said it looked as if her father had been struck with something or pushed, then fell backward hitting his head.

Angela knew the police report didn't tell the whole story. Her father knew trouble was coming. Whoever killed him must have known his habits. Whoever mugged him might have known it might trigger a heart attack. Something had kept him from going to the police with his information and that something or someone had to be the reason he wanted her away and safe.

Only, she had no proof. No facts.

Her only choice was to make a new start and never look back. She trusted her father. If he said run, she would.

The sheriff, in the car in front of her, would be her first friend. This place would become her only home. In three months she'd be so much a part of this wild country she'd almost believe she was born to the land.

CHAPTER TWO

Wilkes
Devil's Fork Ranch

Wilkes Wagner stared at his aging uncle, wondering which of them had completely lost their mind. Common sense rarely ran in the Wagner family, but Great-Uncle Vern's suggestion was ridiculous.

"I've given it some thought, and this is the only answer, boy," the crippled-up old cowboy repeated as if Wilkes were ten and not thirty-two. "Look at it this way, we breed cattle, don't we? Why not just pick out a woman with all the right traits and mate with her? It shouldn't take but a few tries before we got at least one offspring to claim the next generation. And there's a fifty-fifty chance we'll get a boy on the first try."

"You mean marry some woman, don't you?" Wilkes was never sure when his uncle was kidding.

"Of course! There's an order to these kinds of things. You'd need to marry her first, get her pregnant and wait for a son." The old man lit a pipe that looked as if it might have survived the Battle of the Alamo. "Look on the bright side, half your life is about over anyway. If you're miserable at marriage, the last thirty or forty years will seem to move slower with a mean woman around the place and we'll all work harder so we don't come home early."

Wilkes rolled his eyes. He needed another drink. Or better yet give Great-Uncle Vern a few more and with luck he'd pass out.

To humor the cowboy, Wilkes asked, "And what would those traits be that I'm looking for in this breeding-bride?"

Vern smiled as if he'd won the argument. "Stout. You don't want one of those skinny girls who only eats out of the garden. She'll need to have a little meat on her bones. Ain't nothing worse than trying to cuddle up to a skinny gal on a cold night. I did that once in Amarillo, and about midnight I decided driving home in a snowstorm would be warmer."

Wilkes grabbed a pen off the poker table and started writing on the back of his *Western Horseman* magazine. *Not skinny.*

His uncle leaned back in an old rocker that had come to the Devil's Fork Ranch in a covered wagon. "She'll need to know how to cook and clean and sew, too, otherwise she'd be wearing out the road to town buying takeout, hiring housekeepers and replacing clothes she's lost a button on."

"All that might be hard to find these days." The only thing the four or five women Wilkes had stepped out with in the past six years could make for dinner was reservations. He considered them cooks if they knew how to use the microwave for popcorn.

His aging uncle wasn't paying attention. He was busy thinking. "And she needs to be rich. Not just have money coming to her, mind, but already have it in the bank. You don't want to count on her father liking you, 'cause if he don't he might cut her out of the will. Then you'll be stuck with a poor wife with rich habits."

Rich. Wilkes scribbled.

"And dumb." Uncle Vern lit his pipe. "Ain't no smart girl ever going to marry you, even if you are good-looking. If she's got much schooling, she'll want to work at something or sit around and read all day."

Wilkes had humored his old uncle long enough. Vern was the dumbest and the youngest of four children, and all his brothers and sisters claimed he'd been dropped on his head one time too many when he was a baby. He had lived on the Wagner family ranch all of his seventy-seven years. The rule was whoever ran the Devil's Fork also had to keep an eye on Vern. Wilkes's father and grandfather had done it, and now it was Wilkes's turn. The few other relatives, who'd been smart enough to move to the city, never wanted to come back and take over the job.

This crazy idea Vern had tonight was the worst one yet.

Wilkes leaned forward until Vern's whiskey-blurred eyes focused on him. "I'm real busy with the calving right now, uncle. Do you think you could keep a lookout for a possible wife? She shouldn't be too hard to find. She's chubby, eats beef and is rich and dumb. She'll be wearing a homemade dress and probably have freshly made jam dripping down her chins. Oh, I forgot, she needs to be easy to impregnate, 'cause I won't be visiting her often." Wilkes fought down a laugh. "Only, that trait might be hard to prove on sight."

Vern didn't get the joke. He rocked back so far that the forward swing, a moment later, shoved him out of the chair and onto his wobbly legs. "I'll do my best for you! I promise. Might go into Crossroads tomorrow and put up a few signs. I don't think I've been to town since spring and the Franklin sisters always say they miss seeing me."

Wilkes laughed. "You do that, Uncle Vern."

The broken-down cowboy headed toward the massive double doors of the ranch house muttering, "I hated to have this talk with you, son, but you ain't getting nowhere in the breeding department and 'fore you know it you'll be past your prime or dead. Who'll run the ranch? You had a gal once and let her go, so we got to act fast before you get any older and end up sleeping alone the rest of your life."

Wilkes saw it then. The reason his uncle had insisted on drinking tonight and talking. He was afraid he'd outlive Wilkes and no one would take over Devil's Fork. Vern had spent his life living on the ranch, never worrying about money or where his next meal was coming from. He'd hated school so much his mother had let him quit after the seventh grade. He loved working with horses, living alone and driving his pickup until the odometer circled twice. He was afraid of being left out here on his own.

Following his uncle to the porch, Wilkes watched Vern limp toward his cabin a hundred yards away. Light from the second-floor windows of the main house illuminated the old man's path. The massive home had been built fifty years ago to hold a dozen kids. It now held one. Wilkes.

Vern had watched his brother, Wilkes's grandfather, take over the ranch. When he died, Wilkes's father became the manager. Vern said all he wanted to do was cowboy. The job of boss wouldn't suit him.

Uncle Vern had been around all of Wilkes's life, working cattle with the ranch hands, training horses with his father and eating supper every night at the family table in the big house. This life was all he knew. All he wanted to know.

Wilkes shook his head as his heart ached for Vern Wagner, who'd lived long enough to go from being Wilkes's hero and teacher, to friend, to responsibility. His uncle had taught him to ride, cussed him out when he left the pasture gate open and bought him fireworks every year, even when Wilkes's mother said she wouldn't allow them on the ranch. The old guy may have danced with a few girls in his day, but he had never married. He was loyal to the family, loyal to the Devil's Fork brand.

Wilkes watched the lights flick on in Vern's cabin. "I better start looking for a fat, rich wife so I can start breeding Vern's next guardian angel," he mumbled as he downed the last of his whiskey, knowing he was only half kidding. Then he climbed the stairs and slept in the second room off the upstairs landing.

The first bedroom was bigger, the master, but when Wilkes had returned home to take over the ranch, he hadn't felt as if he deserved the master suite. He still didn't.

The next morning as he drove into town to pick up fencing supplies and eat breakfast with a friend, Wilkes thought about the conversation the night before. Vern was right about one thing. Wilkes *had* had a lady once. The perfect one. He'd loved Lexie Davis the minute he first saw her, chased her through high school and college; but she'd never really been his. When he'd left for the army a month after they both graduated, she promised she'd wait, and she had... Only, she'd counted her time in hours. Sixty-three days into his deployment, she'd written him one letter. It said simply she'd met someone else. She'd added five words below *Love, Lexi*: *don't bother to write back*.

Wilkes told himself a hundred times that he was over her. Maybe not everyone was meant to find that forever love. Vern hadn't. But something broke inside Wilkes the day Lexie walked out of his life and he feared he would never mend.

Hell. Vern was right. Maybe he should start thinking about finding a wife, but it wasn't exactly a scavenger hunt. He should make a real list. It'd be pretty much the opposite of Vern's. He liked long-legged women with midnight hair that dropped down to their waist and laughter dancing in their eyes. Women like Lexie.

Lexie, the woman he was over, Wilkes reminded himself.

While he waited for the supplies to be loaded, Wilkes walked along the wide main street. The business district of Crossroads looked as if the stores must have been bought from a clearance rack. All different sizes, ages, styles. Nothing matched. Crossroads was a town more likely to be called quirky than quaint.

He noticed a few new stores since he'd last been in town. Businesses that had filled in where empty gaps had stood. Shiny as new teeth in an old mouth, he thought. The change made the little town look a bit more prosperous.

One empty hull had become the Forever Keepsake Shop. In

his opinion, the only folks who bought knickknacks to sit around gathering dust must be orphans, because every time one of his relatives died, he inherited another crate of "treasured" family keepsakes. Sometimes he wondered if his great-great-grand-parents had hauled their junk from the old country to Texas in a wagon train and not just one wagon. All the old trunks and lanterns and dusty quilts came back to Devil's Fork like ugly buzzards coming home to roost.

Wilkes walked into the new shop hoping he might offer to supply the place. Old tools, butter churns, wall telephones, he had them all in supply.

Two women in their forties giggled when he stepped inside and closed the door. He knew them by last name. The Franklin sisters. They probably had first names, but years ago when his mother would point them out to him, she always said simply, "There's the Franklin sisters. Poor things. Bless their hearts."

He'd been twenty before he found out why they were *poor things*. Apparently, in the late seventies or early eighties, they'd both fallen for the same boy—a good-looking Gypsy kid with bedroom eyes and the last name of Stanley. He ran off with a girl from another Gypsy family in town, and both the Frank-lin sisters were brokenhearted. They swore over an ocean of tears that he was the only man either would ever love and they would never marry.

Some thought that sad; others just thought it was their escape, because the two weren't likely to marry anyway. By eighteen, they both tipped the scales at over two hundred pounds, and at twenty-five, they'd gained another fifty or sixty. By thirty, they both sported faint mustaches.

Even on a dark night no one would mistake them as pretty. But they were sweet as warm toffee. Every few years they took up a new business in town. As far as he could remember, they'd had the Sweet Shop, the Quilting Bee and a used bookstore called the Book Hideout.

Wilkes smiled at the two sisters. "Morning, Miss Franklin

and Miss Franklin." Even round and hairy, there was something about the ladies that was adorable.

Both giggled. "How can we help you, Wilkes?" they said at once.

Wilkes didn't want to seem the village idiot, so he said, "I'm looking for a keepsake to give a friend who is visiting."

"Do you know him well?" the shorter Miss Franklin asked.

Wilkes lied again. "No. He's just someone stopping by for a cup of coffee. He's thinking about going into ranching." Dumb lie, Wilkes thought, but he was too far in now to back out.

"We know just the thing." Each woman grabbed a box from the stacks behind the counter.

Wilkes didn't care what was in the boxes. He picked the smallest and thanked them. Handing them a twenty, he wasn't surprised to get only coins back. They managed small talk about Uncle Vern's health while one sister bagged his purchase.

When they passed it to him, one Miss Franklin started mentioning every relative she had who was still unmarried. "Fran's newly divorced, you know, but she's a treasure."

The other sister chimed in. "Avis is a little older than you, but she's real pretty, and then you know Molly and Doris. I think you went to school with them. Both were engaged last year, but it didn't work out."

Wilkes never knew what to say. He'd been tricked into a dozen meet-the-single-relative dates, and they'd all turned out bad.

The taller Miss Franklin must have gotten the message, but she wasn't ready to toss in her matchmaking wand. "I guess you heard Lexie Davis is moving back."

He hadn't heard. He didn't care, but that didn't stop the conversation.

"Her second marriage didn't work out, you know, and her aunt is poorly. Lexie is hoping to get on at the high school. She can teach both drama and English, she claims, though she's never had to work. Married well both times, you know."

Wilkes had to get out of the store. He didn't want to hear more about Lexie. Not in this lifetime. Besides, how "well" are marriages that don't last two years?

"I wish I could visit, but I've got my hands full this morning." Wilkes had a death grip on his box as he backed toward the door.

They both looked sad.

Wilkes couldn't talk about Lexie. One goodbye letter while he'd been away in the army had been enough to kill any hope of love.

She hadn't waited. He wasn't interested. End of story. Wilkes didn't want to reread that chapter in his life. He'd been home six years and hadn't run into her. She was just a memory now.

He stormed out the door not even remembering if he said goodbye.

With no thought but to escape, Wilkes darted into the next business. The welcome sign clanged like a gong. The smell of hair spray and bleach almost knocked him back outside.

A beauty shop. Wilkes swore. Why couldn't it have been a bookstore, or a Laundromat or better yet a bar?

He looked around at women with aluminum foil in their hair and took a step backward. Alien invasion came to mind.

The gum-chewing girl with green-striped hair darted around the counter and caught up to him. "May we help you, mister?"

"No, thanks," Wilkes managed. "I was, uh, just looking for my aunt."

One of the aliens in the back yelled, "Your last aunt died five years ago, Wilkes Wagner."

Wilkes pulled his hat down and answered, "Then I guess she's not here."

He ignored the laughter and walked out, head high, keepsake box in hand. Thank goodness the next place down the road was a café he knew. Dorothy's Café had been around for as long as he could remember, and the food served was exactly the same. Fried grease with a side of starch. He might be a half hour early to meet his friend, but the café seemed a safe place. He knew it would take a little time to wash Lexie out of his mind.

As he sat down at the first booth, he saw a sign across the street that said Puppy Paradise, Dog Grooming and Training.

No doubt about it, Crossroads, Texas, was growing. Wilkes couldn't wait to show Uncle Vern the new place. Maybe he'd suggest grooming the cattle.

He ordered coffee, then opened the box he'd bought. To his shock, he'd paid twenty dollars for a mug that looked to be about the same as the one the waitress delivered with his coffee.

Only, the mug in the box was obviously worth far more because it read, "You are at the Crossroads of your life."

Wilkes laughed. Nothing had changed in his life in six years. It was hard to see a crossroads when he knew he was born with only one way to travel. He had played four years of college football without managing to pick up much education and served three years in the army without collecting any bullet holes, but by twenty-six, after drifting across the United States and back, he'd come back home to do what he always knew he'd do. Run the ranch. It wasn't as if he'd given up on his dreams; he'd never really had any to begin with.

His folks weren't dead. They were simply absentee landlords. Never around to help or fix things, but calling in now and then to check on what he was doing. They must have started packing the day they'd called Wilkes and found out he hadn't even bothered to look for a job after he got out of the army. He was drifting and they had the solution to his no goal, no direction life.

His mother's folks were aging and needed help downsizing and selling several small businesses. So Wilkes's parents moved to Denver claiming Wilkes would run the ranch while they were gone, since he seemed to have nothing else to do.

He'd agreed, thinking they'd be gone a few months. Six years later his dad looked like an aging hippie and his mother was taking meditation classes so she could teleport. They took cruises

with Wilkes's eighty-year-old grandparents and showed no sign
of coming back to the work of ranching.

Wilkes told himself he didn't care. After all, he had no plans
after the army and he loved ranching.

"Morning, Wilkes," a low voice greeted him.

Wilkes turned to see Yancy Grey coming through the door.
He was a few years younger than Wilkes, but they'd become
friends working on a park project together last year. Yancy had
an awkward way about him at first meeting. He'd talk too fast
sometimes or be unable to find the right words, but Wilkes
didn't mind. When Yancy settled down into a conversation, he
could tell a story with the best of them and Wilkes had the time
to listen when Yancy needed to talk.

"I'm glad you had time to meet me." Yancy slid his thin frame
into the other side of the booth. "I need to ask a favor."

The café was empty, so they weren't likely to be bothered.
Yancy worked across the street as the handyman at the retirement community. The senior citizens seemed to have adopted
him when he was homeless and he looked after them like a hen
with a nest full of chicks.

Since Wilkes was only talking to himself lately, a favor might
pull him out of his slump. Maybe he'd even tell his friend about
Uncle Vern's plan to marry him off to the first chubby, rich,
dumb girl they could find.

"How can I help?" Wilkes had no idea what Yancy needed,
but if it was in his power, he was up for the job.

"I got a history question for you."

Wilkes thought maybe he should warn his friend that just because a man had a history degree didn't make him an expert on
any time period. He'd majored in history because it had sounded
easier than English. "I'll do what I can."

Yancy straightened, took a gulp of hot coffee the waitress
slid in front of him and started. "You think a house can...you
know...draw you to it? Kind of like it's calling you?"

Nope was the first answer that came to mind, but Wilkes

leaned back deciding this conversation might just be interesting. "Tell me about it, Yancy." His friend seemed suddenly far
younger than twenty-seven.

"You'll think I'm crazy." Yancy leaned back as if pulling away.
He'd spent his late teens and early twenties in prison. Sometimes
that lack of trust showed through.

Wilkes didn't judge him for his lack of skills or scars. He had
his own scars.

"I can't help if I don't know the facts, Yancy. Just start from
the beginning without leaving out anything. I'll wait until I
know the details before I call you crazy."

The handyman nodded, took another gulp of coffee and said,
"Last night, like I do a lot of nights, I took a walk down the
north road. The moon seemed to be whispering secrets in the
midnight air, like it does on cloudy nights, you know?"

"I know." Wilkes's brain cells woke up. He didn't know any
such thing, but he'd follow along where this went. He doubted
he would be any help to Yancy Grey, but he wanted to hear
more.

"I went down the road toward the old Gypsy House. You
know the place covered by weeds and long dead trees."

Wilkes nodded.

Yancy continued, "I've heard there are folks who swear they
saw strangers as foggy as ghosts going into the house after dark
and never coming out. According to the retired folks across the
street the place is haunted by dead Gypsies or hippies. No one
knows which. Some say the crumbling old place almost took
four teenagers' lives a few years ago, but I was too much into my
own problems back then and don't remember the details. When
I ask about the house, folks claim evil lived there. One even said
he thought he heard a scream once when he passed the place."

"I've heard the stories, too. Did you feel the evil?" Wilkes
interrupted.

Yancy shook his head. "The house had been drawing me since
I arrived in Crossroads, even before I'd heard it was haunted. I

guess you probably heard I came to town broke, alone and fresh out of prison."

"I heard. Also know you helped the sheriff catch a gang of rustlers who almost killed Staten Kirkland."

Yancy smiled. "Yeah, after that folks accepted me. I'm doing all right now. Got a good job. Hell, I even saved enough to buy a car outright, no payments, but still I walk at night out to that old place. I feel like it's mocking me. Daring me to step inside. Sounds crazy, don't it?"

Wilkes shrugged. "I'm tracking you. Keep talking." He didn't want to admit that stressing over a woman who left him years ago might fall into the crazy folder, as well.

Yancy continued, "As I got close to the house last night, it seemed to grow. Maybe it was in my head, but with every step closer the place looked bigger. I've seen some bad things in my life, but last night I swear I felt a shiver run down my back like someone walked over my grave."

Wilkes smiled realizing, truth or not, the guy could tell a story better than Uncle Vern.

"When I felt it calling last night, I gripped the flashlight in my pocket like a weapon and stepped off the road, determined to get to the bottom of this nightmare. I headed through the high weeds that circle the place like a moat around a monster's castle. I had to do something." Yancy's hands balled into fists.

"I yelled that I was going in, but I sounded like a frightened boy. I'm tired of having bad dreams, Wilkes, and last night I figured to put an end to it.

"The warped frame of what had once been a screen door tapped against the side of the house as if knocking on a crypt's door in a forgotten cemetery. I planted my boot on the porch and stepped up, relieved that the wood took my weight." Yancy took a few seconds to breathe.

Wilkes waited.

"I yelled like I wasn't afraid. 'You don't frighten me.' I took one step toward the door. The boards creaked as if crying out for me to stay back, but I didn't stop. I widened my stance and pulled the hammer I'd brought from the loop on my pants. With as much force as I could manage, I pulled the nails from the two-by-fours blocking the door.

"As the boards rattled across the porch, I took a long breath. What I was doing was probably a crime. The place has do-not-enter signs posted at every corner of the house. But I didn't care. I'd made up my mind."

Wilkes shoved his coffee cup aside. He felt as if he was at the old house with Yancy. His senses hadn't felt so alive since the army.

"Once the boards were off, I shoved the door open and flashed my light inside. Three rotted steps led down onto what looked like a dirt floor. If there was wood beneath the dirt, I couldn't tell. When part of the roof must have tumbled in on the high school kids, no one thought to clean anything up.

"I avoided the steps and jumped down into the lower level of the house. The remains of a staircase leading up to the second floor lined one wall. They reminded me of rotting, broken teeth hanging lopsided in an open mouth. When I passed my light over the floor, I noticed a few old broken chairs and a bed frame.

"All the noise of loose boards rattling and wind whistling through cracks seemed muted inside. I just stood there, too afraid to go farther. If something fell on me, I'd be nothing but bones before anyone thought to look for me in that old place. Then, in the stillness, I swear I felt a hand on my shoulder, a slight tug pulling me deeper into the blackness."

Wilkes could barely breathe waiting for what came next.

"Whatever drew me to the house seemed to want to keep me there.

"Fear stampeded through my blood, I raced out and hammered the boards back across the door knowing even as I did it that I'd have to come back."

Yancy took a drink. "The house calls me, Wilkes, I swear, and it won't stop until I figure out why."

Wilkes exhaled deeply. "That's some story. What's your question?"

Yancy grinned. "Can you help me figure out what it wants with me? I need to know the history of the place and who I have to get permission from to go in without worrying about being caught. I've thought about it all night. You're the only person I know who might go back with me. I remember that night on the Kirkland Ranch when we were waiting for the rustlers in the dark. You said, after the army, you gave up being afraid of anything. Well, now is your chance to prove it. Go back to the house with me."

Their waitress must have been tired of waiting for them to motion her over. She appeared, notepad in hand, ready to take their order. "If you two don't order breakfast soon, you'll have to switch to the lunch menu."

Both men apologized to her and ordered the special. She refilled their coffee and mentioned something about how Dorothy should charge for squatters.

As soon as she was out of earshot, Wilkes smiled. "I'm in. I'll see what history I can find on the house and we'll recon the site one night soon."

CHAPTER THREE

Lauren
Texas Tech University

The strong West Texas wind blasted dirt against her bare legs as Lauren Brigman ran across campus. No girl at Texas Tech wore a dress on days like this, but she'd thought maybe she would see Lucas, her almost boyfriend, today. He had gone home to work every weekend since she'd arrived on campus. Then last week he said he might not be driving home to Crossroads until early Saturday morning, which meant they might see each other tonight.

It meant they could have a date. *A real date*, she thought as she stormed the dorm door and took the two flights of stairs at a run.

She had spent her last two years of high school waiting for Lucas to come home from college so they could start dating. Only, when he did come home, he was always working on weekends and their times together consisted of no more than a few moonlit walks along the lake or early-morning coffee at the café before he headed back. He'd promised that when she joined him at Tech it would be different. *They* would be together, a real couple. Studying wrapped up in one another. Sharing kisses in the dark corners of the library. Late-night phone calls.

Until last month, she'd lived on thirty-minute breakfasts with him before he left Crossroads to go back to Lubbock, and late-night ice-cream runs where they talked in the Dairy Queen parking lot after he got finished working on one of the ranches around town. She'd lived on hope that he'd soon be her real boyfriend. They'd finally both be in college. They'd be a couple. No one could say he was too old for her. A few years difference wouldn't seem so much.

She'd been at Texas Tech over a month and none of her dreams were coming true. Her entire love life had been Photoshopping her and Lucas Reyes's faces onto couples in all the old movies she'd seen. If possible she saw less of him here than she had when she'd lived in Crossroads and he'd dropped in on weekends to work. College wasn't turning out to be what she planned.

As Lauren opened her dorm room door, she wasn't surprised to see her roommate still in bed. After all, it wasn't dark yet.

Polly Pierce rolled over, her black-and-red hair streaking across her face. "You're back already?"

"It's after five, Polly. You missed lunch." Lauren used to say that she missed class, but Polly was on the one-semester plan. She never studied and hadn't bothered to unpack most of her stuff. There was little doubt that she'd be moving back home by Christmas break.

"I know. I'm starving." She rolled over and pulled an empty cracker box from under her back. "I ate all your peanut butter and crackers."

"Where's the peanut butter jar?" Lauren wondered why she even talked to Polly. As an only child raised by her pop, the county sheriff of Ransom Canyon, Lauren had always had her own neat, organized space. Sharing quarters with Polly was like some kind of experiment to see if two different life forms could survive in the same environment.

Polly rummaged around in her mass of covers and found the empty jar. "Don't give me that look," she said, cuddling back under her blankets. "I think I'm descended from bears. It's not my fault the fall semester parallels with hibernation."

Lauren didn't comment on how Polly managed to stay awake all weekend. "Don't you have a date tonight?"

Polly's words were muffled. "Jack texted me and said he had to work, and my backup date has the flu." She sighed. "I could go out looking for a backup for my backup, but it's such a bother to train a new one."

When Lauren didn't comment, Polly rolled over to face the wall. End of conversation.

Lauren pulled out her cell phone, punched in her favorite number and dropped atop her neatly made bed.

As soon as Lucas answered, she squealed. "I made an A on my first big chem test."

"Who is this?" Lucas Reyes answered in a low voice flavored just a touch with his Hispanic heritage.

She could almost see the smile in his question. "It's me."

"Oh, yeah, the only freshman I know," he teased. "Congrats."

Lauren held the phone tight in hope. "Let's celebrate, Lucas. I'll buy the pizza."

The moment of silence told her all she needed to know.

"Can't tonight. I'm headed home as soon as I get cleaned up from mucking out stalls at the agriculture barn. Mr. Kirkland needs me to work at his place all weekend. Probably won't be back on campus until late Sunday."

Lauren fought down tears. He lived half a mile away on campus, and they were still miles apart. The only guy she'd ever really liked didn't like her enough to stay around one evening.

"I'll call you Sunday night and we can talk as I drive in."

"No, don't call. I've got a seven-thirty class Monday." When he didn't try to convince her, she tried another possibility. "I could drive home tomorrow. It would surprise Pop. I told him I wouldn't be back until Thanksgiving. Maybe we could get together after you finish on Saturday night? We could cook out by the lake, then drive over and watch the stars on Kirkland land."

"Doubt I'll have time. Mom says she's going to forget my name if I don't spend a few hours with the family while I'm home this time." His answer made sense, but he was breaking her heart.

Trying to sound as if she didn't care, Lauren added, "No problem. I need to study this weekend anyway." Lucas was her best friend, her first boyfriend, her only love even if she'd never told him. She knew how busy he was. He carried a full load, worked part-time at the campus AG farm on weeknights and left every weekend to work either with his father or on the Kirkland ranch next door. He was working his way through school, no scholarship, no loans.

"I'm proud of you about the A." His warm voice broke the silence between them.

"Thanks." Somehow it didn't seem so important anymore. She'd spent two years dreaming of being at college with him and now, if possible, she was more lonely than she'd been back in Crossroads.

She hung up. All the happiness had drained out of Lauren. In the weeks she'd been at college they hadn't had a real date. Study lunches and Lucas walking her to class a few times didn't count.

She curled into a ball and let silent tears fall. Maybe Polly had the right idea. Sleep your years of higher education away.

The phone sounded. One, two, three rings before she found it in the covers.

"Lauren!" Tim O'Grady's voice reminded her of home. Maybe because he'd been her neighbor in Ransom Canyon for most of her life. "Want to go get something to eat? It's Friday night and, as usual, I don't have a date. You can pick the restaurant. Anything but dorm food."

She wiped a tear off her cheek as she pushed her heartache deeper inside. "Sure." This was Tim's second year at Tech, and it seemed during his freshman year he'd done an extensive study

of the coffeehouses, bars and cheap restaurants in town. "I'll
meet you in the lobby."

"Food," the body under the blankets on the other side of the
room mumbled. "Food."

Lauren frowned. "Can my roommate come, too?"

Tim was silent for a moment, then added, "If she combs her
hair. Last time she tagged along I kept thinking a bush was following us."

"Fair enough. Give us ten minutes. I have to get out of this
dress."

Laughter traveled through the phone. "I've been waiting to
hear you say that for years, Lauren."

She smiled knowing he was kidding. "In your dreams,
O'Grady."

The phone went dead. Lauren stood and began changing
clothes. "Ten minutes, Polly," she shouted toward the other side
of the room, "or we're leaving without you."

Fifteen minutes later, with Polly buttoning her blouse as she
walked, Lauren and her never-friendly roommate headed downstairs.

Tim's dorm and hers were joined by a long lobby and cafete-
ria. When Lauren watched him coming toward her, she could
tell immediately he was tired by his slight limp, something she
knew he'd correct the minute he spotted her.

The limp was a lingering reminder from a night almost three
years ago when they'd both been hurt.

Polly must have noticed the limp, too. She leaned toward Lauren and asked, "What happened to your friend's leg?"

Lauren closed her eyes knowing that, thanks to the echo in
the foyer, Tim probably heard Polly. She thought if she ignored
the question, Polly would forget about it.

No such luck. She asked again.

Only, Tim answered first. "It was a dark and stormy night,
dear Polly Anna." He drew close and sliced his body between
them, giving all his attention to Polly. "Four high school kids de-

cided to break into an old house we thought might be haunted."
He waved his hands. "'Be afraid,' the old Gypsy House warned
them, but they dropped in anyway. Dust filled their lungs and
rotting boards creaked beneath their footsteps, but they were
explorers looking for thrills. Four went in but only three came
out. One was left trapped inside with the ghosts. Me."

Polly looked interested. "What happened?"

"I died." Tim shrugged.

Lauren laughed seeing Polly's horror as if she believed Tim
for a second.

"He broke several bones in his leg," Lauren corrected.
"Thanks to Lucas, I climbed out with only scratches. Reid Collins was with us, too. He didn't have a scratch, just a sprained
ankle."

Polly's eyes widened with true interest. "You two know Reid
Collins? I met him at a party a few weeks ago. What a hunk."

Polly didn't seem to notice both Tim and her shaking their
heads. Reid had been attracting girls for years. In high school
everyone thought he was the hero from that night in the haunted
house. He'd let everyone believe he'd saved Lauren, but it had
been Lucas who saved her from falling through the collapsed
floor. They'd all three let Reid take the glory that night, but
they all knew the truth even if they never talked about it.

Sometimes she thought four kids dropped through a broken
window that night and four different people came out. The accident had changed all of them.

"How'd you do on the chem test?" Tim asked as he turned
away from Polly.

"An A."

He took her hand and pulled her closer for a quick hug.
"Great! I know just the place to celebrate. Chicken fried steak
and all the trimmings. Two for one on Fridays."

She managed a smile as they walked with Polly following behind. "Do you always celebrate after an A?"

"Hell." He slowed and leaned near her ear. "I party after a C.

My folks don't care about grades. They just told me if I flunk out, I'll be working at the new Walmart going in Crossroads. So, I sign up for whatever looks easy and pray for the best. I plan to waste as much time at college as possible, then go home and write a great novel about my wild college days. It might take me a year or two, but I'll be rich and famous by the time I'm twenty-five."

"Can I be in your book?" Polly asked as she circled around them like an out-of-control top.

"I have an opening for one character. She's a nude girl dancing on a table. Of course, you'll have to audition. I need to make sure you can dance."

Lauren laughed and glanced at Polly as the girl asked, "You would use both my names, wouldn't you? Otherwise it could be anyone named Polly."

Lauren changed the subject. "Any idea what degree you're heading toward, Tim? I'm not so sure you'd make it as a writer. They don't usually audition their characters."

"True, but I'm willing to sacrifice for my art." He looked back at Polly. "You got any moles or scars I could put in, Polly Anna? Their detailed description might increase the word count, you know."

Lauren shoved him off the sidewalk. "Focus, O'Grady. What is your major?"

He caught up to her and put his arm lightly on her shoulder. "It doesn't matter. I'm majoring in life." He kissed her forehead. "You want to call this a date? If we do this right, you might make it in my book, too."

"No." She tugged her hood up as fog surrounded them.

"Good. We split the cost of the meal as friends."

Lauren never thought of dating Tim, though he asked from time to time. However, it would be nice if once in a while he acted disappointed when she said no.

The memories of the abandoned house seemed thick in her brain. Tim and Reid had been best friends back then and almost every conversation they had was about football. When Reid Collins suggested breaking into the place, Tim joked about ghosts and went along with the idea. He still bore the scars, physical ones on his leg and arm, and mental ones inside after his best friend left him behind.

"What do you hear from Reid?" she asked, knowing the night at the Gypsy House must be on Tim's mind, also.

"I haven't seen him since we came back to school in August. He's living at the frat house this year." Tim took her hand and they jogged to his Jeep. Polly followed, but didn't try to keep up.

Tim leaned in close to Lauren. "Last time I saw Reid, he was drunk. Cussed me out for caring."

Lauren was glad she couldn't see Tim's face. Whenever he talked of Reid, he always looked hurt.

Before Polly caught up, Lauren said, "Reid called me last week and asked me to go out. Some kind of big party before the homecoming game next weekend."

Tim froze for a moment before asking, low, "You going?"

"I might." She shrugged. "He's from home. Our dads are friends." She'd never told Tim how close she and Lucas Reyes were or that they dated some. Somehow what was between Lucas and her was private, too special to share. Or at least she'd thought it was. Lately she wasn't sure Lucas felt the same.

If he was working every weekend, Lauren didn't want to miss the whole college experience waiting for him. Reid was simply looking for a date, or worse, his old man told him to take her out. Her pop, who'd spent her high school years worrying that she'd date too early, was now probably worrying about her lack of dates. He'd asked her twice if she needed money for clothes. A question Lauren was sure had come straight from her mother. Her mom might have run from raising a kid after divorcing her dad, but that didn't stop Margaret from calling in her motherly advice from Dallas.

Tim pulled into the parking lot of a tiny little restaurant a few blocks away from campus. All the letters on the neon sign were lit except for the *R* in *Restaurant* and the *O* in *Open*. Huge dead elms leaned over the building giving the illusion that the place was caught in a huge spiderweb.

"What's the name of this place?" Lauren didn't make a move to open her door.

Tim stared at it a moment and answered. "Estaurant pen."

"Oh." She wasn't sure she'd want to go in even if it were free chicken fried steak.

Polly leaned forward. "No, guys, can't you see the two letters are out. I can't believe you two missed that."

Tim and Lauren looked at each other silently debating which one should kill the roommate.

"Come on, Lauren, live a little." Tim cut his lights. Before Polly climbed out the back, he whispered, "Only, don't go out with Reid."

"Why? You keep telling me that." She wasn't surprised when Tim didn't answer.

Like always, he changed the subject. They had great fun trying to read the menu in the dark *estaurant* and then laughing at how small the steaks were when the plates arrived. Tim tried to convince Polly the tough pieces of meat were cows' ears. When she believed him, he offered to eat her steak.

Polly flirted with the waiter long enough to talk him into giving her a hamburger. When she got up to go wash her hands, the guy offered her a tour of the place. By the time the burger was served she and Roger, the waiter, were dating.

Polly waved them goodbye as she ate with Roger, who'd said he'd be off in an hour.

Lauren hesitated, then she remembered the dates Polly had come in after, all upset because she couldn't remember the guy's name, even though she'd had her tongue in his mouth for hours.

She'd said, "I always make sure I know the guy's name before I sleep with him. After all, I don't want to wake up married after a night of drinking, like my mother did, and find out I have some stupid last name."

Lauren had only known Polly a week then, but she asked, "Do you sleep with all the guys you go out with?"

Polly had laughed and said, "Of course not. Sometimes I don't go *out* with them at all."

Lauren wasn't sure if Polly was trying to shock her or being honest, but after that she tried not to get too close to her. Only, leaving her here at the *estaurant* with some guy named Roger seemed cruel.

She touched Polly's arm. "Call if you need a ride back to campus."

For a second Polly seemed surprised, maybe even touched by the offer. Then her face hardened. "I never need help," she answered. "Don't worry about me."

Lauren nodded once and followed Tim out.

He pulled her into the night air saying they shouldn't interfere with true love.

"True love?" she whispered.

"Yeah, I have a feeling it hits Polly about every other weekend."

They drove back without talking. Lauren couldn't help wondering if Tim was bothered by Polly's quick hookup more than he admitted.

Lauren didn't know whether to be worried about her or angry that Polly seemed to think so little of herself.

At the dorm doors, Tim kissed her cheek, and Lauren felt as if she'd almost had a date. "Promise we'll always be friends."

He grinned. "Promise."

They usually stood around talking whenever they got together but tonight something seemed to be on Tim's mind and hers was heavy with lost dreams. He tipped his imaginary hat and walked away as she turned and headed up the stairs.

By the time she got back to her room she still hadn't received a message from Lucas. She'd hoped he would have texted just to let her know he'd made it home to Crossroads, but he hadn't.

She did have a text from Reid asking if she'd made up her

mind about the party next Friday night. Say yes, he'd texted, everyone wears black or red to the dinner.

Angry and frustrated and feeling very much alone, she texted back. Yes. I can go.

A moment later Reid answered, Pick you up at six. Bring a coat we'll go directly to the game after the party.

Her first official date at college, she thought. But it wasn't with Lucas. It wasn't even with a guy she liked. All the daydreams she'd had of college and being with Lucas were falling around her like snowflakes vanishing as they touched the rug.

From this night on, she'd build new—real—experiences. Maybe not with a guy she was crazy about. Maybe not forever dreams she'd cherish. But someday when her friends talked of their college days she'd at least have a few memories to compare.

Glancing out her window, she noticed a break in the clouds where tiny stars were shining through. The night of her sixteenth birthday, Lucas had taken her far away from town lights to watch the stars over the lake.

Lauren smiled remembering earlier that same evening when Reid had shown up drunk to her party and tried to kiss her. One swift knee between his legs had sent him to the ground. He'd been a perfect gentleman after that. Tech's stadium was at the far north end of the campus. If he stepped out of line next Friday night, she could always walk back to her dorm.

Leaning back on her bed, she thought of Lucas and how she loved kissing him, but she was his *someday* love. He wanted them to finish school before they got serious. He hadn't believed a sixteen-year-old would know about real love, and in many ways he still treated her as if she was that sixteen-year-old.

Lucas raced through life. He'd graduated early from high school. He would make it through to his bachelor's degree in three years and planned to start law school in the spring. He hinted that he wanted her to be part of his future, but Lauren wanted to be part of his now.

A plan simmered in the back of her thoughts. Maybe if he

saw how other guys wanted to go out with her, he'd pay more attention.

She shook her head. It was a dumb plan. Stupid. But then, being available and waiting every time he called didn't seem to be working.

If she went out with Reid, Tim would tell Lucas. If he reacted, she might just get that real date with Lucas Reyes that she'd been waiting for since she was fifteen years old.

CHAPTER FOUR

Angela

Angela pulled on an old jogging suit and decided to walk around the edge of the lake. She'd spent all week cleaning and moving into her little cabin and had grown to love the lake and the small town a mile away. Tomorrow morning she'd start a new job, a new life. Her years of taking care of her mother, of worrying about her father, were in her past, washed away by a river of tears. Now she had to face her future.

Glancing at the cat trying to spread his fat body across the windowsill, Angela whispered, "This is our new home, Doc. You're going to love it here."

Doc Holliday just stared at her, but Angela couldn't stop smiling.

No one in town cared about her family, and, for the first time since her birth, no family was watching over her. Her mother had smothered her for eighteen years, then she'd passed her off to two old aunts so Angela could attend a small college outside Washington, DC. Her parents said they'd save money if she lived with the aunts, but she'd missed most of campus life. As soon

RUSTLER'S MOON   53

as she graduated, there was never any question that she'd find a job back in Florida and move in with her parents for a while. A part-time job in a small marina museum was all she found and her duties included ordering and cleaning the gift shop as well as giving the grade-school tours.

Then her mom's cancer returned and any possibility of having her own place was forgotten. Her father needed help.

Though her uncle Anthony had offered her a job, Angela had studied to be a museum curator, and even at half the pay, she was glad to be working in a museum. At least she had the title of assistant curator.

Every day she'd come home and tell her parents all about her work at the tiny marina museum as if what she did was fun and important.

Her father rarely talked about his job. She knew he hated it, but somehow he was tied to what he did.

When her mother died, she stayed at home helping him in grief, thinking that they'd move along pretty much as they had before.

One note from her father, written on the day he died, changed all that.

She guessed her aunt and uncle would be glad not to have her around. Surely whatever, or whoever, had frightened her father would not follow her here. She knew no secrets. She owned nothing of value.

As she clicked on her flashlight and began to navigate the uneven shoreline of the lake, Angela felt light-headed with possibilities. Her plan just might work in this quiet little community where cows outnumbered people. She'd fill her new home with her mother's quilts, and the furniture she'd picked up at secondhand stores. She'd fish on the lake with her father's gear. She'd have their memories with her—the photo of her and her dad, his ledger with the leather worn thin and her replica Greek coin necklace. All that would have to be enough.

She decided her father had been right to tell her to leave. She felt newborn here, as if anything were possible, as if life could be somehow fuller, richer here.

She breathed in the night air, the smell of evergreens and lake water. She was stepping into a new world. Walking on a different planet. All her life she'd been a meek homebody and now she was an explorer.

The few dozen houses that stood along the shore didn't seem to have drapes, or even blinds. She felt a little like a voyeur staring into the homes as she walked. Couples reading, playing cards, watching TV. "Yes," she whispered. "There will be a peace here for me."

A fisherman docking his boat stopped to watch her, but didn't wave. A couple cuddled in a blanket at the far end of one of the private docks didn't notice her pass. As the evening aged, she blended in with the shadows.

For the first time in her life, she almost believed she was invisible.

When she passed Dan Brigman's house, she was surprised to see the sheriff with a woman in a flowing dress and heels standing in the room that faced the lake. Dan had mentioned a daughter when he'd shown her the cabin, but not a wife. She'd gotten the impression he wasn't married, yet the woman looked far too old to be his daughter.

The woman was waving her arms as if arguing with the sheriff, then raised her hands in the air and let them drop to her sides as though giving up.

Angela stood frozen as the woman stormed from the room. The sound of the front door slamming and a car starting reached her ears, then the engine roared up the road behind the sheriff's lake house.

She was still staring when Dan Brigman walked out on his deck and looked up at the stars.

She thought maybe, just maybe, if she remained perfectly still he wouldn't see her. But of course, if he looked in her direction, she'd be silhouetted against the moonlit lake. Wild-haired, five-three Peeping Toms were hard to miss.

Angela lowered her head, clicked off the flashlight and walked slowly past his place, hoping the shadow of his dock might hide her from view.

She almost made it to the bend before he called out, "Angela, is that you?"

She turned and watched him jogging toward her in jeans and a sweatshirt. "I thought I'd walk around part of the lake," she managed to say.

He fell into step with her. "Mind if I tag along? I could use a walk." The sheriff looked thinner without his vest and forty-pound duty belt around his waist. He also looked somehow sadder than he'd been last week, even in the shadows.

"Not at all." She clicked back on her flashlight even though the lights from the houses cast a warm glow over a broken path that wandered along between docks and lawn furniture. "You can tell me about the lake."

"Well, legend says this stop was an old Comanche winter camp. After the Second World War some of the men returning home decided to build here. I always thought they were looking for peace. I know how they feel—no matter how hectic the job of county sheriff gets, when I come home and stare out at the lake, the world seems right."

As he spoke, his words slowed a bit and his shoulders seemed to relax. When she asked about his daughter, he laughed and told her that she had a date for homecoming. "I'm finding out just how important that is," he admitted.

"You and your wife must be happy she's adjusting well to college." Angela didn't add that she had no idea how important homecoming dates might be. That wasn't something she'd participated in at college. She'd had few dates, with friends mostly.

"We are proud of Lauren." He cleared his throat. "But my wife and I divorced years ago." He shrugged. "I might as well tell you. You'll hear all about everyone who lives around town as soon as you start work tomorrow. Margaret left me a few months after I took this job. She wanted to finish school, then do an internship at a big company in Dallas. After that she got a job there and couldn't leave the big city and all it had to offer. It took me three years to figure out she wasn't coming back home. It seemed leaving me wasn't a problem."

He fell silent. They just walked. She listened to the water lapping against the shoreline and fish slapping the calm lake as they jumped to catch their supper.

She thought of asking who the woman was that she'd seen in the sheriff's house, but maybe he had a right to his secrets, too. Finally, she broke the silence. "I'd better turn in. Tomorrow will be a big day for me."

At the spot where she turned off toward her cabin, they stopped and he turned to face her. "Angela, don't worry about tomorrow. You'll be fine. We're all glad you're here. When I hand over the museum keys, a few representatives from some of the original families will be there."

He could probably hear her breathing stop, so he rushed to continue. "You've already talked to Staten Kirkland. He's the one who hired you on the phone. You'll meet the O'Gradys and Collinses as well as the Wagners. All from old families who settled here a hundred years ago. They're just showing up to wish you the best."

"Is there anyone I should be worried about?"

Dan laughed. "They are all good people. You might watch out for Wagner, though. Vern's been known to ask any single girl around to marry him."

"How many wives has he had?"

"None. Talk is, after he forgot to show up at the church a few times, every woman in town stopped believing anything Vern said." Dan shook his head. "I don't know if that story is true. Wagner told it to me himself."

"I'll watch out for him."

Dan laughed. "I promise, he's someone not easy to miss."

Angela said good-night and walked down the path to her
cabin trying to remember all the names she'd heard. Kirkland,
Collins, O'Grady and Wagner. Once she got settled in her new
job, she'd look up all their family histories. Though she'd like
to forget hers, most people wanted to talk about their roots.

The next morning she was so early to the parking lot of the
museum she waited half an hour before the sheriff showed up.
While he was unlocking the huge double doors of the museum,
cars and pickup trucks began pulling into the lot.

The sheriff stood beside her as the families piled out and
greeted each other. Dan leaned close to her and quietly gave her
the lowdown. "The couple in the Cadillac are the Collinses,
they own the Bar W Ranch. Both their sons are away at school.
That van with all the kids are one branch of the O'Gradys. Lots
of them around town." He nodded to an attractive couple with
a young son. "The tall couple with the toddler are the Kirklands. Staten owns the Double K. Biggest spread within a hundred miles. Word is his wife, Quinn, is pregnant again. The
two men climbing out of that old rusty red pickup are Wagners.
They own the Devil's Fork Ranch."

Angela fought the urge to bolt. So many people, all coming to see her. Kirkland was tall, big like his voice had been on
the phone. The man called Collins looked bored and his wife
seemed overdressed.

She suddenly had a dozen questions to ask the sheriff, but it
was too late.

People were too near the museum for him to fill her in on
any more details, but she felt as if she had at least put a few
names with faces.

When the sheriff finally opened the doors, she was surprised
to see a banner welcoming her. A long lace-covered table was
set up with red velvet cupcakes, lemon squares and juice in tall
champagne glasses. All made it seem more a party than her first

day at work. Three round little grandmother-types stood behind the refreshments table beaming with pride.

Fifty people crowded into the big two-story open foyer. Angela and the sheriff stood next to the mayor, Davis Collins, and his perfect, much younger wife named Cherry.

Angela fought down a giggle every time the mayor called his wife "Cherry Baby." Everyone in the room, except Davis Collins, could see his wife glare at him. She obviously hated the name and he obviously didn't care.

Everyone except two-year-old James Kirkland stood silently as the mayor said what a grand day it was to have a new curator over the museum they all loved.

With keys in her hand, Angela moved among the people trying to remember names. Everyone wanted to show her their favorite exhibit. After two hours, Angela felt as if she'd had a private tour of every foot of the museum from archives with journals of the first settlers, to the gun collections, to a mock-up of the first wagons. All her years of studying Texas history came alive as she touched artifacts that had survived since the time of the first Austin colony, including weapons that were around during the fight at the Alamo, and Native American clothing now treasured as works of art.

She loved it all. This was where she belonged. She'd grown up with her father and uncle always talking antiques. Every family member's house had tables no one touched and chairs no one sat in. Yet, all these treasures of this Western past came alive as the descendants told stories of how life had been here on this very land a hundred and fifty years ago.

When the last guest finally left, and the three volunteers vanished into a small kitchen in the back to clean up the refreshments, Angela almost danced up the stairs. She wanted to pull the pins from her tight bun and run like a carefree child through her new life.

But of course she wouldn't. She giggled. She'd do what was

expected, at least until everyone was gone. Being here was both terrifying and Christmas morning at the same time.

After stopping at her office to pick up a pencil and pad, she began at the top of the stairs jotting things down that needed to be done and ideas for new displays. It would take weeks to examine all the artifacts, but what fun she would have.

She was so lost in her ideas, she didn't notice a man moving up behind her until she felt his breath on the back of her neck.

"I have a question."

She jumped, almost tumbling into the diorama of the canyon. Her notepad and pencil flew into the air. The pad slapped against the floor, but the pencil jabbed her attacker's forehead drawing a drop of blood.

His right hand shot out, catching her shoulder as his tall frame leaned forward. His grip was strong, digging into her arm as he fought to pull her toward him and away from the display glass.

Opening her mouth to scream, she whirled. Her elbow plowed into his ribs as she found her footing. He folded over and his jaw slammed against her forehead, sending his hat flying into the display.

Both let out a cry. Hers sounded more like a squeal, and his seemed more like swearing, but when they met one another's eyes, both were in pain.

She recovered first. "Mr. *Wagner!*" At over six-four, he was hard to forget. Especially when he'd added boots and a hat to his height. He had towered above her when he shook her hand at the reception, and he towered over her now.

"Mrs. Jones." He gasped as he straightened, rubbing his ribs.

She had no idea what kind of man he was, but she wasn't taking any chances. "My colleagues are in the back. If you are thinking of assaulting me, all I have to do is scream, and they'll come running."

Wagner made an effort to smile. "I doubt your three volunteers have run in thirty years. A cattle prod wouldn't budge them into more than a stroll. As for assaulting you, I'm the one with a hole in my chest from your elbow and several teeth loose from the blow to my jaw." He brushed two fingers across his forehead. "It appears I'm also bleeding. All I planned to do was ask you a question, lady."

She saw his point. Surprisingly enough, she seemed to have won the short battle. "Well, Mr. Wagner, if you're thinking of asking me to marry you, you can forget it. I'm wise to your tricks. I was warned by the sheriff."

The tall cowboy gave up looking injured and stared at her as if she'd gone crazy. Anger flared. "Look, much as I'm turned on by your plain, gray suit and those practical shoes, I'm not in the habit of proposing to complete strangers on first contact."

"I've heard different, Vern Wagner."

Now he looked shocked. Then, to her surprise, he smiled and winked at her. "You do fit the list, Mrs. Jones, except I'm thinking you're too smart. Dumb was a definite on the criteria. That suit looks like it's homemade, and I'm betting you cook. Now that I think about it, we might as well get married, assuming your bank account is hefty and your husband is missing."

She could only stare at the insane man. Maybe there was too much inbreeding in this county. He looked all right, close to perfect, actually. Tall, handsome with his sandy-blond hair and blue eyes. From boots to Stetson he was dressed as if he'd walked off the cover of a romance novel. Too bad he was brain-dead.

"Maybe we should get on with the mating. After all, your being pregnant at the wedding would be a plus." He leaned down to her level as he moved closer.

Angela froze in total shock as his lips touched hers. The few times in her life she'd been kissed, really kissed, were nothing like this. His lips were soft against hers, but he seemed to know what he was doing.

Her entire body warmed. This man was a lightning strike on a clear day.

He hesitated as though just as surprised as she was, then leaned closer letting his body brush against her. One hand moved along her waist. She wasn't sure if he was steadying her, or himself, as the kiss deepened.

She accepted his gift, hungry for a passion she'd never tasted. She had no idea how to kiss him back like this, but for one wild moment in her life, she wanted to learn.

Just as she wondered if crazy was contagious, someone hollered, "Wilkes!" so loud it echoed through the walls.

Wagner straightened and pulled his hat down over his still-bleeding forehead. He was pulling away, straightening to the stranger he'd been moments before, but for one second, she felt his fingers press into her side as if letting go didn't come easy.

She stumbled as she stepped around him and felt his hand rest against her back once more, steadying her after his gentle assault.

An old man limped into the room. "How long do you expect me to wait for you, boy? I got things to do back at the ranch."

She glanced at the man beside her. He definitely wasn't a boy and hadn't been for years, but he didn't seem offended by the old man's tone.

"Angie Jones," Wagner said as if, now that they'd kissed, they were old friends, "I'd like you to meet my uncle, *Vern* Wagner."

The older man took off his hat and smoothed his palm over the few hairs left on his head. "Nice to meet you, miss."

The man beside her leaned close to her ear. "I'm Wilkes Wagner, Angie. My uncle has been proposing to women for years and none have taken him up on it yet. I'm not sure, but I think he made up the part about leaving a few brides at the altar that everyone believes."

He shook his head. "I'm sorry for frightening you. I thought you were in on a joke my uncle was playing on me."

She thought over the odd encounter. She might not know how to fight off a man who wanted to kiss her, but she knew how to be professional. "And what *was* your question, Mr. Wagner?"

Wilkes glanced at his uncle. "I'll have to come back another

time. I'd like you to help me with some research on an old
house."

"I will be happy to," she managed. "Only, please call before
you come. I'm going to be very busy learning the museum."

"I'll try." He smiled, and she knew he was laughing at her.
"Good day, Angie."

She straightened, trying to hold her ground. "My name's not
Angie, Mr. Wagner." Only her father called her Angie.

To her surprise Wilkes Wagner grinned. "It's not Jones, either, Miss Harold, and there's no ring on your finger. If you
didn't keep the man, don't keep his name."

CHAPTER FIVE

Angela
Ransom Canyon Museum

Angela plopped down in her office chair and swiveled around to face her huge window. The beautiful canyon welcomed her, calmed her. She felt the freedom of this place pounding through her blood.

She'd been at work less than three hours and already she'd survived a party in her honor, injured a man she thought was attacking her and had a marriage proposal. Well, the proposal part was a joke, but still he had asked. Maybe living in this little town wasn't going to be as boring as she'd hoped. Maybe she'd be different here. Braver.

"Miss Harold?" Dan Brigman's voice sounded from the hallway. "May I come in?"

She turned toward the office door. Since the sheriff's head was already in her office, she figured the rest of his body might as well be. "Of course." She motioned to the chair in front of her desk, but he walked around to stand at the floor-to-ceiling window.

Brigman looked exactly like what she imagined a county sheriff would look like. They should cast him in a series. He was tall, but not too tall. Brown hair in need of a cut. Boots well-worn and polished, and a weapon strapped to his leg as if it were simply a part of him and nothing more. She'd known the moment she saw him that he was a man she could trust.

"If I had this great a view in my office, I'd never leave." Leaning against the edge of the glass, Dan added, "The town gave you a nice welcome, I thought."

"It was wonderful! The president of the museum board—Staten Kirkland?—said if there is anything I want around the place to just tell one of the volunteers and it will get back to his grandmother, who'll pester him until he gets it done. Strange chain of command, but maybe it works."

Dan smiled. "That sounds about right. Staten can move mountains it seems. The Kirklands are about as close to royalty in these parts as it comes. Legend is Staten's great-great-grandfather bought his wife at kind of a swap meet the outlaws used to have down in this very canyon. The Kirklands come from rough stock, but they're solid."

"Rough stock?"

"Sorry, I forget you're not from around here. Rough stock is mostly a rodeo term these days. Bulls and horses that have never been tamed or broke to ride."

"What about the Wagners? Are they rough stock, too?" She could still feel the tingle of Wilkes Wagner's lips on hers. No man had ever kissed her like that—all out and wild.

"No. The Wagners come from a German family who were carpenters. Very civilized. The first Mrs. Wagner was a midwife who delivered half the babies born in the county back in the late 1800s. Somewhere along the way, a few of the sons or grandsons started farming. The Wagner you met owns the Devil's Fork Ranch. Farms mostly to raise crops for winter as feed. Supplies several of the ranches around.

"Wilkes runs a few head of cattle along with farming over

eight hundred acres, but nothing like the Collins and Kirkland spreads. I've never seen a Wagner who couldn't fix anything that broke. They're good with their hands."

Angela blushed. She could still feel the imprint of Wilkes's hand at her side.

The sheriff pushed away from the window. He seemed to have stretched his skills at conversation to the max. "Well, I'd better get back to work. Call me if you need anything."

He was halfway to the door when she asked, "Where's my staff?"

"Staff?" Dan asked.

"You know, the people who work here?" She'd hoped to meet them first, not last.

"Oh, I thought you understood. You're it. That's why we had to close the place when the old curator left."

"You're kidding." She could not run the entire place by herself.

Brigman must have seen her panic. "Of course. You got help. Nigel Walls comes in twice a week to clean the floors and bathrooms. He also works at the courthouse, so if you need him, I can send him over early.

"The ladies auxiliary holds a brunch here the first of every month and their president assigns two members to the front desk every hour you're open. I think they work in two-hour shifts, but sometimes the ladies get to talking and there will be four to six women at the desk. The county keeps up with donations and bills. We don't charge for our time, but the volunteers keep a count of attendance and give tours. The building is open from nine to five, six days a week. If you take a day off, all you have to do is call one of the board members to step in."

"That's it? That's all the staff?" Angela listed in her mind all the duties that didn't include greeting or cleaning. Kirkland had probably explained it to her during the phone interview but she'd been so excited and tired she must have missed the details.

"Of course we have others. Anyone doing community ser-

vice is sent here to do yard work. The judge tends to make the
hours longer around mid-November to help put up Christmas
lights. But don't worry about the Christmas party, it's still two
months away and the school tours don't get packed back-to-
back until spring."

Angela was glad she was sitting down. She did her best to understand what the sheriff was saying, but invisible boulders kept
falling on her head. She was the *only* employee.

"Anything else I should know about?"

Dan looked out the window. "There is Carter Mayes. You'll
see his little RV parked out here on the museum lot now and
then. He comes every spring and stays till late fall, has for years.
Folks say he's looking for something he lost in the canyon when
he was a kid, but I think he just loves walking the back trails.
Don't worry about him. He's a good guy."

She saw a lean figure far down in the canyon moving slowly
toward the bottom. Carter Mayes.

"Anything else?" the sheriff asked with his hand on the door.

"Yes," she said. "I think I'll go back to my maiden name." It
seemed like a good idea, since she'd never really been engaged to
the man named Jones, who never really existed. "When I talked
to Mr. Kirkland, I thought I'd be married, but it didn't happen."

Dan grinned. "Who knows, Miss Harold, that might have
been for the best. I've been trying to recover from a wedding
for fifteen years. But no regrets. I got my Lauren away at college. If I brag about her too much, stop me."

"I will." She smiled, wondering if her father had ever talked
so proudly about her. Maybe he had.

"Makes sense to clear up the name. Folks would get confused." Dan nodded. "A few started calling you Harold the
minute they heard the bastard didn't move to Texas with you."

She stared at the sheriff. "What makes you think he was a
bastard?"

Dan smiled and stepped through the threshold. "He'd have
to be, Angie, if he left a find like you."

As his footsteps echoed down the stairs, Angela fought back a giggle. That was the nicest thing she could remember anyone ever saying to her.

But her head was spinning. Maybe she had made a mistake changing back to her real last name, but despite her father's warning, why would anyone come after her? The people in Crossroads already knew her real name. She hadn't said anything when she'd signed Harold on the lease for the cabin made out to Angela Jones. Now the fake name on the lease would keep her safe. If she was careful, she could leave little record of her real name.

But then, what did it matter if the people called her Harold now that she was here? They weren't likely to run into any of her relatives half a continent away.

Time to stop worrying about her family and dive into work. This was her new life, her new beginning. She had been so unimportant in her father's family they'd probably forgotten her by now anyway.

Angela grinned, remembering how last Thanksgiving Uncle Anthony's latest wife had moved the family's big dinner and forgotten to mention it to her or her father. Now, if any of them dropped by the beach house on Anna Marie Island, they probably wouldn't be worried enough to ask where she'd gone.

She picked up her notepad and went downstairs. One of the volunteers was giving a tour this afternoon, and she planned to learn as much as possible.

Over the rest of the week, the museum drew her in like a magic time machine to a period in history that she'd loved since she'd discovered *Little House on the Prairie* as a girl. Yet somehow, she felt she belonged in this place. To her knowledge no one in her family had ever come west. She was the first pioneer, even if she was over a hundred years late.

Friday morning, Angela was deep in paperwork when she glanced up from her records to find Wilkes Wagner standing at her office door. He seemed to be blocking the entire entrance with his tall frame and wide shoulders. She had no idea how long he'd been lurking there.

"If you've come to assault me or ask for my hand, Mr. Wagner, I'm sorry, I'm busy. You'll have to come back later."

The cowboy had the nerve to smile and walk in as if he'd been invited. "I haven't recovered from the last beating you gave me, Angie. I've still got a bruise on my rib." He towered over her. "You want to see?" He tugged at his shirt.

"No." She decided the sheriff must have left out dumb when he mentioned the Wagner family traits. Only, he wasn't dumb. Arrogant. Rude. Sexy as hell, but not dumb.

"Well, if stripping is out—" he winked, telling her he'd been teasing "—then I'm here to do some research. You store county records under this roof. I'm looking for details about an old house that may have been one of the first in Crossroads. A friend of mine, Yancy Grey, claims it haunts him."

She stood, trying to look her most professional, but it was hard to pull it off in the baggy trousers and bulky sweater she'd worn for a workday behind the dusty display cases. Any hope that he wouldn't notice vanished when she saw him studying her from the knot of wild hair on the top of her head to her tennis shoes.

"Please follow me," she ordered, her chin high.

He did just that, though she guessed he knew exactly where the museum records were kept. It was a beautiful room in the heart of the building. Although windowless, the walls between file cabinets and bookshelves had been painted sunset yellow. The tall room's lighting had been expertly crafted with low-hanging wrought-iron chandeliers. Local cattle brands were laser cut into the dark iron giving the room a warm, Western glow. The Double K for the Kirklands, The Bar W for the Collins' ranch and many others including the Devil's Fork. Wilkes's family brand looked like the branches of a winter tree that nature had shaped into the lines of a three-tine fork.

She started when Wilkes overtook her a moment before she

reached for the doorknob. He held it open for her and then followed her in. For the first time, she noticed a leather backpack slung over one of his shoulders. "I'm afraid I can't show you around. I haven't had a chance yet to explore all the wonderful records in this room."

He dropped his pack on the nearest chair and sat on the end of the long oak table that sliced down the middle of the room. "Don't worry about it. I've explored these stacks. My mother used to volunteer here on Saturdays, and I always tagged along. I think this place is why I majored in American history in college."

"You went to college?" The words were out before she could stop them. Somehow with his worn boots and old jeans she'd formed the idea that he'd never left the ranch for more than a few hours.

He grinned, that wicked grin she'd seen her first day. "Much as I tried to goof off, I ended up with a degree in history and a minor in math." Sitting on the table, he was eye level with her, which made him impossible to ignore. Men shouldn't be that rugged and that good-looking at the same time.

The memory of their kiss warmed her and she licked her lips. His smile faded, but his eyes darkened slightly, telling her he knew exactly what she was thinking.

Wilkes folded his arms and looked away. One kiss might have been an accident, a part of a game he assumed was being played, but another would be an advance. He was silently telling her it wouldn't happen again.

He was right, of course. It shouldn't have happened in the first place. The best kiss of her life had been a mistake. Nothing more.

She tried to be polite. Change the subject before her cheeks matched the color of her hair. "There's not a great deal you can do with a history degree unless you want to teach, I've heard."

He crossed his legs at the ankle, almost touching her shoes as he did.

She moved a foot away.

"I've no interest in teaching. I want to ranch, Angie. Tried to find something else but waking up to clean air and sounds of the country won out. Maybe I didn't love ranching so much as I simply had no great ambition to do anything else," he said. "Today, I'm just helping a friend who wants to learn about one of the houses at the edge of town. I'm not working on some great research project."

She took another step toward the door. "I'll come back and check in on you later. We have painters down in the foyer and a high school group coming in to look at the wagons."

"Who is the *we*?" he asked.

"Well…me," she admitted, realizing just how alone she was most of the time. Normally, she loved it, but somehow, with him here, she wanted to feel as if there was a crowd around. In an odd way, this rough-around-the-edges cowboy tempted her. He wasn't relationship material, but maybe for that one-night stand all her friends talked about but Angela had never tried. If he made love as well as he kissed, he might be more than she could handle.

Who was she kidding? His old uncle Vern was probably more than she could handle.

Still, she could dream about it, even if she knew nothing would ever happen. Wilkes Wagner seemed perfect to fall in love with for the night and then walk away. He'd never work for long-term but she had a feeling he'd start a fire that would fill her dreams for years.

He stood so smoothly, so silently, she was halfway to the door when he said, "Angie, I'm not going to attack you. I didn't the day we met. You just jumped when I must have startled you." He moved around the table and pulled a chair out as if proving that he'd come to work. "And just for the record, I won't ever ask for your hand. If I come a-asking, it'll be for a lot more than just your hand I'd want, darlin'. I have no doubt there's a woman beneath all those baggy clothes."

Now several feet away, she felt more comfortable. "I wasn't

startled," she lied, not wanting to think about the hand comment.

"You're the most skittish woman I've ever met. Hell, I've seen horseflies calmer than you."

Angela smiled, feeling safe so near the door. "You meet a lot of skittish women, do you?"

"Not many," he admitted as the corner of his lip lifted slightly. "Not any that taste like warm honey."

She walked away, her cheeks burning.

He called out before she closed the door. "Let me know when it's closing time. I don't own a watch and I forgot my cell."

Glancing back, she noticed there was no clock in the room. Wilkes was already busy opening the file drawers, and, to her surprise, he did look as if he knew his way around the stacks of records.

She promised herself she would not go check on him until five o'clock, but a little after four she couldn't resist any longer.

As silently as possible, she opened the library door to find the long oak table covered in books and papers. Wilkes Wagner was sound asleep, his chin on his chest and his boots propped on the chair across from him.

She moved closer and noticed the stubble along his jaw and the wrinkles at the corners of his eyes. He seemed to be a man who laughed often even if he was a puzzle. Why would someone get a college degree and not use it? Why would a handsome man flirt with the likes of her? Why did he let his uncle talk to him as if he were a kid?

As she studied him, she spied a few scars on his chin and one just above his eye. For a man who couldn't be much into his thirties, she was surprised to see so many deep scars on his hands.

A photograph of a house lay next to his left elbow. It was a small two-story, built low into the ground. She'd read early homes often were dug into the plains' sod to save on lumber and to keep the small dwellings warmer in winter and cooler in summer.

Above the photograph someone had written *Stanley House*. Angela began to put facts together like puzzle pieces in her mind. A family named Stanley was listed among the first settlement in the area. They worked as blacksmiths and farriers on the Kirkland spread. She couldn't remember seeing any Stanleys on the current membership list, so they must have died out or moved away.

She left the room quietly and ran to the wagon exhibit she'd just shown on the high school tour. There, at the back, was an old, faded vardo wagon that looked like a tiny house on wheels. A Gypsy wagon made of wood. The name on the plaque read "Stanley Wagon. One of two traveling with James Kirkland in 1872."

She smiled and headed back to tell Wilkes that she'd found something that might help, but a dozen people suddenly filled the foyer. They seemed to be having a small reunion and asked Angela to see their great-aunt's collection of quilts that had been donated to the museum forty years ago. It took Angela and both volunteers, Miss Bees and Miss Abernathy, to find them in the archives. By the time the quilts were carefully folded and put away, it was long past closing time.

As she said goodbye to the older ladies and locked up, she remembered the sleeping cowboy in the library. Maybe she could simply let him sleep the night. No, that wouldn't work. The last thing she wanted was Wilkes Wagner wandering around here after dark.

He'd already spent far too much time wandering around in her dreams.

When she found Wilkes still sound asleep, her next problem was how to wake him. If she frightened him awake, he might jump or attack. Miss Bees told her Wilkes had served three years in the army after college.

Angela had heard of soldiers fighting if surprised.

Maybe if she just tapped him on the shoulder and jumped out of range. With her arm outstretched, she moved slowly toward him, but when she could have touched his shoulder, she corrected slightly and brushed his light brown hair with the tips of her fingers.

It was far softer than she would have thought. Thick, with just a bit of curl circling over her fingers. She could never remember wanting to touch any man's hair before. Most of her encounters with the opposite sex were awkward and none she ever wanted to repeat. But almost of its own will, her hand brushed lightly over his hair once more.

When she finally looked down to his face, his blue eyes were staring up at her, waiting to see what she'd do next.

"Oh! I'm sorry." She leaped back. "I wasn't sure how to wake you."

"Saying *wake up* would have worked," he said, unfolding from the chair. "But I didn't mind you brushing my hair back. My mother used to wake me like that when I was a kid."

"I, um, just needed to let you know that it's long past closing time." She picked up a few of the books, trying not to look at him, then remembered the wagon. "Oh, wait, I wanted to show you something."

He grabbed his pack and shoved a notebook inside. "I can't wait." He grinned that killer grin again, then followed her down the stairs. "Mind if I leave the research out? I'll start again tomorrow."

"You're coming back?"

His gaze seemed to be studying her. "If I'm welcome?"

She straightened, wishing she were taller. "Of course you're welcome, Mr. Wagner."

He grinned as they moved down the stairs. "Want to call me Wilkes, Angie?"

Wilkes must have spotted the paint supplies neatly piled in one corner of the foyer and the front desk that was no longer manned by volunteers. "Looks like we might be alone," he said. "I hope you're not plotting to attack me again."

She ignored the comment as she rushed down the long hallway to the sunny room and the old wagons. "I noticed one of your books had a picture of a house called the Stanley House. I found a wagon you might like to see at the back of the display. The two might have some relation to each other."

She had expected him to be happy, but he was as excited as a kid on Christmas morning as he walked around the old wagon. There were only slight hints of how colorful it once must have been, but Wilkes stared wide-eyed.

"This is great, Angie, but it's not called a wagon. It's called a vardo. Think first mobile home. Just imagine, this one came here almost a hundred and forty years ago. It must have been stored in a barn or it would never be in this good of shape."

"Glad I could help." She couldn't hide her smile.

"I've got to call Yancy. He's the one who wants to know about the old house. He's going to love seeing this. The house's first owner was a man named Stanley, and this is the Stanley vardo. They must be linked."

Angela dug in her pocket and handed him her cell.

Before she knew it a man pounded on the museum door and almost knocked her down running in. He apologized as he rushed toward the wagons. It occurred to her that she had just let a second crazy man into the building.

By the time she made it down the hallway, the two men had examined every part of the old wagon, figuring out how each part worked, and how it had been put together. A neglected piece of history suddenly seemed priceless.

"Be careful," she said, leaning down to where Wilkes lay on the floor examining the underside of the wagon.

His hand reached up and brushed her arm. "I will," he said, letting his touch linger. "Thanks to you, we may have just discovered the value of this old relic."

She stepped away trying to understand how this man's slight touch could affect her so. She couldn't stop watching the way his hands moved respectfully over the old wood.

Wilkes saw its value even through the dust and decay.

She listened as the men talked in low voices as though they were awaking history. Finally, Wilkes turned to her and looked a bit guilty for keeping her so late.

"We have to go, Yancy," he said without looking away from her. "This'll still be here tomorrow and our new curator has had a long day."

She didn't argue.

"I'll walk through all the rooms and turn out lights while you get your things." He was still watching her. "I'll check locks."

She touched the place on her arm where his hand had been. When she looked up, he was still staring at her. Probably reading her mind.

"I'll be right back," she whispered, guessing he probably knew how to lock up better than she did.

"No hurry," he added, probably seeing the exhaustion in her eyes. "I know what I'm doing here. I've worked on this display before. Your treasure is safe with us."

Of course he knew the museum. He was a Wagner. He belonged in this place far more than she did.

As she climbed the stairs, she couldn't stop smiling. Wilkes was a far more complicated man than she'd thought.

When she reached her office, she noticed the message light blinking on her phone. She hit the button as she grabbed a pen to write down the message.

For a moment, there was nothing. Then, in a low voice, a man said simply, "I know who you are. We need to talk." Another pause as if he was thinking about saying more, then a click.

Angela couldn't move. Somehow, someone from her past had found her. She hadn't been gone three whole weeks and they found her. If they'd been tracking her, they must know that she suspected her father's death hadn't been the result of a simple robbery. She could almost hear her angry uncle yelling for one of his assistants to go find the girl and bring her back.

Maybe they thought she took something of value, but all she took was her father's ledger and the picture of them on a fishing trip twenty years ago. Everything else she left with had belonged to her.

Her logical mind began to list everything she'd packed. Her mother's quilts, her father's fishing gear, the ugly cat, her clothes, her small jewelry box with earrings she'd bought herself and her mother's wedding band and the replica Greek necklace that her father had given her.

The money her father transferred to her account was exactly the amount Uncle Anthony had borrowed years ago. Surely her uncle didn't think that it was his now that her father was dead.

Angela's hands shook as she reached for her jacket. Maybe she was wrong. Maybe it was just a crank call. Maybe she had a stalker. There was no one from home who would take the time to follow her. Not for fifty thousand dollars and a few inexpensive pieces of jewelry.

She'd thought she had a stalker once when she was in college, but her mother told her she wasn't the kind of girl who men chase. Only now someone was watching her. The phone message was proof.

The caller might be outside in the dark watching her right now. Maybe one of the thugs who drove the company trucks back home. Her uncle had never liked her, never trusted her with the family matters, and now he, or one of the hired thugs she'd always been afraid of, had tracked her down.

She turned off her office light and stood in the evening shadows staring out at the night wondering if the man behind the message was out there in the dark, watching, waiting for her to be alone.

The shadow of the old man with his walking stick was outlined in autumn's pale grass. The sheriff had called him Carter something. He moved slowly toward the tiny RV he'd parked as close to the edge of the canyon as he could get. Somehow seeing Carter there was comforting. Maybe one person would hear her scream if the caller came after her.

Slowly, she walked down the stairs. The voice on the phone

could be anyone. Maybe her mother was wrong. Maybe someone *was* stalking her. She'd met several men from town already.
She'd even waved at a few fishermen at the lake, and the kid
at the grocery store had politely asked why she had moved to
Crossroads when he carried her groceries to her car.

When she entered the wagon room, she realized she knew
only one thing for certain. The caller was not Wilkes Wagner.
He had no phone.

For the first time since she'd met the man, she felt safe around
him.

Wilkes introduced her properly to Yancy. The thin man was
shorter, maybe a few years younger and not as educated, she
guessed from his speech, but Yancy Grey and Wilkes shared an
easygoing friendship. Maybe it was because they were both tin-
kers. They'd found wonder in the workings of an old wagon.

"This belonged to the family who lived in an old house Yancy
thinks whispers to him late at night." Wilkes stepped over a
wagon wheel and several boards. He must have seen her wide
eyes, because he rushed to add, "We'll put that back on, don't
worry."

He touched her arm in reassurance. This time his touch was
gentle, reassuring, but she still felt the warmth of it.

"Yancy reminded me that you don't know the interesting
part. How could you? You're new in town. Everyone calls the
place the Gypsy House, so it's possible the Stanley family came
in a vardo."

"Some folks think the house is haunted," Yancy added as he
dusted off the wagon's window box. "Others swear it has a curse
on it. But Wilkes says it's just an old house."

"Those are just stories," Wilkes said as if he thought they
might frighten her. In a whisper, he added, "You all right,
Angie?"

She nodded even though she couldn't stop shaking. She
couldn't tell him about the call, not in front of Yancy. She

needed to think about what to do first. "I'm fine. Tell me the stories of the old house."

Yancy called out from somewhere behind the display. "Some kids got hurt there a few years back. Ask them if it's cursed. We'll probably be struck by lightning for just talking about it."

Wilkes shook his head and whispered, "I don't believe in curses or blessings. It's just the luck of the draw, that's all."

"I agree," she whispered. There was no way those long dead could cause any harm. The man on the phone had sounded very much alive.

Yancy was taking apart an artifact and Wilkes was telling her not to worry. If she wasn't already at worry overload about the phone call, she might have screamed at him. But Wilkes and Yancy's crime was no more than a breeze in the tornado rolling around her.

She picked out the first of his conversation to build her illusion of sanity on. "I've met lots of people who feel called to something in their past." There, that made sense.

"Once, I met a woman who found a rocking chair at an old secondhand store. She swore it hugged her as she rocked, as if welcoming her home. When she was buying it, I noticed her last name matched the name carved on the bottom of the rocker.

"We discovered the chair had belonged to her great-grandmother. It had been sold in an estate sale twenty years before the woman was even born." Now she was rattling, Angela decided. That was better than screaming.

Since both men were still staring at her, she added, "As I helped her load it, she said she thought the spirit of her great-grandmother was rocking her."

"Great," Wilkes said. "Angie is just as spooky as you are Yancy."

"I'm not spooky." Yancy shook his head. "I'm hungry and the museum is almost two hours past closing. Maybe we should talk about this over coffee and pancakes. We owe the lady a meal for letting us stay late, and it's all-you-can-eat at Dorothy's tonight."

"I agree." She smiled at Yancy, a silent thank-you for the offer. There was no way she was walking out of the museum alone, so her only choice was to go with Wilkes and his friend.

The men agreed to meet at Dorothy's place. Angie wasn't sure she was part of the gang, but when she locked the museum and walked out, Wilkes was waiting at his car with his passenger door open. "Ride along with me, and I'll bring you back."

She hesitated. "Where's your old red pickup truck?" The Tahoe didn't look like something a poor farmer would drive.

"That old piece of junk belongs to Uncle Vern. He usually won't let me borrow it. Still blames me for wrecking his last one fifteen years ago. He claims if I hadn't rolled the thing in a bar ditch, it would have lasted another hundred thousand miles."

She slid into the leather seat, guessing that an SUV like this probably cost more than her annual salary.

As they drove away, she thought she saw the outline of a black car parked near the tree line.

It looked exactly like a Mercury her uncle had once issued to his top employees years ago.

CHAPTER SIX

Wilkes
Dorothy's Café

Wilkes wasn't sure how to handle Miss Angie Harold. If she'd been more his type, he might have flirted. After all, she was single and so was he, and despite her wild hair and boring clothes, she was cute in her short, shy kind of way. He was drawn to her as he could never remember having been drawn to a woman. She was unique in a one of a kind way that fascinated him.

He told himself flirting didn't require any commitment. He would keep it light until she made the first move. Then, when he knew his advances were welcome, he might move things along fast or do what he usually did when he let a woman get close…run.

If she were beautiful, model thin and black-haired, he would have slept with her without promising anything. He'd found it was easier to walk away when his own lies weren't slowing him down. Only, the last tall, dark-haired woman he'd slept with after the Houston rodeo last year said that he called out another woman's name twice in his sleep. Wilkes didn't want to sleep with a ghost from his past. And for once here was a woman who didn't remind him of Lexie. Nothing about Angie was the same and yet, for some reason, he couldn't stop wanting to get closer to her.

Wilkes wondered how long he'd have to live to outlive Lexie's memory. She hadn't been what he'd thought she was. She hadn't loved him as he loved her. He didn't want to see what she was today. He didn't care. But he still couldn't let go of a dusty memory of what might have been.

Damn, he thought, *I'm a man mourning something that never was.*

Logic told him that he should find someone else. He could be happy. Move on with his life. Problem was, no other woman felt right.

Angie was the first woman he'd bothered to talk to in a long time and she wasn't his type. She didn't seem to be any type. She was pretty, headstrong in a scary kind of way and intelligent to the point he'd never be able to keep up with her. She was also far too short for him and talked way too fast.

He liked being around her when she was yelling at him, though. Then she was cute as a baby rattler. And he loved the way she fired up at the slightest touch. Angie Harold would never be a woman easy to handle, but damn if a part of him didn't want to try.

To cool down, he started listing things wrong with the woman. If they were going to be friends, just friends, he needed to change his direction of thought.

She had the irritating habit of writing everything down in a little notebook she carried in her purse. That was another thing. Her purse was big enough to double as a sleeping bag.

Wilkes hated women who carried big purses. First, there was no telling what they had in them: makeup, lunch, a gun. And second, at some point every woman with a big purse asks the man with her to carry it for her. To Wilkes there was nothing dumber than a man standing in the mall with a purse. He looked as ridiculous as a bull in ribbons.

Now, thanks to Yancy's suggestion, here he was heading to dinner with bossy little Angela Harold next to him. Sunset lights danced in her hair. Folks called her color strawberry blond, but it was really the color of a dying sun. Golden, brown and rich red. She had it tied back but several curly strands were free brushing across her face and curling along her neck.

When they parked in front of the café, he made it around to her door before she got her seat belt undone. "You don't have to do that," she said as he slammed the car door closed behind her.

Just get through this, he thought. Maybe she could be some help to Yancy? Angie wasn't his type. She didn't even let him be polite about opening a door. He hated that. Yet right now, walking into the café, he was fighting the urge to reach for her hand.

He told himself he wasn't attracted to her, but he knew he was lying. Having her within touching distance was strong temptation. What surprised him even more was the realization that she didn't seem to like him. Hell, everyone liked him.

Yancy slid into the other side of the booth from them and started making small talk with her almost as if he were flirting. Yancy had lost his longtime girlfriend to a doctor in Abilene and he struck Wilkes as the type of guy who needed a woman in his life.

Unlike me, Wilkes thought. He'd proved he didn't need a woman. Hadn't said "I love you" to anyone in years.

When Angie asked about food on the menu, Wilkes touched her shoulder while he explained how chicken fried steak didn't have chicken in it. He decided he was sacrificing himself so Yancy would think they were a couple and not get involved with her, but Wilkes had to admit that he did like touching her. It didn't matter what she wore when he touched her, the feel of her was all woman.

He let his fingers brush a loose strand of her hair off her shoulder while Yancy talked to the waitress.

"Does everyone in your family have red hair?" He kept his voice low.

"No," she said. "I have no family. My mother died a few years ago and my father passed last month." Tears floated in her eyes, but she didn't let them fall.

"I'm sorry." If he hadn't been cramped in a booth, he would have hugged her.

She blinked away tears. "I'll be all right."

He fought to keep from pulling her closer. They weren't friends, maybe never would be, but this woman made him feel more alive than he had in a long time.

Wilkes wished she'd share more, but he could put the pieces together. Her dad died, she broke up with her fiancé. There must have been nothing left to keep her there. She was a woman on the run from her life.

"Where did you say you came from?"

Her sadness turned to alarm. "I didn't."

Wilkes swore silently. So much for casual conversation.

"None of my business," he said as he mentally moved away even if he couldn't leave physically.

"Right. I just don't want to talk about me."

This woman's emotions were wired with so many land mines he'd be lucky to survive long enough to understand her.

"Keep it professional. No personal questions."

"I agree."

Something about the way she straightened and nodded made him want to kiss her senseless, but every brain cell shouted that kissing her might not be a good idea.

"How about we start as friends?"

She finally seemed to relax. "I can handle that."

When Yancy turned back to them, he seemed totally unaware that they'd been talking while he'd been flirting with the waitress.

They continued in casual conversation like old friends. Wilkes was still confused why he liked being near her and, worse, why he didn't want Yancy flirting with her. Yancy flirted with every woman in town under fifty.

Then, probably just to mess with his brain, Angie acted as if she didn't notice he was sitting two inches away from her. If he touched her any more often, she'd think he had a twitch.

She'd spent most of the meal ignoring him and asking questions about the old house. Yancy didn't know much, and Wilkes handed over all he knew. When he went for more coffee, he came back to find Yancy and Angie staring into each other's eyes.

"You're right," she said. "One of your eyes is gray and the other green."

"I told you. Someone said that means I could have Gypsy blood in me. Maybe that is why the house calls me. It knows I'm blood."

Angie laughed. "How exciting."

Wilkes didn't want to look in Yancy's eyes and he wished he could think of something about his Wagner ancestors that was interesting.

By the time he paid the bill, Wilkes was frustrated. He was used to women playing up to him but Angie made no attempt. It was as though she didn't care if he was there or not. He told himself he would turn her down gently anyway, but it was a shot to his pride that she didn't even try.

Several times during the meal she'd glanced out the window. He had the feeling she was watching for something. But what? She hadn't lived in town long enough to make an enemy.

The wind had turned cold by the time they left the café. Wilkes pulled his hat low as the first hint of rain splashed across the windshield of his Tahoe.

Yancy waved goodbye and darted across the street to his apartment in the front of the retirement community.

Wilkes walked close to Angie and opened the door for her.

"I told you, you don't have to do that."

"Do what?" he asked innocently.

"Open doors for me. No one does that anymore."

"We do here," he said. "Where did you say you came from?"

"I didn't, but I... I was born in New York, and I grew up in Florida. If everyone stopped to open doors in New York, the whole city would come to a standstill."

"So, you liked living in New York?" He was finally making progress. She'd told him something about her background.

"S-sure."

She had hesitated just long enough to make him wonder if she were telling the truth. She seemed so innocent, almost newborn to the world, but there was a shadow following her. The lady had a past.

"I'm just being polite when I open doors." He fought the urge to touch her again, just to make sure she was all right. "All you have to say is thank you."

"Oh, I see. I have to say thank you for something I didn't ask for."

There it was again. That smart mouth just under her shy act. Once she lost her fear of him, she'd probably cut him to shreds. Damn if he didn't find the lady's attitude sexy.

Wilkes circled around his car thinking he needed to get in as fast as possible. If she started arguing without him, he wouldn't have a chance at keeping up. Maybe his mind had been sharp enough to handle a woman like her when he'd been in college, or even right after he got out of the army, but not now that his brain had been rusting for years.

An old memory danced across his thoughts. When he'd been in college, his steady girlfriend, Lexie, used to talk on and on about nothing. At the time he thought it was cute. She even talked during sex.

Thinking about it now, Wilkes decided that wasn't cute.

He used to think that he knew every thought in Lexie's head. Obviously not. She dumped him within two months of his deployment. Friends claimed she'd already roped a new guy before he was out of United States airspace. Some commented that she did the same between husband number one and husband number two.

Angie was a totally different kind of woman. She didn't flirt, or play silly games when she talked. He decided maybe she was the never-marry type, or maybe one of those women who marry someone years older and wiser so they can have long evenings of conversations. He figured he was out of luck if that were the case. First, he wasn't that much older than her, and second, he'd always thought his communication skills were more on the nonverbal side.

Wilkes had a feeling she'd love one man if she ever decided to love at all, and he wasn't ready for an all-out kind of love. Maybe he could talk her into being just friends. No, better yet, friends with benefits.

No, she'd never go for that.

To say he didn't understand her was an understatement. They weren't just from different planets; they were from opposite solar systems. She was mad at him for opening her door. Hell. That made no sense. And besides, she hadn't mentioned much of anything about her fiancé. He thought all women ran down every old lover within the first two hours of meeting anyone new. It was a comparison-shopping kind of thing.

"Okay, Angie, you don't have to say thank you." He kept his voice calm. All his anger was turned inward as he realized he'd been dating girls by their bust size and not their IQ. He wouldn't be surprised if a few he'd picked up at the Two Step around closing time didn't know *how* to open a car door. He usually drove them home and gave a quick kiss, then spent the rest of the night wondering why he'd put his tongue in the mouth of someone who was brain-dead.

"Fair enough," Angie said, unaware he wasn't paying attention to her as they passed down the main street of Crossroads. "I had fun talking with you and Yancy over dinner. I usually eat meals alone. Just me and Doc Holliday."

"Doc's been gone for quite a while, Angie. You talking to his ghost?"

"Doc Holliday is my cat."

Damn! Now he felt sorry for her. She ate all her meals with a pet. "You should try eating meals with Uncle Vern. He'll make you long for silence."

"How long has he lived with you?" she asked, as if just making conversation.

"All my life. But he doesn't live with me. He has his own place on the ranch. I think my grandfather built it for him when he was about thirty and hadn't moved off. I can't believe I'm admitting this, but when I was in the army, I missed the old guy. My folks were always busy with their lives. I was simply an accident they had to raise, but Uncle Vern always had time for me."

Wilkes almost laughed aloud. "Some of his stories go on for days. He can remember every detail about the blizzard of '72, but can never find his truck keys. Even in his seventies, he's still the best cowboy around. Last winter we were in the saddle for days during a storm. Heifers were dropping calves in the snow. He found twice the number I did and brought them home to his cabin so the newborns could thaw out. If it's below freezing, ice forms on the calf's mouth and he can't suck."

She didn't ask any questions as they turned down the road toward the museum. He guessed he was telling her more information than she wanted to know.

Wilkes expected her to ask about what he'd done in the army, but she didn't. Which was fine. He'd been telling his stories for so long he wasn't sure which were memories and which were lies.

An hour with Angie reminded Wilkes of what a boring man he'd become. He'd earned a degree. He'd traveled all over the world, mostly to places no sane man would want to go. But he couldn't keep a conversation going with this clever woman who had a love for history, a subject he once majored in.

When he pulled up to the only vehicle left in the museum parking lot, he lowered his voice. "Angie, I don't want to frighten you, but there is a car parked near the entrance with a man sitting in the driver's seat. Not something we see around these parts. He had to pull off the main road and into weeds to park there."

She leaned over the console and looked out his window. "I thought I saw it sitting there earlier. It looked like a Mercury Marauder."

"Could be some guy just pulled over to check his phone messages."

She shook her head, brushing away her curly hair that had long since tumbled out of the hair band. "No, the car was parked there before dark. I'm surprised you noticed it at night. I barely saw it."

"There was a time I was trained to notice things out of place. Old habits die hard." Like now, he thought. He'd never forget the smell of her hair. No hair spray or dye, just fresh as a spring breeze.

Even in the dashboard lights he could see the tension in her face. The car frightened her. Maybe everything frightened her. She'd been afraid of him when they'd met. But in the café, she'd seemed calm.

"Maybe he's waiting for the museum parking lot to be empty so he can rob the place." Wilkes doubted his own idea. All the items in the museum were priceless to the folks around here, but they would be a hard sell on an open market.

"Maybe." She didn't sound as if she believed him. "Can I ask a big favor?"

"Sure." If she wanted him to confront the guy in the car, he'd take the .45 in his glove box with him. If the guy was simply checking his messages, he would have stopped at the historical marker a quarter mile back, not in the weeds behind a line of trees. Only, from the marker he wouldn't have been able to see the front of the museum.

"Would you drive me home?" she whispered. "If he stays here when we leave, I'll notify the sheriff to watch the museum."

"And if he follows us, you think he's looking for you, right?"

Wilkes couldn't help but wonder what kind of trouble someone who looked so innocent could be in. Cupcake thief? He
frowned. Maybe the Mercury belonged to the ex-fiancé who
never got over her honey kisses. Maybe Jones changed his mind
about the marriage and moving to Texas.

"Right," she whispered again. "He could be looking for me."

Wilkes frowned. Damn if her voice in the darkness wasn't
turning him on. "So, I take you home and lose the guy on the
way. That's the plan."

She nodded. "If he knew where I lived, he'd be waiting for
me there."

Wilkes pulled out of the parking lot and headed through the
entrance. The stranger's car pulled in behind him. He grinned,
already knowing exactly where he was going. "How about a
tour of the canyon, Angie? Within ten minutes I'll have him so
lost on the trails, it'll take him till dawn to figure his way out.
Once we're at the bottom, I'll speed up and lose him."

Angie turned in her seat so she could look out the back window. She watched the car following them as they took the winding road down into the canyon.

The black car dropped farther behind, probably trying not
to be noticed. When Wilkes reached the bottom, he turned off
the main road taking first one trail and then another, speeding
up on the turns. The black car couldn't have caught them even
if he'd tried. Then Wilkes took a sharp right into a camping
area, killed the engine and turned off his lights.

Minutes later the Mercury raced past, barely making the
curve.

Wilkes took her hand in the darkness. "He's gone, Angie.
You can breathe now." His thumb moved over her small fingers in comfort.

After a moment she straightened and pulled her hand away.

Using only the moonlight, Wilkes slowly retraced his path,
watching the dark outlines of brush on the sides of the dirt road

as his guide. When he made it back to the main road, he flipped the lights on low and drove out of the canyon.

"We lost him," she whispered near his ear as she watched out the back window.

He reached over and brushed her cheek lightly. "And we know two things. One, he's not planning to rob the museum, and two, he is looking for either me or you."

"Do people ever chase you?" she asked.

"Never." He turned his head slightly. For a moment he just breathed her in.

Then, slowly, she turned those summer-green eyes at him, and he had no doubt Angie guessed what he was doing. She shifted back in her seat without a word.

He turned his eyes back to the road and felt like an idiot. They weren't a couple of teenagers on a first date. He was simply helping the curator out.

Twenty minutes later they were at her cabin. He grabbed a flashlight from the backseat and climbed out of the car a few seconds behind her. She could follow his flashlight beam as he circled the house, then returned to the car. Angie stood and held up her hand as he walked toward her. "Thank you, but you don't have to walk me to the door."

Wilkes closed his fingers around her raised hand and lowered it to her side as if he were opening an invisible gate latch. "I was checking the perimeter to make sure no one has been here."

"Oh," she whispered.

Wilkes studied her outline in the shadows. She had the sexiest whisper without even trying. If he were a blind man, he'd fall for her with that voice alone, and the way she smelled and how her kiss tasted and the soft feel of her skin. Hell, if he'd been a blind man, he might not notice that she was too short.

He tried to relax, hoping she would, also. "I guess I should give you your hand back," he said, without turning loose of her.

She laughed, and he felt a little of the tension between them ease.

He slipped her hand, still surrounded by his, in his pocket.

"On second thought, I think I'll keep it. I like the feel of your skin, Angie."

She tugged and his whole body moved closer to her. "You have to give it back, Wilkes. I'm afraid it's attached to the rest of my body."

This wasn't the time or the place, but he leaned close against her cheek and whispered, "Kiss me, Angie. I need to know if you still taste like honey."

"I…" She might be trying to think of how to say no, but her body moved closer and she was no longer trying to pull her hand away.

"You can, if you want to, Angie. I wouldn't mind." For some crazy reason he wanted her closer. He was positive he wasn't attracted to a woman like her, but his body hadn't gotten the message.

"I don't want to," she said and stepped back.

He let her hand go. Her fingers slid out of his pocket, and before he could react, she was hurrying toward her door.

Wilkes stood on the first step and stared at her blocking the doorway. If she wasn't going to kiss him, he doubted she would invite him in. "Thanks to the rain it was easy to tell no one has been around here. I found some deer tracks out behind your cabin and a few more on the trail to the lake, but nothing else. My guess is this isn't a place even locals could find easily, and Mr. Mercury is not a local."

"How do you know?"

"If he was, he wouldn't have been dumb enough to follow me into the canyon after dark."

"Thank you for checking for me," she said.

"You don't have to thank me, Angie. I'm happy to help. We're friends. Well, almost anyway." He headed toward his car. "You got a phone in there?"

She nodded. "A landline left by the owner. The sheriff said he usually rents the place in the summer, so he leaves it on. I've also got my cell."

"Good. Call the sheriff and tell him what happened, then ask him for a ride to work in the morning. If a black car comes down the hill to the lake, it will have to pass Dan's house. My guess is before it pulls down your drive, there will be a sheriff's car following it."

"What about my van?"

"Don't drive it until I have a chance to take a look at it. Leave it exactly where it is. If he was waiting for you, he might have messed with your van just to make sure you didn't run off."

Angie stepped out onto the porch, her arms wrapped around her waist, her head shaking. "I'm afraid, Wilkes."

He knew he should stay away from her, but in three steps he reached her. If ever there was a woman who needed a hug, it was Angie.

He wrapped her in his arms and held on tightly, half expecting her to bolt.

But she didn't. She rested her head on his chest and cried softly. She must know something he didn't. Maybe she knew the reason someone might be following her.

"Want to tell me why someone's looking for you?" he asked as his hand cradled her head.

"No. I can't," she whispered. "I don't have a clue."

Several ideas of what she might have done came to mind, but none of them fit. She hadn't committed a crime, or the police would have walked right up to the museum and arrested her. She couldn't have escaped from a biker gang, no tattoos. However, he wouldn't mind doing a complete search. Just for the sake of making sure, of course.

"Don't worry, you're safe here." He doubted he was right, but the words might help. "If you get scared, run to the sheriff. If he's not home, there's a back road by the dam. It dead-ends at the north corner of my land. Cross over the cattle gate and you'll be able to see the lights of my house."

She straightened. "Thanks. I'm sorry I fell apart. I'm usually stronger than that."

"No problem." He moved his thumb over her cheek to wipe away a tear. "You don't happen to want to kiss me, do you?" If she did, it might be interesting. If she didn't, at least it would take her mind off the black Mercury.

She laughed, just as he hoped she would. "No, thanks."

To his surprise Wilkes felt greatly disappointed.

CHAPTER SEVEN

Lauren

Friday night of homecoming seemed magical. Lauren could almost feel the excitement in the dorm. Both her mother and her father had sent money for a new dress, and, for once, Lauren spent every penny. Red dress, black shoes and red-and-black wrap that cost almost as much as her dress.

Her date might not be the one she'd hoped for, but she was still excited. Her first real party on campus. Her first college game. Part of her saw this as the caterpillar she'd been all through high school finally turning into a butterfly.

She told herself she would have talked it over with Lucas if he had called, but she hadn't heard from him all week. Lucas was special to her; he had been since the night he'd saved her life two and a half years ago, but he never once said they were boyfriend and girlfriend or that they shouldn't date others. Maybe he *did* get in late Sunday night and maybe he *did* work every weeknight at the AG barn, but surely he could have called. They could have talked, or met for coffee downstairs.

Her roommate, Polly, sat across the room watching Lauren

get dressed. "Now, let me get this straight," she said. "The guy we went out with last Friday isn't the one taking you to homecoming. You know, the redheaded one. Tim, right?"

"Tim is just a friend and he is *not* my date," Lauren said.

"And the guy who calls, the one you talk all mushy-like to, isn't the one taking you." Polly looked terrible, hungover and depressed, but she seemed to be trying to get her brain working enough to figure out Lauren's dating life for some reason.

"Right. Lucas is the one who calls and he's working this weekend." Lauren didn't want to mention Reid Collins's name because Polly would only ask more questions. "I'm just going with someone from back home. He probably asked me because his dad and my dad are friends."

"Okay, but why didn't he ask you out for a hamburger and not to a hundred-dollars-a-plate dinner if he's just being nice?" Polly frowned. "Oh, never mind. My head hurts too much to care, so I'll just get to the big questions. How come you have a date tonight and I don't? I've been going out every night since we started rooming together. Now, the biggest date night ever, and I'm left behind."

"I don't know, Polly. Gotta go. See you." Lauren grabbed her wrap and decided to wait downstairs for Reid. Every conversation she'd had with her roommate was always about Polly. The girl couldn't have passed second-grade science. How could the planets rotate around the sun when Polly was convinced the world revolved around her?

Tim was the one waiting for her in the long lobby with its scattered, uncomfortable couches and a few study tables. In a sweatshirt and jogging pants, he obviously wasn't going to the spirit dinner or even the game.

"Hi, Tim." She smiled. "I can't go hang out tonight. I'm going to homecoming with Reid, remember?"

"I know. I just dropped by hoping to get to tell you one more time not to go." He looked defeated. "I know I'm wasting my breath, L."

He'd used her initial, something he hadn't done since middle school.

She didn't appreciate his concern. Just because Reid and Tim were no longer friends didn't mean she should turn Reid down. She'd gone to every one of Reid's birthday parties since they were five. She'd known him as long as she'd known Tim. The only guilt she felt tonight was that she hadn't had a chance to tell Lucas. Maybe, since they weren't really dating, he didn't have a right to know if she went out with someone else. But deep down she knew she should have told Lucas.

Before Lauren could answer Tim, Reid came through the far door looking Bond-like in a black suit with a Texas Tech tie. He was one of those rare people who'd been born into a family where everyone was good-looking, and he wore his genetic gift as easily as a second skin.

When she turned around to see Tim's reaction, her old friend was gone. Vanished amid the columns between the seating areas.

"Evening, Lauren. You look hot!" Reid smiled. "Spin around for me. I've never seen your hair curled like that." He made little circles with his finger. "You're going to look good on my arm tonight."

She twirled round, letting her long hair float like a cape. "I know I look better than in high school. My boobs finally filled out." She laughed remembering how he'd teased her about being flat chested.

"I hadn't noticed." He took a deep breath and asked, "Lauren, just for tonight…could we forget that we've known each other since we were kids? I'd just as soon my frat brothers think I lucked out in finding a pretty and smart girl for a change."

His compliment made her blush. "So no stories about how you lost your trunks in the town pool or how you…"

"No stories. I promise to be a perfect gentleman." He took her hand. "I already got the call from my old man and your dad warning me that if I step out of line, they'd take turns killing me. Dad even said that since Charley is finally acting halfway sane, I could easily fall out of the favorite-son chair."

"Really?"

Reid stopped walking long enough to stare at her. "Which really? That our dads called or that my oversexed brother is finally getting his life together?"

"The dads didn't really call, did they?"

"Yeah, I'm afraid they did. Your dad said he'd shoot me in the privates if I made his little girl cry, and my dad just promised to murder me. He's not too creative. Neither seemed to have any faith in my behaving tonight."

Lauren almost felt sorry for Reid. "You're lucky my mom didn't have your number. She's into torture. She's been practicing on my dad for years. I think they separated when I was five just to allow him to bleed out slower."

Reid shook his head. "Lauren, you really do look great, but you should know from the start that we'll never make it work more than a date now and then. I don't think I could handle a sheriff for a father-in-law and a mother-in-law who is a dominatrix."

"I agree. For the sake of your health, you might want to avoid me as much as possible." She smiled, thinking that on her part it wouldn't be much of a sacrifice. "Two dates a year, tops."

"I can handle that. I picked this one and you can pick the next."

He offered his arm as they walked out as if they were off to prom, but Lauren guessed neither of them was disappointed they wouldn't last. By the time they were at the dinner in the Frazier Alumni Pavillion just outside the station, Reid was back to his usual egotistical self, telling her how lucky she was to go out with him.

Reid never had a problem with ego.

They sat with a group of his fraternity brothers. All nice guys, she thought, but by the time dessert was served Lauren had the feeling she wasn't in the right place. There was somewhere her heart would rather be.

They all walked over to the game together. Reid was the life of the party and didn't seem to notice when she grew quiet.

The football game was chaotic; everyone was yelling and cheering, making conversation impossible. Reid spiked his Coke, but didn't insist when she refused his offer to add whatever was in his flask to her drink. The game turned from long to endless. A man behind Lauren tumbled into her, spilling his drink all over the back of her new wrap. A woman passing in the narrow space in front of Lauren managed to step on both her feet. Lauren lost all interest in the game and in trying to carry on any conversation with Reid.

Finally, gratefully, the date was over. Tech won, but the group she was with seemed too tired, or too drunk, to really care. Conversations and laughter circled in the cool air as lovers cuddled in the evening shadows and bells rang from the tower. Car lines snaked slowly down the roads through a campus decorated in red streamers.

Reid took her hand and walked beside her, but he spent most of his time talking to the others in the group. At one point one of the girls, who'd been flirting with Reid all night, asked Lauren if she had a roommate.

Lauren assumed the girl asked so she could lean across Reid, but she answered, "I was assigned one. Polly Pierce."

The dozen people walking together all seemed to inhale at the same time. "Oh, really," the girl who asked offered as a reply.

"Do you know her?" Lauren already knew the answer. None of them were looking at her, not even Reid.

No one answered her question. They just changed the subject and kept walking.

When she and Reid broke off from the others, he put his arm over her shoulders. "You cold? I probably should have taken my car, but I swear parking for the game is farther away than the dorms. You'd like my new car. Dad got it for me last spring when I pulled off B's in every class."

She wasn't interested in cars. "What does everyone know about Polly that I don't know? Everyone went silent when I mentioned her name." Lauren had held the question in for as long as she could.

He didn't answer for a minute. "It's not something I should talk to you about, but you might not want to tell people who your roommate is. She showed up at one of our open house parties last week and it didn't turn out well."

"Why?" Lauren knew Polly was wild, so she doubted anything Reid said would surprise her.

"Because half the guys at the frat house have slept with her. Or maybe *sleep* is the wrong word. She made it clear when she showed up that she was there to drink and..." He seemed to have lost the right word. "Party," he finally ended.

Lauren stared at him. "Did you, uh, *party* with her?"

He hung his head. "Well, yeah, but it was just a... We just hooked up for a few minutes one time in the upstairs hallway."

"Oh. So it didn't mean anything to you." Lauren was torn between being mad at Reid and feeling sorry for Polly.

"Right." Reid relaxed as if he finally made her understand. "It's just something guys do in college. Look, I'm not proud of it. I would never treat a girl like you that way."

"A girl like me?"

They were at the dorm. The date was over and so was the interrogation.

"I had a nice time," Reid lied. "We'll have to do this again sometime."

That was it, she realized, not a very eventful first date, but she hadn't expected more. Luckily, he wasn't even going to try to kiss her or set another time to go out. She felt as if their date had been nothing more than an obligation he had to fulfill. If her pop asked, she'd say he was a perfect gentleman.

"Thank you for inviting me, Reid," she said stiffly. "I'll never forget my first homecoming." As he waited, she added, "Don't worry. I won't say anything to anyone about you and Polly."

He smiled. "There was no me and Polly. Just sex in a dark hallway. When it was over, she said I was number six for the evening. Made me feel real special." His laughter bore no humor. "Tell you the truth, I don't even remember what she looked like, it was so dark. Is Polly pretty?"

"Does it matter?"

"No, I guess it doesn't." He straightened. "I won't be doing that again."

"Let's forget you ever told me about it. More than I wanted to know." Lauren moved toward the door. "See you around, Reid."

"See you around," he said, already turning away.

She found Polly curled up on her bed. As Lauren flipped on the light, Polly threw her arm across her eyes to block the sudden light. Lauren saw a long smear of red dripping on the blankets, and what looked like broken glass everywhere.

The big mirror Polly had nailed on the wall over her bed must have fallen and shattered. A million points of light sparkled over the covers and the rug beside her bed like fresh fallen snow. Blood dripped from a long gash that ran from Polly's wrist to her elbow and crimson bubbled like fat freckles across her face. Polly let out a low cry like an animal in pain, but didn't open her eyes.

"Polly!" Lauren dropped everything and dialed 911 on her cell, then grabbed her scarf and wrapped it about the open wound as tightly as she could. "Polly, what happened? Polly? Where else are you hurt?"

In the panicked silence, Polly opened one eye and asked sleepily, "How was your date?"

"Fine," Lauren answered, so angry at her roommate she didn't want to talk to her. "What happened? Did you do this, Polly? Did the mirror just fall?"

She seemed to be struggling to keep her eyes open. "I don't know. Maybe I hit the damn mirror. It was looking at me. I thought if I couldn't see me, I might get lucky and disappear. I thought it was a good idea at the time. Didn't know it would hurt so much."

A stampede of footsteps sounded from the other side of their door. Lauren stumbled over the shattered glass in her heels as the first responders rushed in. She stood out of the way as they worked, talking to Polly, checking her vital signs, lifting her onto a gurney.

In less time than she thought possible, they were all gone, and her new wrap lay on the floor covered with blood. They'd gone, leaving all the blood and glass and chaos behind. When they'd asked Polly what happened, she'd simply whispered, "Accident."

Lauren picked up her phone and dialed Tim.

"How was the date with Reid?" he asked, still sounding angry.

"Tim, listen. When I got home, Polly was all cut up and bleeding. Can you take me to the hospital? I don't think she knows anyone who'll sit with her."

"What happened?"

"I'll tell you on the way."

Lauren pulled her winter coat from the closet and slipped it around her. The night couldn't be much below sixty degrees, but she felt cold all the way to her bones.

She waited for Tim by the main door. When their eyes met, he didn't say a word. He just wrapped his arm around her and held on tightly until they reached his old Jeep.

With all the traffic from the game on campus, they would have made better time walking the few blocks to 19th Street, which bordered the university. From there they could have run across the busy street and down a few blocks to the hospital. By the time they drove in the traffic, found a parking place and located the emergency room, Polly had been moved into one of the examining rooms.

A nurse said they could go in for a few minutes. As she walked them down the hall, she asked, "Were you with her when the accident happened?"

Lauren hesitated, then said, "No. I must have come in just after. She was under her covers."

"Lucky. That probably prevented further cuts from the falling glass," the nurse whispered as she pushed the door open. "If she'd lost much more blood, she might have died."

The nurse pointed to an open door, then disappeared on down the hallway.

Polly looked so young, so small. Lauren could see a bit of the little girl she must have been, before college, before dark hallways and frat boys, before having no one, not even a roommate who cared.

Lauren tried to erase what Polly had said from her thoughts. *I thought if I couldn't see me, I might get lucky and disappear.*

"She's so pale. How'd it happen?" Tim whispered.

I don't know if it was an accident, Lauren wanted to say, but she couldn't. Like it or not, Polly needed someone to be on her side tonight. Reid had commented that Polly wasn't like her. Did he mean that Polly was of no value? No one cared about her? Polly had told her that her parents had found the farthest college from home to send her to.

Tears silently rolled down her face and dropped onto her winter coat.

To Lauren's surprise, Tim moved closer to the bed and took Polly's hand. "Hey, Polly Anna, you should have called if you weren't doing anything. We could have gone back for more chicken fried steak ears."

Polly's eyes opened just a bit. "That stuff was terrible." Her voice sounded weak, sleepy.

"Yeah, but think of all those earless cows walking around so they could serve it every weekend." Tim patted her bandaged arm.

Polly gave a tiny laugh and looked down at her arm. "It doesn't hurt. I didn't even feel the stitches." She closed her eyes for a few minutes, then whispered more to herself than them, "I had a fight with a mirror and I think the mirror won."

"No, you won." Tim squeezed her hand.

"I did?" she said without opening her eyes.

"I'm glad you did, Polly Anna, but you look like you could use some rest. You won because you're still here."

Tim didn't turn loose of her hand. "Promise me you'll call the next time you have a free night. We could go eat, then come back and shoot some pool."

"Are you any good?" she whispered.

"Are you?" he asked.

Polly shook her head.

Tim smiled. "Then I'm great."

Lauren watched Tim talking to this girl he barely knew, trying his best to make her feel better. When the nurse finally dropped by to tell them that it was time to leave, Tim stepped into the hallway to answer his phone and Lauren took his place at Polly's side.

"Take care of yourself," she said as Polly seemed to drift in and out of sleep. "Who do you want me to call? Family? Friends? They'll want to come help."

Polly shook her head. "No one." After a long pause, she added, "Thanks for coming. How was your date?"

Lauren grinned. For the first time, Polly asked a question. "To tell the truth, it was a disaster. Not fun at all."

Polly nodded. "I've had a few of those lately, too."

"Promise you'll get better, Polly. I don't want to have to break in another roommate. I'm used to you."

Polly had drifted to sleep and didn't answer.

As Lauren and Tim left the hospital, she leaned over and kissed his cheek. "I love you, you know. You were magic with Polly."

"I know." Tim laughed. "Redheads are always irresistible."

"Who told you that?"

"Another redhead."

As they walked to his old Jeep, she thought about what he'd

done for Polly, a girl who hadn't even bothered to talk to him the night she'd gone to eat with them.

"Swear to something, Tim?"

"Anything, L," he said casually.

"Promise we'll always be friends."

"Only if you'll take my advice about not going out with Reid."

"I've already decided that. The dinner was nice, the game fine. I even liked his friends, and he played his part, didn't even try to kiss me good-night. But, you know, the whole time I realized I wasn't where I wanted to be."

"So he was a perfect gentleman?"

She nodded, and he checked his phone.

One text blinked bright in the darkness. One text from Reid Collins.

Got lucky tonight.

Lauren couldn't breathe. "My pop is going to kill him."

Tim swore. "He'll have to get in line."

CHAPTER EIGHT

Carter

Carter Mayes leaned against the red jagged canyon wall and tried to ease his aching back. He had run out of aspirin two days ago, but he refused to stop. His quest was too important and the fact that he was tired, aching and in his seventies didn't matter.

"Come on, Watson, we got to keep going. If we make another half mile today, we'll sleep good tonight." Carter tested the ground with his walking stick and took one step.

The dog didn't answer, as usual. Watson was far more interested in the occasional rabbit or squirrel than his owner's great quest.

Since he retired over ten years ago, Carter never had a problem talking to himself. "We'll give it until dark tonight, and maybe most of the day tomorrow. We should be near the lake at Crossroads by then." He didn't like the idea of quitting, but even his cleanest clothes were too dirty to wear, and Watson needed real dog food. "We'll pull the trailer into one of the rental spots on the lake, hook it up and relax for a few days. Maybe do some fishing. How does that sound, boy?"

Watson trailed along as Carter examined every crack in the canyon wall.

A month after he retired, Carter set out on his quest. When the weather allowed and he was feeling good, he walked the tiny offshoots of the Palo Duro Canyon and Sunday Canyon, and now Ransom Canyon, searching for a memory.

He had been about five or six when his father started taking him hiking on weekends. His mostly absentee dad was a tough man and hated people in general, or so Carter's mother used to say. So, every weekend when he wasn't drunk, which was a fifty-fifty shot, his dad would pick up his kid and they'd camp out.

The weekends had been hell, until Carter learned to stop complaining and stay out of his father's way. Even during the bad times, the fresh air beat staying home with his mother's boyfriend-of-the-month. Carter would load his backpack down with drinking water, an extra jacket and Snickers bars. His kindergarten mind figured if he had something to drink, eat and a way to stay warm, he could survive his old man's total neglect for two days.

Carter learned how to make camp, skin and cook a rabbit, and keep his mouth closed about what happened on weekends. He also learned to mark the trail into the canyon so he could find the car when his father was too hungover.

By the time Carter was eight, he loved the outdoors and was tall enough to see over the steering wheel. He could drive home when his dad was passed out in the back of his old Ford.

That was about the time they stumbled on a cave way back in an offshoot of a canyon. In his mind, Carter could still see the strange drawings on the cave's rounded wall. Stick figures drawn too high on the sheer rock to be pictures children had done.

He and his father had spent a rainy night in the cave along a trail rarely traveled. They'd built a small fire at the mouth of the cave, but over sixty years later Carter could still remember the sound of the wind howling through the cave like a low growl or the dying cry of an animal. The slice of an opening was jagged, just tall and wide enough for a man to pass through. The floor of the cave was smooth, slick with a trickle of water running over rocks.

His dad had finished a bottle of whiskey that night. He passed out near the fire, but Carter took his flashlight and went exploring. With his beam of light pointed down, he almost missed the drawings until he tripped and found them when his light danced wildly as he fought to keep his footing.

The markings shone bright in the black cave as the flashlight's beam moved over them. The stick figures almost seemed to come alive, creeping toward Carter in the unsteady glow. Big round heads and blank circle eyes atop bony bodies.

Carter sat staring at them until dawn, never sleeping. He couldn't remember even blinking. In his child's mind he feared if he closed his eyes for even a second, the figures might move a step closer.

He remembered the rain turned into a foggy soup about noon the next day, and the wind stilled, making the cave as still as a temple.

Carter and his dad crawled out of the cave and made their way along slippery rocks and muddy paths to an old trail pounded down by deer. His father swore most of the way, claiming his head hurt. Carter remained silent, but he kept glancing back to make sure one of the ghostly stick figures wasn't following them.

When they finally made it to the flat land above the cave, he remembered seeing a rock corral about two feet high and twenty feet square. He asked his dad why the rocks were there, and his old man simply told him to get in the car.

Carter drove away from the canyon on a road that was simply two ribbons of crushed grass winding around bunches of short trees heavy with fruit. It was dark by the time they pulled onto a farm-to-market road.

For years afterward, Carter would ask his father where the cave had been, but he either simply liked pestering Carter, or couldn't remember. The old drunk died never revealing even what canyon they had been in that night.

As he grew, Carter never mentioned the stick characters on the canyon wall to anyone, but they haunted his dreams. He and his mother moved south to Galveston about the time he entered his teen years. Carter went to college, then to Vietnam. The stick men followed him halfway around the world. He married and raised three daughters, but two things he never did—he never forgot what he saw in the cave, and he never took one drink of alcohol.

The year he retired, his wife, Bethie, died. His daughters were in Dallas, all with lives of their own. Carter thought about it for a month, then he sold his house in Galveston and bought a small RV and a good pickup to pull it. One bed, a tiny kitchen and the world's smallest bathroom. Just enough room for Carter and Watson. In the winter he parked at an RV village in Granbury located smack in the middle of his three girls. He played golf on warm days and poker on cold ones. He did odd jobs his daughters needed done around their homes and waited for spring.

From the Ides of March until the first snow, he relocated to the Texas Panhandle and searched for what he remembered seeing as a boy. If it took him the rest of his life, he'd find that wall inside the hidden cave. Maybe it would be a great archaeological discovery. Maybe it wouldn't. But before he passed on, he was determined to find that cave and see those strange stick figures one more time. They were a part of his childhood, a part of his nightmares, and he needed to know they were real. They'd followed him in his thoughts and dreams through his whole life. The hollow eyes mirrored his childhood—the good, the bad. A part of what he was. A memory he needed to know had been real when so many memories had faded to may-have-beens.

CHAPTER NINE

Wilkes

By Sunday night, Wilkes felt as if he was wearing out the Saltillo tile in his big house worrying about Angie. She had two phones with her at the cabin, and he hadn't bothered to ask for either number. If he drove over there without calling, he'd probably frighten her to death. If he waited here, he'd die of stress fretting over the little museum curator.

Something about her drew him. Maybe it was simply that she needed him, and no one had needed him in a long time. After the breakup with Lexie, he'd pushed everyone away and given up on trying to understand women.

But worrying about Angie was starting to look like his part-time job.

He didn't want to admit how attracted to her he was. The smell of her hair. The way she sounded when she whispered. He wouldn't mind listening to that all night long. And her eyes. Even her wild hair was growing on him. It felt so good when it had brushed his jaw. He'd like to dig his fingers deep into the curls.

Wilkes swore. He was sounding like an idiot picking her body parts apart as if she were a Lego doll.

Finally, he grabbed his keys. Maybe he couldn't go to her place and he couldn't call without a number and he wasn't about to ask the sheriff, but he could drive around. If he found a black Mercury, he'd confront the driver. Knowing Angie, the stalker was probably some asthmatic, underweight accountant who'd fallen in love with her at her last job and hadn't had the nerve to tell her how he felt. Maybe it was the coward Mr. Jones who'd broken up with her as she was packing to take a new job.

Wilkes wouldn't mind putting a few dents in that guy's head. Angie might not be his usual type of woman, but she had her own beauty, and the guy should have seen that.

Halfway to town, Wilkes realized that any way this turned out tonight, he'd be playing the part of a hero or the fool. He might be confronting a bad guy who preys on shy, short women, or he could be getting between two lovers making up after weeks apart. Problem was, Wilkes wouldn't know which until it was over.

He told himself to calm down as he drove through town, circling the parking lots of every place that was open. If he saw no old Mercury, he would go back home. If Angie needed him, all she had to do was look up the Devil's Fork Ranch in any old phone book or online.

As he drove, he thought about how Angie hadn't kissed him, even when he'd asked her twice if she wanted to. Something was definitely wrong with the girl. He'd been told a few times that he was a great kisser, but in truth he was so out of practice he may have lost his edge.

If Wilkes were being honest, he'd also been told he was not so good at staying around by the few women he'd taken out since he'd been back. His last three-date girlfriend told him he had the shelf life of squash. But he'd been faithful to one woman once, and she'd dumped him. He didn't plan to ever get that involved with a woman again. To say Lexie Davis had stomped on his heart was an understatement. When she'd written to tell him she'd found someone else soon after he'd left for the army, Wilkes was lost. He'd built his whole life, his future, his goals, his dreams around her.

Every time he went out with a new woman, part of him would begin to calculate how long it would be before she left so that he could leave first.

So far, the plan had always worked. Only, Angie Harold wasn't following the rules of the game. She didn't seem to be falling for him, but then again she'd kissed him all out that first time in the museum.

He told himself he could handle one night with her, he might be willing to go for two or three, but she'd have to understand that there would be no love involved. It hurt like a cannonball to the heart.

But the way she kissed could almost make him forget the pain.

Pulling out of Crossroads, Wilkes decided to drive over to the Two Step Bar thirty miles away. Only locals knew about the place, and Sunday nights at the bar were usually slow. Sports played on every TV. He always felt lonely there, but at least he was lonely in a crowd.

Sunday nights Ike Perez and his wife, Velma, always served homemade tamales with a southwest sauce hot enough to take the hair off a trucker's chest. They were one dollar a tamale, usually ordered by the dozen, and the beer was a buck a bottle.

Surprisingly, tonight the Two Step was packed. The only thing that would have made the crowd better would be if Ike allowed dancing. But Ike and Velma were Southern Baptist. And while they might serve beer, they drew the line at dancing on Sundays.

Wilkes looked around and spotted Yancy Grey talking to an old man at a corner table. He wound a path to his friend. Beer and football might take his mind off the little curator.

For a moment his brain went rogue and pictured Angie in

bed. Not a possibility, logic screamed. He wasn't into breaking hearts. Hers or his. The two of them would never work. But one night might be a paradise he'd spend years reliving.

He rubbed the bruise Angie had given him on his side as a reminder of their first meeting. A man would have to have a death wish to take Angie to bed. Wilkes told himself the only reason he was worried about her might be because curators willing to come to Crossroads were not easy to find. If he didn't watch out for her, with his luck, he'd have to serve on the committee to find another one.

Lying to himself didn't work any better than usual.

Yancy stood as Wilkes neared, dragging a chair over. "Have a seat, Wagner. I've got someone you'll want to meet."

Wilkes didn't want to meet anyone, but company while drinking always seemed like a good idea. He shook hands with the old man sitting with Yancy.

"Carter Mayes is exploring the canyons," Yancy said by way of introduction. "He claims there's a cave with stick men painted high on the walls."

The old man looked up, his eyes filled with hope, but he didn't say a word in greeting. "I spent five years in the Palo Duro and three in canyons east of here. My dad took me camping somewhere near Crossroads about seventy years ago. We parked up top on grassland by a road, and it wouldn't have been too far down or a hard climb. I was just a boy, and Dad was too fond of drinking to camp far from the car. One rainy night, I saw the painted men on a cave wall we took shelter in."

Wilkes shook his head. "I've never seen anything like that, but you might ask my uncle Vern. I've seen old maps of roads back before the Second World War scattered around his place."

Carter Mayes nodded. "I've collected quite a few maps myself, but there are still some private roads through ranches that I might not know about."

A waitress passed by to take their order. It wasn't too hard.

Beer and tamales were the only two things offered. All she needed was a count.

Wilkes ordered a dozen for the table and a beer. Yancy already had a bottle of Coke sitting in front of him, and Carter had water. Wilkes changed the subject. "Didn't I see you parked at the museum, Carter?"

Carter nodded. "It's an easy walk down into the canyon from there. I go down to the last viewing overhang and take pictures, then blow them up on my laptop, looking for any caves. 'Course, the museum wouldn't have been there when I was a kid."

Wilkes wasn't interested in caves or stories of cliff paintings. "Did you happen to notice a strange car parked out by the museum?"

Carter nodded again. "I sold cars for a living for forty years. I spotted it Thursday night when I came up top. It wasn't dark yet, and I wondered what a car like a Mercury Marauder would be doing parked off the road by the trees."

"Was the curator's old junker of a van still in the parking lot?"

"It was. I'm surprised that thing runs. I can hear the rattles in that engine from half a mile away. In fact, Angela was walking to her van when I climbed up. I waved to her and followed her out of the parking lot Thursday night. The Mercury pulled in behind me. When he honked at me for not making the light on Main, I looked back. Couldn't see him clearly, but it was a man and from the way he was waving his fist I'd swear he was cussing me out for not rushing through the light."

"What did you do?"

"I sat through the green light, too. He tried to go around, but there were cars on both sides of my camper."

Yancy shook his head. "What would you have done if he'd got out of his car? Some folks get killed because of road rage."

Carter smiled. "I would have sicced my dog, Watson, on him. Town's only got one light, might as well enjoy it."

All three men looked down at the dog asleep beside Carter's

chair. Wilkes chuckled, guessing that Carter had unknowingly kept the stalker from following Angie's van.

As the food arrived, Wilkes asked if Carter had a cell phone.

"Of course. My daughters insist if I'm going to explore, I always carry one."

"Mind calling me if you see that car again or any trouble near our curator?"

Carter took a bite of his tamale, then downed half his water before saying, "I will."

"Thanks." Wilkes didn't want to go into details so he changed the subject again. "Carter, if you want to drop by my place tomorrow night, I'll have my housekeeper make something not as spicy and we'll talk to Uncle Vern about your cave. No one around knows this part of the country better than he does."

"I could drive him out," Yancy offered as if Carter didn't have his own transportation.

"Good idea. I'll set another place." He thought for a moment and added, "Why don't you stop by and pick up Angie, too. She'd probably like hearing about a secret cave. Pick her up at the museum and I'll drive her home after dinner."

Yancy grinned and nodded once as if he'd figured something out.

Wilkes didn't wait for the question. "No, I'm not seeing her. We're just friends, I think."

Carter snorted. "What is this, grade school? In my day, if a man liked a woman, he just grabbed her and kissed her. If she didn't run, he married her."

"Nowadays they call that assault," Wilkes answered. "I have a firm rule. The woman has to kiss me before I make a move. Then I know she's interested and I'm in control." He didn't want to admit that he'd broken that rule with Angie three minutes after he met her.

Carter laughed. "Having three daughters I appreciate the thoughtfulness, Wilkes, but it makes you sound like a bull just circling the corral waiting to be roped. Any man who thinks he's in control where women are concerned needs to think again."

"Not me," Yancy broke in. "Since my last and only love left me six months ago, I've been circling the corral with the lasso around my neck just hoping someone will pick up the lead."

"You sound desperate, son."

Yancy nodded his head. "Oh, I am. I do have a few strikes against me, so I can't afford to play it cool. I live in a retirement community with a dozen old geezers looking out for me. I was in prison once, and my eyes don't match. If a girl even glances my direction, I'm slicking my hair down and smiling using all my teeth."

Wilkes laughed and drained his second beer.

Yancy nodded at him and added, "If a good-looking cowboy like you can't find a woman, maybe we should all just give up women and start roaming the canyons like Carter."

Wilkes laughed and the conversation turned to legends. He told the old story about how Colonel Mackenzie came up on a tribe of Comanche warriors. They'd left their horses on the plains to graze and slipped down to the floor of the canyon to set up a winter camp.

"Mackenzie didn't have enough men to round up the horses and climb down the canyon walls to attack the Comanche. He knew if he didn't control the horses, the Comanche would ride away and the Indian Wars would continue. So, he ran the horses off the walls of the canyon. They tumbled hundreds of feet to their deaths."

"I've heard that legend." Carter nodded soberly. "Folks say on cloudy nights you can still hear the horses' screams echoing off the walls."

Wilkes sat back in his chair. "They say that act saved hundreds, maybe thousands of lives, both Comanche and settlers."

"The night I found my stick men in that cave, I heard howling all night long." Carter lowered his voice, and the younger men leaned in to hear. "I thought it was the wind. I held the light on the figures, afraid they'd come for me if the cave went dark. When we climbed out the next day, I don't think we even had a trail to follow for a while. Then my dad found a path that looked like animals made it."

Wilkes ordered another round of beer, planning to drink all three himself. "Uncle Vern told me once that he found a rock corral near where Ransom Canyon wiggles along the north side of our place."

Yancy frowned. "What does that have to do with anything?"

"Early Mexican ranches raised sheep. With no wood for fences handy, they built rock corrals. When the ranches were burned out, the sheep could have run into the canyon. If a small herd lived wild, they could have made a trail up and down. Up to graze, down to hide out." Wilkes was just guessing. Sheep in this part of the country wouldn't have much of a chance to survive with all the wolves and coyotes around. "Maybe that trail you found was a sheep trail."

"You think your uncle can remember where the stone corral was? I remember seeing one once."

"He might. You can ask him tomorrow night. I think I'll head on home." Wilkes stood waving the three beers he'd ordered away and dropping a ten-dollar tip. He hadn't had near enough to be drunk, but he'd had too much to force his mind to stop thinking about Angie.

He climbed into his Tahoe thinking that half the women in Crossroads were more his type than the little curator. She didn't know how to dress or fluff her hair. Every female in Texas was born knowing how to wear boots and jeans. You'd think Angie would look around and notice jeans are worn tight, not baggy.

He headed straight toward the lake and her tiny little cabin. He decided it was simply to check to make sure no Mercury was parked anywhere near, but in truth he wanted to see her.

Maybe he'd just ask for her phone number so he could check on her. That made sense, but tonight his sense seemed a quarter shy of a dollar even though he'd only had a couple of beers.

When he came down the hill to the lake, he passed the sheriff's place. All the lights were on, but he didn't see Brigman.

A few minutes later when he pulled onto the dirt road that wound around trees and natural rock formations to get to her cabin, Wilkes relaxed. No Mercury.

There were lights on inside the cabin, but when he knocked, no one answered.

"Angie!" he called. "It's just me checking on you."

It occurred to him that she might not know who *me* was, but he'd feel like an even bigger fool yelling out his own name.

He knocked again.

No answer.

He walked around the cabin looking in every window like an impatient Peeping Tom. No one inside, but the cabin still had its usual explosion of color. Huge Texas Star and pinwheel-patterned quilts hung on the walls. The old leather couch he'd seen two nights ago was now covered with an afghan, and the table he'd seen by the front window now looked elegant covered in antique lace.

Wilkes sat down on the front step, leaned against a support log, lowered his hat and went to sleep. This seemed as good a place for a nap as anywhere.

Before he was settled into a dream, someone started shaking his shoulder.

He bolted and tumbled off the top step. When he recovered enough to realize nothing was broken, he found Angie staring down at him. "Must I forever be waking you up, Wilkes Wagner? Don't you have a bed to sleep in?"

Wilkes slowly stood dusting off clods of mud. "Didn't I tell you that all you have to say is *wake up*? You don't have to knock me off the porch."

She glared at him. "What are you doing here?"

"I was worried about you and forgot to get your phone number." That excuse sounded lame even to him. "I also wanted to ask you to my house for dinner tomorrow. There's an old guy searching the canyon for what might prove very interesting to the museum."

Finally, she seemed to relax. "Are you talking about Carter Mayes?"

"You know him?"

"No, but I heard one of the volunteers mention him and I've seen him a few times around where steps go down into the canyon's viewing area. I'd love to meet him." She hesitated, then added, "Thank you for inviting me. I'm sorry I knocked you off my porch."

Wilkes rubbed his head. "Angie, maybe we should try starting all over again. We seem to have gotten off on the wrong foot and at this rate I might have permanent injuries before I get to know you. I think I'd like it if we could be friends. Good friends." He knew he wasn't being plain enough, but he had to start somewhere. Asking her to sleep with him seemed a little forward at this point.

Angie laughed, and he thought it was a nice sound.

"Do you want to come in for a cup of coffee before you drive home? Maybe it will keep you awake."

"Sure." He dusted off his hat and headed in behind her. "Mind my asking where you've been?"

She moved around the tiny area that served as her kitchen as she made coffee. "I like to walk over to the water's edge and watch the sunset. It reminds me of my parents' home. They lived on a sliver of an island in Florida."

"I thought you were from New York."

"We moved to Florida when I was in grade school. My father had lost his job and his brother offered him one in Florida. Dad had loaned him money a few years before, so I guess he figured he owed him."

"Nice of your uncle."

She shook her head. "Not really. They might have been brothers, but they never got along. My dad hated the job, but my mother got sick, so he stayed. Then after my mother died, he stayed on because it was all he knew."

Wilkes wanted to know about her. What made her interesting mixture of character traits? "Which did you like better, New York or Florida?"

"Both. Neither." She laughed. "I had friends before we moved, but never found any in Florida. When I went back to visit New York, it wasn't the same. I didn't really have much in common with my childhood friends." She stared out the window. "Every place has its history, its magic, its own sounds. Here, after dark, the sounds of the lake fascinate me. They're lonely sounds."

"You lonely out here?" He had the feeling Angie had been alone most of her life. An only child who got moved from place to place.

"No." She shoved away from the window. "I have my cat, remember? Plus I'm growing to love Texas more every day. It's a place to breathe, you know."

He agreed. Every place he'd traveled had made him feel as if he couldn't draw a deep breath. "I have half a dozen cats, you know." To his surprise she smiled and touched his arm in almost a pat, almost a hit. He wasn't sure if she was trying to be friendly or about to beat him senseless.

"That's great," she said. "Most men hate cats."

"Not me." He patted her arm back, feeling as though they were kids on the playground. He didn't dare tell her that his cats lived in the barn and now and then Uncle Vern pancaked one driving out in his pickup.

Angie leaned across the table to pour the coffee.

Wilkes wouldn't have noticed if the coffee was made of mud. He was too busy watching her. He guessed she was in her mid-twenties. She was a smart, accomplished woman, but something about her didn't fit. Besides being shy, she didn't seem to understand, not just him, but men in general. If she had, she would have been aware of how her blouse opened at the neck as she leaned forward.

He reminded himself that if he were a gentleman, he wouldn't have noticed. Wilkes knew he'd have to be dead to be that much of a gentleman.

"Where'd you go to school, Angie?" he managed to say when she sat down across from him.

"In Washington, DC. I lived with my two great-aunts. We had a grand time."

Proving his theory about how sheltered she probably was, he thought, as he said, "Tell me about it."

She moved her head back and forth and blushed. "Well, we always got prepared for the snow. We'd buy fabric and yarn and all kinds of crafts just for fun. I was in charge of the snow-day movies. I'd order a dozen sometimes. When the bad weather came, we'd hole up and sew or quilt while we watched movies. It was a fun time."

"I can bet," he said. "You stayed with them all four years?"

She nodded, sending her curly hair bouncing. "I did. My aunts moved to a retirement home a year after I left. I miss them terribly."

She glanced down, and he had the feeling that she was worried about something.

"What about your fiancé? Do you miss him?" Wilkes watched her closely. Obviously the guy she left behind hadn't crossed her mind.

"No," she said a bit too fast. "I'm over him. To me he never existed."

Wilkes was starting to wonder if he ever had. Women like to pick apart all that was wrong with an ex. She'd never even mentioned this guy Jones's first name. This born-yesterday woman was starting to fascinate him like no woman had in years. But if he were to stay around her, he would have to slow down, back down.

No matter how jaded Wilkes was with the game men and women play, he couldn't go stomping over a heart that was newborn.

CHAPTER TEN

Lauren

All the bells and cars honking for homecoming had long faded by the time Lauren got back to the dorm after visiting Polly at the hospital. Tim walked her to the elevator in the lobby without saying much; maybe he was as shaken as she was over Polly's attempt at suicide, if that's what it had been. The hospital might believe the mirror had fallen, but Lauren and Tim had put pieces of what Polly said together, and neither was sure the tumbling mirror had been an accident.

"Why do you think she did it?" Tim finally asked.

"I don't know," Lauren answered. "We've been rooming together for over a month and as far as I know her mom's only called once. For all the parties she goes to, and guys she goes out with, I think she's lonely."

"Yeah." Tim didn't look at her when he added, "Aren't we all. This time is supposed to be the most exciting of our lives. The years we live fast and do outrageous things so we can talk about it the rest of our lives. But if this is as good as it gets, I don't know, I might start hoping for a mirror about to tumble."

"Don't say that, Tim. Don't ever think that." Lauren fought back tears.

He looked at her and saw the effect of his words. "I'm sorry, L. I didn't mean it. You know me, I was just trying to be funny."

She attempted to smile, letting him know he was forgiven. It had been a wild night, starting with the strange date with Reid Collins and ending with Polly in the hospital. She couldn't even remember how long they'd stayed with her, an hour, a day.

Tim sat on the arm of one of the chairs by the elevator. Silently, as if there was nothing else to say, they watched girls return from homecoming parties. Some looked happy, even dreamlike. Most looked tired or sad. A few simply looked drunk.

"Sometimes I think the world is packed with lonely people walking around, bumping into each other but never really seeing anyone." Tim shrugged.

She kissed his cheek. "I'm not lonely. I've got you. Thanks for coming with me to the hospital. You knew what to do. You made Polly feel better. I'm glad you were there, Tim."

"Always." He smiled. "You're the only girl who calls me to go out, and where do we go? The hospital." He grinned. "I've tried dating a few times, but the girls either don't get my jokes or they expect me to pay for them. What is the fun in that? I run out of money twice as fast and they go buy a new pair of shoes. If you're not married by thirty, will you promise to marry me? I have a feeling I'll still be single."

"I promise I'll marry you if I'm still single and we'll grow old together wondering why no one else wants us." She giggled, releasing nervous energy and worry.

He took both her hands in his. "We'll build a house on the lake between my folks and your dad and have redheaded babies."

"Wait a minute. Is sex part of the deal?" She laughed.

"Hell, yeah." He winked.

"I may have to reconsider."

He stood and walked toward the open door. "It's part of the deal, babe, take it or leave it."

She pushed the elevator button and said, "We've got over ten years to negotiate. Good night, Tim."

"Good night." He walked out the open front door and into the shadows.

She watched him go. When the elevator opened, she just stood there, staring into the night wondering why Tim hadn't crossed the corridor to the other wing.

It was late, very late. Maybe he didn't want to take the chance of seeing anyone if he crossed through the inside passage between their dorms. Maybe he felt as she did. All of her emotions had drained, leaving a tired ache that melted into her bones.

When she turned back to go upstairs, something caught her eye. Someone was standing there a few feet away, almost invisible between the building's corner lights.

She waited. Hoping. Fearing.

"Hi, Lauren."

She'd know his voice anywhere. Low and rich with the slight hint of his heritage whispering in his words. The one voice that always made her heart beat faster.

"Lucas," she answered, remembering the first time she'd become aware of him. It had been a night like this, starless and cold, two and a half years ago. Only, it had been spring, not fall, and she'd had no warning of how much she would grow up in one night.

Several of them had been working on a project for 4-H. When their ride didn't show up, they decided to walk home. Reid and Tim were talking football, but Lucas talked to her. He'd been a senior about to graduate, and she'd been a sophomore. They were both planning to simply walk and talk, but thanks to a bad suggestion from Reid Collins they'd ended up breaking into that old abandoned house. She'd gone along, thinking she'd have a story to tell on Monday, and Lucas said he'd agreed so he could watch over her.

They dropped into the old house from a window. Part of the floor gave way and Lucas had saved her life that night.

After that, now and then when he was home from college,
they'd talk or take an hour to watch the stars. Her father thought
they were friends who called each other sometimes. No one
knew that they were far more. Promises unspoken, but felt. A
few dreams of what might be bound them. More than friends
and less than lovers. Purgatory.

He moved closer but remained in the shadow of the doorway.
"You all right, Lauren?" he asked.

She took a step closer to him. Lucas Reyes was standing in
front of her just as much of a shadow in life as he was in her
dreams.

"I went upstairs looking for you," he said as his tall, lean body
moved toward the light. He was dressed in worn jeans and a
faded Western shirt. She guessed he'd come straight from working cattle all day. "One of the girls on your wing said you took
your roommate to the hospital."

There was so much she wanted to tell him, but Lauren didn't
know where to start. "The ambulance took her. I caught a ride
with Tim. Polly was hurt pretty bad."

She wanted to scream at Lucas for not being there for her tonight. He should have been the one to take her to the game. He
should have helped her with Polly, but no promises had ever been
spoken between them. Maybe they'd only been in her mind.

She wanted him to care so deeply that seeing her was as necessary as breathing, but he didn't and she couldn't bear that he
didn't.

Lauren was suddenly angry and guessed Lucas would be, too,
after overhearing her promise to marry Tim, but he wasn't. He
simply moved slowly to her until their bodies touched, then he
circled her in a hug and pulled her against him.

It felt so right to be in his arms. It always had. She breathed
him in as if he were her first fresh air in a month.

With tears falling, she told him all about her night. How Tim
told her not to go out with Reid Collins and how she hated

football and how she found Polly. She even told him what Reid said about the hallway sex he had with a drunk Polly.

Slowly, her body relaxed against Lucas, but he never let go of her, not even when she repeated what Reid had texted after their date. "I didn't even kiss him," she admitted and then felt bad at her need to explain.

Lucas remained calm as he always did. Sometimes she swore he was far more than two years older. He had his life all planned out and the world around him was no more than a soap opera he sometimes had to walk through. She'd never seen him angry or hurt or even frustrated. He'd been tired sometimes after work and excited when he told her of his plans after college. Reason seemed to rule his emotions, and she wondered if Lucas had ever snapped.

"Aren't you upset about Reid saying he got lucky tonight?" she asked.

Lucas wiped away her tears. "No. Anyone who knows you won't believe it, and anyone who knows Reid knows that he lies. Remember how he pretended he saved us all the night at the old house? The whole town turned out to call him a hero, but you, me and Tim knew the truth."

"It was sad to watch how Reid had played a trick on the entire town," Lauren admitted. "Tim still doesn't want to talk about that night. He not only got hurt bad, he lost Reid as his best friend. I guess it was hard to be a town hero with Tim limping beside him knowing the truth. Reid never even called to check on him. Not once."

"It's ancient history now." Lucas pulled away and took her hand. "It's also after midnight, but walk with me awhile. We'll stay close so you can go in as soon as you get cold."

She nodded, doubting she'd be able to sleep tonight anyway.

As they walked around the complex of dorms, he told her all the news from home and that Mr. Kirkland had him working from dawn till dark at his ranch. "Rain's coming in hard in a few hours, so I doubted I'd be able to work tomorrow. I knew I couldn't study at home, so I drove back, thinking we might spend the afternoon studying tomorrow. When we used to talk about you coming to Tech, I always thought I'd show you around, but you've been here over a month and I haven't even started."

Lauren breathed deep of the cold air. "That sounds wonderful."

He tugged her into the shadows of an aging cottonwood and kissed her, slowly and gently.

For the first time, Lauren wanted more. She pressed against him, wrapped her arms tight and traded gentleness for passion. They were no longer children and she needed to feel Lucas against her.

To her surprise, he matched her need. His hands moved down her sides as he leaned her against the tree with his body. Their kiss turned wild as if they'd both been dying of thirst and a dam broke over them.

His hand brushed over her body lightly at first, then he unzipped her coat. She didn't feel the cold. His fingers were warming her as he cupped her breasts.

She trembled with the sudden feel of him unbuttoning her blouse to get closer. This was a side of Lucas she'd never seen, a side she'd hoped was there behind all his calmness and logic.

Time slowed as her heart raced. She was growing, changing, awakening. Each touch, each taste, each feel of him was making her a little more woman…a little less girl.

She fought to catch her breath as his hands moved over her skin and his lips returned again and again to her open mouth. She could count the number of kisses they'd shared before tonight on her fingers, but none had been like this. He was showing her just how much he wanted her and she was lost in the joy and the passion of it all.

Suddenly, Lucas pulled away. For a moment he just took in deep gulps as if fighting for control. "We can't be doing this, Lauren."

She couldn't speak. His words had been an order, not a request, but she feared if she protested she might just break his resolve.

The cold air rushed between them, freezing out all they'd shared.

Lucas was the oldest child, the one always taking care of his brothers and sisters. The one who took care of her. He lived by a standard. He had his life set. All he was, she admired, maybe even loved. She wasn't sure who either of them would be if she changed him now.

The knowledge that he'd lost control, if only for a few moments, frightened her a bit at the same time it gave her an ounce of hope that she might matter more to him than even he realized.

Lauren stood perfectly still. She wouldn't push or force more between them. She couldn't, for both their sakes. For right now just knowing that such an attraction was there seemed enough.

Without a word, she took his hand and they walked to the nearest door. When she reached to open it, he braced his hand above her head and held it closed. Then he leaned toward her and brushed his lips over hers.

To Lauren it felt as if it was a goodbye. When it was over, he straightened an inch away and held both of her hands in his.

"Driving back tonight, I thought about something I should tell you. Now I know it has to be said."

"Okay," she whispered, fearing he was about to say something she wasn't going to like.

"I've never told you, but my dad went to Tech. He planned to be a vet. He and my mom started dating in high school and she got pregnant with me just before he left for school. They married and tried to make it work, but even with two jobs it wasn't easy for him to stay in school. Before his second year, Mom was pregnant again and Dad had to quit and take a full-time job."

Lauren didn't know what to say. Now his actions made sense. Maybe he thought he'd already ruined their lives and didn't want to have his and Lauren's added to the pile.

Lucas continued, "Dad says he never regretted it, but I decided

I wouldn't give up a dream of forever for now. I don't mean the getting pregnant part. I mean the getting so involved in another person that I give up my goals. And worse, you'd give up yours, too. Some people drop off the right path and never find their way back. For as long as I can remember, I've sworn I'm never going to let that happen to me."

Lauren's heart was threatening to break her rib cage from the inside out. Lucas couldn't be saying what she thought he was saying. She'd waited two years to make it to Tech so she could be with him. She'd kept their meetings, their conversations, their caring for each other a secret from everyone. She'd waited long enough but she could wait some more.

"I'll wait." She didn't need much of his time. She'd be happy with a slice. Just some. Just a little. Just enough to keep her dream alive.

"I can't ask you to wait. It's not fair to you. I stood in the dark tonight waiting for you to get back and hating myself. I wasn't here to help you with Polly. I didn't take you to homecoming." His laugh held no humor. "I didn't even know it was homecoming.

"Don't you see? If you wait, you'll miss too much. For me to keep my dreams on track, I can't be here every time you need me. If we started dating, I'd either be missing work and not be able to afford to come back next semester, or I'd miss studying and not have the grades. If I saw half as much of you as I want to, I'd be chipping away at my whole future, and it would crumble. I have to give me a chance before I can even think about giving us a chance."

Lauren fought back tears. Lucas saw life as either-or and she was losing. She was being set aside for another time. He thought he could simply lock away their feelings. Love and passion had to wait. It didn't matter now. She didn't matter now.

"Then why did you kiss me like that, Lucas?" she whispered, not really expecting an answer.

"It won't happen again. I swear." He straightened and she saw the strength in him, the strength in the man he'd be one day. She feared his goals would always come before her and she realized that until this moment her only goal had been to be with him.

Not any longer.

For the first time in two and a half years, she hated Lucas. "So you're giving me up." It wasn't much of a loss for Lucas, since he never bothered to come around anyway. He'd said such sweet words on the phone late at night when he was driving back from Crossroads. But apparently, they were just words to him.

She'd been building a future with his words when he'd simply been passing the time on the long drive.

He reached for her, but she pulled away. She had to think. Maybe she was taking this all wrong. The night had been endless and her nerves felt raw and sharp as if they might break the surface of her skin at any moment.

She had to think.

"We can still be friends," he said, hammering the first nail into the coffin of their bond. "We can talk on the phone. Study together. The time isn't right for us to be more than that, Lauren, can't you see that? If we're meant to be, it will happen when it is right for both of us."

When she didn't answer, he opened the door and they crossed through the main corridor back to the elevator. "Have you got a room you can sleep in tonight?" In the light his words were cold now, a stranger's questions. Not a lover. Never a lover. Not even a boyfriend. Only someone she thought she knew. Only a high school girl's dream of what might be.

It was time for her to wake up.

She remembered his question. "The girl two doors down doesn't have a roommate. I don't think she'll mind if I bunk in with her." Lauren didn't look at him. Tears were dripping off her chin, but she would not wipe them away. She let them fall.

"Good." He sounded relieved that he didn't have to worry about her. "When you wake up, call me. I'll bring coffee. We'll clean up the glass together." He leaned down to kiss her cheek but she stepped into the elevator before he could.

"When you've had some sleep, we're going to have a talk about your promising to marry Tim." He smiled. "Tomorrow you'll see that what I'm suggesting is best for us both. We'll have our time. We don't need to rush."

She pushed the up button. "Too late about Tim. A promise is a promise."

Lucas frowned for a moment, "*Mi cielo*, are you all right? Do you understand?"

The door closed without her answering.

She used to love it when he called her *mi cielo*, *my sky*, even if she'd just learned that she didn't mean as much to him as he did to her. Lucas had been her hero, her first love, and he didn't even know it. He was also the first to break her heart.

Tim was right about one thing earlier tonight. These are supposed to be the best times of their lives. Only, if they are, why are so many lonely people walking around?

And now Lauren could add her name to the list. For the second time in her life, she felt it. That growing up all at once was happening again. She suddenly felt years older than she had this morning, and she knew there was no going back. The girl might cry herself to sleep tonight, but the woman in her would wake up tomorrow and pick up the pieces.

Too soon, dawn blinked through open blinds onto her borrowed bed. Lauren slipped into an old pair of jeans and a sweatshirt, then tiptoed down the hall to her room. Mirrored glass shone in the morning light like slivers of memories that no longer fit together. Polly's blood had dried dark, spotting the rug, smearing across blankets.

At some point last night someone must have stepped into the blood for footprints tracked over the hardwood like dance steps pasted to the floor for a song that had no rhythm.

As Lauren cleaned up the glass and the blood, her phone rang.

Lucas. The excitement at seeing his name wasn't there today and she was too tired to wonder if it would be there tomorrow.

Lauren let it ring.

CHAPTER ELEVEN

Angela

Facing down Doc Holliday with her leftover cereal bowl half full of milk wasn't easy but Angela had to set some boundaries. After all, this was her place, and the cat was only a guest, even if he obviously saw it the other way around. "You've got to come in at a decent hour, Doc. Every night since we've been here at the lake, you're out running wild."

At the beach house in Florida he was perfectly happy to lie out on the deck, but since they'd been in Texas, Doc was climbing trees, darting around as if he was on a hunt; and last night he'd tracked in mud.

Her parents had adopted Doc Holliday from the old lady next door when she had moved. She said he'd had his shots but wasn't sure how old he was. Angie had always planned to take him to the vet, but at the time, with her mother ill, life seemed too full for errands and other things that had to be done.

She lowered the cereal bowl to cat level. "All right, here's your favorite, Cheerio-flavored milk. Now, in return I want you to stay close to the cabin today and guard the place."

Doc didn't even bother to look up from the bowl.

Angie collected her purse, sweater and lunch. Going to work would take her mind off the possible stalker and her nervousness about going to Wilkes's house for dinner. She had no idea what to expect at the Wagner ranch, but it was a dinner party and she planned to go dressed appropriately.

He might live in one of those shacks that had never seen paint on the boards, or he might have a big ranch house. People in this country didn't dress to impress anyone, so she didn't know how rich or poor he might be. A hat wasn't considered comfortable until the band was sweat-stained, and jeans were bought looking new and worn thin after weeks of work.

Miss Bees, one of the ladies at the museum, told her folks often talk poor because only a fool brags to his neighbors. Angie liked these people. The slow way they talked, their giving nature. She loved the humor they saw in the smallest everyday events of life.

Mrs. Kirkland greeted her with an honest smile as she walked into the museum. "You're two minutes late," she teased. "Must have been the traffic."

Mrs. Butterfield, dressed in pink and bling, agreed. "Probably a hangover from too much coffee with Wilkes Wagner." She winked. "Nothing gets past us."

Mrs. Kirkland giggled. "We live in the center of town right across from the café. How could anything get past us?"

Angela relaxed and laughed. Why worry about a stalker? She didn't need surveillance cameras; she had the Evening Shadows Retirement Community retirement home watching her.

"I was up talking to Wilkes and Yancy last night," she said. "They've got some ideas for the old Stanley wagon."

Both women rolled their eyes and Mrs. Butterfield's took their time coming back around.

"Two good-looking single men at a time," Mrs. Kirkland exclaimed. "And she hasn't been here a month yet."

"I don't think I have to worry about Yancy or Wilkes. They

both seem more interested in history. I'm going out to the Devil's Fork to look at Vern's old maps tonight."

Mrs. Butterfield laughed again. "I did that once in my twenties. It was very entertaining."

Angela had a feeling she wasn't talking about maps at all.

Mrs. Kirkland shook her head. "Don't worry about Wilkes. His great-uncle is the man to watch out for. Vern Wagner is walking, talking sex appeal in an aged bottle."

Angie simply smiled but inside she was afraid she wouldn't be able to look at Wilkes's great-uncle without laughing tonight.

On her lunch break she rushed home and rambled through half her wardrobe, finally picking a pretty silk dress of rich, swirling fall colors along the shoulders and hem. It was V-necked with three-quarter sleeves and was the right length to show off her legs to best advantage. She told herself she didn't care what Wilkes thought of her, but it seemed every time she saw him, she looked as if she'd borrowed someone else's clothes. This one dress was all her. Angie had known it the moment she saw it. The warm hues slimmed her figure, and the rustic golds brought out the shine in her hair.

High heels completed the outfit, but she'd packed her flats in her purse just in case they got too uncomfortable at the museum during the afternoon.

When she pulled into the museum parking lot, she couldn't stop smiling. A cool breeze greeted her with midday sun sparkling off the canyon walls. If this place was so beautiful in late fall, she couldn't wait to see it in spring. This was her new life. There was nothing left for her back in Florida or up in New York. Here was where she'd have to start over. Here was where she wanted to start over.

. The two afternoon volunteers were waiting for her. Angie couldn't remember their first names, but both were O'Gradys by marriage. They spent their time talking about everyone else in their family while they were on duty. When she ran up the steps, they both told her how pretty she looked. They made such a fuss she almost believed it.

The afternoon was busy with work. No message light blinked on her phone. No black car hid in the trees. Angie was beginning to think maybe she'd made too big a deal of a car following her. After all, who would want to bother her?

Only, the words in her father's note kept whispering in her mind. *Run. Disappear. Vanish.* Had he written it the night before he died, maybe as he feared for his life and hers? Was he so pressed for time that he couldn't explain? But he had prepared.

His note behind the picture. The money he'd deposited into her account. The way he died. All were pieces of a puzzle she couldn't make fit together. Almost from the day of her mother's funeral, he'd talked about moving. He'd never said why, but she knew he wanted away from his brother. But the time was never right. Something held him in Florida with his brother.

That last night while he worked in his office, he'd taken a few minutes to move the money he'd loaned his brother to start the business. He'd put the note where only she would find it.

But he hadn't even mentioned the priceless necklace that was rightfully his, and now hers. Obviously, her getting away was more important to him. She'd left the Greek coin circled in diamonds behind in the store's display case. It hadn't been important to her father. Her disappearing was. He must have thought her very life depended on her vanishing. But why?

She touched the replica Greek coin that now hung around her neck. The real one didn't matter. She suspected it had always been a bone of contention between her father and Anthony, but for generations the coin had been passed down to the oldest child; otherwise, it would have been sold and the money split.

Now her uncle could have it for all she cared.

Maybe he'd written the note because he wanted her to move on with her life. Maybe he'd been afraid his brother's family would try to run her life, or ruin it by having her work for the family. It seemed as if every time she saw her uncle after graduating college he'd complained that she should have gotten an accounting degree, and not studied museum management.

He'd frown and say, "I could have helped you then, Angela. I could have brought you into the business."

Angie had never answered. How could she tell him she'd rather die than work for him? She'd seen how much her father hated it.

Whatever the reason why Uncle Anthony complained, he was right. There was nothing left in Florida for her. But here, in this little town, she could belong.

She forced her questions about her father's death and home to the back of her mind. They were in her past now.

Midafternoon Angie decided to take the lunch she'd forgotten to eat outside and enjoy the warm sunshine on a rare, windless day. As she walked toward the seating area near the edge of the canyon viewing, she saw Carter Mayes climbing down out of his RV. His movements were slow as if forcing aching bones to function.

"Morning, Mr. Mayes," she called.

He waved and walked over. "I know I'm meeting you for supper, but mind if I join you for a snack?"

"Not at all." She offered him her extra bottle of water as he pulled out fruit from his pack.

"I usually eat down in the canyon. Take fruit so there's no trash to have to carry up." He laughed. "Every year I plant seeds down by the water, but I've yet to see a peach or apple tree growing, and I'm not even looking for an orange tree down there. Even if one sprouted it'd never make the winter."

She smiled, but he was no longer looking at her. Following his gaze she saw something flapping against her van's windshield.

"Looks like you got a ticket." The old man pointed as if she might miss it.

"Probably just a suggestion on how to improve the museum. Everyone seems to have a few ideas for me." Angie set her lunch aside and walked over to her van, then without opening the envelope, she hurried back to Carter.

She tore it open and unfolded the piece of paper. Words typed in all caps read simply: YOU KNOW WHAT I'M HERE FOR, ANGELA HAROLD. WE NEED TO TALK SOON.

Angie stared at the words feeling her whole body turning cold. Whoever wrote the note wasn't interested in talking. If he had been, he could have called or dropped by the museum. This note was left to frighten her, maybe make her run again. She could almost feel her blood freezing. If she ran, she'd be totally alone. No volunteers around all day. No sheriff watching over her at night. No senior citizens keeping an eye on whom she was with at the café. No Wilkes...

"What's it say?" the old man beside her asked.

She couldn't move. The words blinked in and out of her sight and a brooding darkness seemed to surround her as she fought not to pass out. She could no longer pretend that the voice mail had been a prank or the car hadn't really been following her. It was time to see reality. She was in trouble, real trouble, and she had no idea why.

"Is it a ticket?" Carter asked.

"No. I have to go. Please excuse me." Collecting her lunch, Angie hurried back into the building. Without speaking to the ladies at the desk, she rushed to her office.

There, silent and protected by the walls around her, she tried to control her breathing. The stalker wasn't gone. He was still out there, watching her...waiting for her. Maybe he'd parked his car and walked over to plant the note, or maybe he'd driven in with one of the dozen cars that had stopped by this afternoon.

Standing, she stared out her huge window looking for answers. She decided that her father must have told her to run because he knew she was too much of a coward to face whatever trouble was out there. And she *was* a coward, hiding in her office.

Anger suddenly boiled inside her, keeping tears from falling. All her life her parents had protected and sheltered their only child, and now she wasn't sure she'd ever be strong enough to face danger.

She tried to think of why someone was torturing her. Maybe it was a stranger in town who saw how frightened she seemed of the world and this was all a joke. Maybe her uncle was mad at her for taking the money her father had loaned him twenty years ago. She'd heard them arguing a few times, over money or store policy.

Her hands shook as she looked down at the note. Part of her wanted to run again. She'd be smarter this time. She'd leave in the middle of the night. Drive in circles. Change cars every other day until she knew it was safe to buy something she could keep.

Maybe she would ship her belongings and travel by train somewhere, then ship them again and again until she knew no one would be able to follow the trail. That might work next time. Whoever was bothering her might not be able to track her if she changed names, maybe dyed her hair. Or she could walk away from everything and hitchhike with truckers across the country.

Angie laughed at her own thoughts. She was hiding in a safe office in a safe building in a safe town. She'd never be able to go on the run.

Besides, she'd already spent a third of the money her father had deposited into her account, and if the Mercury found her again, she might not have enough to escape a third time.

A knock on the door made her jump.

She didn't answer.

It came again. Harder, faster.

She didn't breathe.

"Open the door, Angie." Wilkes sounded worried. "I know you're in there."

She straightened, lifted her chin, opened the door and ran into his arms.

Wrapping her in a bear hug, Wilkes lifted her off the ground.

For a long time he just stood there holding her. When he finally
lowered her to the floor, he said, "Tell me all about it."

Angie showed him the note and watched as he read. There
was no reaction until he looked up at her. For a blink she saw
anger in his blue eyes, then it was gone, as if he had been well
trained to hide emotions. "Any idea who put this on your van?"

She shook her head.

"No old boyfriend or jilted lover? Some guy you forgot to
give the ring back to when you broke up?"

"No."

Wilkes looked frustrated. "Did you ever take anything that
wasn't yours?"

"No."

"What about Jones's name when he didn't come along with
you? Maybe he's pissed."

She didn't meet his gaze when she answered, "No. He's not
the one stalking me."

Wilkes stroked her arms as if warming her. He pulled her
close and kissed her forehead, letting his words brush gently into
her hair. "You got your secrets, lady. I guess we all do, but I'm
afraid this one might get you hurt, and for some crazy reason
I'm not going to let that happen."

She managed a smile. "Thanks, but I don't need a knight in
shining armor. I'll settle for a friend."

"That's a good place to start. I can be that. When the sheriff
gets here, we'll come up with a plan to find this nut. The easi-
est way to stop this guy is to have a talk with him. If you have
no idea what he wants, maybe he's got the wrong person."

Angie didn't think she'd get that lucky. "Wait a minute.
How'd you know I was in trouble?"

"I told Carter to call me if he noticed anything. On my way
over here, I called my uncle Vern and told him to call the sheriff and both to meet me at the museum."

Angie shook her head. "It was just a note on my car. I'm

causing too much of a fuss." She'd spent her life being invisible, never the center of attention.

"You're not alone now. I don't like seeing you so afraid. None of us do."

"Thanks." She leaned in and kissed his cheek. "But I can take care of myself." The lie was so obvious she wouldn't have been surprised if he rolled his eyes.

He smiled at her. "Any chance you stole that old cat of yours from someone back home, Angie? People get real attached to their pets."

"No. The old lady who gave him to me said she'd found him when she moved in and planned to leave him in the empty house when she left."

Before Wilkes could ask any more questions, Dan Brigman appeared at her office door. This time the sheriff was all business. One call could have been a wrong number. A guy following them into the canyon might have simply been going the same way, but a note on her car had the markings of a crime about to happen.

Wilkes filled Dan in on all the facts, then offered to stay at the museum until closing time.

The sheriff said Uncle Vern had already stationed himself at the front door with the O'Grady women and the two volunteers for the next shift. When Dan passed by, he said the old cowboy was trying to talk them into playing Spin the Bottle and they were all acting as if they weren't old enough to know what he meant.

All the attention made Angie uncomfortable. "This isn't a siege on the museum. It was simply a note on my car." She faced both men. Now that her panic was over, she felt embarrassed and just wanted to forget the whole thing. "I've decided that maybe you're right, Wilkes. Maybe whoever this is has the wrong person. I haven't stolen anything. No one is looking for me."

Wilkes studied her. The caring in his gaze surprised her.

Dan didn't look up from his notes. They might not know all

the facts, but she had no doubt they were both taking this seriously.

If someone *was* following her. She knew it all the way to her bones. They must mean her harm. *Just like they had her father.* She could almost see them waiting for him out in the alley that night. Had they planned to kill him, or just beat him before the heart attack did the job for them.

"No one is looking for me," she said again, no longer believing her own lie. Her father's old ledger crossed her mind. Maybe it held a secret someone would travel half a continent to keep hidden.

Someone had broken into her father's house in Florida. Someone had shattered his office window. Was it possible that someone might have tracked her here?

But why? She had nothing. She knew nothing.

When neither man could offer an answer, she walked out of her office and left them to think it over.

Fifteen minutes later the sheriff found her in the kitchen making more coffee for Uncle Vern and three shifts of volunteers who refused to leave the front desk.

Dan leaned back against the counter and folded his arms. "I didn't mean to worry you, Angie. I'm sure you're right. This may be nothing, but we need to take precautions nevertheless."

"Wilkes doesn't think so. He seems to want an around-the-clock guard on me, and I don't think that is needed." Her emotions were jumping around in her mind like hot popcorn but she didn't want the panic to show.

Dan studied her and finally asked calmly, "What else besides the note and the call?"

Angie couldn't lie and she couldn't tell the whole truth. She had no proof. So, she stuck to the facts. "The day before I left Florida, my house was broken into."

"Did you report it?"

She nodded. "My father died a few days before and my aunt told me his office was also broken into, but I don't know if that was reported or if anything was taken. My aunt said the windows were broken and papers were scattered everywhere."

"Any chance your fiancé did it?"

Angie almost laughed. Her imaginary ex-fiancé was getting a rap sheet all of his own. "No. It wasn't him."

Dan wrote down a few facts. "How did your father die?"

"He was mugged and suffered a heart attack." She didn't want to tell him her suspicions.

The sheriff was silent for a few heartbeats, then he lowered his voice and said, "I'll check a few things out, Angie. In the meantime, let the Wagners watch over you. Wilkes is a good man. He seems easygoing, but near as I can tell he hasn't cared about anybody in a long time. He's been sleepwalking through this life, and for some reason he woke up and decided to care about you."

Angie glared at the sheriff. "What are you saying, Dan? That somehow my stalker might be good therapy for Wilkes?"

"No, of course not." The sheriff held his hands up in surrender. "But there is a chance this problem is real. This guy hasn't committed a crime—yet. I can't do much until he does. The bottom line is, I can't be everywhere. All I'm saying is let Wilkes help. Let him care about something for once." He lowered his hands and his voice. "Let him care about you."

CHAPTER TWELVE

Lauren

Lucas Reyes had been right about the rain coming in. Lauren could hear the tapping on her dorm window as she put new sheets on Polly's bed.

"Rainy days and Mondays." Lauren thought of the old song her pop sometimes played in his study. He'd said his mother used to dance with him in her arms to the Carpenters' song, and he'd done the same with Lauren when she was a baby. For the first time since she'd moved into the dorm six weeks ago, she missed her father.

Maybe she'd go home next weekend and tell him she got the Thanksgiving dates mixed up. Knowing Pop, he'd probably order a turkey dinner for two.

Lauren finished dressing. She didn't want to call and tell Lucas about the rain. The kiss they'd shared after midnight last night had changed her somehow. She'd tasted passion, if only a drop.

Lucas's words still hurt. She needed time to think it all out, to cry, to decide if she wanted anyone, including Lucas, to chart her life.

All her problems could wait. She had Polly to deal with first.

By the time Tim picked Lauren up to go to the hospital, it was pouring rain as if the whole world were crying.

She'd packed Polly a bag of clothes and anything she saw that she thought Polly might need. As an afterthought, she added two pairs of socks and the shoes she'd cleaned the blood from earlier.

When Lauren climbed into Tim's old Jeep, he asked, "You think she's getting out today?"

"No. I called to ask what she wanted me to bring up, but a nurse answered. Polly locked herself in the bathroom when they said she had to stay at least two more days. Apparently, her steady diet of alcohol, no sun and pills has left her anemic. She's got two infections. You don't want to know where. And the nurse says Polly refused to call in any family. She told the hospital we're all she has."

"Me and you?" Tim wiped his face, but rain still dripped from his red hair. "We got a kid and I don't even remember the sex?"

Lauren laughed. "If you're her dad, I have to tell you, we messed up. Our daughter is locked in the bathroom."

Tim tried three times before he got his Jeep started. It finally rattled to life, sending rain through the rips in the canvas roof as the heater blew a blast of cold air. "Is it too late to put her up for adoption?" he asked. "I can't afford a kid."

Lauren leaned back in the worn seat. "You know, Tim, I think this is one of those 'step in' or 'step out' moments. My pop told me about them. When you see someone who's sick or hurt or down, you can step in and help, or you can step out and send flowers."

Tires splashed through puddles as Tim drove. "I think I'm a 'step out' kind of guy, but I know you, Lauren. You'll step in."

She nodded. "You're right."

He looked at her when he stopped at a red light. "Like you and Lucas, you know, when I was hurt. If it hadn't been for you both dropping by all the time, I would have gone out of my mind. My leg was broke, but my mom would have spoon-fed me if I'd let her."

Grinning, she offered her hand. "So we're in?"

"We're in." He shook her hand and squeezed it as if making a silent bargain.

Lauren didn't let go for a moment, and he held on, too.

Lauren almost didn't recognize her roommate when they got to her room. A white bandage covered her arm, but nothing else looked like the girl who'd checked in twenty hours ago.

Polly had somehow managed a shower. Her hair was clean and braided into pigtails. No smeared makeup. No sexy clothes, only a white T-shirt that said Lubbock Rocks across the front. When she smiled up at Lauren, Polly looked about sixteen.

"Morning, roomie," she said.

Lauren set down the clothes bag. "An hour ago they said you were locked in the bathroom."

"I know. Turns out the nurse didn't seem to care. I think she would have left me there. After ten minutes of standing around in that gown with the back gaping open, I took her up on her offer to help me take a shower. I called down and asked if the gift shop could send up a shirt." She looked down. "This is what I got."

Tim perched on the edge of her bed. "You look great, sunshine," he lied.

Polly smiled. "No, I don't."

No one in the room argued. The dark lines under her eyes were still there, and her arms looked bone thin even though they were partly covered by the T-shirt.

Polly turned to Lauren. "Did they say I could leave? I'm dying of hunger. The food in here is worse than the dorm. Can you believe it—they bring the tray by at six? Who in their right mind gets up at six?"

Lauren didn't want to tell Polly she might as well get used to it. She wasn't leaving.

Thankfully, Tim jumped in. "The good news is they want

to keep you a few days to fatten you up, Polly Anna. Make sure the wound is healing correctly, I'm guessing." He took her hand. "The bad news is you've got me and Lauren to keep you company. And I'm wild about Star Wars movies. Once the nurses get finished poking on you, I'll bring up my laptop and we'll watch them all. If you're still alive by dark, I'll smuggle you in chili fries."

Both girls looked at him as if he'd gone mad, but since it was the only plan presented, they went with it. Two hours later, with the laptop propped on her tray table, Polly and Tim were watching a movie, and Lauren was studying in the corner.

Every time Polly fell asleep and missed a part, Tim would rewind and she would groan. After dark, Tim ate her hospital dinner, then went out in the rain and bought the girls hamburgers and chili fries.

Lauren was used to Tim, she'd known him most of her life, but Polly had to adjust to his humor and his endless chatter about nothing. When he suggested another movie, Polly said she'd agree to it just to get him to stop talking, but the nurse had to give her a sleeping pill first. She didn't want to take the chance of seeing the entire movie.

Half an hour later, Tim whispered, "Lauren?"

She looked up and saw Polly curled against his shoulder, her arms circling one of his as if he were her teddy bear.

"She's not so bad when she's asleep," he whispered and smiled as he brushed a stray hair from her face. "The nurse said they may keep her until Wednesday. Apparently, even without the cut, she was one sick girl."

"I didn't think she put up too big a fight to get out. Maybe she doesn't want to go back to the dorm. It's a shame her family couldn't come."

"Couldn't or wouldn't?" he whispered.

Lauren shrugged. No one had helped Polly move in. No calls, no letters, not even any emails that she knew about from family.

"We could take her home," Tim whispered. "Not the dorm,

home-home. I could skip my Friday lecture. I usually sleep through it anyway. You could join her after class Friday if you don't want to skip."

"But…"

"My mom is well trained at smothering the sick, and your pop has an extra room if she wants to stay at your house. A few days away from here would do her good, and from what I hear her grades couldn't get much worse."

Lauren thought that was a terrible plan, but she couldn't think of another one. "You know, Tim, she's not a stray kitten we're taking in."

He carefully tugged his arms free and covered Polly's shoulders with the blanket. "Step in or step out, Lauren. Make up your mind."

She tugged on her coat and answered. "I'll pack her books. If we take her to the lake, there will be nothing for her to do but study. I'll see if I can't get her professors' permission to help her with her work online for a few weeks."

Glancing back at Polly, Lauren thought about the haunting possibility that she'd tried to kill herself. Polly had told everyone it was an accident that the mirror fell on her. Everyone believed her.

Everyone except Lauren and Tim.

CHAPTER THIRTEEN

Wilkes

Tuesday afternoon in the museum dragged by for Wilkes. He had a dozen things he needed to do at the ranch, but he didn't want to let Angie out of his sight.

Grinning, he admitted watching her move wasn't a bad way to spend his time. She looked great in a dress. This was the second day she'd worn one. He hadn't commented, but he thought of suggesting she burn all her other clothes. The dress she'd worn yesterday had been the colors of fall, but today's dress was dark blue, almost black, and he liked the way it swayed around her legs like midnight water.

They'd postponed the dinner party to Tuesday night after all yesterday's excitement. Angie had insisted on going back to her cabin. She said she couldn't leave Doc Holliday alone. Wilkes thought it would be safe with the sheriff near, but when he'd seen her, he could tell she hadn't slept.

By noon when Wilkes took over watching her, she was wound up on coffee and doughnuts.

Keeping up with her turned out to be harder than following a rabbit in the middle of a wildfire. She, unlike he, was working. He finally gave up trailing her from room to room and set up a desk by the open door of the records hallway. At least he could search old newspapers for any mention of the Gypsy House, which he now knew had been owned by a man named Stanley.

From just outside the archive's door, he could hear her high heels tapping across the hard floors downstairs and see her circling through the foyer as she rushed from one project to another.

He liked her heels. She still didn't come up to his chin, but she didn't seem so short, and the dress was far easier to look at than those baggy pants she must have stolen off a street performer. The sweaters had made her look boxy. The dress showed off her curves.

Wilkes frowned. If he didn't stop thinking about the way she looked, Dan would probably arrest him for being some kind of pervert. Lusting after a curator was bound to be a crime.

Finally, when he realized he'd read the same page three times, Wilkes packed up and asked her if she'd consider leaving early. "I've got a dinner party to get ready for," he added, "and you look like you could use a little rest."

To his surprise she didn't argue. Maybe the caffeine and sugar were winding down.

Vern agreed to watch over the museum, and the six white-haired ladies at the desk swore they'd be his backup if trouble came calling.

"Who's watching the ranch with both of you here?" Mrs. Butterfield asked.

Vern answered before Wilkes had a chance to explain about the four ranch hands who always worked this time of year. "We got a rule." Vern winked at Mrs. Butterfield. "When we're gone, the cows promise to watch themselves. If one steps out of line, the others butt him into submission."

All the ladies giggled and batted their eyes at him.

Vern paced in front of them like a rooster impressing the hens.

"While there are no visitors in the museum, we got work to do, ladies. I want you all to call your families and tell them to be on the lookout for a black Mercury. Crossroads will never need the FBI to investigate anything. We'll watch out for each other. People like the Franklin sisters know everything that happens in town as far back as the sixties. Someone call them and ask about cars."

Wilkes took Angie's hand and rushed out the front door. Vern was having way too much fun and they needed to escape before he gave them an assignment.

He walked close beside her to his car. "Did you sleep at all last night?"

She shook her head. "I kept thinking I heard something moving around outside, and once, I swear I thought I heard the doorknob turning. I must have gotten up three or four times to check all the locks." She climbed in without complaining about him opening her door.

"Sit back and relax. I'll watch over you." When he started the car, he rested his hand over hers. Her fingers were cold, but that wasn't the only reason he held on tightly, he loved the feel of her hand in his.

By the time he reached the turnoff for his ranch, she was sound asleep.

He called the ranch headquarters to make sure his housekeeper had prepared the chicken enchiladas, beans and Spanish rice for their dinner, then told her to take off early and leave the front door ajar when she left.

Five minutes later he carried a sleeping Angie through the front door. He liked holding her. Something about her felt so right. As carefully as he could, he laid her on the big couch in his game room and covered her with a blanket.

He couldn't resist brushing the tips of his fingers along her cheek. He swore she looked like an angel. No girl had affected him so completely since Lexie Davis. He wanted to hold Angie, protect her, make love to her so completely that they'd both lose themselves to passion.

Wilkes stood. This wasn't him. He hardly knew her. But there was something about Angie that touched a place inside him that no one, not even Lexie, had ever found. Maybe it was just that she seemed lost and needed him, or maybe he'd just been alone too long. But this wasn't just a woman he wanted to date or sleep with casually. This was his Angie. If she walked out of his life today, he had a feeling it would be a long time before he stopped missing her.

Wilkes walked to the kitchen trying to figure out if he should try to tell her how he felt, or maybe just declare himself crazy.

For two hours she slept while he set the table and made a salad. When everything was ready, he sat watching her sleep. Finally, reluctantly, he stood and leaned over to wake her.

He thought of how she'd touched his hair once to wake him. So he moved his hand over her curly hair loving the way it tickled his palm. "Wake up, sleepyhead."

She opened those huge eyes.

Kneeling down level with her, he whispered, "You fell asleep, so I brought you inside. I let you sleep as long as I could before dinner."

Watching her rub her face as she sat up, he said, "If you want to freshen up, there's a bathroom that way. I'll be in the kitchen that way." He nodded once in each direction. "Dinner guests should be arriving soon."

Without a word she vanished down the hallway to the bathroom.

At exactly seven o'clock, Yancy showed up with old Carter Mayes. Following them in came Uncle Vern, complaining that he thought he'd never get those women out of the museum so he could lock up. The three were in their work clothes, stained and dirty, but when they saw Angie, all dressed up, they straightened. Vern even went to the kitchen sink and washed up.

The group started talking about Carter's quest to find the

cave from his childhood while Wilkes made drinks. By the time he returned with all their orders, Angie had nestled in the middle of them. She looked rested and seemed fascinated with Carter's story.

"I swear they would have come for me if I'd blinked, but I didn't," Carter swore. "I kept my eyes on them all night."

"Are you sure you saw them?" she asked. "You were only a kid."

"I saw them that night and I've seen them ever since in my dreams. They were real and I'm going to find them."

Vern joined in. "They were probably painted there by aliens."

Yancy said there was no such thing as aliens but Vern wanted to argue the point.

Their conversation lasted until Carter had the opportunity to corner Uncle Vern. Amazingly, the two men remembered each other from grade school. Suddenly anyone who wasn't over sixty might as well be part of the furniture.

Wilkes told Yancy to be the bartender. Since all he was serving was beer and sweet tea, Yancy should be able to handle it until the last guest, the sheriff, arrived.

Pulling Angie into the kitchen, Wilkes asked if she felt up for the party.

He noticed shadows under those big green eyes.

"I do feel better. Thanks for letting me take a nap," she said. "I didn't see Mr. Mercury today, but I swear I can feel him out there watching me. I must have spent half my day staring out the museum windows. I keep asking myself what I'll do if he shows up. Talk to him, see what he wants or just run?"

Wilkes saw the fear in her gaze. She was no more than a mouse being chased by a cat. Without any thought of his safety, he took a step toward her and opened his arms for the second time.

She came to him like a cannon shot. Before he had time to blink she was pressed against him, her face buried in his chest and her wild hair brushing against his chin. If he hadn't held on, she would have knocked him off his feet.

Damn if it didn't feel good to be needed. He must be losing his mind.

First clue, he decided, was that giving Angie comfort ranked up there with petting a porcupine. When he brushed her hair back, she stared up at him with those green eyes, and he would have gone to war for her any day.

Second clue that no brain remained in his head was that all he could seem to do was stare at her lips. She had the most kissable lips. He swore he could still taste the honey of those lips.

"It's all right, Angie," he said as he kissed her forehead. "Nothing is going to happen." He touched her soft cheek. "The guy is probably long gone by now."

Just as he was moving closer to her mouth, thinking that he might distract her from her worries with a long kiss, she pulled away.

"You're right," she said. "I'm being foolish. Some guy tracking me makes no sense. I can handle this. I'm twenty-seven. If I set some rules, I shouldn't have to worry." Like a little general, she began pacing across the kitchen. "I'll make sure I leave with the volunteers after work. I won't go directly home if I see the black car again. As long as he doesn't know where I live, he can't follow me, and I'm safe enough while at the museum."

"You're welcome to stay here," Wilkes offered. "It's so quiet out here you can hear a car turn onto my land."

She froze as if fearing she'd fall into an invisible trap with one more step. "I'd be safe here with you?"

"You'd be safe from anyone following you and you'd have nothing to fear once you're on my land." Those big eyes of hers made her look as if she were Little Red Riding Hood and the wolf had just offered a room at his bed-and-breakfast. "I've got five bedrooms upstairs, Angie, and they all have locks on the doors." Now that he thought about it, he kind of liked the idea of her sleeping under his roof. If nothing else, it would prove interesting. "I'll give you a gun to put under your pillow."

"Can Doc Holliday come? He's very shy. Hides under my bed most of the time."

"Sure," he said, thinking that he could put up with an invisible cat in the house. "I'll drive you back to your place tonight so you can pick up what you need. No sense waiting until you're in danger to come over. You could stay a few days until you know it is safe."

She nodded as if following his flawed reasoning.

"How about we keep this our secret, except for maybe the sheriff? The fewer people who know where you are, the better." The town gossips would be all over this if they knew. Wilkes had never brought any woman to the ranch since his folks left.

"Thanks for the offer, and you're right, we should keep it a secret. If news that I was staying with you got out, my little volunteers would think that I've lost my mind."

He decided he didn't want to know the "why" to that statement. Handing her two hot pads, he pointed at the enchiladas. "Mind carrying those in? I'll get the bowls of beans and rice."

"How many people are coming to dinner?" She stared at the huge pan.

"We're all here except for the sheriff. My mom always said to cook for a few extras when you're serving supper, since you never know if the guests are bringing guests."

As they set out the food, Dan Brigman showed up with his ex-wife, Margaret. Apparently, she'd been over to see their daughter in Lubbock and stopped by Crossroads to fill her husband in on what was going on at college.

Dan whispered that when he said he was having dinner at the Devil's Fork, she decided to come along. The sheriff looked sorry for the trouble, but Wilkes assured him it wouldn't matter. In truth Margaret didn't look as if she'd eat more than a half of an appetizer.

She was tall and thin, too thin, he thought. Wilkes had met

her a few times and decided the sheriff probably dodged a bullet when she left.

Wilkes didn't think Dan and his ex-wife looked as though they'd ever gotten close enough to make a child. Margaret made a point of taking the seat farthest from his. Wilkes watched them frown at each other and decided the Brigmans painted marriage, or the aftermath of it, in a dark light. If she'd come armed, there would probably be a duel before dessert.

The rest of the guests in the room soon became audience to the ringside fight.

"A mirror falling on Lauren's roommate is *not* nothing, Dan. Polly had to spend a few nights in the hospital." Margaret glanced around at the jury and explained. "Our daughter's roommate was hurt this weekend. I think Lauren should come home for a few days or, if she likes, she could come visit me. Either way that would give poor Polly time alone to recuperate. But Lauren insists on staying with this…this girl she barely knows. She's even talking of bringing her here to the lake this weekend."

Wilkes grabbed the salad off the counter and rushed back to the dining room. He didn't want to miss anything. He'd been around the Brigmans before, and their fights were better than watching *Survivor*.

"It was an accident, Margaret. Accidents happen. Polly's not contagious." Dan always sounded tired when he talked to his ex-wife. "With a deep gash down one arm, the poor girl might need help and Lauren's a good nurse."

"Well, I didn't raise Lauren to be a nursemaid to a clumsy girl," Margaret sniffed.

Brigman's voice was low. "You didn't raise her period. You left, remember?"

Margaret opened her mouth to argue, but no words came out.

Wilkes stepped between them. "Dig in, everyone. Hope you all enjoy the meal. My housekeeper is used to cooking for roundup, so there will be plenty. Can I get anyone another beer?"

The sheriff took a long breath and began talking to everyone at the table except his ex-wife. Nothing like bringing an ex to a party to make every bachelor in the room swear off marriage. The only one who didn't seem to understand what was going on between the sheriff and his ex-wife was Uncle Vern.

But by the end of the meal, Wilkes had to admit, when she wasn't snarling at Dan, Margaret was one beautiful, classy lady. She'd managed to enchant Carter. And Vern, who started flirting with Margaret halfway through dinner, was now patting her hand.

Wilkes stood, told everyone to enjoy visiting while he got dessert.

Everyone but Angie followed orders. The little strawberry blonde picked up a few of the dishes and followed him to the kitchen.

"I can handle these," he insisted.

"I know," she said wearily. "I just needed some air."

It hadn't occurred to Wilkes that Angie might not be enjoying herself, but since Margaret showed up he couldn't remember her saying a word. He'd seen it many times when he'd been with Lexie. The outgoing ones take center stage and the shy ones disappear. Only tonight Angie hadn't disappeared in his eyes. He'd been watching her all evening.

The thought crossed his mind that he'd spent his whole dating life watching the performers and missing the real women.

He handed Angie an apron and welcomed her onto the cleanup crew with a wave of his hand. They worked in silence for a few minutes before he said, "The Brigmans make an interesting couple, don't they?"

Angie nodded. "Were they happy once?"

"Not that I know of." Wilkes shrugged. "They seem to hate each other, but it's strange how neither remarried."

It occurred to Wilkes that even hating Margaret might make Dan feel more alive than trying to love someone else. If Wilkes looked inward, he'd have to admit that being lonely lately was better than feeling hurt. He remembered being that crazy kind of "in love" with Lexie in college. She was always on his mind, and no matter how much time they spent together, it was never enough. When he got that damn Dear John letter from her, something died inside him. For a while he didn't even feel the pain, he was just numb. Then the hole where his heart had once been settled into a dull ache.

By the time he got out of the army and started bumming around, he'd realized he was like the Tin Man. Only, he didn't need the Wizard to tell him he didn't have a heart.

Wilkes looked down at Angie. She was nothing like Lexie. She was the kind of woman he could be friends with. That was all he had to offer anyway. If he told her he wanted to get closer to her, it wouldn't be fair. A woman like her deserved much more than he could offer. Maybe he once thought he was, but now he doubted he could be that kind of guy who'd love someone forever.

Wilkes didn't think in forever terms. He thought in seasons, maybe. Since the army, he'd never had a girl longer than one season. Looking back, he couldn't remember if a single seasonal girl ever walked out on him. He'd been the one to leave.

Only, Angie seemed so different. He might like to try to cuddle up with her in winter and still be holding her beneath the stars in summer. If she'd be open to the idea. Which was doubtful.

He smiled as she served dessert, mothering Uncle Vern and Carter with her kind ways. One by one they finished off the cobbler and coffee and said good-night. Margaret even hugged Wilkes as if they were close friends, leaving Wilkes to wonder with her big job in Dallas if she had time for any friends.

When he finally walked Angie out to his Tahoe, Wilkes decided he was glad to be alone with her. He didn't feel as if they had to be talking to each other all the time.

Halfway to her place she seemed to need to break the silence. "I can help with Carter's search."

"He's got me," Wilkes added as if she'd forgotten about him.

She didn't even look his direction. "If he found the drawings, surely someone else has, too."

"Some folks don't see what's right in front of them."

She seemed to get the point. "I see you, Wilkes. You're a hard man to miss."

He smiled at her, but she didn't smile back. He guessed what she was doing. Counting the minutes until they'd be at her place. Waiting until she could say goodbye.

After a long stretch of silence between them, he voiced his thoughts. "Angie, are you still afraid of me?"

Her laughter seemed forced. "No, Wilkes. I know it looks like I'm afraid of everything, but not you."

He smiled hoping her words were true as he headed down the incline to the lake and her cabin. They passed the sheriff's place. Wilkes slowed. "Margaret's car is still parked out front."

"That's surprising after how they avoided each other all evening."

He agreed and turned toward Angie's cabin. "I don't want to ever be like that," he said. "I'd rather not marry at all."

"I agree. When my mother died, my dad never got over it. I asked him once about his sadness and he said it didn't matter. He'd take the grief for the pleasure of having been with her."

Wilkes pulled up in front of her cabin. "You think couples get to be in heaven together?"

"Maybe a few. If they loved enough."

Wilkes walked around the car and laughed as he opened the door. "Dan and Margaret better hope for heaven 'cause if they end up in hell the devil might skip the fire and brimstone part and simply put them together."

He offered his hand and she laced her fingers in his.

A good sign, he thought. She was proving she wasn't afraid of him.

As they reached the porch, he pointed to the sky. "See that quarter moon? That's called a rustler's moon. Enough light for rustlers to slip onto a ranch and steal cattle, but not so much that anyone on guard would see them clearly."

She leaned back and stared up at the sky. "And what would you do, Wilkes, if you could move unseen beneath the rustler's moon?"

"I might steal your heart, pretty lady," he answered, halfway kidding.

She laughed. "Not likely."

"Then I'd settle for a kiss." The words were out before they'd passed through his mind. "I don't know why, exactly, but there is something about you, Angie, that I find downright kissable."

To his surprise, she met his stare. In the shadows he couldn't tell what she was thinking. Maybe something like they didn't fit together or she had enough problems without getting involved. He didn't want any complications, because it wouldn't take long for her to figure out that his heart had shriveled up and died a long time ago.

"I'm not interested in playing games, Wilkes."

"I'm not asking for forever, Angie, or even tomorrow. I just thought it might be a nice way to end the evening."

She frowned. "So the kiss is just the after-dinner mint?"

"Something like that." It was amazing how quickly she could make him feel like an idiot. "Never mind."

Her hand reached out and brushed his shoulder, stopping him in his tracks.

"All right. If it doesn't mean anything. No forever or even tomorrow. One friendly kiss."

She wrapped her arms around him. The fact that holding this woman always felt like an attack registered in his mind about the time the softness of her pressed against him.

He realized he'd been waiting for this moment all day, maybe all his life. To kiss a woman for no reason other than it might feel good. No strings. No promises. Just the pure pleasure of holding Angie.

Her lips were one inch away, but Wilkes couldn't move in to

claim the kiss. The sudden realization that he did want more made him hesitate.

He laughed as he carefully lifted her off the ground. They were almost the same height now. For once they weren't so mismatched.

"One kiss," he whispered to himself. *One kiss.*

He set her feet on the first step and pulled her tighter against him, wanting to see her face in the moonlight until the moment their lips met.

She smiled and tilted her head in invitation.

When his mouth lowered over hers, he kissed her slow, taking in the waves of her feelings moving from surprise to a hesitation at his boldness to passion. He didn't know much about her past, but he had no trouble believing that she was naive to this kind of kiss.

And surprisingly, he felt the same.

Wilkes pulled away, kissing across her cheek to her ear before he whispered, "That was unbelievable, Angie. Maybe the best kiss I've ever had."

She looked shy as she moved away and climbed up the steps of the cabin. "Where'd you learn to kiss like that?"

He was so busy trying to get his head around what had just happened, he didn't think to answer. The touch of her lips hadn't set off fireworks. No chills or light-headedness. Just a slow hunger he feared might take a lifetime to satisfy.

"I don't think I've ever kissed anyone like that. Never. Usually a kiss is just something moving on to the real action, but this...this was..." He had no ending to the sentence.

She didn't say a word. She moved a few feet away and sat very still on the porch railing with her hands in her lap.

He couldn't stop staring at her. Maybe she couldn't figure the kiss out, either. Hell, for all he knew she was praying the night would end.

Without a word, she stood and went in the cabin.

He waited on her porch hoping she was packing a bag and loading her cat in a carrier. If she was ending the evening, surely she would have closed the door.

Wilkes stared into the night wondering if it was too soon to ask to kiss her again. Or, maybe he wouldn't ask, he'd simply kiss her. After all, they were two adults, not kids on a first date.

He looked up at the rustler's moon. "I've gone brain-dead. I'm sounding like a teenager. Maybe I should go home and ask Vern to shoot me before I lose the three brain cells I have left."

The light went out in the cabin and Wilkes ended his one-sided conversation.

"We're ready," Angie said as she stepped out of the cabin and handed him Doc Holliday.

The cat hissed, and Wilkes growled back. They were off to a great start.

On the drive back Wilkes talked about Yancy's house that called to him. They even drove past it, but in the black of night there wasn't much to see.

"I'm not afraid of ghosts," she announced.

He pulled away from the house and headed back to his place. "What are you afraid of, then?"

She laughed. "Pretty much everything else."

Thinking about it for a mile, he finally said, "Promise you'll never be afraid of me, Angie. I never want to see the fear I saw in your eyes that first day we met." He'd startled her. She'd jumped, falling into the display. He'd only meant to stop her tumble, but it had frightened her.

"I'll try not to be." She grinned in her shy way. "I am getting used to you, Wilkes."

A few minutes later when he showed her to the bedroom farthest from his, Wilkes was polite and funny. He even swore Doc Holliday would love all the dust bunnies under the bed.

As he left her to unpack, he said, "Coffee will be on in the kitchen by seven. Uncle Vern will be sitting at the table waiting for a cup, so don't let him startle you."

"Thanks for everything," she whispered.

"You're welcome." He glanced over his shoulder and found her staring.

"And for the best kiss I've ever had." The words were so low he felt as if he read her lips more than heard.

He took a step back toward her as she slowly closed her door.

"Anytime," he said, knowing she could no longer hear him.

Part of him wanted to pound on her door and grab her in another kiss, but he couldn't rush this. It was too special for him and maybe for her.

He was coming alive again and he wanted to enjoy every minute for as long as it lasted. A day, or forever.

Wilkes walked to his end of the hall and whispered what he'd been thinking since he'd held her for a few minutes beneath the rustler's moon. "One kiss is never going to be enough, Angie. Not by a long shot."

CHAPTER FOURTEEN

Carter

By the time Yancy dropped Carter Mayes off at the campsite a quarter mile from the museum, Carter was almost too tired to walk up the three steps into his mobile home.

Mid-October's wind whispered of winter moving closer, and the old man knew his time in West Texas was almost up for the year.

"You all right?" Yancy yelled from the open window of his car. "Maybe Wilkes's chicken enchiladas didn't agree with you."

"I'm fine. My old bones just ache when the temperature drops. Come sunrise, I'll be ready to go again." He unlocked his door, and Watson met him. "My dog will keep me company for the rest of the night."

Carter watched Yancy drive off, and the night became inky black. He turned on one reading light over his bed and told Watson all about the dinner party. The shaggy old shepherd didn't seem all that interested.

He stripped down to his underwear, crawled into his blankets and called one of his daughters. He knew it didn't matter which one because whomever he called would notify the other two. His girls were close, and their main hobby, since their mother died, was worrying about him.

"I'm sorry I'm late, sweetie," he began. "I had dinner with some friends."

He closed his eyes and listened for a few minutes. Like her mother, his daughter April had the habit of listing, in order, everything she'd done all day. Finally she ended with a question. "What friends did you have dinner with, Dad?"

"Oh, I know lots of folks here, you know. I've met the new curator of the museum, nice girl, and an old fellow I went to school with seventy years ago. You're not going to believe this, sweetie, but he's got more maps of this area than I do."

He wiggled deeper into the covers. "I'm having a great time as always. I swear the canyons get more beautiful every year. Tell your sisters not to fret. I've been coming out here so many years half the people in town know me by name. I like to move the RV around now and then so as not to wear out my welcome in one spot."

He listened to his daughter talk about his grandchildren. All together he had seven granddaughters under ten years old. He called them the seven dwarfs and couldn't have named all seven if his life depended on it, but that didn't mean he didn't love every one.

Almost dozing off, Carter broke into his daughter's account of her youngest. "I'd better call it a night. I'm tired tonight, but I'm close to finding the cave. I can feel it. Another week, maybe two. After that it'll be too cold here, and I'll come home for the winter."

Carter pulled the covers close around him feeling the season's change all the way to his bones. "Good night, sweetie. Tell your sisters that I'll call one of them tomorrow night." He laughed. "You know, I almost said to tell your sisters and mom that I'll be home soon. Sometimes, when I'm really tired, I forget that she's gone. In my mind, most days I think that maybe she's home waiting for me when fall is over."

He smiled as his dear daughter said good-night, then Carter laid the phone down and turned off the light as he added, "I love you all, too."

When he passed into dreams, the stick figures with huge round heads and hollow eyes walked beside him. He never spoke to them, but they no longer frightened him.

The sound of a car pulling up behind his little mobile home was the last sound that registered in his thoughts before he slept.

CHAPTER FIFTEEN

Angela

Walking out onto Wilkes's ranch house porch at dawn, Angie felt as if she were floating on her own private cloud. Somehow Wilkes and she had discovered something totally new. She had no doubt they'd both been rattled to the core by that one kiss last night.

They'd stepped on an uncharted planet at the same time. This new feeling wouldn't be all that unusual for her, she'd had a very sheltered life, but Wilkes was one of those men who'd been around. He'd probably had a dozen girlfriends and flirted with hundreds. Surely he'd kissed someone before as he'd kissed her last night.

Yet when he'd looked down at her after the kiss, he looked as if he wasn't sure what had happened. She might have dreamed about that kind of kiss, but she knew Wilkes never expected to be so shaken by it.

He left a note by the coffeepot saying he wouldn't be able to take her into work. He was sorry, but the sheriff would drop by about eight thirty to pick her up.

She sighed. Maybe she'd read too much into last night. So much for any feelings growing out of one stolen kiss under a rustler's moon. It was time she stepped back into the real world. Fairy-tale endings don't happen to practical girls like her. Wilkes was simply offering to help out.

Shy women like her didn't have romantic encounters or passionate love affairs. She was like her mother, or at least she always thought she was. She'd find someone one day who shared the same interests, wanted the same things. They'd marry and have a good partnership. No drama. No complications. No passion.

Men like Wilkes were the stuff of fantasies and dreams. She had a feeling she'd relive that one kiss a million times in her mind. Wilkes, on the other hand, would move on to one of those model-thin girls with perfect hair and cute shoes. Either he was avoiding her because he feared lightning might strike again and he'd be tempted to do something foolish, or the kiss had meant nothing and, as he said, there was no tomorrow.

She was still trying to figure it out when the sheriff arrived at Devil's Fork to pick her up. He was easy to talk to, but she couldn't imagine discussing a kiss with him. So all the way to the museum he told her about his daughter, Lauren, and how she'd come up with this half-baked plan to bring her crazy roommate home to the lake to recover.

"The girl streaks her hair," Dan complained. "I can't tell if her natural color is brown and the red is painted on or if it's red and she paints in the brown. Polly doesn't look old enough to be in college, but once I saw her eyes, I swear she's one of those old souls people talk about. Only apparently, she's a slow learner and has to keep coming back again and again to learn the same lessons. Proving not all old souls are bright."

Still focused on Wilkes, Angie wasn't really paying attention. She'd probably never meet the girl. Simply smiling and nodding now and then seemed to be enough for the sheriff.

"We're running early, Angie," Dan said as he pulled up in

front of the county offices. "Mind if I check to see if a report has come in?"

"No, of course not." She planned to stay in the car, but he pointed to the keepsake shop a few doors down.

Angie got the hint. "I'll be in there when you're ready."

She wandered into Forever Keepsake as they unlocked the door for business and met the Franklin sisters.

Angie wasn't surprised they knew who she was. The sisters might be in their midforties and as wide as they were tall, but they reminded her of the two aunts she'd lived with outside of Washington. There wasn't a topic the sisters weren't prepared to talk about, whether they knew anything or not, and they never met a stranger. They swallowed her up in conversation as if she were an old friend.

When the door chime sounded, they were laughing. Angie turned expecting to see the sheriff, but a tall woman with long black hair to her waist stood at the door grinning as if she expected a round of applause for showing up.

The sisters seemed to have turned to stone.

Angie had no idea what to do. From their stares, the Franklins could be looking at an armed robber. Only, the lady's perfectly tailored dress was far too tight to allow for a concealed weapon.

Her red-lipped smile never slipped as she held out her arms. "Hello, Miss Franklin and Miss Franklin! Or should I say Rose and Daisy? After all, I am all grown up now."

Neither woman answered.

The beauty didn't seem to notice. "I just had to stop by and give you two a hug while I was in town. It's been years and years since I've seen you, and I swear neither of you has changed a bit. The boring life in a dead town must slow aging."

Angie moved out of the line of fire. The taller Franklin, Rose, Angie guessed, since she wore a rose pin on her collar, looked as if she might explode.

Daisy, the shorter Franklin, glared as if fearing the beautiful woman might kill them at any moment.

Rose recovered first. She waddled forward, no smile but a sweet voice. "Why, child, I didn't recognize you. It *has* been years. We used to see you when you came home from college, but when your parents moved away, I think you only came back to see your aunt once in the past six or seven years. It was while Wilkes was in the army if I remember right."

At the mention of Wilkes, Angie doubled her interest in the new customer.

The tall lady gave Rose an air-kiss, kind of like what movie stars give each other. Almost touching. Almost caring.

Daisy stepped forward and got her almost hug, too. "You've been gone a long time, Lexie. What brings you back?"

Angie seemed to have become invisible, so she simply watched.

The woman called Lexie brushed an invisible tear off her porcelain face and said low and sad, "Since dad died, it's hard for me to return to Crossroads. My mother moved into a senior living home near me in Dallas and swears she'll never come back here."

Both the Franklin sisters nodded like dueling bobbleheads.

Lexie lifted her chin, putting on a brave front. "Only now my aunt is very ill, and I'm afraid I'm her only relative. It's my duty to be with her during her last days, no matter how busy I am in the city."

Daisy Franklin nodded, but added, "'Course, your aunt has had dementia for three years, so she don't remember you. Last I heard, when they moved her to the nursing home in Bailee, she thought she was going on a cruise. Thinks her doctor is the captain. She told someone the waitresses dress in white and serve her an afternoon drink on the deck along with appetizers and her pills." Daisy smiled sweetly. "They also say she plays bridge with old lady Wilson, who has been cruising since she was ninety-three. Apparently, they're both party animals, even at the home."

Angie watched Lexie frown. Obviously the "poor me" act wouldn't work with these two. She tried another approach. "Still, I'm visiting her every day while I try to clean out that enormous house of hers. I was wondering if you two ladies would like to help me appraise some of her things. I'd give you first option to bid on anything."

Angie wanted to yell "bingo." Lexie had finally gotten down to the reason she'd walked in the door.

Before the women could answer, the door chimed again and the sheriff rushed in with a gust of wind.

Angie almost laughed as he took one look at the beautiful woman with the midnight waterfall of perfect hair and froze. Angie had no doubt that if he thought he could step backward and disappear before anyone noticed, he would.

But the sheriff wasn't a coward. He nodded once and said, "Lexie, you're back. What's it been? Ten years?"

"Seven, actually," Lexie said as she looked him up and down from boots to Stetson.

"Time flies," he answered and turned his attention to the Franklin sisters.

Not exactly a welcome home, Angie thought. This lady was getting more interesting by the minute. It was as if they gave her a parade when she left, and now she'd returned, they all wanted their streamers back.

Angie swore she saw the woman push out her breasts slightly and arch one of her perfect eyebrows. "Well, Dan Brigman, you haven't changed one bit since you came here the year I turned eighteen. New sheriff that played everything by the book. Tried to arrest Wilkes and me for driving through the canyon one night. We were just kids having fun."

Dan didn't smile. "You might have been eighteen, but you were going over eighty. Wilkes told me it was your idea, but he worked a month to pay off the ticket."

"Of course it was my idea. Like I always say, I don't have to go to the party. I *am* the party. Every wild thing Wilkes did was because of me."

When no one in the shop commented, Lexie must have felt the need to stay on stage. "That man never had a spontaneous or romantic thought in his head. Then one day he just says that he joined the army, like it wasn't something I should have had a say in."

"He wanted to serve his country like his dad and grandfather had. I'd call that responsible more than wild." Dan frowned as if he was thinking of pulling his weapon.

"Always the drama queen, Lexie." He took a deep breath. "Ever wonder what the town talks about when you're not around."

She struck a pose. "In fact I do. I imagine keeping up with my life is the only thing that keeps half the people in this town from dying of boredom."

Angie wished she were recording this. How could she have thought there would be no drama in a small town? She felt as though she'd stumbled into the middle of a soap opera.

The beauty laughed. "Yeah, I heard the speech. Even my dad thought I should have waited for him, like I had three good years of my life to waste." She flipped her mane like a stallion on parade.

Angie simply stared. If being self-centered had a smell, the room would need fumigating.

Lexie seemed tired of waiting for a compliment. She twisted her hair in a long rope. When that got no reaction, she crossed her arms to push up her perfect breasts, then widened her stance. Her dress tightened over perfectly shaped legs. If anyone had taken a picture, she'd be on a cover somewhere. "Tell me, Sheriff Brigman, did you ever get over your wife? If so, you might just know where the parties are around this dull town."

Dan didn't look as if he even heard her questions. He turned to Angie. "If you're finished shopping, Miss Harold, I'll be happy to take you to the museum."

Lexie jerked, almost tumbling off her five-inch heels. Pretty ones, of course. She looked at Angie as if a frog had just appeared in the room. "Oh, I'm sorry. I didn't notice you."

Angie blamed it on that five-foot-three thing again, but really, how could someone miss a whole person in a twenty-by-thirty shop?

The sheriff stepped between them. "Angie, meet Lexie Davis."

Before Angie could say anything, Lexie laughed. "Well, give the girl a few details, Danny. I'm as close as this town ever got to having royalty. I'm sure she'd want to know who she's meeting." She turned her full attention toward Angie. "I was runner-up for Miss Texas eight years ago. I'm married to a very successful plastic surgeon in Dallas now, but all this town seems to remember is that I used to date Wilkes Wagner. We were kind of a thing a while ago."

Daisy Franklin added, "Dated him almost five years. Broke up with him when he was away fighting for our country. Folks don't forget that."

Angie bit back a smile at the expression on Lexie's face. She looked as though she might have bopped the little Miss Franklin on the head if the county sheriff hadn't been standing so close.

"We broke up," Lexie announced. "We went in different directions, and guarding an embassy isn't exactly like being at war. It's not my fault Wilkes didn't move on. I did."

Angie's brain was on overload. Lexie was exactly the kind of woman she'd thought would belong on Wilkes's arm. Beautiful, tall, nice shoes. Maybe she should have been jealous, but Lexie was simply reminding her of what she'd known all along. Great-looking men don't go for mousy women. She was angry for even daring to hope.

Rose got a word in. "I heard this husband of yours, the doc, is moving on, too. You already shopping for number three?"

Lexie opened her mouth as if she planned to say something ugly to the Franklin sisters. "Do you know, I believe I've reconsidered," she announced with a false smile plastered across her perfect lips as she moved toward the door. "I don't think I'll need an appraisal after all, ladies."

She pivoted, her perfect hair brushing against her perfect bottom as she walked out the door. "Good day, Miss Franklin and Miss Franklin…and whatever your name was."

Angie looked back to Dan in time to see the sheriff wink at the Franklins. "She forgot me," he whispered. "How lucky can a guy get?"

Rose and Daisy both tried to hide their giggles.

"Angie." He smiled. "You're going to be late to work. I'd better do my duty." He offered his arm as if he were a formal escort to a ball.

The two women watched as Angie walked out. She thought she heard one of them whisper, "Wish we could have told that Lexie that our Wilkes has him a new girl."

As the door closed, she whispered to Dan, "That's not true. Wilkes and I are not together."

The sheriff leaned near. "The Franklin sisters are never wrong. If they say you are, you are."

Angie blushed and changed the subject. "Did your paperwork come in?"

"Yep." Dan smiled. Somehow seeing Lexie had changed his dark mood about this daughter. "I've already sent it to Wilkes. He's picking up Yancy, and they are on their way to Austin."

"What?"

Dan grinned. "Don't worry, he'll be back in a few days and tell you all about it. In the meantime, he told me to ask you to stay at his place. It's safer. And don't forget to feed Uncle Vern. The old guy can handle cereal for breakfast and a sandwich for lunch, but he needs something for supper."

"But I don't even know…"

Dan interrupted, probably guessing her next question. "You'll find your way around the kitchen. The housekeeper keeps the place well stocked. I'm guessing the old guy will eat anything you make." He hesitated. "You'd be doing Wilkes a big favor. He doesn't like to leave the old guy alone and Vern hates it if he thinks Wilkes sent a babysitter. This way he can think he's guarding you while Wilkes is gone."

Angie felt as if she'd been reading a spy novel and somehow skipped a chapter. All she could do was nod as she muttered, "Doc Holliday and I will keep an eye on the place."

CHAPTER SIXTEEN

Lauren

The Saturn her father gave her for graduation was loaded down. Lauren was only taking Polly home for a long weekend but they were prepared for anything. Computers and books for studying, clothes for the unpredictable weather, boots, rain gear, bathing suits if they lucked out and had a warm sunny day on the deck.

Polly was riding with Tim in the Jeep ahead of Lauren. He'd packed a backpack and a bag of Cheetos. Right now they had the top down on the Jeep and kept waving back to her. Now and then a Cheetos would hit the windshield as though they were passing a snack back to her.

The doctor said that Polly should take it easy for a few days, eat regular meals and stay away from alcohol.

Lauren felt as if she was watching a robot slowly turning into a human. Step by step Polly Anna, as Tim called her, was changing. Cussing less, even smiling now and then. The trashy clothes were gone, but the red stripes in her hair were still there. Polly wanted to be the center of attention and Tim gave her that, but she refused to answer any questions about her past. It was almost as though she was born the day she walked into Lauren's dorm room.

Lauren tried to make up a past that fit her. Polly's father had beat her. Her mother had sold her into the sex trade. She was older than she looked, and this was the fifth college she'd flunked out of. She was younger and wanting to go wild a semester before the school found out she was a genius.

Not one of Lauren's theories worked.

When they reached the lake, Lauren moved Polly into what Pop and her called "Mother's room." But, except for a few nights back around her sixteenth birthday, her mother had never slept in this house on the lake. Lauren and her father had moved in while she was in elementary school. Margaret had come out for moving day, hauling some of her books and things as if she was really moving in, but even at five years old Lauren knew something was wrong. Margaret had left that night.

She thought her mother didn't want the lake house, but it turned out after a few years of lies and excuses that Margaret Brigman didn't want them. Lauren decided Margaret didn't want to be a mother, but Lauren feared her pop thought she left because she didn't want to be a wife.

Logic would have predicted that she and Pop would have been miserable, but it wasn't that way. They kept each other's spirits up. All her childhood memories were of the two of them living life in the small house. Now that she'd been away from home she realized how precious those years were.

She never, not for one minute, doubted his love.

Like now, Lauren thought. Pop had complained about her bringing her roommate home on such short notice, but he'd stocked the kitchen with snack food. He'd been angry when he found out Lauren was skipping class to come in Thursday, but then called back to tell her to check her tire pressure and make sure she had plenty of gas.

They pulled in and Tim immediately found the kitchen and announced they were having lunch on the deck. He wrapped

Polly in a quilt and carried her to the deck despite her protests, then lugged out a card table of snacks.

In the cool shade of autumn leaves, they watched sunlight dance over the water, and Lauren smiled. She was home.

A little after five her father showed up wearing his uniform and a huge grin.

"Your dad's a hunk," Polly whispered as they saw him heading toward them.

"No, he's not," Lauren whispered back.

Dan Brigman shook hands with Tim and smiled warmly at Polly as he told her she was welcome to stay as long as she liked.

When he excused himself to lock up his service weapon, Polly whispered again, "Hunk."

"No way," Lauren answered.

Tim broke into the argument. "Since I'm the deciding vote, I stand with Lauren. To me he just looks like a sheriff, and if you knew how strict he was, Polly, you'd stop staring at him like he was puppy-cute."

They all laughed.

The rest of the evening was cooking hot dogs on the grill and telling old stories about people in town. Lauren knew all the stories, she was even in the one Tim told about the Gypsy House, but she loved listening anyway. Tim had a way with words. He was a natural storyteller.

While Tim and her pop cleaned up, Lauren took Polly for a walk along the lake. She introduced her to a few of the neighbors and even met the woman who had just moved in a few weeks before. Polly seemed fascinated that Angie Harold was a curator. She even asked if she could take a tour of the museum later.

"Of course," Angie said. "Drop by anytime."

"I will." Polly smiled. "When I was a kid, babysitters used to drop me off at the museum by our house and pick me up at closing time. I loved wandering the place and picking my lunch from the vending machines."

The curator was busy loading up her car, so Lauren didn't

want to take up too much of her time. "We'd better go," Lauren said. "You look like you're busy."

"I'm just loading up a few supplies. I'm house-sitting for a few days and want to use my own pots to cook in."

Lauren wanted to ask why, but didn't. First, no one in Crossroads hired a house sitter. They just told their neighbors to keep an eye on the house. Second, what did it matter which pot you used. She'd met two curators in her life and both seemed odd. This one who only cooked with her own pots and the old one at the Ransom Canyon Museum who never stopped talking. Anyone who went in the museum found out he followed them around like a living portable headset.

As they walked back in the dark, Polly thanked her for bringing her to such a quiet place.

"I needed this," Polly whispered.

"I know," Lauren answered as they picked their way along the path between boat docks. She waited for her roommate to say more.

Finally, Polly added, "I wish I'd grown up in a place like this. My house is more like a war zone when my folks are home, which isn't often. They travel all over the world on photo shoots for magazines. I've heard coworkers say they never fight on the job, but the minute the day is done, the yelling begins."

"So who looked after you?"

"Babysitters when I was little. A housekeeper once I was in school during the day. It was a revolving door. I got to where I called them all Betty. No one stayed long. Once, when I was six, the old lady my folks had hired to stay a month died before the first week was out."

"What did you do? Call the police? Go to the neighbor's house?"

Polly shook her head. "I was afraid I'd get in trouble. I lasted almost a week on cereal and popsicles. But the old lady's sister kept calling to check on her. After about a dozen times of me saying I didn't know where she was, the sister called child welfare."

"Oh, my god! How terrible that must have been for you. Your parents had to come back early?"

"No. My parents were working and apparently didn't want to be bothered. They refused to take the call. I had nowhere to go and the cops wouldn't let me stay at the house alone."

"What, no friends or relatives?"

Polly didn't say a word.

Lauren had her answer.

"Welfare put me in a group home. It wasn't so bad. Kind of like the dorm. When my folks came back, I talked them into putting me in boarding school so they could do as they pleased."

"How'd that work?"

"Fine. I got in trouble a lot. Finally, I just ignored everyone. Once you're marked as a troublemaker, you learn to go with the flow."

Lauren took in everything Polly had said. The girl was right about one thing, Lauren had been very lucky to grow up here with her dad. "Polly," she said as they neared the steps up to the deck. "You're welcome here anytime. My pop said it and he means what he says."

In the low glow of the porch light Lauren thought she saw a smile from Polly.

"Don't tell Tim," Polly whispered as she nodded toward Lauren's dad and Tim cleaning up the grill. "He already feels sorry for me."

Lauren thought of telling her Tim felt more than just sorry for her. She'd seen it in his eyes. Tim cared for Polly, even if he didn't know it yet. At first he might have been just helping Lauren out with her troubled roommate, but it had grown to something else. Something between them that had nothing to do with her.

When Tim finally crashed out in the living room and Polly

was sound asleep in her room, Lauren heard her pop playing his old CDs.

She walked into his study and leaned against the door frame. For the hundredth time, she said, "You need to buy some new music."

"I always feel at home with the music my mom used to play." He switched to the old Carpenters' song she'd thought about Monday when it was raining.

Without a word she moved into his arms and danced to "Rainy Days and Mondays." When she was little, he used to carry her when they danced. When she grew tall enough, she would stand on his boots as they danced. When she was finally in her teens, he taught her how to twirl and dip as if the living room was a ballroom.

As the music circled round them, he said, "I've missed you, kid."

"I know, Pop. I've missed you, too."

"You know any rainy day you ever have, you can always come home no matter how old you get and tell me your problems."

"I know, Pop." She hugged him tighter, wishing she could tell him about how scared she'd been when she saw Polly bleeding, and how hurt she was when Lucas backed away from even trying to love her.

But maybe she didn't have to tell him. Maybe his just being there and offering was enough.

CHAPTER SEVENTEEN

Austin
Wilkes

Wilkes felt as if he and Yancy had been chasing ghosts since early Wednesday morning. As he drove through the streets of Austin, Wilkes tried to put it all in order.

He hadn't been able to sleep the night Angie moved in. About four, he'd given up trying and gone downstairs to work on his computer. He wanted to find out more about the Stanley House that drew Yancy. If the wagon at the museum had been owned by the Stanley family and they had arrived with the first cattlemen, then they were like family. They stood with the Kirklands and the O'Gradys and the Collinses and his ancestors, the Wagners. Now that he'd seen the wagon at the museum, it made sense that the Stanley family might have been called Gypsy.

About six o'clock a link blinked on that Wilkes hadn't noticed before. A family named Stanley joined with another family to form a blacksmith and farrier business in early Texas. They'd even put an ad in the Austin paper in 1872 saying they'd be willing to travel for employment. That same year Kirkland drove his herd onto this part of Texas. Surely he would have brought both a blacksmith and a farrier along, and as fast as the population grew they'd be in demand.

Sweat broke out on Wilkes's palms when he saw the second family's name: *Grey*.

He picked up his cell and dialed Yancy Grey.

"Hell," Yancy said after four rings. "Do you have any idea what time it is, Wagner?"

Wilkes didn't waste time. "Do you have any living family?"

Yancy grumbled a few seconds and answered, "None that I know of. My mother's family all died off, and she never bothered to tell me my father's name. Just said they ran off when they were still kids, never mentioned marriage. Mind telling me why we're uprooting my family tree at six o'clock in the morning?"

"Because—" Wilkes tried not to yell "—the Stanley family who built that old house you keep saying calls to you were once partners with another family, and their last name was Grey."

"You kidding?"

"Would I call you while it's still dark to kid about something like that? Get dressed. I'll pick you up in an hour. I found a few Stanleys living in Austin, and it might be worth a trip to find out if they were related to anyone who lived in the house."

Wilkes had wanted to wake Angie before he left, but after the way he kissed her that night, he figured she'd shoot him through the door if he came knocking. She had to know how much he wanted her. One kiss and he couldn't sleep. If they ever did make love, he'd probably self-combust.

Besides, with luck, he might be back in a day or two. Once he calmed down, maybe the feeling would cool. He'd had it happen a few times before with women he swore he wanted but by dawn he couldn't get away from fast enough.

Only, Angie wouldn't be like that. Once wasn't what he wanted. He wanted more.

As he tossed a bag in his car, he decided to worry about other things for a few days. Get his mind off her.

But his mind didn't want to budge.

A little after seven he and Yancy hit the road. Wilkes called and asked Dan to pick Angie up and take her to work.

"Look out for her, would you, Dan?"

"I'll watch over your girl," Dan promised.

"She's not mine." Wilkes almost wished she was his. It had been a long time since he'd thought of anyone as his even for a night. The one girl he thought would be his forever hadn't been. Lexie hadn't waited for him and Wilkes had been trying to shake the feeling that he wasn't worth waiting for ever since.

When he explained to Dan where they were headed, the sheriff didn't seem too excited. "You two do realize that this is an old trail you're trying to follow?"

"I know," Wilkes agreed, "but for Yancy's sake we have to see where this leads."

The sheriff added, "Tell Yancy that relatives you don't know are usually relatives you don't want to find."

Wilkes ended the call already wishing he was headed back home but knowing he had to give it a try.

Only, when they got to Austin, they ran into one dead end after another. Frustrated, Wilkes booked them both rooms at the Driskill Hotel and, after a good night's sleep, they began again the next day and the next.

He checked in with Dan daily. No sign of the black Mercury. No more phone messages and nothing else left on Angie's van. The sheriff seemed to think that there was a good chance that whoever had been watching her had left town. But Wilkes wasn't so sure. If the stalker wanted something from her, he was taking his time.

When Dan mentioned that someone had messed with Carter Hayes's brakes, Wilkes couldn't stop asking questions. The sheriff didn't know much about the brake problem, but Carter's reasoning made sense. Either it was kids playing around and hoping to push the little travel trailer off the side of the canyon, or someone was simply hoping Carter would leave.

The old man swore he'd heard a car pull up near his camper one night, but he'd thought it was probably just kids parking or a drunk sleeping it off out by the museum.

"Did he leave?" Wilkes asked. "I've got another reason someone might want Carter gone. He's a natural lookout for what's happening at the museum."

"Might be," Dan agreed. "But he's safe now."

"Where?" Wilkes didn't like the idea of the old guy being in danger.

"He took his trailer into the shop and is staying out at your place." Dan laughed. "Seems Uncle Vern is running a bed-and-breakfast now he found out Angie can cook. I've even picked her up early the past few mornings. Best omelets I've ever had."

Wilkes frowned. For Angie's safety, he couldn't tell Dan to back off no matter how much he'd like to. "I'll be home tomorrow. And I'm betting on your second theory. It wasn't kids. The man stalking Angie doesn't want the old man around. I'm guessing he's near, just waiting for his chance to catch her alone."

After Wilkes ended the call, he thought about Angie's bodyguards. One sheriff with way too much to do as it was. One old broken-down cowboy who loved flirting with the volunteers. One retired car salesman who was probably unarmed and believed stick figures were chasing him.

"We're heading home as soon as we can," he told Yancy.

"I agree. This can wait."

Wilkes drove back to their hotel, lost in thought.

The way Angie kissed made a man lose all common sense. Hell, at the rate he was going, Wilkes might be Angie's next stalker. He couldn't get her out of his head. Every moment he wasn't trying to find a Grey in Austin, he was thinking about her. Listing things he didn't like about her and things he liked. After two days without her the "didn't like" list began to get shorter.

He told himself he wasn't looking for a forever woman, and even if he were, it would never be someone like her. Petite women always made him nervous. Her hair seemed to have a mind of its own. She talked too fast when she talked, and when she was shy she almost disappeared. Hell, she even had a cat. Since she wouldn't let Doc Holliday out of the house, the damn beast insisted on following Wilkes around. Keeping her safe came with a price, he decided, and cat hair on his office chair was part of the bargain.

But Angie was taking care of Uncle Vern. Wilkes called to check on him while he waited on Yancy to load his gear into the truck.

The old guy told him not to bother coming back because he was eating food cooked in heaven every meal.

Several hours later, when they stopped for gas, Wilkes checked in with the ranch while Yancy picked up snacks.

After a dozen rings Vern answered and said he'd asked Angie to marry him.

Before Wilkes finished laughing, Vern mentioned the trouble in town.

"What kind of trouble?" Wilkes frowned. Crossroads was too small of a town to have problems. Maybe the one streetlight was out?

Vern took a deep breath, then delivered the bad news. "Lexie Davis is back. Everyone in town has seen her, including Angie."

Wilkes fought not to react.

"You're sure?"

"Yep, Rose Franklin called Miss Bees at the retirement village and she told Miss Abernathy, who told Cap. We used to fight grass fires together, me and Cap, and he knows how bad Lexie hurt you. I guess he felt the need to call and let me know."

"We were over years ago, and by the way, I hate living in a small town. No one ever forgets anything. If I'd been born with a birthmark on my ear, I'd be that boy born with the funny ear for the rest of my life."

Vern's answer was simply, "You ain't got no birthmark on

your ear, boy. What you've got is a beauty queen who grew up to be a bitch."

"She's not mine. The beauty queen or the bitch. She never was."

Wilkes fought down a few cuss words and went back to the real problem. "I haven't seen Lexie since I left for the army." He could still picture her crying at the airport swearing she'd be waiting in the exact spot when he got back. He learned later that she had a date with some guy that night. "I'm not interested in Lexie, and besides, she's married."

It crossed Wilkes's mind that one of the reasons he didn't come home when he got out of the service was knowing that he'd have to walk past the spot where he'd kissed her goodbye, and she wouldn't be there.

Vern cleared his throat. "Something is up with that girl. Rose Franklin thinks she might be getting a divorce. Seems to need money. After two husbands she couldn't boss around, maybe she's decided to come back and give you another try."

"You got any facts about her moving back, or just the Franklins talking?" Wilkes didn't have to fake the little interest he showed.

"Well, one thing, she's not in Dallas. Two, she's trying to sell off her inheritance and her aunt's not even dead yet. Seems to me if she's still with that rich doctor, she wouldn't be here."

"I really don't care." Wilkes was ready to hang up but he had to ask one more question. "She still as beautiful as ever?"

"I don't know. I ain't seen her," Vern answered. "But she'd have to really ugly up to go down past pretty."

Wilkes hung up and dialed the museum. He hadn't realized how over Lexie he was until this very moment. There had been a time when he would have taken her back, but not now.

Angie's hesitant voice answered on the third ring. "Hello, Ransom Canyon Museum."

"Angie." Wilkes grinned just hearing her voice. "Everything all right?"

"Yes. Thanks for letting me stay at your place, Wilkes. Your uncle set up a cowboy patrol around the place just to make me feel safe. He's a funny old man. Thinks he has to hug me good-night every evening before he turns in, like we're kin."

"Thanks for feeding Uncle Vern. And, Angie, you are a very huggable woman." This wasn't what he wanted to say to her. He wasn't even sure why he called. Maybe he just wanted to hear her voice and now he was remembering how great she felt.

Wilkes gripped the phone and mentally pulled his thoughts off Angie. "How are things at the museum?"

"Fine," she answered. "The ladies are planning to do a Country Christmas theme in the foyer. We're going to hang quilts everywhere there is a wall. I'm even putting one of my mother's in the mix."

Wilkes closed his eyes. She was all right. She was working and happy. He could relax. She didn't need him.

"I guess Dan told you what we were doing here in Austin. We're not having much luck. Lots of records of Stanleys but none we can trace back to the house in Crossroads. Appears the house may have been passed down several times from one Stanley to another."

"I thought Yancy said his mother spent a few years in Crossroads when she was a kid. Maybe she was born here. If so, she could have had relatives who lived here. I could do some checking."

"That might help." Wilkes didn't want to hang up, but he was at a loss for what to say. "Angie, unless we find something, we're heading back tomorrow. How about going out to eat with me when I get home?"

She hesitated, then finally asked, "Is this a payback for feeding your uncle or a date?"

"It's a date. Don't mention it to my uncle. He said he's getting fat on your cooking. It won't hurt him to skip a meal. I miss talking to you." He closed his eyes, trying not to be too obvious. "Just me and you," he added.

"Just talking?" She laughed, and he thought about how much he liked the way she laughed.

"Among other things. I like the way you feel in my arms."

"Wilkes, you've already reminded me there is no forever or maybe even tomorrow where you're concerned."

Her replaying his words hurt. "Angie, I..." What could he say? That he'd reconsidered? That he'd changed his mind? He hadn't known her long enough to even be thinking about tomorrow.

Lexie walked through his thoughts. She hadn't waited. Would Angie if he asked her to?

"The date is on, Wilkes, but nothing more." Angie broke up his worrying.

"Fair enough," he said. "I'll call you with details."

The next morning they might be leaving Austin, but his thoughts were already home.

A little before sunset when Angie and Wilkes walked into Dorothy's Café, Wilkes wasn't surprised to see Uncle Vern and Carter sitting at one of the back tables waiting for them.

He leaned close to Angie. "You told him."

"No, I didn't. I simply said I had a date."

Wilkes grinned. She'd given Vern the only clue he needed to figure it out. What Wilkes had hoped would be a few hours alone with Angie vanished.

To depress him even more, Angie hugged them both and then sat down between the old guys. She pulled a tattered book from her purse and began showing them early sketches of the canyons.

Wilkes took the last chair across from her and listened as she told them about a man in the 1920s who had written about caves along one of the shallow canyon walls.

After they ordered, Angie pulled a red stone from her pocket and laid it on top of the worn book. "What I can't figure out is why I found both this book and this rock in the safe. Neither seems particularly valuable." The rock looked as if it could have easily been picked up in the canyon, and the old book might go for a hundred dollars in a rare book auction if it were in better shape, but it was as worn as her father's ledger book. "It took me an hour to figure out how to turn the combination to that huge walk-in safe in my office and this is all I found."

Wilkes watched both his uncle and Carter lean back in their chairs as if Angie had set poison on the table and not simply a dirty old rock.

"What is it?" she asked.

Uncle Vern took a deep breath. "I don't know about the book, but the rock is not something you want to keep. I had a cowboy show me a stone like that once. He was part Cree or Comanche, I forget which. Said the rock is called a bloodstone."

Carter nodded. "I've seen pictures of rocks like that. Vern's right. It's nothing but bad luck."

Wilkes had enough and picked up the rock. "How can a rock the size of an egg hurt anyone?"

"It doesn't hurt. It steals." Vern crossed his arms over his chest. "Bloodstones steal your memories."

Wilkes thought of Lexie. "There are a few memories I wouldn't mind forgetting."

Carter shook his head. "No. It's the good and bad memories that make you what you are. You got to take them all or it's not you. When the stone does its dark magic, it takes them all a little at a time."

Vern took the rock from Wilkes's hand and set it back on the book. "The cowboy with Native American blood running through him told me he found a stone like this in the pocket of a man who was lost. Said the man was half dead and couldn't remember his name or when he last ate."

"But why would anyone put an old book with pages stuck together and a rock in the safe?" Angie obviously didn't buy into the superstition.

That night as the wind seemed to howl outside the café, they talked of legends. Wilkes had heard all the stories; out here they were bedtime tales, but Angie was drawn in to every one, so he just sat back and watched her. Those big eyes. That sweet mouth. That quick mind trying to make sense of stories that were nothing but campfire entertainment.

When Wilkes stood to pay, the wind blew in a woman dressed in a long red cape as if she was going to an opera in a big town.

"I got your order ready, Lexie," Dorothy yelled through the open window to the kitchen. "What kind of salad dressing you want? We got Thousand Island or French."

Wilkes turned and came face-to-face with the one woman he felt he'd spent half of his life trying to forget.

"Wilkes!" Her voice held surprise, but her eyes did not.

She flew into his arms before he could draw in a breath. Her mouth covered his and the kiss had nothing to do with hello. Her lean body slid against his as her arms wrapped around his neck. If he didn't know better, he'd swear she was staking a claim on him and he had no say.

He finally got control and broke the kiss. All he'd done was lower his chin, and they were nose to nose thanks to her heels. She whispered something about how much she'd missed him and how she never stopped thinking about him.

As if they were the only two in the place, she pressed her mouth against his ear and added, "You haunt my dreams, cowboy. It is so good to see you."

Wilkes, on the other hand, felt as if the eye of a tornado had just passed over him, leaving everyone else in the place untouched. The smell of her, the taste, the feel were all the things he'd thought he'd die missing, but he felt nothing in the hole where his heart had once been. Nothing.

This Lexie Davis was no more than a stranger.

He gently pushed her away. "I heard you were in town." A few other questions came to mind, but he didn't want to get into the past.

"I came hoping to see you. I thought we might..."

"I'm busy." Whatever she was selling, he wasn't buying.

"Oh, but..."

Wilkes cut her off again as he glanced back at the table he'd just left. "Angie, I'll take you back to the museum if you're ready. We might as well take your van back to the ranch."

Vern grabbed Angie's elbow and pulled her up. "Sounds like a plan. Time we all left." The old man was suddenly in a hurry to leave. "I've been wanting to look at the engine of your old van. It don't sound right, and we don't want our Angie having car trouble, do we, Wilkes?"

"No, we don't." Wilkes, and everyone in the café, could easily read through the lines of Uncle Vern's chatter, but Wilkes had to give the old guy credit for trying. Even though he wanted Wilkes married off, apparently just anybody wouldn't do.

Lexie reached for him, but he stepped away. Out of the corner of his eye he saw her straighten. She was not a woman anyone backed away from. Whatever she wanted, he wasn't interested. If he could grab the bloodstone right now, he'd hit his skull hard, hoping the rock or the crack in his head might allow him to forget every memory he had of Lexie Davis.

For the first time, he saw what she really was, who she was, all wrapped up in pretty ribbons. The gift she was offering only looked good before it was unwrapped.

He nodded once to Angie. She quickly gathered up her things and for once didn't argue as he opened the door. They were at his Tahoe before he glanced back. Lexie was standing at the counter staring out at him and this time he didn't see her beauty.

In the darkness, as they headed toward the museum, Angie asked, "Are you all right?"

"I don't want to talk about it." He fought to keep the anger from his voice. He could think of a hundred things he should have said to Lexie but all he thought about was getting away from her.

Glancing over, he saw Angie sitting all proper, her hands folded in her lap. He'd frightened her. He half expected her to say she was staying at her own place tonight. All he'd thought about was getting back to Angie and now, apparently, he couldn't seem to talk to her.

"All right," she agreed. "We don't have to talk at all."

When they got to the museum, she climbed out. "Thank you for the dinner." She was so formal ice seemed to rattle out with her words. "I need to put the book and the stone back in my office before I follow you to the ranch. If you'll make the coffee, I'll be there by the time it's ready and we can all have dessert. I promised Vern chocolate cake tonight."

"All?" He tried to sound relaxed. "Does that mean me, too?"

She grinned. "I showed Vern the cake earlier, and he said he'd invite Carter over." She walked up the steps of the museum.

He cut his engine and stepped out, planning to follow her in. "I'll go with you."

"That's not necessary. Nigel Walls is still in there cleaning. I'll be safe." Her words were formal again as if he were no more than a stranger.

Wilkes felt like a jackass. "I'm sorry, Angie. I guess I wasn't prepared to see an old girlfriend tonight." He took the steps two at a time and caught up to her. "I hate that she kissed me like I still mattered to her. Like I ever mattered to her."

"I understand. You're still in love with her. Look, Wilkes, we're just friends. It's okay."

"No. It's not okay, Angie. You don't understand. I'm not still in love with her. I haven't been for a long time." He touched her shoulder and smiled when Angie didn't bolt. "I wish I could wash the taste of her kiss away."

She didn't move. Those big eyes just stared up at him as if trying to see into his soul.

"I wish…" He touched her strawberry hair so soft and curly it was almost fuzzy. "I wish you'd been the one to kiss me tonight."

He leaned in and almost touched her mouth. "I want to remember the taste of honey tonight."

She shook her head. "Don't use me to forget. I don't want to be anyone's second choice."

He kissed her forehead knowing she was right. He didn't want to kiss her with Lexie still in his thoughts. "I'm not using you. But I've no way of proving that to you." Now wasn't the time to tell her that she'd been all he thought about for days. "How about dinner tomorrow night, just us? We can drive over to Lubbock, where no one will know us."

She smiled. "You going to bring Uncle Vern and Carter along?"

"Nope."

"But what will we talk about?"

He grinned. "We'll think of something."

"Then I'll go."

He fought to keep from touching her. "Want me to wait out here while you go in?"

"No. The sheriff says the stalker hasn't been seen for a week. He's long gone. I can't spend the rest of my life having everyone worry about me. I'm sure I'm fine. After dessert at your place, I think I'll move back to my cabin." When Wilkes didn't move, she added, "The janitor will see me to my car as soon as I run up to the office, and if I see anyone following me, I'll call."

"All right." Wilkes knew she was safe and there was no time to talk about why she wanted to go back home tonight. "I'll drive slow. If you hurry, you might even pass me before I turn off for the headquarters."

As she walked away, Wilkes had the feeling he'd screwed up what had started between them. Surprisingly, his loss of something he'd never had, hurt.

CHAPTER EIGHTEEN

Angie

As Wilkes drove away, Angie climbed the stairs thinking again how this town was different than anywhere she'd ever lived. Everyone's lives seemed connected here. Maybe she'd talk to Wilkes about it over dinner tomorrow night. It would be fun to just talk without any problems or emergencies in the way.

Smiling, she thought about how dearly she'd enjoyed studying him from across the table. He was one good-looking man, but something haunted his eyes and now and then she swore she could see his scars. When he'd kissed Lexie, Angie couldn't help thinking that they fit together perfectly. Strong, wild, rich men like Wilkes didn't pick workhorses like her. They picked the racehorses like Lexie.

She could hear Nigel Walls polishing the floors down one of the long hallways and guessed he hadn't heard her yell hello, but if he started to lock up, he'd see her light on upstairs and check.

When she reached her office, the tiny desk light left burning lit her way. She'd left the old walk-in safe open, since she'd taken the only two things inside. Carefully she set the bloodstone and the old book on the shelf where she'd found them and turned to leave.

The outline of a man sitting in the chair at her desk made her jump.

Her first thought was to run, but the intruder was between her and the door. If they scuffled, Nigel might hear. If he'd turned off the machine. If he didn't have his headphones on.

Angie fought to keep calm as the man slowly stood. His face was in shadow, but she could make out the broad shoulders and the dark tie against his white shirt. Not exactly the attire of a murderer, or a thief. Only, what would he steal. The old book? The bloodstone? One of the wagons or sewing machines or plows?

Of course, if he were a murderer, his choices were somewhat limited. Nigel or her. Since he hadn't already killed Nigel while she was at dinner, Angie's best guess was her.

"What do you want?" She tried to guess his height and weight just in case she lived and had to identify him later.

"I'm not going to hurt you, Miss Harold," he said in a calm voice. "I'm just here to talk." From the sound of his voice he was probably in his forties or fifties, and the slight accent placed him from the Northeast, not the South or Texas.

"That's probably what all killers say." She backed up a step.

He laughed. "You run into a lot of criminals, do you, Miss Harold?"

She reached back into the safe and lifted the bloodstone. It fit in the palm of her hand. Not much of a weapon, but it was all she had. If he grabbed her, she'd hit him as hard as she could between the eyes.

"You mind if we turn on a light?" he asked and leaned over the desk clicking on the desk light.

The warm glow lit up his face. Short hair. Clean shaven. She didn't recognize him. No gun, at least none showing. About forty. Angie didn't relax. He didn't need a gun to kill her. He could choke her, or snap her neck, or... Stop! She wanted to scream, fearing she might start rattling off options for her own murder.

"If you would stop trying to figure out how I'm going to kill you, I thought you might sit down and listen."

"You read my mind?"

"It wasn't all that hard." He smiled and surprisingly looked like a normal person. He pointed at the chair across the desk. "Take a seat, Miss Harold."

She sat down with a plop and looked up at him as he reached inside his coat. Angie hid her face. *A gun.* He was going to shoot her. She couldn't stand the thought of dripping blood all over her own office.

"Look at me, Miss Harold. I'd like to show you my badge before you talk yourself into dying of fright."

She picked up the badge. Agent Dodson, FBI. Maybe it was real, she thought. Maybe not. If he was a fed, why didn't he just call and ask her for a meeting? Why hide out in her office?

"I'm here to ask you a few questions, not kill you." He sounded weary, as if he doubted he was getting through to her. "You might be in danger, Miss Harold."

Great! The killer was telling her what she already knew.

He stared at her. "You don't believe me."

She shook her head and then decided arguing with a murderer was probably a bad idea. "I believe you, Agent Dodson. I just wonder why you were sitting in the dark waiting to warn me about something I already know."

The guy in the suit smiled. "No, you don't believe me. Let me fill you in on a few facts you don't know. We've been investigating your father and his brother's business for months. We even have an agent working there keeping an eye on things. Three months ago your father came to us for help. He'd connected the money trail to drugs, but he had no hard proof."

"My dad was a spy?" Now the fake agent had gone from being frightening to crazy. Her father had never done anything brave in his life. He wouldn't even ride a roller coaster. He'd wanted to quit his job almost since he moved the family to Florida, but he was afraid to face his quick-tempered brother. The security of a job he hated was better than no job at all, and if he made his brother mad, he'd have no family at all, either.

The agent leaned forward. "Your father gave us all the information he knew, but he couldn't tell us how the drugs were coming in or where they were being stored. Evidently your uncle Anthony didn't want him in on the real business, but your father was smart enough to see that the items sold in the shop didn't match with the money being deposited."

"How does any of this affect me? Did my uncle kill my father?" The idea had been in the back of her mind since the beginning, but it didn't seem possible. "Tell me the truth, whoever you are, or go away and stop frightening me."

Even a mouse can get fed up with being scared.

"No," the man answered too quickly to be telling a lie. "It appears your father's death may have been just what it seemed, a mugging gone wrong. Whoever did it must have disappeared when he heard he'd be charged with murder and not robbery if he was caught."

Agent Dodson stood and walked to the window. He didn't look so threatening now. "The link between the drugs and your father's death is that he feared his brother might have found out he'd talked to us. He went up to his office in a dangerous part of town that night, worked later than usual because he wanted to find all the evidence he could. Time was running out for him. He thought his brother was watching his every move."

"I'll ask again. Why are you here? I don't know anything about the business. I was away at college, then home taking care of my mother. I didn't work for my uncle and my father didn't talk about his work except to complain about it or that he never seemed to get finished with the books."

"We wouldn't have bothered to find you, but our informant says your uncle has sent a man after you. He said the word is you took something very valuable, and your uncle wants it back."

The agent smiled. "I'm hanging out in the dark, miss, because we're not ready to tip our hand. We want to catch this guy, not frighten him off. So think about it. What do you have that someone would track you down to get?"

The ledger book. Of course. It might contain proof of her uncle's crimes. But if she told this suit and he wasn't one of the good guys, she was back to trying to guess how he'd kill her.

"What kind of car do you drive?"

"I rented a Ford when I landed in Amarillo yesterday. I parked it by the loading dock out back of the museum."

"Have you tried to contact me before?"

"No." Dodson pointed his finger. "But you are a hard lady to catch alone. Seems like people have been around you all day. I always thought a curator would be a solitary job. But not for you, Miss Harold. Perhaps I should warn you that the fewer people who know about this investigation, the better. The FBI needs to remain invisible until we know what is going on."

She moved toward her phone. "You wouldn't mind if I call the sheriff, would you? I want to make sure you check out before I talk to you any more. I'd feel better if the sheriff *is* with us. He's someone I do trust."

Agent Dodson smiled at her. "Go ahead. He can check me out, then maybe, Miss Harold, we can work together. All I ask is you don't say anything to anyone else. In fact, your cabin might be a good place to meet him. If whoever is looking for you sees me, we may force him into doing something rash."

Her hands shook. "How did you know about my cabin?"

"I'm from the FBI. It took about ten minutes. Only two places were rented in the area in October. Electric transferred over to an Angela Jones. Address was on the bill. Let me give you a hint—when you're on the run, change more than your last name."

Angie used her office phone to call Dan. The FBI guy turned to stare out at the canyon as if he were offering her some privacy.

"Hello, Sheriff Brigman." She tried to sound calm as she pulled her cell from her pocket.

"What's wrong?" Dan said, obviously reading the panic in her voice.

"Is there any way you could meet me? Right now? I need your help with something. You don't have to change. Keep your uniform on."

Angie prayed he'd figure out that meant "bring a gun."

"I'd love to get out of here. Lauren and her roommate are here and I seem to have adopted Tim O'Grady for the weekend." He lowered is voice. "Are you all right?"

"I think so," she answered a bit too slow. "I just need your help."

"I'll be outside my house waiting," Dan said.

"No. Meet us at my cabin."

Dan hung up and she knew he was already heading that way. He'd be waiting when she reached her cabin.

Angie kept talking into the dead phone about Dan's daughter and her friends being home from college as she texted Wilkes on her cell. I'm fine. Don't worry. See you soon.

She lowered her cell under the desk and pressed Send as she said into the office phone, "We'll be there in a few minutes. Goodbye, Sheriff."

CHAPTER NINETEEN

Wilkes

Doc Holliday was curled up on the leather jacket he'd left on one of the kitchen chairs when Wilkes got home. The fat old cat didn't seem the least bit interested in moving. After yelling at Doc and issuing a few threats that went unheard, Wilkes picked up the cat and walked him out to the barn. It was time Doc Holliday met a few of the outlaws living in the hayloft.

"I hate cats," he muttered as Doc took off like a prisoner just released. "But you, Doc, are starting to grow on me."

The only good thing about Angie going home tonight was that she would take the not-so-invisible cat with her. The first night, Doc had jumped on Wilkes's bed, waking him. When Wilkes tried to ignore the cat, Doc decided to share the pillow. Wilkes couldn't tell if the cat was snoring or purring.

When Wilkes walked back into the kitchen, Uncle Vern and Carter Mayes were waiting for the chocolate cake that Angie had made. She'd left it on the bar, covered with a glass dome. Which, around the Wagner home, meant hands off until after supper.

"That girl can cook," Vern said, staring at the cake. "She ain't made a bad meal yet." He glanced at Wilkes. "And believe me, I've had enough to know what bad is."

Carter brushed down his whiskers and lifted his fork when Wilkes reached for the plates. "My daughters can cook, but with all the granddaughters running around it's like trying to eat in a tornado. Food's usually flying. Two of them live under the table like wild squirrels foraging for food. The little one is always crying and the oldest one has a Cinderella complex. When daughters have daughters, it's like the drama is multiplied."

Wilkes cut them each a piece of cake. When he walked back over to his coat, he realized that while he'd been gone today, Doc Holliday had walked on all the furniture and clawed anything he could reach. He decided cats were smarter than humans. They always knew when someone didn't like them. Doc was probably just trying to make it plain that he didn't like sleeping over at the ranch.

When Wilkes's cell fell out of his pocket, he noticed he had a message from Angie. She should have been pulled up in front of his place long before now, not sending him messages. He'd been so busy with the cat he wasn't even sure how long ago she'd texted him. Ten minutes? Fifteen?

I'm fine was all he had to read to know Angie was in trouble.

As Wilkes grabbed his hat, Uncle Vern yelled from the kitchen. "Where's the coffee?"

"Fend for yourselves, boys," Wilkes answered. "If Angie shows up here, call me. I think she might need me."

Both men laughed. Vern mumbled, "I think it's more like you need her, son, but you'll figure that out soon enough."

He hit ninety on the way to the museum. When he got there, she was gone. The place was closed up for the night. Nigel was loading up equipment at the side door.

Wilkes yelled, "Did you see Angie leave?"

"I did." He took the time to scratch his beard before adding, "She headed out about ten minutes ago with a guy in a suit. He parked in the loading dock like he thought he owned the place.

You might have some competition, Wilkes. Wouldn't hurt to buy a new hat."

Wilkes fought the urge to strangle the janitor. "Did she say anything to you?"

"Yep. She said 'good night.'" Nigel kept scratching. "No, that's not right. She just said 'night,' or it might have been just 'bye.' No, come to think of it, she said 'night bye.' No, that don't make any sense."

Wilkes jumped back in his car. He'd kill Nigel later. Right now he had to find Angie. Ever since he'd met her, he had the feeling she was a guppy in a shark tank.

If her van was gone and she hadn't come to his ranch, Wilkes could think of only two places she'd go. The sheriff's lake house or back to her cabin. He checked in with Uncle Vern as he drove through town. The dessert was half gone, and they hadn't seen Angie.

Only a few low lights shone at the sheriff's place. Wilkes parked farther down the road thinking he could walk into the back of both the sheriff's place and Angie's cabin. That way, he'd see trouble before anyone saw him.

When he climbed out of the Tahoe, he pulled his .45 from the glove compartment and shoved it deep into his coat pocket. It was the first time he'd felt the weapon in his hand since the army. The army, where he'd learned to work hard and not feel. After Lexie's letter there was no joy and tired muscles seemed to dull the pain.

When he'd first heard about Angie's trouble, he'd thought it was all in her mind or simply some jilted boyfriend, but tonight he swore he could smell trouble in the air. His muscles tightened preparing for anything that might come.

His hand closed around the doorknob, and he burst through the back door of Dan Brigman's house without knocking and came face-to-face with teenage lust.

The O'Grady boy, who should be away at college, was wrapped around a female body with most of her clothes missing.

For a second, in the shadows, he saw the red hair and thought it was Angie. Only, nothing else fit. The color was off, and brown hair was mixed in with the red. The body wasn't rounded in all the right places as Angie's was and the girl didn't look as if she needed the bra that now lay across the coffee table.

Wilkes tried to remain calm. The young couple simply froze.

"Is the sheriff here?" he asked as if he hadn't seen a thing.

Tim O'Grady, to his credit, moved in front of the girl. "He left ten or fifteen minutes ago, maybe more, Mr. Wagner. I wasn't watching the clock." Tim grinned. "We figured we'd hear a car when he came back. Didn't know you'd be breaking into the place, but I'll be sure to let the sheriff know you did."

Wilkes didn't know which he hated more, that he hadn't found Angie or that he was now Mr. Wagner, marking him as one of the older generation. "Sorry to bother you, kids," he started. "I was just looking for a woman."

Tim smiled. "Might try a bar or church. That would probably be your best bet, Mr. Wagner."

"I'll consider that. I'll leave you two before your girlfriend freezes."

He was gone before either of them could say goodbye. As he ran down the deck steps, he glanced back and saw the two shadows blending together again.

When Wilkes made it to Angie's cabin the lights were on, but no one was there. Carefully he circled the place. Two cars had pulled up, leaving fresh tracks, and two cars had pulled away. Three sets of footprints. One was Angie's small feet, he guessed, and the others were two men. If the sheriff hadn't returned to his house, there was a good chance he was with Angie. If so, she was safe. Only, who belonged to the third set of prints?

Wilkes walked back to his Tahoe and climbed in. Maybe he should go back to his ranch and wait. After all, she'd texted him that she was fine. He always seemed to be overreacting with Angie. Maybe it was because she seemed so helpless. Maybe he

just hadn't cared about anyone in so long that he was overdo-
ing it.

"Mr. Wagner?" a girl's voice whispered out of the darkness.

Wilkes turned and saw Lauren Brigman a few feet away.
"Evening, Lauren," he tried to say calmly as if teenagers often
walked out of the night and scared the life out of him.

"I thought that was you," she said as she came near his window. "My dad rushed by here a few minutes ago. He climbed
out of a van and hurried to his cruiser. When he saw me, he
said he had to run to the office for a few minutes."

Wilkes started his car. "He have a woman with him?"

"Yes, that new woman who works at the museum. She was
driving the van and it looked like someone was following behind her. Are you with them?"

Wilkes nodded trying to make sense of what was going on.
"Did the woman look frightened?"

Lauren shook her head. "No. She smiled at me. We met once
before out here. If you're heading to my dad's office, mind giving me a lift? I'll ride back with Pop." Her voice cracked as if
she was about to cry. "I haven't been alone with him much this
weekend."

Wilkes didn't have to ask why. "Sure, hop in. If he's not in
the office, I'll bring you back." If he didn't find Angie at Dan's
office, he'd circle by Angie's place again. She'd said she would
be packing and moving back to her cabin tonight. Maybe she'd
just asked Dan to check out the place for her and left the lights
on so she wouldn't have to come back in the dark. She'd mentioned once that it looked as if someone had tried to get in her
back door. Angie had laughed and said they either couldn't get
in or had broken in and found nothing to steal.

Wilkes tried her cell again. No answer. He called the ranch.
The only change there was Vern's account of how the cake had
disappeared.

The third set of footprints by the car tracks at her cabin bothered Wilkes. Dan and Angie were not alone. Nigel had men-

tioned a man in a suit was with Angie when she left. She must not have trusted him if she'd stopped by to pick up the sheriff. She must still not trust him if the sheriff was following her.

He tried the sheriff's cell. It went to voice mail and by the time he left a message he'd be at the county offices.

Angie's cell went right to voice mail. She must have turned it off.

Wilkes needed to think, but that wasn't easy to do with a college freshman riding along with him. He managed to be sociable enough to ask her how she liked school, and she never stopped talking.

He didn't really listen, but when he saw Angie's van parked in front of the county offices, Wilkes relaxed. He even managed to wish Lauren a great year as he climbed out and headed for the sheriff's office.

Lauren waved goodbye to Wilkes as a carload of screaming teenagers pulled up. They ran to hug her as if she'd been gone a year.

When he stepped inside the county headquarters, Angie, Dan and some stranger in a suit were all leaning over a book on the sheriff's desk.

All Wilkes saw was Angie's smile. He didn't care about the rest. One smile was enough.

The sheriff introduced him to Agent Dodson from the FBI and explained that Angie was being asked to help in an ongoing investigation back in Florida.

Wilkes noticed none of them went into any more detail, which didn't bother him.

Angie grinned and said now that she understood what was happening, and she'd turned over something the agent said would be helpful, she had no worries. There was no reason for anyone to be looking for her.

The agent agreed. "Thank you, Miss Harold. I'll make sure your father's ledger gets into the right hands." He lifted the book as if it were a treasure.

Dan didn't seem convinced. "Someone was following her. How do we know they'll go away now that the ledger is in the *right hands*? That might not even be the reason he was here."

"Of course it is, Sheriff," Agent Dodson explained as if he was speaking to a child and not a fellow officer. "I'll make sure we announce that we've found the crucial evidence tomorrow. Once they know, whoever is following her will see no reason for hanging around. They might have planned to break into her office or cabin, but apparently that wasn't as easy as they thought it might be." He looked at the two men who stood beside her. "Miss Harold, it appears you have your own body-guards, but trust me, I've worked many cases like this. Once whoever is bothering you realizes he has no chance of getting what he wants, he'll disappear."

She kissed both the sheriff and Wilkes on the cheek. "Thank you both."

When they walked out, Agent Dodson told them he was driving back to Amarillo so he could catch the first flight out. Dan took his daughter's hand and asked her if she was up for a banana split. Wilkes and Angie were left standing outside the offices.

Angie stared at him, then climbed into her van. She lowered her voice, though no one could have overheard. "I think I'll just go back home tonight. If you'll keep Doc, I'll pick him up tomorrow. Thanks for everything, Wilkes."

Wilkes knew the routine. She was making it easy on him. Giving him a way out. Letting him know there were no ties. Damn. Didn't she know he didn't want an easy way out?

He was so mad at her he couldn't say a word. He just closed her door, climbed into his own car and followed her to the lake.

When she got out of her van, she wiped her eyes on her baggy sleeve as she walked up her steps. "You didn't need to follow me. I'm fine."

Wilkes was getting tired of those two words. Maybe she was fine, but she didn't look fine and he sure as hell didn't feel fine.

He stormed up the steps and caught her arm. "I got something to say first."

She turned. "I know, whatever we had is over, right? I can guess what's coming. You don't have to spell it out. I got it the moment you kissed Lexie. It just took me a while to let it sink in. I'm sorry I was so much trouble, but thank…"

"Angie, shut up." He pulled her against him and kissed her hard.

She didn't try to pull away, but after a moment he realized she wasn't kissing him back, she was simply waiting for him to stop.

When he straightened, she whispered, "Wilkes, I don't want to be the substitute. I saw the way Lexie kissed you. I could never compete with that."

Lexie hadn't been on his mind since he walked out of the café. Her kiss had been nothing but cold. Only done for show. She wanted him back because she thought she could have him, but he'd been on the leash before.

"This isn't about anyone but me and you, Angie, but you're right, you can't compete with Lexie. You could never get that low." He moved his hand up and lightly brushed the curls away from her neck. "When I kissed you the other night, it scared me half to death. Not because I could feel again, but because I could feel so much more than I've ever felt. It was like someone opened a window, and I took my first breath of fresh air."

His fingers played along the tense muscles at the back of her neck. "All I've thought about the past few days is what my life would have been like if I hadn't found you. What if I'd married Lexie and never known the feeling I had with you after one kiss."

She shook her head. "You're moving too fast."

He knew he was. In truth he had no idea if the one kiss was simply a bolt of lightning that would never hit again or an every time kind of thing that would leave him half drunk on her for the rest of his days. Either way, she was right; they couldn't rush this between them. Not this. It was too special.

Wilkes knew he'd been rushing into things all his life. One date with Lexie and they were a couple. One night after graduation he joined the army. He hadn't even asked Lexie if that was what she'd wanted. And finally, when he couldn't find happiness, he'd rushed into running the Devil's Fork, and into feeling nothing. Hell, he even took pride in holding everyone away.

Slowly, he lowered his hand from her throat and took a step back. "Your kiss meant something to me, Angie, but you're right, I am rushing you. How about this—we continue to see each other as much and as often as it feels comfortable, but I swear I won't touch you. I'll give you time. We'll get to know each other. We'll talk. Hell, we might even fight, but no matter what we give these feelings a chance to grow."

"All right," she answered with measured doubt in her voice. "I think I'd like that."

"There is a 'but' to this agreement," he added.

She waited, her hand shaking slightly in his. The fear in her eyes told him she was afraid to hope.

"When, or maybe if, you do come to me, you come full out. No holding back. No playing games. No maybes. I've had a lifetime of games and promises that weren't meant to be kept. I'm always jumping into things. This time, I'll take my time. But you, Angie, once you know for sure, you have to run headlong into the wind."

"Anything else?"

"Yes." He looked down into those big eyes and hoped he could hold to this agreement he was making. "Don't kiss me on the cheek, Angie. I hate that. It's an almost affection."

"So no kissing at all."

"None that I initiate, but if you want, you can kiss me anywhere, anytime." He winked. "I wouldn't mind that at all. I'm a hard man to resist. I will not start it or end it. You have to do both, but while you're kissing me I promise I'll be kissing you back." He had to give her the reins in this or she'd bolt.

"This is the strangest bargain I've ever heard of. You're not going to touch me, but I can kiss you or do whatever I want to you." She hid her smile with her fingers. "That might give me a wild idea or two."

"Do you agree, Angie?" If she said yes, he'd just signed up to be tortured.

She tilted her head first one way and then the other. Curly hair bounced. "All right. I think I like this plan. And when we are alone I might just take you up on your terms. I think it might be nice to be in control for once in my life."

She turned to go inside, then paused and faced him. "I'll be by to pick up Doc Holliday tomorrow."

"All right." He watched her, feeling as if this one bargain might keep him from rushing for once in his life.

She followed him to the edge of the porch. "Take one step down," she ordered.

He backed up.

"Another one," she added.

He moved down one more step. Now her face was even with his.

"Did you mean it? I set the pace? You'll not advance, but only welcome my kiss."

"I meant every word."

Without another moment's hesitation, she leaned slightly and pressed her mouth to his. The kiss was quick, but it was a real kiss.

When she took a step back, she smiled, obviously proud of herself for being so brave.

"Good night, Angie," he said with a grin.

"Good night, Wilkes."

CHAPTER TWENTY

Lauren

Smiling and stuffed with ice cream, Lauren kissed her pop good-night. It was late, but they'd had so much fun pigging out on banana splits that they'd stayed in the booth at Dairy Queen and talked for over an hour.

She told him about her date with Reid Collins, leaving out the part about Polly's meeting with Reid in the hallway at the frat house. She'd told him all about what it had looked like when she got back to the dorm and found Polly bleeding. Only, she left out any hint that it might not have been an accident. She talked about Tim and Lucas and all the other kids from Crossroads who were also at Tech, leaving out how Lucas had kissed her wildly and then broken up with her, even though he probably never thought they were a couple anyway.

Strange, Lauren realized as she walked out onto the midnight deck and stared at the moon dancing in the water. She had a feeling that for the rest of her life she'd be leaving out parts of every story she told her pop. There was a time she'd rattled on

about everything that happened at school. Now he was getting
the PG version of her almost R-rated life.

Everything in her life seemed to be changing, like sand shift-
ing beneath her feet. For the first weekend in years, she didn't
know if Lucas was in Crossroads or still at Tech. He hadn't
called.

She saw the light go off in her father's bedroom and knew she
was the only one still awake. The decision to come home had
been a good one, not just for Polly, who seemed to be coming
back from the dark side, but for her, too.

She walked along the shore and spotted Tim sitting on a rock
that jutted out almost into the lake. When they'd been little,
they would climb up on that rock and make up stories. Since
both were only children, Tim was probably as close to a brother
as she'd ever have.

"Evening," she said as she climbed up on what they called
storyteller's rock. "It's too cold to be moon-bathing tonight."

"No kidding. I'm afraid to try to stand up. My butt's frozen
to the rock."

Lauren laughed.

"It's not funny, L," he complained. "In the morning some
fisherman will come along here and notice my butt left out here
frozen. He'll say, 'Wonder who lost their bottom out here over-
night? Must have been a left-behind.'"

Fighting down a giggle she said, "That's about the saddest
joke I've ever heard."

They sat in silence for a while, not really needing to talk.
Finally, she asked, "How did you get on with Polly tonight?
Sorry I disappeared on you guys. I ended up spending some
time with my pop."

"We made out," Tim answered, giving only the facts.

"What? Tim!" Lauren found that hard to believe. Oh, not
about Polly, she had sex in hallways and elevators, but about
Tim. He'd had very few dates and usually woke her up when
he got home just to tell Lauren how bad it was.

"Don't worry, we didn't go all the way, but it might have happened if I hadn't stopped."

"Let me guess, Polly has no stop button?"

Tim nodded. "Right. She was built to go full throttle. I don't even think she comes with brakes. Before I could even think about what to do next to her, she was already doing it to me."

"And did you like it?" Lauren asked.

"Of course. It was wild. Remember the last girl I went out with? I politely asked if I could kiss her and she said, 'Do I look that desperate?' Nothing gets a guy over that kind of hit like a girl climbing all over him. Polly even ripped two buttons off my shirt."

"Are you interested in her?"

"I was. I am," he admitted. "But I don't want it to be that way between us, at least not all the time. If there is ever going to be an 'us,' I want more out of it than just make-out sessions. I get the feeling, that for Polly, relationships are measured in hours, maybe minutes sometimes. I don't want that with any girl."

"What *do* you want, Tim?"

He was quiet so long, she didn't think he was going to answer. Finally, he said, "I want someone to hang out with, to talk to, to fall asleep with during a late movie and to have sex with. I want to know that sometimes it's making love and not just sex. I want the whole package deal. I want to grow into loving someone so much that I can't imagine spending my life without them. When I'm old, I don't want to just remember the wild times I had in college, I want to talk about them with the person sitting next to me."

"You're one in a million, Tim. How could any girl not love you?"

He laughed. "I can think of one. Polly took 'slow down' for goodbye. When we head back tomorrow, she'll probably be riding with you. I don't think she wants to ever see me again."

He leaned back and put his head on her outstretched legs. "I did enjoy it tonight for a while. Polly's breasts are small, but..."

Lauren covered his mouth with both her hands. "TMI, Tim!"

"Sorry, L. I thought we could talk about anything with each other."

"Not my roommate's breasts, okay?"

"Okay, but you don't have any problem with me thinking about them, do you?"

Lauren kicked him off her legs and stood. "I think you and your frozen butt had better head home."

He stood and offered a hand to help her off the rock. "All right. See you in the morning. My mom's sending over cinnamon rolls for breakfast. The plan is to help Polly study until it's time to head back to school."

Lauren walked home thinking how Lucas had put his hand over her breast last weekend and wondered if he'd told anyone about it. She doubted it.

If she ever saw Lucas Reyes again, maybe she'd ask him.

CHAPTER TWENTY-ONE

Carter

Dawn broke through a web of gray clouds, and Carter Mayes knew he wouldn't be walking the canyon today. He was too old to get wet this time of year when the wind blew cold from the north and any moisture rested against his bones. Reason told him it was about time to head back to Granbury and his daughters. Before he could get settled in there, it would be Thanksgiving.

The holidays were always painful in a good way. He missed his wife's pumpkin pie and the way Bethie always got excited about putting up the old Christmas tree as soon as the Thanksgiving dishes were put away. He missed how she talked about what to get her daughters and how she always watched everyone else open gifts and forgot her own. Each year was just as painful as the first one he'd had to go through without her, but it was a good pain. He wouldn't have missed the memories even if he had to live another ten years with the loss.

Mostly he liked the winter months when he had time to read and play cards with friends at the trailer park, but he usually spent the afternoons napping and waiting for spring. His hunt for the white stick figures on the wall of a cave far northwest of Granbury had long ago become his only mission. The hollow-eyed bony skeletons no longer frightened him as they had when he was a boy. And the nightmares he endured in 'Nam, where the stick figures managed to come with him, were long gone. Now his goal was simply to find a memory, a slice from his childhood.

Funny, how one little thing follows you all your life, he thought as he stared out the café window at the rain falling. Now and then a drop shattered on the sidewalk as if it were made of crystal. The first hint of snow moved in with the rain, but he wasn't ready to leave just yet.

He hadn't told anyone about what he'd seen as a kid until his wife died. Got too busy living life to worry about the stick men painted hundreds of years ago.

When he'd told his daughters, they'd been all for him spending a summer searching, but as the years passed, they'd tried to delay his trip each spring and always called wanting him home sooner.

Carter didn't know how to tell them that he felt more alive searching one day than he felt all winter waiting.

"Howdy, partner," Vern Wagner called over when he came in the front door of the café. He took off his hat and shook like a dog coming out of the rain. His skinny, tough body reminded Carter of a thick slice of wet jerky.

"Stop that, Vern Wagner," Dorothy yelled from the pass-through. "You're getting water all over the floor. At your age I can't tell if you're trying to get dry or having a stroke."

"Coffee!" Vern yelled back as he limped toward Carter. "When it gets cold, my joints start to rust up."

By the time he made it to the table, a waitress was pouring him a mug of hot coffee.

"Pour an extra cup. Jake Longbow is climbing out of his truck."

The new waitress who'd replaced Sissy last year glared at Vern as if she thought she might be wasting a cup. "You gentlemen just having a cup or planning to wait out the rain?"

Vern grinned. "I've been waiting out the rain all my life. Make a fresh pot, darlin'. We're going to be here awhile."

Carter tried to figure out if she thought Vern was lying about needing the extra coffee or if the old man climbing out of a huge truck might not live long enough to drink it. He'd seen the trucks before, huge Dodge Rams with a Double K brand. The Kirkland Ranch.

Jake Longbow walked slowly in the rain, enjoying the stroll. His Comanche blood showed in his high cheekbones and long nose. He'd tanned over a dark complexion for so many years his skin looked more like bark. Vern might be a cowboy who loved the land, but Jake Longbow was different. He seemed more a part of the land, a part of all around him, even the storm.

While Jake hung up his hat and coat on the rack by the door, Vern pulled out an old map wrapped in plastic and spread it out on the table in front of Carter.

"Longbow and I have been talking, and we think we can find that rock corral you talked about. The road heading out in that pasture was fenced off fifty or so years ago, but we could get close to it on a four-wheeler." Vern stopped long enough to down half his steaming coffee.

Carter decided Vern's lips hadn't just thinned out over the years. He must have burned them off drinking coffee. Carter cleared his throat as Longbow sat down. "I want to thank you two for agreeing to meet me here. It means a lot to me. I'm not even sure which canyon around here the cave might be in. But I do remember that I saw rocks in a square the next morning."

"No problem," they both said at once.

Three gray heads leaned over the old map and began to talk. Their knowledge of the land and the history of the canyons blended with their familiarity of maps.

Carter could feel his goal almost within reach. If the first snow would hold off until after Halloween, he'd have time for one last search before winter.

Vern downed the rest of his coffee and motioned for the waitress to bring more. "One thing we've decided, Carter," he said. "Me and Jake are going down with you. Three sets of eyes, even my nearsighted ones, are better than one. If we find the rock corral, we'll know we're close to the cave and, if you've no objection, we'll climb down with you."

"I'd be honored to have you along on this crazy journey."

All three smiled. For a moment they weren't three old men in their seventies. They were wild boys looking for an adventure.

That night Carter dreamed of the stick men dancing. In his dream he imagined that they'd be as excited to see him as he was to see them.

CHAPTER TWENTY-TWO

Angie

The following Monday, Agent Dodson called Angie at work. He told her the case against her uncle was progressing. The ledger helped them follow the movement of money through her uncle's company. Apparently, her uncle was only one link in the chain, and they planned to pull several people in with the net they'd cast.

When Angie hung up, she thought of calling her aunt back in Florida, but she decided they weren't really part of her family anymore. They'd proved that by sending someone to track her down and harass her. The ledger her father kept wasn't part of the official books and if her uncle hadn't been doing something wrong he wouldn't have worried about it.

She had the feeling that her aunt and uncle would try to blame everything on her father. After all, he was dead, he couldn't defend himself. Maybe they'd planned that from the first and deep down her father knew if he exposed what was going on he'd be the one to take the fall. If so, his getting killed must have messed up their great escape plan if the smuggling was discovered.

All her life Angie had wondered if there was a place she could find where real people lived who cared about one another. A place where being related wasn't an obligation, but a blessing and a true friend.

She'd found it here. There was no need to look back. Dan, Wilkes, the volunteers, even Uncle Vern, didn't have to help her, they just did.

Her cell rang.

She picked up, smiling. "Wilkes. Did you find my cat?" She'd dropped by his place twice and both times they couldn't find Doc Holliday. Vern swore he'd seen the cat around and all Doc's food had disappeared from the porch, so Angie wasn't too worried.

"Yes, I finally found the darn cat. He was up in the barn loft playing poker with my wild cats. He's okay, but I think he's about half drunk, because he's walking funny."

"Don't let him out of the house again."

"I won't. How about I bring him over to your place when I pick you up for that dinner in Lubbock I promised you?"

She hesitated. "Would you consider dinner at my house? I haven't really had a chance to cook there and it might be fun."

"You mean just me and you alone? No one else to talk to. Nobody watching us. I might consider it. What time?"

"Seven." She giggled. "And the only company we'll have will be Doc."

Angie thought all morning about what she'd cook and how Wilkes would look sitting at her little table in her little cabin. She even rushed home at lunch to put the sauce in the slow cooker so it could simmer all afternoon.

She'd also thought about their bargain. She had all the control and he'd said he'd welcome her kiss or touch at any time.

She'd always been shy, never knowing where she stood with a man. Some must have thought she wasn't interested, others tried to move too far, too fast. One of her greatest fears in dating was that she'd make the first move only to find out that the guy didn't see her in that light. Wilkes had made it plain how he felt about her and that she'd be the one to set the pace.

Every time they'd been together he'd found a way to touch her. At first she hadn't seen the attraction. His first kiss was hesitant when they'd meet. But the last one had warmed her to the bone. She'd relived it several times a day since that night, but it was his touch that caused the slow heat moving through her body. His hand on her waist warming her even through her clothes. The way he leaned into her as if he wanted no space between them. And when he pulled her against him, their communication became full body contact.

Angie stood and turned down the heater. It might be a cold day, but she didn't even need to wear a sweater. Tonight, she'd surprise him. She'd take that power he'd given her.

She might not be long-legged sexy Lexie Davis, but she might try to be bold for once in her life. After all, Wilkes wanted her. He'd never suggested that she change a single thing. He wanted her just the way she was.

For the first time in her life, Angie felt beautiful.

By the time she left work an hour earlier than usual, the rain had slowed. She stopped for fresh vegetables and a bottle of wine, then decided to drop in at Forever Keepsake to borrow as many quilt frames as they could loan her. The museum's theme of Country Christmas was taking off with all the volunteer staff. If they planned to have everything up by the first week in December for the party, the ladies auxiliary had to start now.

The Franklin sisters greeted her with hugs. They were so excited to be able to help. As they worked wrapping old frames up to fit into her van, one of the sisters asked her how Wilkes was.

Angie didn't want to talk about their strange bargain, so she picked another subject. "He was in Austin for a few days last week trying to help Yancy Grey with a project he's been working on. He's looking for anyone who might know who owns the Stanley house. You know, the old fallen-down place out on the north road."

Both sisters stilled, listening to every word Angie said.

"Yancy feels a pull from the old place and has no idea if it's a blessing or a curse. He says he's got to find out what happened to the family who lived there. It seems to have become a quest."

Both sisters stared, wide-eyed as if Death walked across in front of their store window. Rose Franklin finally asked, "You're talking about the old place they call the Gypsy House?"

Angie nodded.

"I don't know Yancy, just seen him from a distance a few times, but I think he would be better off to forget about that place." Rose looked frightened. "Bad blood must have been sprinkled there. It would do no one any good to look into the house's history."

Angie decided she'd better agree. "You are probably right, but he's determined. Do you two know anything about the place?" She knew they did. She could see it in their faces and body language. The two sweet ladies seemed to be on guard.

Rose straightened. "This Yancy's not from around here. I heard he just rode in on a bus and stopped here by accident. That old house should have been torn down years ago."

"I'll tell Yancy Grey that," Angie said. "But I don't think it will stop him from searching."

"Did you say this Yancy's last name is Grey?" Rose asked slowly. "I don't believe I've ever heard anyone say before. Folks just call him Yancy and we all know who they are talking about."

"Yes. He's Yancy Grey." Angie might not be able to read minds but she knew something was going on between the sisters. It was almost as if they were silently passing invisible notes. Rose had her top chin stuck out as far as it would go and Daisy looked as though she was about to cry.

Angie swore the air in the little shop changed. She took a gulp while some oxygen remained. These two were hiding something.

"All right, ladies, tell me what you know about it," Angie said, unsure if she wanted to hear whatever they hid from her. "Any detail will help Yancy," she said as she thought about whether a family had been killed there or devil worshippers had mutilated animals in the house that called to him.

Rose shook her head, then turned to her sister for support. They seemed to be reading each other's mind again, only now it seemed more like an argument. Finally, Rose straightened like a judge about to pronounce a sentence. "We'll tell the horrible story once and only once if it will help. Evil lives in that place, and anyone interested in it needs to know that."

Daisy didn't look at her sister as she whispered, "No. Let what happened be dead and buried, Rose. It's none of our concern."

"It needs to be told." Rose folded her arms. "If only for Yancy's sake. If he's a Grey, he might need to know it."

"All right. Once. Then the story dies."

Angie stared at Rose. "Can you two come to my house in an hour? I'll have Yancy there if you think it's something he needs to hear." She wasn't sure their tale would help Yancy, but Angie didn't want to be alone when the sisters told what they knew. "I'm making supper for Wilkes and you'd be most welcome to join us." If the sisters were only telling the story once, she needed others there.

"We'll be out to your place as soon as we lock up tonight," Rose said.

"And we'll bring dessert. It's only proper if we stay for dinner," Daisy added.

Angie studied the pair. How bad could this story be if no one else in town knew it? The Franklin sisters were probably blowing it up.

An hour later, Wilkes, Yancy and Dan Brigman all stood in her tiny living room. Three long-legged men in boots all tried to fit into her furniture. Wilkes finally gave up trying to look comfortable and simply stood leaning against the wall.

Angie faced them all with a wooden spoon in her hand.

"Now, don't any of you frighten Rose and Daisy or I swear you'll regret this."

None of them looked bothered by the threat. Dan even laughed, probably imagining a fight between the three of them and the two middle-aged ladies.

Wilkes shook his head. "Angie, honey, I've known the Franklin sisters all my life. They love spreading gossip about everyone in town. I'll be shocked if there is one story about this town that they haven't told a hundred times."

Dan agreed. "They file a police report on at least one person in town a month. Usually crimes they haven't actually witnessed, but they've heard about or suspect. Things like Dorothy serving cat food at the café on Wednesday, or the principal stealing trash cans out of the roadside parks, or the volunteer fire department watching X-rated movies on their training nights. They are always wanting me to go out and investigate something they think is going on."

Angie was beginning to think she'd fallen for a trick. Maybe the Franklin sisters were just telling stories. "What do you think, Yancy?"

He shrugged. "I don't know the ladies except by sight, but I'm hoping they know something, because I'm out of ideas. The sheriff says I can't explore the place without permission from the owner, so all I can do is hope information falls in my lap. But don't worry, Angie, I'll be nice to them. I can smell supper cooking and hope I'll be invited."

"You're all invited. I made enough spaghetti for a dozen." She wanted to tell them about how her mother always made a big pot of sauce on rainy days, then froze servings for meals later, but she doubted the three men would care.

Wilkes moved to the kitchen as if to help. She handed him the spoon and nodded toward the pot of sauce.

When Dan and Yancy started talking about the problems at the roadside parks, Wilkes leaned close to Angie and whispered, "This wasn't exactly what I had planned for tonight."

"Me, either, but this is exciting. Just think, you might find out something about this town that you don't know. I've got the feeling the sisters have never told this story before. Daisy looked like she didn't want Rose to mention anything."

He shook his head. "Not likely."

Ten minutes later the sisters rushed in. Their little folding umbrellas did nothing to keep the rain off their tent dresses. The wet material clung like shrink-wrap over bodies rich in bulges.

The men moved away from the fireplace so the sisters could sit close to dry their clothes. Angie served cocoa as they all pulled up kitchen chairs and sat down in the little living room. The rain outside, the fireplace crackling, the warm smells of home cooking, all made for a night of storytelling, but from the tears sparkling in Daisy Franklin's eyes Angie wasn't sure this would be a tale anyone would want to hear.

For a few minutes they talked of nothing, the day, the rain, the upcoming holidays. Then, as if he were the judge over the proceedings, Dan took the lead. "Miss Franklin," he said to Rose, who usually did most of the talking for the two sisters, "we understand you have news about the old house on the north road."

Rose nodded. "I promise to tell the truth, the whole truth and nothing but the truth. Very few know this story and I'll only tell it once. I wouldn't be telling it now except Yancy's last name is Grey, so my sister and I finally agreed that he has a right to know."

Angie saw Wilkes roll his eyes as if to hint they were playing it up a little too much.

"Take your time, Miss Franklin," Dan encouraged. "We're looking for anything you might know about the old Stanley house or the people who once lived there."

Everyone waited except Daisy Franklin. The poor woman looked as if she might bolt. This subject was obviously not one she wanted to talk about. Her little umbrella made a clicking sound like a tiny chime as she twisted it back and forth in her hands.

"I'll start with what everyone in town probably knows." Rose ignored her sister's panic. "Almost thirty years ago my sister Daisy and I fell in love with the same boy. He worked for our father." She looked at Daisy. "We had a small dairy farm and he mostly made deliveries. Rose or I would go along and collect the money. He had a kindness about him that made us both feel special just to know him."

"What was his name?" Dan asked.

"His name was Galen Stanley. His family could trace their roots all the way back to the original folk who were among the first settlers. He said his great-great-grandfather had been the first blacksmith in the area.

"Galen was a good person, but something was wrong with his old man. He'd served time in prison, and most said he wasn't right in the head after that. He'd grown up with the Grey boys down the road but they had a falling-out twenty years before when they were all young and running wild. Poor farm kids with nothing to do."

Daisy interrupted. "We don't know why the two families hated each other. That happened before Rose and I were born."

Rose nodded and continued, "As the years passed, the two families grew to hate each other more and more."

Daisy sliced in again. "Teachers used to make sure there were no Greys and Stanleys in the same class."

Yancy moved to the edge of his chair. "I'm a Grey. Maybe it's the hate I feel when I walk near the old house if it was owned by the Stanleys. Only, I've never heard of any Greys or Stanleys who live here. Seems like if they were both big families they'd have some descendants."

"There ain't any anymore," Daisy whispered. "Left more than twenty-five years ago, I'm guessing."

No one commented on Yancy's speculation about why he might sense hate from the house, and Rose continued, "Galen's father was a mean, mean man. He was hard on his only child. We all saw it. Even when he was a kid, Galen would come to school all beat-up. Not from just a whipping or a slap, but deep bruises that lay on top of each other."

Daisy decided she wanted to break in again. She waved her hand until her sister noticed her and let her have the floor. "My mother said Galen's father got messed up on drugs in the early sixties. The house he'd inherited was known for wild parties. But by the time Galen came along, his dad had straightened up some. He'd married a girl fifteen years younger, claimed he wanted her young so he could finish raising her right. No one in town saw her much after she married. She had Galen within a year. There were no other children. Word was she miscarried a few times. Some claimed she fell a lot.

"Galen was a good kid despite his mean father. Tried to do what was right, made good grades, but it wasn't easy with a drunk for a dad. When he was seventeen, he fell hard for a girl who claimed her heritage was Gypsy, too. She was from the family the Stanleys hated. She was a Grey."

Tears slid down Daisy's cheek as she continued. "Story goes that Galen and the girl ran off one night. Their fathers set aside the feud and went after them. When they found them, the account was told to my father that they stripped the girl and tied her to the front of Galen's pickup so she had to watch them take turns beating him. Every time he'd fall or crawl out of the headlight beams, one of the men would drag him back so she could see how bad he looked. His own father snapped a bone in Galen's arm just to hear her scream. She passed out before the beating was over. If she knew what happened next, she never said.

"No one in town saw Galen again. My father said the few who knew of the beating thought his own mother wouldn't have recognized him anyway when the fathers finished with him. One told my father that Galen's own father killed him that night. Another claimed Galen just started running and never stopped. The girl's father drove her home still tied to the truck."

Rose broke in. "Our dad believed that what the fathers did that night put a curse on both families."

Daisy nodded. "Galen's father died before Christmas that year, and when the girl's family found out she was pregnant, they disowned her. A month later her father, Mr. Grey, was paralyzed in a car wreck. His wife loaded him up and moved away the next spring, even before the baby her daughter carried was born. No one knows where they went but I'd bet that they're both dead.

"After that, all Greys and Stanleys either moved away or died off. A house fire killed a few. Layoffs made some leave. Two Stanley brothers who supposedly witnessed the beating killed each other in a gunfight. Within a year no Stanleys remained alive except Galen's mother. She lived in the old house you've been asking about. Kept it dark all the time and only walked into town a few times a year. Folks said she was ghost thin."

"What happened to the girl? The one Galen got pregnant. The one who had to watch the beating," Yancy asked.

"She had the baby. Lived with Galen's mom for a few years in that old house on the north road. The Grey girl was no more than a child having a child. Then the town lost track of her. They say she just left one night with the baby. A few years later, four or five after Galen's beating and maybe even his death, a postman found Galen's mother's body. She'd been dead so long she wasn't much more than bones laid out in her garden."

The room was silent. Finally, Yancy asked, "What was Galen's wife's name?"

Rose straightened and looked directly at Yancy. "I don't know if she and Galen had time to marry when they ran off. Her name was Grey. Jewel Grey." A tear ran down Rose's chubby cheek. "I believe she had a son. He would be about your age...if he's still alive."

Yancy put his head in his hands. Everyone in the room sat silent. Angie guessed that no one had any trouble putting the pieces together.

Suddenly, Yancy bolted for the door before anyone could stop him. He was gone in a flash. Everyone let out the air they'd been holding at once. They all knew that somehow this wasn't just the story of the old house. It was Yancy's story.

While Dan was saying they should all give Yancy time, and the sisters were commenting that Yancy looked a little like his father, Angie tossed the wooden spoon at Wilkes and whispered, "Finish up dinner. I'll be right back."

He looked as if she'd just asked him to do brain surgery, but she didn't wait around to hear any argument.

She didn't have to look too far. She found Yancy standing on the edge of her dock. Walking up behind him, she said quietly, "If you're thinking of jumping in, I should warn you it's only about four feet deep."

Yancy didn't turn around. "Go away."

The pain in his voice made her brave. Without a word, she put her arms around him and hugged him. When he tried to tug away, she held on tighter. He swore, not at her she knew. She simply tightened her grip.

The cold air, thick with rain, seemed to move over them both, soothing cracks in their souls and washing away the horror of the story.

Finally, he whispered, "Please go away."

"Can't do that," she said.

"Didn't you hear about my family? They were terrible, terrible people. No wonder my mom was a druggie. Can you imagine what she suffered at the hands of her own father? My grandfather was in prison, a loser like me. Sounds like he was abusive to his young wife and his only son. Maybe he even killed my dad."

Yancy swore at the world, but Angie just hung on tight.

"I always wanted a family, but not this one. I don't want any of them. You can take the sisters' story and keep it. I don't want any part of it."

When he dropped to his knees on the dock, she tumbled down with him. She didn't let go, but she shifted around until she could look him in the face. All she saw was dark eyes and dark shadows.

"I come from a family the wolves wouldn't claim," he cried out. "All my life I've always wanted to know who my people were and now I know they were no good."

Angie shook her head. "That's not what I heard. The sisters said your father, Galen, was kind. They both loved him so much they never married. All he did wrong was love a girl, your mother. And she kept you. No abortion. No adoption. So she must have loved you. And your grandmother on your father's side took her in. That must have been very brave."

"You think my father's dead? I don't have his last name, so they didn't marry."

Angie thought about it. "I think he is or he would have come back. I also think he didn't know about you, because if he had, he'd have come back to see what a fine man you've become. All the residents at the retirement home love you. I even heard one of the volunteers say she wished you were her grandson."

"You don't understand," he whispered more to himself than her.

She laughed. "Hey, I've got an uncle about to be arrested by the FBI and a father who did the books for a drug business until someone killed him in an alley. I've got an aunt who would step over me if I were dying, and complain about the mess I was making. If we all let a few relatives define our lives, we'd probably all be in jail."

"I think I would have been happier thinking I had no relatives," Yancy said.

"Me, too." She took his big, rough hand. "Since we're both out here alone, how about we decide to be each other's family? I could be your sister and you could be the brother I always wanted to protect me."

"That mean I can come to Thanksgiving dinner?" Yancy finally raised his head to look at her.

"Sure, and I'll call whenever I need anything moved or fixed. You may count me as only one sister, but I'll keep you busy."

"That sounds like a good plan. I've always wanted a little sister." Tears were still shining on his cheeks, but Yancy smiled.

He stood, pulling her to her feet. "Speaking of food, I'm starving. Nothing makes you hungrier than digging up all your dead relatives."

She knew he was putting on a brave face, but she let him.

As they walked back to the house in the dark, Yancy added, "Thanks, Angie, for not letting go of me back there. I was tumbling into a dark place. I think I can handle this now. Do you really come from a messed-up family?"

"Anytime, brother. We'll eat tonight and rebury all the bad relations tomorrow." She laughed. "And yes, I was telling the truth about my family. The whole truth."

"Maybe it shouldn't be, but that's real comforting to know." Yancy put his arm over her shoulders. "Thanks for coming out in the rain to get me."

Angie began to run as soft rain blended with the tears she hadn't noticed. "It's raining! My hair really gets curly when it rains!"

When they got to the porch, he stopped. "You know, one thing I learned in prison was no matter how bad things get, they can always get worse." He squeezed her hand. "Well, tonight I figured out that having one person who won't let go can make the trouble bearable."

CHAPTER TWENTY-THREE

Wilkes

Wilkes watched Angie and Yancy walk back in holding hands. If he'd been younger, he might have been angry or jealous, but he recognized it for what it was—Angie had cared enough to help.

The rain had made her hair look as if she had a strawberry-colored halo. The urge to hold her was so great he feared he'd have to break at least one leg to keep from running to her.

The woman had no idea how beautiful she was. She'd helped Yancy when no one else in the room knew what to do for a man whose world was falling apart.

Yancy walked over and hugged each of the Franklin sisters, then they all sat down at the little table made for four. Elbow to elbow they broke bread together as friends.

Wilkes had done his best to finish up the meal. He'd had to scrape the burned part off the garlic bread, and the spaghetti was overcooked, but no one really noticed the food anyway. They were all trying to make Yancy feel better, and the best way to do that seemed to be to not talk about the old house.

The Franklin sisters giggled when Wilkes teased them. Dan

promised he'd pull his weapon if Yancy told one more joke he'd heard at the retirement community where he worked. They all corrected one another on the proper way to eat spaghetti. Angie laughed so hard her sides hurt and Wilkes told her the only cure was wine.

The meal ended with the Franklin sisters announcing they'd brought s'mores for dessert. Rose roasted the marshmallows and Daisy divided up and stacked the graham crackers and chocolate.

As soon as the dishes were done, everyone hugged goodbye. Wilkes was happy to finally be alone with Angie.

She talked about her day as they put the furniture back in order. He could hear her growing love for the museum. He could also see how tired she was. The story the sisters told had drained everyone. No matter how much he wanted to touch Angie, he decided maybe tonight wasn't the night.

"This plan of a dinner for two didn't work very well," he said, smiling. "How about next week we try Lubbock. Just once I'd like to look across the table and see only you."

"Sorry."

"Don't apologize. This was hard on Yancy, but now he can start looking ahead and not behind him."

She nodded.

Wilkes wasn't surprised to find Doc Holliday asleep on his coat when he dropped back to the bedroom to retrieve it.

"I'd better call it a night," he said when he walked back into the tiny living area. "I've got a full day tomorrow, and Uncle Vern's already told me he's not going to be there to help. Plans to join Carter Mayes in his search for the stick people."

"You think he'll ever find them?" she said as they moved to the door.

Wilkes shook his head. "If they existed, someone would have found them by now. People have been wandering around the canyons for hundreds of years."

He pulled on his coat and moved to the door. The night had been interesting but not what he expected. In a way, he'd learned

a great deal about her. The kindness she showed the sisters and
Yancy had surprised him. He'd known these people all his life.
She was new here but her heart was open. They had been an
odd group that he never would have thought would blend together, but they had.

She handed Wilkes a take-home container of spaghetti for
Vern.

Wilkes just stood by the door waiting. He'd said she'd have
to make the first move, and he was a man of his word.

The thought that they might spend the rest of their lives as
friends crossed his mind. He'd never be able to survive in a
world where he couldn't touch her. Even tonight with the sheriff on one side of him and Rose Franklin on the other, Wilkes's
thoughts were definitely X-rated. At one point he missed the
punch line to Yancy's joke because he was busy thinking of how
much he wanted to brush Angie's hair away from her throat and
kiss his way down to her...

"...still raining," she said.

He had a feeling there was a first part to the sentence. If she
didn't touch him soon, he'd go mad. He thought of trying to
say something about what she might have been talking about,
but gave up and just said, "I love your hair that way."

She smiled as if knowing what he was doing and took a step
closer to him.

Slowly, she stood on her tiptoes and kissed him so awkwardly
it was downright cute. "Good night," she whispered.

He waited, fighting the urge to reach for her.

She leaned closer and said, "Come down closer so I can reach
your mouth."

When he did, she kissed him again. Soft, with a hesitance
that he found touching.

She took Vern's food from Wilkes's hands and moved until
their bodies barely touched. "You want to touch my hair?"

He grinned. "You know I do." He didn't question the invitation. His long fingers moved into her curls. He loved how

soft her hair felt, and the way she leaned near, barely touching him, was driving him insane. Leaning down, almost brushing her lips, he whispered, "You want to kiss me?"

He felt her little laugh against his mouth a moment before she closed the space between them. With his hands in her hair, he turned her head just right and the kiss deepened to the heaven he'd been waiting for since that first real kiss that seemed to have been ages ago.

She melted against him and he could feel her breathing.

"Closer," he whispered with his lips still brushing hers.

She opened her mouth wider as her breasts pressed against him and he felt both their hearts pounding.

When she circled her arms around his neck, he lowered his hands to her shoulders and slowly moved down her body pressing her to him. He wouldn't have cared if the kiss never ended. They'd find two skeletons bound together in the door of her cabin before he'd be the one to stop. He loved the way she felt, the way her hips curved, the way her breasts flattened against his chest.

When she finally pulled away, her big eyes sparkled. "Can we do this again?"

It took all his effort to straighten and pull even an inch away. "Anytime, Angie. You're welcome to come to me whenever you want. I can think of nothing better in this world than holding you. Just tell me when and where."

He didn't care if they came back here to have leftovers or went out for a fancy meal. He just wanted to be with her.

"I'll call you tomorrow. Maybe we can get away Friday. I've heard rumors that couples do manage to get together on that day." Her hand laced in his.

He agreed and walked with her out to the porch. If he'd had his way, he'd sweep her up in his arms and kiss her senseless, then carry her to that little bed ten feet away and let her know just how much he wanted her, but he wasn't setting the rules. He'd given her the power, and he had no doubt that she loved it.

Wilkes had to keep it light before he said the wrong thing. "Tell Doc if he wants to come back and play with the boys, he's welcome anytime. You could even stay over to keep an eye on him."

"I might sometime. I think he liked your place. Good night." She let her fingers brush softly over his cotton shirt, then crossed her arms against the chill and let him walk away.

On the drive home Wilkes felt all pinned up, like a football player who never got off the sideline. Angie was starting to matter to him. If he let himself care again, he'd be opening himself wide-open. But he could never turn her away. The ache to have her near was building every time he saw her.

As he drove past the old Gypsy House, he spotted Yancy standing in the weeds staring at the crumbling ruins of what had once been his father's home.

Wilkes circled round and climbed out of his car to stand beside his friend.

"A lot of evil lived here once," Yancy said sadly.

Wilkes shook his head. "The evil lived in the people, not the house. If you still want to go in, I say we bring some ropes and flashlights over and have a look. After what the sheriff heard tonight, he's not likely to arrest us for looking around."

Yancy sighed. "I got to think about everything I heard tonight. I'm a product of all that happened here. I've heard folks say that this man or that one came from good people. I can't make that claim. Some of my relatives were really bad." He laughed without humor. "And apparently they are all dead because of a curse."

"That's right, you can't claim good relatives, Yancy, but I'm thinking your children might be able to claim it."

Yancy laughed. "First, I'm a work in progress. I've tipped the scales in both directions and I'm not out of my twenties, so who knows how I'll turn out. And second, I don't even have a woman, so not much chance of children."

"Oh, but you will," Wilkes promised.

"How do you know?"

Wilkes smiled. "Don't you know? The Franklin sisters are the best matchmakers in town. They'll find you someone before spring."

"If they do, I'll let both of them be flower girls in my wedding."

Just the thought of that sight made both men laugh all the way to their cars.

CHAPTER TWENTY-FOUR

Lauren

As far as Lauren could see, the love affair between Tim and Polly was over. Her roommate got up cussing Tim O'Grady in the morning and fell asleep swearing she'd kill him tomorrow when she had the energy. Her undying hatred was born out of a passion that Tim seemed to insist on: studying.

He walked Polly to class, went over her homework, scheduled every makeup test she'd missed and helped her write every research paper. At meals he drilled her on facts that kept falling out of her brain. By the end of the week Polly said she'd decided not to color her hair again, since she'd have it all pulled out by the end of the semester.

After over a year in college, Tim had taken on a project. Polly. He'd finally become passionate about something. He just smiled when Polly went into a rant as if waiting for the break to be over and the studying to pick up again.

On Friday, when she'd passed her first test in any class, all three decided to take off for Crossroads to celebrate. They'd pig out on junk food and watch old movies. And, Tim pointed out, study for a history test Polly had coming up next week.

Funny how the very place Lauren had dreamed of getting away from was now her retreat. When she called Pop, they were already an hour down the road. Her father didn't sound all that excited, and Lauren wondered if she was interrupting a secret life she didn't know about.

Surely not. Pop lived for his job and her. If he did have a secret, it was something like online gambling or reading romance novels. Nothing bad. Nothing illegal.

"I have a meeting I have to attend tonight at the county offices," he said. "Do you guys think you can cook without burning the house down?"

Lauren made a face at the phone. He'd been saying that since she was five. "Of course. We're almost there, but we have to stop off to pick up a few things for Polly, so don't worry about getting snacks. We'll save you time."

"What kind of things?"

That was her pop, always interrogating.

"Polly left her bag at the dorm. We'll get things like pajamas, maybe a sweatshirt and pants, since it's cold. Underwear, makeup, you know."

Tim commented from the front seat. "She doesn't wear underwear."

Lauren covered the phone hoping her father didn't hear him.

After a pause, Pop said too calmly, "Tim's coming home, too?"

"Yes," she answered.

"Any chance he'd stay at his place this time? It's only a few hundred yards away, and I'm sure his parents would like to see him. I fell over him sleeping on the floor before dawn last Saturday."

Lauren laughed. "Not much chance, Pop, but I'll tell him he has to go home to sleep."

"Great. Charge the snacks to me and remind Tim to get out of my house by ten."

Lauren ended the call fighting down a giggle. Her father was not going to handle it well when, or if, she ever got a real boyfriend.

They pulled off at a Walmart a few miles later. Tim grabbed a cart and said he'd get snacks. Lauren and Polly hit the racks. Since Polly was a good five inches shorter than Lauren and their styles were completely different, Lauren was no help. Polly picked out simple pj's with Minnie Mouse on the front, a few T-shirts and a cheap pair of tennis shoes. After ten minutes of searching, she found a dull blue-hooded sweatshirt and baggy pants in the boys' department.

"It'll keep me warm out on the deck," Polly said. "Who knows, I might pick up your habit of walking our lake."

Lauren felt a very childish reaction settle over her. For a second she thought about saying, "It's not *our* lake. It's *mine*." Polly had already taken over Tim, and after last weekend she had started calling Lauren's father *Pop*. What was next?

Tim pulled up beside them with a cart full of frozen pizzas, cookies, chips and Halloween candy. "Since your dad has a meeting tonight, I've got an idea. Why don't we invite a few friends over and have a party. The World Series is on."

Lauren wanted to say no, but how much trouble could pizza and the World Series be? "Sounds like fun."

Polly shook her head. "I really don't feel like being around people."

"What are we, Polly Anna?" Tim asked.

"Friends," she answered with a smile.

"Well, how about you meet some of your friends' friends. You can meet them tonight, and on the way back Sunday we'll tell you everything that ever happened to all of them. It'll be like a biography of a dozen boring people, narrated by me. The only ones home this time of year will probably be the ones who went to work after high school or flunked out of college."

"Or were a year younger than me," Lauren added.

"Fine." Polly rolled her eyes dramatically.

Lauren thought about calling her pop back, but he was working. She'd just surprise him. With luck, the party would be over before he got home. County meetings sometimes lasted until midnight.

It occurred to her then that maybe the meetings didn't always last so late. Pop might have somewhere or someone he went to after work now and then. She shook her head. Impossible.

Three hours later Lauren decided the party was a bad idea. Several of Tim's high school buddies dropped by. Tim acted as if he was glad to see them, but in truth, she sensed he didn't have much in common with them after being away for a year. They all had nine-to-five jobs, and Tim's goal in life seemed to be putting off work as long as possible.

A few girls, still in high school, stopped by acting as though they'd been Lauren's best friends last spring. They wanted to know all about the boys at Tech. Not one seemed curious about classes.

A little after nine, Reid Collins showed up. Unlike everyone else, he wore slacks and a dress shirt. He said hello to everyone, but his gaze kept searching for Lauren.

She could feel him watching her. Finally, he made his way to the kitchen, where she was pulling out the last pizza from the oven.

"Hi, Lauren," he said politely. "I had to come home for a party my parents were having. A political thing. I heard you were back for the weekend. Thought I'd just stop by and say hi."

Lauren didn't know what to say. He'd been polite enough two weeks ago at homecoming, but then Tim showed her the text Reid sent out. She wasn't sure if she should be mad at him or just ignore what he'd texted.

Reid watched her. "You and Tim dating now?"

"No," she said. "We're still just friends. He drove my room-

mate and me home for a weekend off. You know my roommate, Polly."

Reid looked around. "I doubt she'll even remember me. Ancient history."

"Kind of like us." She leaned close so that no one would hear.
"And how you 'got lucky' after the homecoming game."

Reid looked surprised. Then understanding hit him. "Oh,
God, Lauren, that wasn't about you. I hooked up with the blonde
who had a date with one of my frat brothers. You remember the
one. She flirted with me all during the game."

Lauren smiled. "Don't look so horrified. I know you weren't
talking about me, but anyone who knew we had a date might
have come to that conclusion."

To her surprise, he honestly looked sorry. "No wonder Tim
gave me a 'drop dead' look when I saw him the next day."

Lauren didn't feel sorry for Reid.

"What can I do to make it up to you, Lauren?"

She shrugged. "Stay away from me and my roommate."

"Done." He grinned. "After all, you and I aren't due for another date for a year."

"But be polite to her if you do see her." Over Reid's shoulder, Lauren saw Polly heading her way. "Which might happen
sooner than you think."

He nodded again. "If this gets back to my dad or the sheriff, you'll stand with me on what really happened, won't you?"

"I'll stand with the truth, Reid, but don't even think I'll cover
for you. I don't plan on being that kind of friend."

"Got it," he said to Lauren as Polly backed into him.

"Oh, sorry," she said when she saw his face.

Reid shot a quick look at Lauren before turning to Polly.
"No, it was my fault for standing in the middle of the room."
He took the empty popcorn bowl. "Polly Pierce, right? I think
we met once, but I can't remember where. I must have been
very drunk."

She nodded, obviously surprised that he remembered her name. "You know Lauren?"

Reid glanced at Lauren knowing he'd need to be careful and not give too much away. "Everyone from Crossroads knows everyone else."

Several people rushed for fresh pizza and Lauren lost track of Polly and Reid. When she circled the room, she saw Reid watching the game. She thought she could see Polly, dressed in her navy sweat suit, step off the deck and head out near the water.

"She all right?" Tim said from just behind Lauren.

"I think so. Last week she walked along the shore and said she liked it. Maybe she just needs a little alone time."

"Reid didn't say anything to her, did he?"

"No. I don't think so."

An hour later the game was over, and everyone decided to leave. After all, there was only so much fun they could have at the sheriff's house.

Tim, Lauren and Reid started cleaning up. As they worked, Reid asked where Polly was.

"I introduced her to the peace of walking along the lake," Lauren said as she washed the last of the pans.

"She's been gone a long time. Shouldn't one of us go look for her?"

Lauren had already been thinking that, but who? She didn't want to leave Reid and Tim alone. Tim wouldn't like the idea of leaving her with Reid, and she wasn't sure she wanted Reid to go after Polly anyway. Sometimes he could be so polite, like when he said he didn't remember where he met Polly, and other times he was a first-class jerk.

The problem was solved when her father walked in the door. "Hello, kids," he said as if they were still sixteen. "Have a nice time?"

When no one spoke, he looked around. "Where's Polly?"

Lauren answered slowly. "She went for a walk an hour ago, but we're starting to worry that she got lost."

Pop didn't seem too concerned. "The lake makes a circle. She could walk it twice in an hour. Maybe she's just sitting out watching the water like you used to do. Give her a call."

Lauren dialed Polly's number and they all heard a cell ringing in the kitchen. She'd left her phone on the counter.

Her pop was an organizer. "If you're worried, we could go look for her. She may have stopped to talk to someone."

"We did meet the curator who lives in one of the back cabins, but Polly wouldn't have stayed an hour there." A sinking feeling washed over Lauren. "We need to look. It's dark. She could have fallen and hurt herself."

"She does tend to be accident prone," Tim voiced her fears.

Pop nodded and handed out flashlights. "Tim, circle toward your house. Reid, go the other way. Lauren, stay here. If anyone finds her, call Lauren. She'll notify the others." Her father was in his element. He knew what to do. "Keep your lights on so we can see each other moving. I'll take the back trails that lead to cabins not on the lake. We should find her in a few minutes."

Lauren stood on the deck and watched the search begin. She tried to think of reasons Polly would still be out in the dark. None made sense. It had been thirteen days since the mirror fell. Beneath the sweatshirt she wore, her arm was still wrapped in white bandages. She wouldn't have gone for a swim in the cold water, and she wasn't a "stop and visit" kind of person.

The rumbling fear she tried to push aside was that Polly might have tried to hurt herself again. Lauren had no proof, but what if the mirror hadn't been an accident? Polly could have hit it in anger, then taken a piece of glass and cut her arm. If she had, would she try again? The lake would be an easy place to end a life and have it look like an accident. Fifty-foot drops onto rocks from the top. Water would be an almost painless way for Polly to die. She couldn't swim. One step off the dock would end her life.

Miniature lights danced along the edge of the lake. Tim's to the right, Reid's to the left. Both were moving slowly checking out decks where she might have stopped. Any warmth had left with the sun. If Polly were still outside, she'd be cold.

When they'd met the museum curator last Sunday when they'd been out walking, Polly had acted interested in the museum. Maybe she'd planned to go back to the cabin, but took the wrong turn.

Lauren shook her head. No matter how she turned she couldn't miss the lake or the lights along the edges.

Maybe Polly had twisted an ankle and stopped somewhere.

Lauren waited. With each minute, trouble seemed closer.

A car pulled up a few feet farther down the road from their drive. She recognized Wilkes Wagner's Tahoe as he folded out of the driver's seat. "Evening, Lauren. Any chance your father's home?"

"He's out looking for my roommate. She went for a walk and, uh, got lost," Lauren explained as she walked toward Wilkes. "You can reach him on his cell."

Wilkes frowned. "I forgot mine. Could you call him? I have an emergency here."

Lauren hit her Pop's number and handed over her phone. She thought of telling him that they were already dealing with an emergency, but losing Polly might not seem as much of a problem. After all, Polly wasn't a lost child, and the lake wasn't a dangerous place.

"Dan," Wilkes said into the cell, his voice loud enough to carry around the lake. "Someone broke into Angie's house. Ransacked the whole place. I don't know who was there at the time, but no one is there now, and there's fresh blood pooled in a few places on the porch. From the looks of it, there was a struggle right at the door."

Wilkes looked concerned, but he didn't seem to be panicking. Lauren leaned closer.

Wilkes listened, then answered, "Angie's fine. I called from her cabin, and she's still at the museum. Thank God she was

running late. I told her to stay at her office until I can get there."
He listened again and added, "I'll meet you at the cabin first."

He listened again, then added, "I agree. If it was just a robbery, there shouldn't have been blood."

Wilkes handed back the phone. "The sheriff said for you to round up your friends and get inside as soon as you find Polly."

The tall cowboy didn't wait around to answer questions.

A crime scene at the lake made no sense, Lauren thought. There had to be an explanation. Maybe a bobcat came down along the canyon. Maybe he killed a cat or dog. Maybe a burglar cut himself trying to break in, but in all the years she'd lived here she'd never heard of a crime happening here.

She looked out over the lake and saw the two tiny beams from the flashlights meeting on the other side. Tim and Reid had made it halfway around the lake and neither had called in.

Where was Polly?

Lauren could sit and wait no longer. She had to move. Take action. Help.

With everyone searching the lake, the only place for Lauren to look was the road toward town. Maybe Polly decided to walk into Crossroads.

It didn't make sense, but then Polly didn't always make sense.

CHAPTER TWENTY-FIVE

Angie

By the time Wilkes picked her up at the museum, Angie was near panic. Not only had someone broken into her cabin, he'd apparently hurt himself. She didn't know whether to be mad or feel sorry for the criminal.

Angie laced her fingers and tried to hold them still in her lap. Wilkes was talking to her as he drove, but she kept asking him to repeat every detail he knew. The burglar had tried breaking the window first, but he couldn't make a big enough opening to climb in, so he kicked down the door. It took him several tries. Wilkes described a half-dozen dents in the door.

"Dan Brigman has called in backup from Bailee," Wilkes said for the third time. "He told me to take my time picking you up so they can check out the crime scene. Want to stop for a malt?"

"No." She sounded frustrated.

"Why not?" he asked.

"My house is a crime scene!" Angie closed her eyes. "How can you think of eating or drinking?"

"I worked through lunch imagining how we'd be ordering

appetizers at a fancy restaurant about this time. Now I know you're okay, I'm hungry." He grinned. "Think about it, honey, what is some burglar going to steal? Your quilts? Your fishing gear? Your food? He must have had the wrong cabin. Once we board the place up, we go eat."

"Right," she said. "I'm sorry about the date. Are you starting to think that maybe we weren't meant to go out? This is the third time we've tried."

"No," he answered. "The night's not over, Angie. It just got off to a bad start. Even if we drop by Dorothy's when this is over, at least we'll be alone and have something to talk about." He hesitated, then admitted, "I want this time between us more than I've wanted anything in a long time."

Wilkes circled around town. When he stopped at the only light, he covered her hands. "It's going to be all right, Angie. I'm right here with you. And before you start arguing, I'm telling you right now, you're sleeping at my place tonight."

"No argument." She almost wished he was inviting her for other reasons and not just because she was in danger. Lifting her chin she forced herself to think logically and not start dreaming of what-ifs.

"Was Doc Holliday at the cabin?"

"I didn't see him, but you know how he hides. Besides, someone wouldn't kick the door in to get Doc."

"They might. I don't have anything of value. Surely they could look in and see that there was nothing worth stealing."

Wilkes agreed with her but that didn't seem to calm her down.

When they got to the cabin, four lawmen were trying to figure out what had happened.

"Anything missing?" the sheriff asked as she looked at piles of broken dishes and mounds of clothes that had been pulled from the closet. "Whoever did this was looking for something. Every drawer and shelf has been swept clean. Even every cup was pulled down from the rack and dropped on the floor."

The place looked just like her parents' little house had a few months ago in Florida. Nothing taken but everything pulled apart.

Angie didn't care about the clothes or the dishes. She walked directly to her bed and coaxed her cat out. "Doc Holliday must have seen it all," she said. "Too bad he can't talk."

She handed the cat to Wilkes and walked around making sure her mother's quilts were all there and that nothing from her father's fishing box, now spilled across the floor, had been taken. The whole scene felt unreal. Someone had pulled the sheets from the bed, and the flipped mattress was sideways, but on her nightstand a book and her pearl earrings were left untouched.

One by one she moved through all her things. Some were broken or bent or wrinkled, but as near as she could tell, everything was there.

Dan took a call, then stepped back into the cabin. "Polly, my daughter's friend, is still missing. She went for a walk about an hour ago. I'm sure she's fine, just doesn't know her way around out here."

One of the deputies from Bailee asked, "What does she look like?"

Dan stared at Angie. "She's about Angie's height. Last time my daughter saw her, she was wearing a sweatshirt and baggy jogging pants. Navy blue." Dan looked straight at Angie. "When I saw her out walking last week, I thought she was you for a moment. One curl of her dyed red hair was sticking out of her hood."

Everyone in the room was silent. They all seemed to come to the same conclusion. Polly might have been kidnapped. Whoever had taken her must have thought she was Angie.

"Impossible," Angie whispered, but deep in her gut she knew it could be true.

Dan moved into action. He hit one number and got the county dispatcher who handled all emergency calls for thirty miles around. "We may have a real emergency, Delynn. Get this down fast. A missing girl, about eighteen, small build, wearing dark sweatpants and a hoodie. May be injured or abducted. Last seen near my house. Call the volunteer fire department. Tell them to knock on every house at the lake. Ask if anyone has seen anything. Have the homeowners search their property and those who aren't able, have the volunteers look."

He was silent for a minute, then shouted, "No, Delynn, this is not a joke. Her name is Polly Peirce. She's been missing over an hour."

He turned to one of the Bailee deputies. "Set up a roadblock at the top of the hill. It may be too late, but I want to know everyone and every car going in or out tonight."

Angie fought back tears. "If Polly was taken, what will happen when they find out she's not me?"

No one answered her question.

Finally, Wilkes put his arm around her. "No one knows about the girl yet, Angie. She could just be sleeping in one of the picnic areas. There are a dozen trails around the lake where she might have headed up before dark and then not known how to get back.

"Right now, I've got to get you somewhere safe. If someone did take Polly thinking she was you, when he figures out Polly is not the woman he came after, he might head this direction."

"I'll call the FBI and let them know their investigation might not be as over as they think it is," said Dan.

"This is how my house in Florida looked the night before I left," Angie whispered. "Someone is still looking for me and I have no idea why." All the reasoning that the things that had happened to her could be a mistake vanished. She was being hunted.

The sheriff nodded at Wilkes. "I've got my hands full here, can you keep her out of harm's way?"

"It's done. I'm taking the back road to my place now. Within thirty minutes there will be an armed guard at every gate into my place."

She couldn't breathe. Not only was she in danger, someone might have been hurt because of her. The world started to spin.

She was barely aware of Wilkes picking her up as if she were a little kid and carrying her out into the night air. "There is nothing we can do here. You're coming home with me."

CHAPTER TWENTY-SIX

Lauren

As Lauren jogged along the road to town, she heard a fire truck siren.

She moved off the road not wanting to attract any attention. A moment later the volunteer fire truck raced past her heading toward the lake.

She thought of turning back, but she was only a few minutes from town. Polly might be at the mini-mart buying the root beer she'd been craving earlier, or she might have walked a few blocks for a malt. Three people were looking for Polly at the lake. Lauren's best chance at being helpful was to search in town.

Lauren walked in a soft carpet of leaves as she approached the lights of Crossroads.

Polly had said she didn't want to be at the party. She must have been upset when Reid showed up. What if she decided to walk into town and hitchhike back to Lubbock? That sounded like something she'd do.

Lauren saw the old Gypsy House in the distance. She weaved

among the trees not wanting to get too close to the house, and hoping to stay far enough away to not be seen by passing cars.

Ever since that horrible night, the place gave her the creeps. Lauren didn't believe in ghosts, but the house seemed to moan into the night. She refused to look toward the house and found herself tiptoeing as if the house might hear her passing.

"This is as good a place as any to stop." An angry voice came from the direction of the house.

Lauren froze. All the stories of ghosts and devil worshippers she'd heard filled her head. Slowly, she turned her head in the direction of the Gypsy House.

"Damn it, woman, be still." The voice came again. Ten, maybe fifteen feet away.

Lauren moved between the trees, inching closer in the midnight darkness.

A man, not the house, was talking, she reminded herself. He must have parked behind the old house so no traffic would see him from the road. She watched as he pulled someone out of the trunk of his car.

The man was big, but the other person was small, a woman. From the way the woman moved awkwardly, Lauren knew that her hands were tied in front of her.

Lauren heard a slap. Then another, harder. The woman's head fell first one way and then the other.

"That should sharpen your memory, girl." The man raised his hand again. "You want a few more? We can do this all night."

The woman shook her head, and Lauren thought she heard the word *no* blend with the wind in the trees.

The man pulled the woman's body up as if straightening a mannequin.

"That's better. If you pass out on me again, I'll leave you in the trunk for the night." He batted at her face as if teasing a wounded animal. "Tell me where it is, Angela, or I swear you'll end up just like your father did."

Lauren inched closer as a slice of moonlight broke through the clouds.

The sight she saw made her shake and she held in a gasp. The man was holding the woman by the front of her shirt. When she didn't answer, he slapped her again and then shook her. "Talk!" he ordered. "Or I swear more than your nose will be bleeding."

The girl didn't say a word. Her body swayed like a rag doll in the man's grip.

Lauren knew she shouldn't be watching this, but she couldn't move. She'd seen the blue sweatshirt. The dark hair tipped with red was all too familiar.

"Stop acting like you've fainted," the man roared as he grabbed his victim's arm and twisted it above her head.

The woman's cry was quickly silenced by a fist slamming against her jaw.

When the woman's body went limp, he began shaking her violently as if he could wake her up. For a blink the hood slipped.

"Polly."

Lauren wasn't aware she'd said the name out loud, but all at once, the man looked around.

"Who's out there?" He shoved a limp Polly toward the car's trunk and took a few steps into the trees.

The moment he loosened his grip on her, Polly seemed to come alive. She jerked away and tumbled against the open door of the trunk.

Lauren panicked. If she answered, she'd be caught like Polly. If she ran, she'd be leaving her friend.

The man took another step trying to see into the shadows.

From behind him, Polly rose with something in her hands.

Lauren opened her mouth to scream, but no sound came out as Polly swung what looked like a bat through the air.

The weapon connected against the side of the man's face. He fell backward, screaming and swearing. Polly just stood three feet from him staring at him.

"Polly!" Lauren rushed forward and grabbed her roommate's hand. "We've got to get out of here!"

It took several steps, but finally Polly was running with Lauren.

The man's yelling and cussing raged behind them like rolling thunder.

"Faster," Lauren said, pulling Polly into the trees on the other side of the road.

"If...he...catches...us..." Polly gulped out a cry.

"He won't." Lauren sounded far more determined than she felt. She pulled Polly down and they rolled under a barbed-wire fence. A few feet later they were on the edge where the canyon dropped down toward the lake. Lauren quickly untied Polly's wrists. The path looked like no more than an incline where water ran off the pasture above.

They slid down the incline to the lake. Branches, left bare of leaves, scratched and tugged at the girls as they worked their way down. Finally, they reached the lake. Hand in hand they ran along the water until they reached the back door of Lauren's lake house.

Even in the low lights of the deck, Lauren could tell Polly's bandaged arm was bleeding, and dark bruises were coloring the side of her face. They ran all the way to Polly's bedroom, damp with sweat even on the cold night.

"Get under the covers," Lauren said softly. "Do you think you'll be all right for a minute until I can get help?"

Polly nodded. Blood began to drip across the white sheets, but she didn't cry. "Thanks for finding me," she whispered.

"Just rest for a minute. I think we're safe now."

Polly's nod was jerky as if adrenaline still bounced through her body. "I'll get Pop. I'll be right back." Lauren stared, trying to take in all that had happened. "You're going to be all right, Polly. You put up one hell of a fight. He must have thought you were Angela, but I don't think he's going to be bothering any-one again for a long time."

Polly pulled the covers around her. A grin brushed across her bloody lips. "Go find Pop. I'll wait."

CHAPTER TWENTY-SEVEN

Angie

Wilkes flew down the dirt road along the back of the dam. He clenched his jaw in concentration and worry. Finally, he turned off on another trail that couldn't even be called a road. Wilkes crossed over an old cattle guard that rattled as if it might fall apart at any moment, but he kept going.

"Before they built the dam, this was the main way into town," Wilkes said without expecting her to comment.

No lights from town glowed in the distance. The night seemed to close in around her. She had to keep reminding herself she was going to safety, not hunting danger.

Wilkes slowed. "We're in the Cottonwood Pasture now. Have to go slow and watch out for cows."

He was silent for a while, then his voice came low and calm. "If you look up ahead, you can see an old oak mixed in with the cottonwoods. It's well over a hundred years old. When all the leaves finally fall, you'll see the thick branches are in the gnarled shape of a fork. That's why we called the ranch Devil's Fork."

Angie knew what he was doing. Trying to calm her. Trying to get her mind off what had happened at the cabin.

"Uncle Vern says that when he was a boy, he knew of several trees around the area that were bent or twisted in strange shapes. He said some of the Plains tribes used them as signposts pointing the way to go. Tribes were nomadic, traveling by the seasons to different camps or to follow the herds of buffalo."

Angie didn't want to talk, but she had wondered how on such flat land people could tell directions. On cloudy days it would be hard with no ocean or mountain range, or even hills for as far as a man could see.

She saw the light of his headquarters in the distance.

Doc meowed from the backseat.

"You remembered Doc." She smiled at Wilkes. In all the excitement, she'd forgotten about the cat.

"I put him back there while you were looking around your cabin. Figured you wouldn't be staying there tonight, no matter what. When I told Doc he was going back to visit his friends in the barn, he got real excited."

"We'd better keep him in your house. He might run off."

"He didn't run off last time. He was hiding in the barn." Wilkes met her stare. "Besides, when he sleeps in the house, he wants to share my pillow, and a cat is not who I'm willing to share it with."

As they pulled into the circle of lights around the house, she saw something in his eyes. A need. A longing like she'd never seen before when a man looked at her. "Are you saying I'm overprotective of Doc?" she managed to ask even though she knew the cat was not on his mind.

"Maybe," he said as he turned his attention back to parking.

She watched his profile and told herself she'd imagined the way he'd looked at her. Wilkes was probably right about letting Doc out of the house, though.

Angie came from a long family of people who were overprotective. But the world seemed a frightening place. She never rode her bike alone. By the time she could date, she was afraid to go out with boys. Even her aunts always had her call when she left the campus, so they could time her drive home.

Wilkes pulled the car under the pergola attached to his house and walked around to open her door. She slid out just as he neared.

"You want something to eat or drink?" he offered.

She shook her head. "Can we wait out here until the sheriff calls?"

He motioned to an old swing in the corner of the porch. "If I turn off the yard light, we can watch the stars." While she settled in on the swing, he went inside and grabbed an afghan.

When he sat down beside her, he opened his arms and she cuddled in next to him. It felt so right to be here with him. She felt so protected.

"Angie, I know I was a little early tonight, but why were you still at the museum? I thought we agreed I'd pick you up at the cabin?"

"I would have been there, but I got a call asking if I wouldn't mind holding the museum open a few minutes later than usual. A man said he wanted to show his wife a picture of his relatives on the Pioneer Wall. I thought it odd, but since the volunteers offered to stay late with me, I agreed. We'd already waited over thirty minutes when you called me from the cabin phone."

Wilkes was silent for a while, using one boot to rock them both in the swing. The slight tapping sound and the gentle swaying were like the steady beat of a heart, calming her.

"Maybe whoever called asking you to stay open late was the same person who ransacked your place. That way he'd know he had extra time, and he knew where you were."

"But why? I've already given that agent, Dodson, my father's ledger. He said it would be helpful in the investigation and that was why someone was stalking me. He said that I would be safe now."

Wilkes tugged her to him. "Go over everything you brought

with you. There must be something you have that is worth committing a crime to get."

Resting her head on his chest, she began. "My mother's quilts, most of which are old. One set of dishes plus coffee cups I'd collected over the years. My father's fishing equipment almost too old to use. A pair of pearl earrings I got for graduation. A necklace that is a replica of an old Greek coin. My clothes. Books I've kept and loved. My mother's sewing machine, a featherweight Singer." She looked up at him. "I can sew, you know."

"I never doubted it," he answered with a funny smile as if she'd told a joke.

"Where is the sewing machine?" Wilkes asked.

"I saw it still in the corner of my bedroom."

"Where is the necklace?"

"I left it in my desk at work. It sometimes gets in my way when I'm leaning over my desk doing detailed work." She sighed. "That's all except the food in the fridge. I didn't have much to pack when I left my parents' home. I tried to leave as soon as possible." She couldn't tell him why. He'd think her a coward, for running away from home, afraid of her own shadow. Afraid of what truth she might find if she looked too deeply.

Angie's phone rang. "Hello," she answered tentatively.

"Angela, it's Dan Brigman." The sheriff's voice came through so loud she had no doubt Wilkes could also hear. "We found Polly. She's safe. You guys all right?"

"We're fine." Angie let out a long breath of relief. "What happened to her?"

"How about I fill you in tomorrow? I've got my hands full right now. Tell Wilkes to keep close to you and stay armed until we catch whoever got into your place tonight."

"Will do," Wilkes answered. His head touched hers as he listened.

The sheriff rang off, and Angie smiled. "The girl's safe. I'd love to know what happened."

"I would say call the Franklin sisters, but they'd blow the

story up so much, you wouldn't recognize the truth. I'm guessing she just fell asleep in one of the deck chairs. We'll hear all about it tomorrow."

"What about the blood at my place?"

"From the looks of it, the burglar was an amateur. I'm guessing the blood was his."

Wilkes rocked back and let the swing fly. "You know, all I was hoping for was a dinner with you alone. No excitement. Just you and me. At this rate, we'll be into middle age before we go out to dinner alone."

Angie raised her head. "Where's Uncle Vern?"

"He's sleeping over at the Kirkland bunkhouse. Carter Mayes, Jake Longbow and he are heading out at dawn to find an old rock corral, and from there they plan to search for Carter's cave. They shouldn't get into too much trouble, since they're taking a four-wheeler. If I know Kirkland, he'll make sure Jake has everything he needs to take care of all three old guys."

"Wilkes," Angie whispered. "We are alone. I'll go pack that basket you've got stashed above the cabinets, and we can have a midnight dinner anywhere on this place. Alone. If only for a short time, I need to feel normal."

"Aren't you tired?"

"No, I'm still keyed up. I'm tired of waiting to be alone with you."

By the time she made their picnic, he'd spread blankets in the loft and set up hanging lights that made the barn look almost romantic.

"I decided if Doc Holliday loved it out here, we might give it a try." He took the basket and climbed up far enough to lift it into the loft. Then he retraced his steps down the ladder and stood close behind her as she climbed up. His arms braced her on either side of the ladder. "I like how you feel," he whispered as they reached the top. "I think I have since that first day in the museum when you attacked me."

She had no idea how to answer. She simply ignored his words

and tried not to notice the way his hand rested lightly on her waist as he guided her to her place on the blanket.

They used the picnic basket as their table to eat what he claimed was the best meal in the world. Cheese, crackers, grapes and cold slices of brisket she'd put between leftover breakfast biscuits. She'd even thought of paper cups and wine.

They talked and laughed as they ate. He told her of life out here where they seemed to be the only two people in the world. He loved the ranch and was proud of all he'd done in the years he'd been running the place. His love for history surprised her when she talked of the museum.

Doc pestered them out of all the scraps, then curled up on the corner of the blanket when only wine was left.

Angie couldn't stop smiling. This was the most romantic time in her life. Wilkes was unlike any man she'd ever met. Strong and good with a stubborn streak that made him believe he lived in the best place in the world.

She couldn't stop touching him. First his arm as they talked. She liked stroking her fingers over the muscles just below the cotton of his shirt. Then she moved to his jaw, running featherlight fingertips over his whiskers.

When she laid her hand against his heart, he stopped pretending he didn't notice her touch.

When the moon was high, Wilkes floated another blanket over them both, and they sat in the opening of the barn's loft to watch the stars. Her hand rested on his back and his arm warmed her shoulders.

They might not be talking as much, but they were learning more and more about each other. She loved the feel of him near. The way he smelled of fresh air. The way he leaned his face against her curls and breathed deep as if taking her in.

Wilkes held her close and moved his hand along her side, almost touching her breast, almost brushing over her hip. "You're so beautiful, Angie."

"No, I'm not," she whispered. "You don't have to say that

just to make me feel better. I've never been beautiful or sexy or any of that stuff. The few men I've dated said I was *cute* or *nice*, but never beautiful. My father always said I should be practical, never lift my head in the clouds. That kind of thing is not for girls like me." She knew she was rambling, but she couldn't stop. "And don't look at me like you did earlier in the car. Like you were longing for me or hungry to touch me."

Wilkes laughed. "Shut up, Angie, and kiss me."

She lifted her chin. "All right. I will, but not because you said it. I was already thinking about kissing you anyway."

She leaned in to him and kissed him. A quick kiss just to prove that she was doing it because she wanted to and not because he told her to.

He waited, just staring at her, after she broke the kiss. "You're wrong, Angie. You are beautiful, and I do want you."

Shaking her head, she whispered, "Men like you aren't interested in women like me."

Putting his big hand around the back of her neck, he pulled her to him and began brushing the curls that had come loose from her bun long ago. "Men like me want a woman who is real. A gentle kind of beauty that no amount of makeup can cover or improve." His thumb moved up and brushed the line of her jaw. "You're wrong. There is something very sexy about you."

His hand moved over her shoulder and along her arm. "I love touching you. I can feel every cell in your body react to my touch." He lifted her hand and kissed her palm. "When Lexie kissed me the other night, it was like I finally woke up. I couldn't push her away fast enough. I knew she wasn't what I wanted. If I kissed her every day for the rest of my life, it wouldn't have made me feel like I felt when you kissed me."

Angie had all she could take. She didn't know if she believed this handsome man or not, but for once in her life she didn't want to protect her heart. "Shut up, Wilkes, and kiss me again like you did the other night."

And he did.

He kissed her long and tenderly in the cool shadows of the barn and again on the porch.

He kissed her like no one had ever kissed her. He kissed her better and deeper than she'd even imagined in her wildest dreams.

"It's late," he finally whispered. "I have to let you rest."

"One more," she answered, knowing one more would never be enough.

He leaned her against the door and pressed close. "One last kiss."

But he lied. They made it halfway down the hallway to her room before he pulled her against him and lost control once more.

When she finally pulled away, he took her hand and walked her to her room. "If I touch you again, I won't be able to leave and you need rest." Then without a word, he handed her one of his shirts to sleep in and walked away.

Angie closed the door and leaned against it smiling. She knew he would have stayed with her if she'd invited him, but she needed to treasure tonight for a while. Her body could feel his hands still moving over her. He hadn't tried to take off any of her clothes, but he'd let her know how much he loved touching her. She could feel his strong fingers moving over her hip with a need to pull her closer that shocked and surprised her. Boldly he'd pressed his hand over her breast and circled just below her waist as if promising her there would be a time and a place for more: bolder caresses, longer kisses, deeper loving.

He was waking her to desire. After the heat of his body, she was left cold when she stepped away. She wanted to return to his arms and never run again.

He hadn't tried to talk her into anything. He'd simply shown her how he felt about her.

Standing behind the door, Angie knew she couldn't move. If she did, she'd be running down the hallway to his room, begging him to hold her for just a little longer.

The words he'd whispered seemed to move through her, warming her blood. "I love touching you," he'd whispered over and over. "I love the feel of you. I love the fire in your eyes when I do this."

As she remembered every word, she could almost feel him pressing against her as his hands moved from her hair all the way down her back. He made no effort to hide his need for her, but he never pushed for more than she willingly gave.

And when he'd kissed her at the door, he'd whispered, "Thanks for letting me know perfection."

He'd said it as if she'd given him a gift and not the other way around. She'd started to argue, and he'd closed his mouth over hers and given her one last long kiss. This time, he'd held her away. Only the kiss. Nothing more. As if one more brush of her body to his would have been more than he could bear.

More than he could resist.

CHAPTER TWENTY-EIGHT

Lauren

The first light of day broke slowly from the east, stealing away at the darkness where Polly and Lauren had hidden all night in the corner of Lauren's father's deck. They'd wrapped up in a sleeping bag after Dan had one of the firemen rebandage Polly's arm and doctor her split lip.

"My body feels as if I fought a long battle during the night, and I'm now so battered and sore I can't straighten," Polly whispered with little more than her nose poking out from the zipped-up bag.

Lauren was too tired to open her eyes. "You're all right, Polly. Just a few bruises. That's what happens when you fight with a burglar in the dark." Lauren giggled. "I bet he's feeling worse this morning than you are. He's got the imprint of a tire iron across his face."

"You think I killed him? He could have bled to death."

Lauren opened one eye and saw solid bruises along Polly's jaw. "No. He was cussing too loud. And he still had enough brains to drive away before Pop got out there. You, on the other hand, don't look so good."

"Thanks for reminding me. I'm fine, by the way. It wasn't my first fight."

"Why'd you leave the party? Upset about Reid or just bored?"

Polly swore. "I'm not as messed up as you and Tim think. I swear. Not usually anyway. Last night, after seeing Reid again, maybe I was frustrated. He was so nice to me. When we met before, I thought he was so hot and last night I wondered why. Not my type."

"Not mine, either." Lauren giggled. "Reminds me of something I heard Miss Butterfield say about his dad once. She said if he could buy himself for what he was worth and sell himself for what he thought he was worth, he'd make a million."

Polly groaned. "My head hurts too much to even think about that."

Lauren sat up so she could see Polly's face. "I told you last night he's not worth thinking about."

"So if he's a jerk, why did you go out with him? Tim told me Reid was your date to homecoming."

"I don't know." Lauren was too tired to remember. "My brain is as foggy as yours."

Compared to all Polly went through last night, a date with Reid seemed pretty minor. "Tell me again what happened last night after you left the party."

"I already told your dad twice."

"Then tell me," Tim said as he bounced onto the deck. "You were being patched up by some big fireman before I knew you'd been found. The sheriff told me to go home before he booked me for trespassing."

Lauren looked at Tim. "What are you doing here? Dad's right. Don't you have a home?"

Tim glared at her. "Anybody ever tell you that you sound just like your old man? I woke up early and decided to come over to check on both of you. I didn't know when you two would be up, but I wanted to be here when you woke. I've got a few questions. Like why are you two sleeping on the deck, for one?"

Polly sat up. The moment she moved her arm, she winced in pain.

Lauren gave up on any attempt at sleep. "I'm here because Polly couldn't sleep in her bed. I had her curl up there while I called Pop. It's got blood all over it and we were too tired to try to find sheets."

Tim sat down between their chairs. "Okay, why was she bleeding?"

"The guy who tried to kidnap her twisted her arm and pulled out several stitches. The fireman butterflied them together but it took him a while to stop her nose from dripping red. We couldn't both fit on the couch, so we collected the sleeping bags and came out here so we couldn't hear Pop talking on the phone. Evidently he was up most of the night."

Tim looked at Polly. "Hanging out with you is like visiting the set of *The Texas Chainsaw Massacre*. Blood seems to be everywhere."

"Last night I was starting to think I was in a horror movie. You're not going to believe what happened." Polly showed him her new bandage and her split lip. He could see the bruises without any help.

Tim pulled his chair closer to her and said, "Tell me the details, Polly Anna."

She shrugged. "I got tired of the party and took a walk."

"What was your state of mind?" Tim asked as if suddenly the psychiatrist in the group.

"I was down. Thinking of jumping in the lake and forgetting to come up. I'm a total screwup. My arm hurt and I couldn't find anything to drink around this place. Bad night all around." She glanced at Lauren and they both laughed at Tim's shocked face.

Tim interrupted their giggling. "Okay, forget your state of mind. Tell us what happened."

Polly glared at him. "All right, CliffsNotes. About the time

I got close to that cabin hidden in the woods, I heard banging. So I took a walk down the road and saw this guy kicking the crap out of the door. But he wasn't very good. He had on dress shoes and a suit. One sleeve of his jacket was all ripped from where he must have tried to knock out the glass in the window beside the door. It was too thick and all he'd accomplished was a mess of elbow-size holes.

"I should have run, but instead I yelled, 'What do you think you're doing?'" She glanced at Lauren. "I thought he'd run or explain what was going on. That's what they do in movies. But this guy turns around and takes off after me. I make it about twenty or thirty feet before he tackles me. He starts beating on me like I'm a punching bag and asking questions I had no answers to. When he figured out I wasn't telling him anything, he started dragging me toward his car."

Tim and Lauren were now on either side of her listening to every word.

Polly smiled, loving the attention. "I had a feeling this guy was going to kill me. I don't have much reason to live, but I'd be damned before I let this thug take my lousy life away from me. He was dragging me by one leg and complaining about how I was way too much trouble."

Polly leaned back in the deck chair. "I must have passed out, because when I woke up, I was in total darkness. It didn't take me long to figure out I was in the trunk of a car. We drove around awhile. Pop says he was probably trying to figure out how to get out of the lake community without going past the sheriff's house.

"When he stopped and opened the trunk of his Mercury, I think his plan was to keep beating on me until I told him what he wanted to know."

She giggled. "When Lauren saw us, she yelled my name." Polly looked at Lauren. "Great strategy by the way. While he was distracted, I hit him with the first thing I found in the trunk. I think I caught him in the eye and nose. Blood went off like an automatic sprinkler on full power.

"Next thing I know, Lauren grabbed my hand and we were off running. When we made it back here, the sheriff took over. He's probably still out looking for the guy."

"Shouldn't you two be all locked up in the house?"

"Pop said the safest place in the area is here at the lake. The volunteer fire department woke up the whole community. The deputies from Bailee have a roadblock at the entrance and are checking every car."

Polly agreed. "When we first came out, we watched all the lights coming and going. Then I dozed off knowing Lauren would watch over me."

Lauren shrugged. "It appears to be my job."

She leaned close to Tim. "Can you take over for a while? I need to make a call."

She went to the kitchen and dialed Lucas. When she got his voice mail, she whispered, "Sorry I didn't return your calls. Can we go back to being friends?"

The machine beeped and she closed her phone.

CHAPTER TWENTY-NINE

Angie

Angie woke to the silence of the country. She'd spent most of the night reliving every moment in the barn with Wilkes. Despite all the trouble, the late picnic dinner was a memory she'd cherish. Wilkes made her feel beautiful.

It was after nine when she made it to the kitchen. Wilkes probably had finished breakfast hours ago and was working in his study. She tiptoed past his door, not wanting to disturb him.

"Morning, beautiful." He swiveled around and smiled.

"Morning."

"Make yourself at home in the kitchen. I'll be finished in a minute, then I'll drive you to work." He turned back to his computer.

He was polite during the drive, but the magic of the night before was gone. They talked of the weather and what she had planned for the day, but he didn't touch her.

Once they got to the museum, he set up a guard station on the second floor of the museum so he could see both her office and the front door. Several of the ladies auxiliary were in the foyer trying to make up their minds on which quilt should go where and what each card should say beside the quilt.

Angie knew she couldn't say a word to Wilkes without it drifting down to the ladies, so she worked in her office. She usually left at noon on Saturdays, but today she wasn't sure where to go. If the police were finished looking around her cabin, she probably should go home and start the cleanup.

Absently, she twisted the necklace her father had given her in her hand. He'd told her to take care of it because no matter what happened in life, it would remind her of her mother and him. She did remember her mother wearing the original coin now and then, before they knew how valuable it was.

Having it appraised had probably started the feud between her uncle and father. Her uncle thought it should belong to the family, but her father wouldn't turn loose of it. Finally, they'd agreed to display it in the store and sell replicas of it.

The day her father placed it in the case, he seemed to say goodbye to the one thing he'd inherited. He never went by to look at it again that she knew about.

Angie stood and placed her copy of the necklace in the old safe at the back of her office. Her one memory of both her father and her mother belonged on a shelf with an old book of the canyon and the bloodstone. The quilts and the fishing gear wouldn't last forever, but she could pass this down if she ever had a son or daughter.

She pulled the safe almost closed and cried, really cried, for the loss of her parents for the first time. It was no wonder she had trouble knowing what was real or fake about people. Her one treasure from her parents was a fake necklace.

Moving to the window, she tried to get control once more. The beauty of the canyon always calmed her nerves. With each passing day, the feeling of belonging here in this wild land grew inside her.

She didn't turn as she heard Wilkes walk into her office.

His warm hand slid along her waist. "You all right, Angie?"

I'm fine," she answered, loving the way she could feel the warmth of him even though he was an inch away. Of course he'd heard her crying in the silence of the museum. And he'd come to comfort her.

His chin rested atop her hair as he stood behind her, pulling her gently back against his chest. "I know you don't believe it, but all this mess with the stalker will end. He'll either give up looking or we'll catch him."

Leaning into him, she agreed. "I have nothing of value. He's bound to give up soon."

Wilkes kissed her temple. "I don't know about you, but I'm holding something in my arms that I consider of great value. There is a kindness in you, Angie, that amazes me. A loving way that silently pulls me to you."

They heard footsteps coming up the stairs. For a moment he held her tighter as if not willing to let her go, then he stepped away as one of the volunteers hurried in.

As she helped Miss Bees with her question, she looked up to see Wilkes in the doorway. He stared at her and for a blink she read something new in his gaze. She'd seen anger, and desire, but this was different.

Just for a moment Angie saw love.

Wilkes spent the afternoon in the museum hallway staring at a journal he'd opened hours ago and had yet to read a page. What in the hell did he think he was doing? He should have never kissed or touched Angie like that last night. She wasn't some girl he picked up at the Two Step. He had no plans for his future. She was definitely a woman who wanted to grow roots and he had no idea if he'd be any good at long-term loving.

He stared at the book remembering the way she'd fit so well beside him as they leaned back on the hay and watched the stars. It had been cold, and he'd told himself the first time he touched her that he was simply keeping her warm. But she felt so good in his arms, and when she kissed him just because he told her to, he lost any sense of reason.

She did look beautiful. He hadn't lied about that. He could so get lost in those big eyes of hers. He loved the feel of her against him and the way she reacted when he touched her. It took him a while, but he finally figured out she wasn't afraid of him. The feelings he was making her realize were frightening her.

He loved waking her up to passion. Each time they kissed, it was a fraction deeper, a little more. He could never remember feeling so alive. When he'd moved his hands over her hips, she stopped breathing for a moment. He froze, until he saw her slow smile and he knew he'd done something right… No, not just right, something prefect.

Later, when he pressed his full palm over her breast, she'd let out a little cry. When he pushed harder against her sensitive flesh, she'd gulped for air and the desire to do the same thing without clothes pounded in his whole body.

But he didn't go too far. He'd kept control, he told himself. Only now he knew he'd gone too far for his own sanity. She deserved more than a man without a heart.

He'd been awake all night thinking about her. The way she'd known how to help Yancy. The way she worried about Uncle Vern. How all the volunteers loved her. She'd become one of the town.

Wilkes stood up from his makeshift guard post and began to walk around the museum, wondering how he'd be able to beat himself to a pulp if he hurt Angie. And of course, he'd hurt her. That's what he'd done to every woman since Lexie.

Never get too close. Never care. And if they started to care about him, Wilkes walked away.

Only this time, when he walked away, he had a feeling they'd both be hurting.

What had he done?

CHAPTER THIRTY

Carter

The canyon had a haze to it Saturday morning that Carter had never quite seen before. So beautiful, as it had been when he'd camped out by an open fire as a boy.

The air smelled of fall. The coffee in his tin cup tasted better than any cup he'd paid five dollars for in Dallas.

At times like this, where there were no mirrors or other people around to remind him of how old he was, Carter straightened tall, thinking himself still a young man. Inside he remained the soldier who went to war, and the father who carried his daughters on his shoulders and the husband who'd given one woman all his love and a lifetime of laughter.

He took a deep breath and realized how lucky he was.

This trip down into the canyon would be his last until next spring. And, for the first time since he'd gone down with his father, he wouldn't be going alone. Jake Longbow and Vern Wagner were with him.

Jake had been up before dawn checking out the four-wheeler. Vern was frying up a dozen eggs. He'd dunked biscuits popped from a can into butter and cooked them in a Dutch oven. Not exactly the way cowboys of old did, but they'd taste great when they browned.

"Grub's ready," Vern yelled as if the camp held a hundred cowhands. Jake and Carter gathered round to fill their plates and sit in canvas folding chairs with holders on the arms for their coffee cups.

They'd found the rock corral last night before dark. While Vern made camp, Jake and Carter had circled around and found what could have been a road at one time. It was overgrown, but the ruts in the earth were still barely there. Then, just before dark, they spotted what looked like a trail leading down into the canyon. With their walking sticks, they figured it would be easy going.

It was all Carter could do to keep from heading down right that minute, but Jake said they'd go at full daylight.

Now Carter had to fight to stay still and eat breakfast. He knew the canyon wouldn't be safe this early. They needed full light to see every step. But he was close. He could almost feel the stick figures near. They were waiting for him.

"Tell us again, everything you remember," Jake said.

That was no problem, since Carter had gone over it in his head a million times. "We parked off the road by a pile of rocks that looked like they'd been stacked up into a square. Dad walked along the edge of the top of the canyon until he found a path going down. The plan was to climb down and make camp. Then he'd drink and I'd run around. But about the time we found a site for the camp, it started raining. My dad knew it would be dangerous climbing back up, so after we were soaked to the bone, he noticed a cave. The opening was long and narrow, just about right for a man to pass through.

"Dad built a small fire from branches and leaves that had blown into the opening. I think he must have passed out then. I took the only flashlight we had and went exploring. I slipped on wet rocks and the flashlight rolled. When it stopped, the light was pointing high on the wall. I saw these figures painted in white. Stick men with round heads and hollow eyes."

Vern lifted an old pack that looked as though it had made it through at least one war. He stuffed it with water, then he finished off the eggs left in the skillet.

Jake's pack looked new. It had the Double K brand on the flap. He packed flashlights and an emergency med kit. He also left most of his eggs for Watson.

Carter lifted his pack loaded with fruit and pulled out the map. "Now it's light enough, let's go over our route one more time." Carter always marked his route and tried to follow it. Over the years he'd been lost a few times down in the canyon. He didn't want that to happen today.

Finally, three old warriors stood as Carter whistled for Watson. The dog bounded out of the trees ready for an adventure.

They took the four-wheeler to the canyon edge. Jake planted an orange flag so they could see where the four-wheeler was even from the canyon floor.

One by one they started down. Stopping often to study the walls and outcroppings where a cave might be. Carter remained in the lead. He might be moving slower than usual, but he now had three sets of eyes watching. If his cave was down this path, there was a good chance they'd find it today.

The old familiar excitement he always felt ran through his veins and whispered that maybe today would be the end of his quest.

Carter guessed they were probably moving at half the pace a younger man and his son might have moved, maybe even less. If this was the spot where they'd climbed down almost seventy years ago, the wind and rain may have changed it, but only slightly. These canyon walls had been here for thousands and thousands of years.

A rock slide could have covered the opening of the cave. The water could have eroded the opening making it wider. But some hint of what had been here might still show.

Step by step they moved down into the canyon. What looked like an animal trail was still visible, but rocks the size of bowling balls blocked the path now and then.

Jake spotted a rattler curled on a rock five feet from the path. The snake seemed to be enjoying the last warm day. They left him alone and moved on down.

Two hours into the descent, Carter spotted a clearing big enough to pitch a tent. That's where his father would have picked for a campsite. Only that day seventy years ago, the rain had started before they'd reached the site or pitched a tent. They had been too far down to climb back up, and there was great danger if they stayed on the path.

Carter felt his heart pounding, remembering how frightened he'd been. What if this was it? He and his father must have made it to about this spot.

"Let's stop here." Carter raised his hand. "We can rest and study the walls."

Vern and Jake lowered their packs, but Carter stood impatiently.

He was too excited to rest. For once, after all the years of searching, this spot felt right. He took one more step and then another. Three more, and he saw what he thought was a shadow on the rocks.

For a moment he just stared, then he made out the opening not much taller than a man.

"I think I found something," he yelled and the other two joined him.

All three stared. Maybe thirty feet off the path, hidden from three sides by rock overhangs, was an opening to a cave. Exactly as Carter remembered it.

The men moved slowly toward it. Vern stumbled once over a rock, but he caught himself with his hand. He left a bloody print, but he didn't stop. He simply pulled the bandanna from his back pocket and wrapped the hand.

When they were three feet away, Vern and Jake stopped.

Carter glanced back at them.

Jake spoke first. "Go on in, Carter. This is your quest. You should be the one to see it first."

Vern nodded his agreement. "We'll give you time to walk in and say hello to your friends, if the stick men are there. When you're reacquainted, if you've no objections, Jake and I would like to be introduced."

Carter clicked on a flashlight and started in. He was a little boy again, afraid of the dark, afraid of what he might find in the cave.

Two feet inside, the air turned cold, and he heard the wind whistling through the cave and swore there was almost a melody to the sound. He could hear water dripping off the ceiling of the cave one drop at a time and knew if he caught a drop, it would be cold in his hand.

He carefully took one step after another. His heart pounded so loud he had no doubt his friends could hear it outside the cave.

Deeper and deeper he moved into the darkness until he saw no light from the opening. There was a stillness here. As if all the world had vanished.

No turning back now.

He raised his flashlight knowing the stick men were waiting for him with their big heads and hollow eyes.

And they were.

CHAPTER THIRTY-ONE

Carter

"We need to be starting back," Vern called to Jake and his voice echoed through the cave.

Carter knew his friends were at the opening of the cave waiting for him. They'd walked inside and stared at the stick men, then they'd left, giving Carter time alone.

Carter wasn't sure if he'd stayed an hour longer or more. But he didn't want to leave. He couldn't stop staring at the stick figures for which he'd searched for so long.

All the years he'd thought about this place. All the summers he'd walked over the canyon looking. How could he turn away from the drawings on the walls? They were exactly as they'd been seventy years ago when he'd first stumbled upon them. Still watching him with their hollow eyes.

Carter felt his heart slow. He could die happy now. Right here in the cave where he'd finished his quest. Maybe Vern and Jake would leave him here with the stick men? That would be all right.

He let his breathing grow shallow. This was a great day to

die. He'd done what he set out to do more than ten years ago. He'd found the cave. Bethie would understand if he didn't go back to Granbury to be buried next to her.

He thought of his daughters with their own lives. They'd miss him, but it was nature's way that they'd outlive him. When they heard he was dead, they'd hold their children tight and cry.

Slowly, he leaned back on the cool rock floor and took one last breath. As he closed his eyes, he imagined the stick men moving closer, watching over him now, knowing that he'd be joining them in the forever world where time had no meaning.

His finger twitched and turned off the flashlight. He didn't need to see now. He knew where he was and that he was not alone.

One more breath. One more thought and then he'd let go of this world.

Only, thoughts flooded in all wanting to be the last in his brain. The war when he'd seen his friends die. The first time he made love to Bethie and neither of them knew what they were doing. The sight of her nursing their first daughter. The day he walked his youngest down the aisle. The moment he knew Bethie no longer held his hand even though her fingers were still entwined in his. Last winter when his three-year-old grand-daughter asked him if she could be a monkey when she grew up.

One more breath. More memories came. The day he killed a man in battle. The night he thought of killing his middle daughter's husband. The pain of watching his children move away on their own and the joy of realizing he and Bethie had the house to themselves.

One more breath. A hundred more memories.

Carter could hear his two friends talking somewhere beyond the blackness. He knew the stick men were watching him in the dark with their empty eyes.

"It is time to let go," he whispered, almost expecting the painted men to answer.

Silence. Then one drop of water plunked on the floor of the

cave. Far into a dark corner of the cave he heard the wind whistling. Another drop fell.

Slowly, Carter sat up, feeling near his leg for the flashlight. One tired muscle at a time he straightened. Turned on the light and stood.

He took one deep breath taking in the cold damp air as though it was pure oxygen.

One step at a time he moved toward the opening. Just as he saw the afternoon light shining at the entrance, he turned for one last look at the stick figures. He'd have all winter to remember them.

"You about ready, Carter?" Vern Wagner asked. "Looks like we got bad weather coming in. Clouds boiling like they're about to spill over."

Carter moved closer so he didn't have to shout. "I thought about dying back in that cave. Figured I was ready."

Both men were old enough to understand.

"Why didn't you?" Jake asked.

"I almost did. Got down to my last breath a few times, then memories started pestering me. I got this son-in-law who needs straightening out now and then. I got one granddaughter who wants to be a monkey and there is no telling what the two wild ones who live under the table have torn up since I've been gone. I still got things that need doing. Plus, when I do lie down for good, I think I'd like it to be next to Bethie."

The men moved out into the daylight. Vern took the lead this time as they headed up.

Carter was last, taking one more look at the entrance. He couldn't stop smiling as he caught up with the other two. "I always thought the stick figures were waiting for me," he told Vern and Jake as they moved one step at a time like a rusty old cog train rolling up a steep incline. "It had crossed my mind that they could have taken my soul that night when I was a boy and they were still waiting for me to come back."

He squinted at the sky. "But it turns out, they didn't want me."

"I'm glad," Jake yelled down from a few feet farther along the trail. "I wasn't looking forward to having to drag your dead body back up."

"Me, either," Vern voted. "How about we climb out of this canyon and head over to the Two Step for a few beers?"

Carter grumbled. "All right, but no Mexican food. I was up half the night last Sunday after eating one tamale."

"No salt for me," Jake said.

Vern swore. "You guys are no fun. How about we forget the beer and pick up a few younger ladies?"

Jake nodded at the idea, then frowned. "The only two women I know younger than us and unmarried are the Franklin sisters, and I doubt all three of us could lift one of them."

They laughed as they climbed out of the canyon.

Carter couldn't quit smiling. Maybe the adventure in life wasn't over for him yet.

CHAPTER THIRTY-TWO

Lauren

Sunday passed at the lake, and no one suggested going back to school until almost dark. Lauren and Polly had a great day doing nothing. Tim worked on Polly's homework and Pop slept in his favorite chair.

He'd been up the past two nights trying to find the guy who had hurt Polly and probably broken into Angie's cabin. A man with a tire-iron mark across his face shouldn't be that hard to find, but the guy seemed to have vanished.

Lauren knew her father. He wouldn't stop looking until he found him.

Polly took a morning nap. They all took afternoon naps. Now she knew if she didn't start the gang moving toward the Jeep they'd all be asleep by sundown.

Pop hugged everyone, including Tim. Lauren didn't miss the fact that Tim hugged Polly goodbye as if she wasn't riding back with them to Tech.

A few hours and several stops later, they made it back to the dorm.

Tim waved good-night and walked away saying, "Thanks for the restful weekend, L. Remind me next time not to go if you've got something planned. I don't think my heart could take any more excitement."

She laughed.

After tucking Polly into bed she decided to go for a walk. Lauren loved the campus on cold nights. Fog was in the air and all the lights that outlined the buildings seemed fuzzy. The campus was a bubble all on its own. She had the feeling that no matter where she lived in her life, she'd always miss this magic world. Beautiful. Alive. Haunting. College was like a spaceship slowly drifting, constantly moving you from one world to another.

The fear she'd felt when she'd seen Polly being beaten was still with her. The knowledge of seeing violence and fearing she couldn't help, still lingered. The need to find some way to make the world safer grew inside her.

Her father must have seen far more. That might explain why he couldn't leave his job. Lauren remembered hearing her mother say once that if Pop had just quit his job he could have moved to Dallas and done something where he didn't have to carry a gun. Margaret didn't understand him at all, but after seeing Polly being beaten, Lauren thought she did. His job wasn't just fighting the bad guys, it was helping those who couldn't protect themselves.

She'd done it again, she realized. She'd grown all at once. She wasn't the same person she'd been Friday when they'd left the dorm.

Lauren realized she was changing in the two months she'd been in this world, in this bubble. She knew she could never go back to looking at things as she had before.

Walking along the lighted paths through the campus, Lauren wished she could talk to Lucas. He must have known she'd change and grow. Maybe he was simply waiting to see how she turned out.

As she circled back toward the dorm, she saw him standing

outside the main door. His collar was up and his hands were shoved deep in his pockets. He looked as though he'd been waiting for a while.

"Lucas," she said. "How'd you know I was here?"

Lucas studied her. "I went by your dad's house. He said you'd left an hour earlier." He couldn't seem to stop staring at her. "I should have called earlier today. I thought we might ride back together."

"I rode back with Tim and Polly."

"I figured that. You all right?"

She wasn't surprised he knew about the trouble at the lake. "You probably know more about what happened than I do."

"You want to go somewhere and talk about it?"

She hesitated. "No."

They just stood looking at each other. The night he'd kissed her seemed a million years ago. "I don't want to talk about the trouble at the lake, but I'll go somewhere if you're offering food."

Lucas smiled. "I'm offering."

She laced her arm in his and they walked to his pickup. For three hours they talked of nothing and everything.

When he walked her back to the spot where he'd picked her up, he said, "Lauren, you've changed."

"I know and I'll probably change again and again and again. I can't stay that frightened high school girl you saved in the old Gypsy House almost three years ago. If you're going to be my friend, you have to be in through the changes, Lucas."

"I think I'd like that."

She realized she was stronger than she ever thought she was. "If you're my friend, you won't run just because we kiss." This was it, the moment where he made up his mind. He was no longer in control. He'd take her as an equal or nothing.

"Fair enough." He faced her as he always did, straight on. "But, Lauren, someday I'm going to have to admit that I don't want to be just your friend. I want to be more, a great deal more."

"Fair enough," she said as she kissed his cheek, then turned and walked to the dorm.

CHAPTER THIRTY-THREE

Angie

Three weeks passed without any hint of the man who'd broken into her cabin and later kidnapped Polly. He seemed to have disappeared completely. Angie went back to work and cleaned up the cabin on her lunch breaks, but after dark every night, she always decided to spend just one more night with Wilkes, vowing it would be the last one.

Every morning she'd plan to go home after work and not spend another night at his place, but something always seemed to come up. First she had to wait until she had time to buy new dishes, then Vern came down with a bad cold and she felt she should stay on and watch over him. Then there were dinners with friends and Wilkes wanting to teach her to ride.

She became aware of how hard Wilkes worked. Since he had to watch over her, she knew he was working late into the night. Angie hadn't really given it much thought, but there was a great deal of computer work involved in running a ranch.

Each night, they built a fire in the six-foot-high fireplace in what he called the game room. They'd plan to play pool or

watch a movie, but before the fire burned low they always decided to cuddle on the couch and talk. Slowly, piece by piece,
they learned each other's lives. Tenderly, one caress at a time,
they learned each other's body.

Every night, when he kissed her one last time outside her
room, she knew she fell a little more in love with Wilkes Wagner.

Finally, they stopped thinking up reasons for her not going
back to her cabin and just enjoyed being together. The talks
and dinners and rides across the land at sunset were nice, but
Wilkes's good-night kisses were addictive.

They might have gone further, but Uncle Vern's cold dragged
on until both Angie and Wilkes figured out that he thought
he was acting as chaperone. His bedroom, in the main house,
was in the middle of the long hall and his door tended to swing
open if he heard a sound.

Angie thought it was cute. Wilkes mumbled that maybe it
was time for Uncle Vern to move to the retirement home or at
least back to his place.

Thanksgiving was only a week away and Wilkes had decided,
since Angie could cook, they should invite all their friends who
didn't have families. They spent the weekend planning and re-
organizing his house.

Angie walked into her office at the museum the Monday
morning before Thanksgiving thinking about the groceries she
needed to buy. The moment she saw the message light blinking
on her phone, she paused.

Probably nothing, she almost said aloud. But the old fear crawled
up her spine. She must have told Wilkes a hundred times she
was all right. She told herself that the reason she stayed with
Wilkes was because she loved being with him, but deep down
she knew she was also a coward. She was afraid to go back to
her little cabin on the lake.

Slowly, she sat down and lifted the phone. When she pushed

the message button, a familiar voice from the county clerk's office made her let out a long-held breath.

"Call me back as soon as you can" was all Carol said.

Angie returned the call.

"I've got the paperwork, Angie. You want me to run it over to you?" Carol had a twang in her voice that was pure West Texas. "Yancy is going to be excited."

"No, I'll pick it up on my way to the café. I'm meeting him and Wilkes for lunch."

Three hours later Angie rushed down the stairs of the museum. As she knew he would be, Vern Wagner sat at the front desk entertaining the volunteers. He came to work with her a few days a week, acting as bodyguard, he said, but in truth she knew he just loved visiting.

"Hi, little darling." He grinned. The ladies had made him an official badge. "How can I help you?"

She smiled. "Can I borrow your pickup so I can meet Wilkes for lunch? I'd ask you to go with me, but someone needs to be on guard while I'm gone."

Vern handed her his keys. "Since I've had two of Millie's rolls this morning and one of Sandy's scones, I'm thinking I might go take a nap in your office while you're gone. I might need to build up my strength before the afternoon goodies arrive."

"The door is open now, but you might want to close it if you nap. I think a group of O'Gradys are coming in to work on their family tree. A band of their children think the upstairs is a playground."

"I'll do that." He winked at her.

Angie pulled on her coat and started out. Before she closed the front door she heard Vern telling the ladies how Angie fussed over him.

As she hurried down the steps, she saw several carloads of O'Gradys climbing out of their cars. It should be an interesting afternoon. They'd brought the preschool kids along.

Angie maneuvered around the children and climbed into

Vern's old truck. It started on the first try and purred as she drove to the county office, picked up an envelope and rushed into Dorothy's café.

Wilkes and Yancy both stood as she blew in. She loved the way Wilkes's face lit up when he saw her. His arm moved around her as if he couldn't wait to touch her. It seemed impossible to her, but she'd become his addiction, too.

"I've got something for Yancy," she said as she slipped into the booth.

They waited until the waitress took the order, then Angie passed Yancy the envelope. "It took a little digging but we found this."

Yancy looked interested, but not excited. He pulled an old black-and-white picture and held it up. At the bottom someone had written: *Home of Adam Stanley.*

"That's what the old house you say calls to you looked like in 1944."

Yancy studied it. "Place looks nice. Must have been white at one time with shutters and a long porch. Look, the trees were once all in a line, not overgrown like they are now."

"I think that's a garden out back and, look, they had a chicken coop." Angie leaned over the table pointing out details. "It was just a normal house then, nothing evil."

Yancy reached for the other piece of paper in the envelope. "What's this?"

"It's your birth certificate." Angie fought to keep her excitement from exploding.

Yancy stared at the paper, his eyes wide. "This couldn't be right. It's got my birthday, but my mom always said I didn't have a middle name. It says here I'm Yancy Adam Grey."

Wilkes looked at the certificate. "Footprint is way too small, too."

Angie hit his arm and they all laughed.

"Yancy, look down and read who the mother was."

"Jewel Ann Grey."

"And the father," Angie said.

"Galen Yancy Stanley."

No one at the table moved. Finally, Angie whispered, "Your grandmother Stanley lived in that house for twenty years before she died. She left what money she had in the bank to pay the taxes." Angie let him digest her words, then she added, "She left the house to you, Yancy."

"Mom said she lived in Crossroads when she was just a kid. I thought she meant little kid, but it must have been until the year I was born. She said she hated it. She never mentioned that she lived with my father's mother."

Wilkes was figuring out the gaps. "Granny Stanley knew your name. She thought her son was dead, so who else would she have left the house to?"

Yancy shook his head. "Are you saying I own that old falling-down house?"

"Yes," Angie said. "The house and the five acres around it."

Yancy stood, leaving the photo and birth certificate on the table. He pulled on his work coat and hat.

"Where you going?" Wilkes asked.

"To have a look at my land," Yancy said as he walked out. "I'll be back for lunch."

Wilkes hugged Angie close. "I don't know how you did all this research, but I wanna tell you right now how great you are."

She laughed. "I think Yancy's in shock. Maybe I should have broken it to him a little at a time. He has his father's middle name and his great-grandfather's first name. The house is his."

"He'll be all right," Wilkes said. "For a man who owns nothing to suddenly find out he has land must be a lot to take in."

"Until he hears the rest," she added.

Wilkes pushed a curl away from her forehead and asked, "What rest?"

"Even with the taxes coming out every year, Granny's account still has over two hundred thousand dollars in it."

CHAPTER THIRTY-FOUR

Wilkes

Wilkes got up to pay Dorothy for his and Angie's lunch. Yancy had returned but hadn't stopped asking questions long enough to eat. He asked Angie the same questions over and over as if he couldn't quite get his brain around the facts. Had he really been named after his father and great-grandfather? Was the house really his? When could he start working on it?

Wilkes's phone beeped and he picked up as the waitress handed him his change.

"Hello, Sheriff," Wilkes said. "Have I got some news..."

Dan didn't let him finish. "I'm headed to the museum, Wilkes. Is there any way you could leave Angie with Yancy and meet me there as soon as possible? We've got an emergency on our hands."

"I'm on my way." Wilkes didn't have to ask, he knew there was big trouble. He also didn't bother to ask how Dan knew he was with Angie and Yancy. The sheriff could see the café from his window.

Wilkes walked slowly over to the booth and leaned in between Angie and Yancy's conversations. "Angie, if you'll stay here, I have to run an errand. I want to hear all about the plans when I get back, so don't you two go anywhere."

They both nodded and went back to their plans of what Yancy should do next.

Wilkes took off for the museum.

When he walked in, all the little volunteers looked upset.

"Your uncle's in the kitchen," one said. "The sheriff's with him."

Another little lady pointed. "Just follow the blood."

Wilkes ran to the back area. What if Vern had fallen or had a stroke or... Wilkes couldn't breathe. He'd thought it was a great idea to have Vern come up here a few days a week. The old guy needed some rest. But obviously Wilkes needed to re-think his plan.

As he opened the door, he saw Vern sitting in a chair, his head back, a bloody hand towel across his face.

"What happened?" Wilkes rushed forward.

"I don't know. I only beat you by three minutes," Dan snapped. "You're uncle isn't talking."

Vern waved his hand as if pushing them away. He lowered the towel and looked at them with bloodshot eyes.

Wilkes saw the bruise on his cheek and the blood still drip-ping from his nose.

"I'm all right, boys, don't fuss over me. I had to come in here to keep the ladies from smothering me." Vern dabbed at his nose. "I think the bastard must have broke my nose. Double damn. I'm not ready to lose my good looks."

Wilkes relaxed. If Uncle Vern was cussing and fussing, he wasn't too hurt. "Tell me what happened. And this better not involve a fight with any of the O'Gradys, Uncle Vern."

"No, it ain't the O'Gradys. Half the ones I used to fight with are dead and the two still living can't hear nothing even if I did insult them."

"Mr. Wagner," the sheriff said. "Start at the beginning and tell us what happened. Who hit you?"

"One question at a time," Vern complained as he dabbed his nose along the towel, making red circles.

Wilkes and Dan waited.

Finally, Vern stopped dabbing. "I was up in Angie's office taking a little nap. I'd turned her chair around and propped my feet up on her file cabinet." He looked at them both as if expecting them to say something. "I've done it before."

"Go on." Dan frowned.

"Well, I thought I heard the door, but I wasn't sure. I didn't turn the chair around for a minute, then I heard movement over near the safe. Ain't nothing of value in it, so I wasn't thinking a robber might be sneaking up on me.

"When I swiveled around, one of my legs slipped off the cabinet and hit the floor. This stranger dressed in a suit and looking like someone hit him with a fence post jumped me. Before I knew what was happening he had his hands around my throat demanding I tell him where some necklace was."

Wilkes glanced at Dan and knew they were both thinking the same thing.

Vern didn't notice. He went back to dabbing.

"What happened next?" Wilkes shouted.

Vern frowned. "What do you think, son? Ain't nobody man enough to put his hands on me. I jumped up ready for a fight and told him I didn't know where his necklace was.

"He hit me when I wasn't looking and probably broke my nose. Then he shoved me back in the chair and said he wanted Angela's necklace. Before I could fight, he pulled a gun and I decided I'd be wise to sit still. I probably could have taken him but only a fool fights a man with a gun."

Wilkes began to pace. "You're lucky to be alive. What happened next?"

"Well, I'd seen Angie wear an old coin necklace once or twice and I'd noticed it was on a shelf in that open safe in her office. So I told the guy where it was."

"You what?"

"You hard of hearing, boy? I said I told him where it was."

"You let someone get away with stealing her necklace." Wilkes was thankful that Vern was alive but just letting a thief walk off with something didn't seem like Vern's style.

"Yep. He's got it. I'd bet it's in his hand right now."

Dan picked up his cell. "Do you know what kind of car he's driving? What way he went when he left the parking lot?"

"Nope," Vern said. "Didn't see his car and he didn't leave the parking lot."

"Where is he?" Dan lowered the phone.

"I'm not sure, but when I left Angie's office he was in the safe. When he stepped in to grab her jewelry," he said proudly, "I simply closed the door and turned the dial!"

CHAPTER THIRTY-FIVE

Wilkes

A light snow danced in the wind as Wilkes stared out the kitchen window of his home. He loved his land. It had taken him six years to figure out he was living right where he wanted to live for the rest of his life. Though his parents had signed the deed to the Devil's Fork over to him, he knew he wasn't the owner but the caretaker of this slice of Texas. For as long as he lived, he'd take care of it so that someday he could pass it down to his kids.

"Wilkes," Uncle Vern yelled from the dining room. "Where's the gravy?"

Wilkes reached for the gravy bowl and walked into what had been his game room a few weeks ago. The big-screen TV was gone. The pool table. The leather couch and chair had been better suited to one of the bedrooms that Angie now called the media room. The big room now had a long dining table that could seat a dozen.

Change was happening. The house was turning into a home. He took a deep breath thinking that he'd missed the smell of home cooking all his life.

He looked to the other end of the table and saw Angie laughing with Lauren and her roommate home for Thanksgiving.

Angie had done a great job of putting this all together. The meal, the friends, even the flowers on the table. And strangely enough everything she moved or tossed out Uncle Vern followed right behind saying he'd thought that needed to happen.

The loneliness that had settled in Wilkes's soul years ago was gone now. The friends had always been there. He just hadn't appreciated them, as he hadn't seen the beauty of the land until he showed it to Angie.

"So," Lauren was saying to Angie, "you had the real necklace all along?"

"Right, and my uncle didn't even know it." Angie laughed, touching the Greek coin set in diamonds around her neck. "It seems he wanted me to come back home and put the money my father transferred over to me the night he died into the business account. Only, one of the men who worked for him discovered the necklace on display was a fake. He decided I must have had it, so he came after me."

"And that was the man who kidnapped me?" Polly giggled. "I made a lasting dent in him."

Vern patted her hand. "Don't you worry, little darling, I took care of him. When I finished beating him up, I tossed him in the safe at the museum. By the time we got him out he was so desperate for fresh air, he confessed to everything."

"Are you going to keep the necklace or sell it?" Lauren asked as everyone began passing the bowls and platters around for second helpings.

"I think I'll pass it down to my children." Angie smiled.

The conversation turned to other things, but Wilkes couldn't take his eyes off Angie. He was still staring at her when they walked down the hallway to her room hours later.

"You know, it took me a while, but I've discovered something."

"What's that?" She giggled, always excited when he was close enough to kiss her.

"All my life I thought there was one type of woman I was attracted to, but I was wrong. There is only one woman I'm interested in. She's not my type, but she's the one. The only one I'll never get enough of touching." He moved closer and leaned down, loving the way she came so easy into his arms now.

His hands moved over her body, craving the feel of her. Loving the way she reacted every time to his touch.

"Angie, we need to give some thought to who you're going to pass that necklace down to. A daughter, or a son."

She kissed him for a while and then whispered, "That's not something I have to think about tonight, Wilkes."

He moved the fingers of one hand through her soft hair. "I was thinking we could get started on the plan tonight, but you've got to answer one question first." His hand moved up from her waist to just below her breast. He knew she'd let out a little sigh and open her mouth just wide enough to welcome one long kiss.

Over the weeks he'd learned her well. The kiss would grow deeper when he covered her breast, then she'd melt into him.

When he finally broke the kiss, he pushed her against her bedroom door with his body, loving the feel of her rapid breathing and the way she closed her eyes and smiled. He lowered his mouth to her throat while she whispered how she loved the feel of him.

As he pulled her blouse open so he could continue down her throat, he whispered, "Answer my one question, Angie."

"What question?" She giggled.

"If we have this talk on which we'll have first, a boy or a girl, you have to promise to marry me come morning. I don't ever want to think there is any chance you might disappear again." He shoved the lace of her bra aside as he kept raining light kisses. "I think we should start on getting at least one baby on the way."

"I'm not going anywhere, Wilkes. I'm home. I think I knew that the first night Doc and I moved in."

He loved the way her skin grew warm where he'd kissed. He loved this woman beyond reason. "If you're home, open the door and invite me in."

He moved a step back and studied her. Her hair was a mess. Her blouse open almost to her waist. Her face flushed. And her big eyes had a longing for him that almost drove him mad. "If you open your bedroom door, there will be no going back, no halfway. You'll be silently saying you are running full out toward me and I'll never let you go."

She turned the knob.

———

CHAPTER THIRTY-SIX

Angie

Dawn drifted through the window. Angie lay perfectly still beside Wilkes. He needed sleep and she needed to relive every moment of their first night together. All her dreams could never measure up.

When she finally shifted to see his face, she found him smiling at her.

"Morning," he said. "Today is our wedding day. You're marrying me. That was the deal if you opened that door."

Giggling, she whispered back, "We've already started out the honeymoon. Do you think we made a son or daughter last night, or maybe early this morning?"

He pulled her body against his. "I doubt it. We'll have to keep trying, and trying and trying." His hand moved along her body and she knew his hunger for her grew once more.

"It's almost time to get up."

He kissed her cheek. "Almost is enough time." He gently pushed her against the pillows just as they heard Uncle Vern shouting from the barn.

In a flurry of flying clothes they dressed as they rushed down the hallway. Wilkes grabbed her hand as they ran to the barn thinking the old cowboy might have fallen or hurt himself or finally had one of his horses kick him in the head.

Vern was on the floor of the barn, kneeling low in a corner. Wilkes couldn't tell if he was laughing or crying.

"What is it?" Wilkes slid down beside the old man.

"Are you hurt?" Angie asked.

"Look." Vern laughed. "Doc Holliday just had kittens. Ain't that something."

Wilkes lifted Angie in his arms and headed back to the house. "Don't bother us again, Uncle Vern. I don't want to hear you or see you until noon and then you'd better be in your best clothes."

"Am I getting married?" Vern yelled.

"No, I am. In case you didn't notice, I love this woman and I've talked her into hanging around."

"Oh, I noticed, son," Vern crowed. "Ain't a person for a hundred miles around who hasn't." He lowered his voice. "No surprise there, but what I can't understand is why she'd pick you when I'm still available."

★ ★ ★ ★ ★

Want more of the dramatic
RANSOM CANYON *series?*
Turn the page for a sneak peek at Jodi Thomas's
LONE HEART PASS

CHAPTER ONE

Washington, DC
November

The Georgetown street outside Jubalee Hamilton's office looked more like a river of mud than a beautiful old brick lane.

"Why does it always have to rain on Election Day?" she said to the life-size cutout of her candidate.

The few volunteers left in the campaign office were cleaning out their desks. The polls hadn't been closed an hour, and Jubalee's horse-in-the-race had already been declared the loser.

Or maybe she was the loser. Two months ago her live-in boyfriend, the man she'd thought she'd someday settle down with and have the requisite 2.5 kids, had said goodbye. David had called her a self-absorbed workaholic. When she'd denied it, he'd asked one question. "When's my birthday, J?"

She folded her arms as if to say she wasn't playing games. But this time her normally mild-mannered lover didn't back down.

"Well?" He stared at her with a heartbroken gaze.

When she didn't answer, David asked again. "We've been together three years. When is my birthday?"

"February 19," she guessed, knowing in her gut his assessment of her was right.

"Not even close." David picked up his briefcase and walked out. "I'll get my things after the election is over. You won't have time to open the door for me before then."

Jubalee didn't have time to miss him, either. She worked so many hours on the election she'd started sleeping at the office every other night. Sometime in the weeks that followed, David had dropped by the apartment and packed both their things. She'd walked in on a mountain of boxes marked with *J*'s and *D*'s. All she remembered thinking at the time was that she was glad he'd left her clean clothes still hanging in the closet.

A few days later the boxes marked *D* were gone and one apartment key lay on the counter. There was no time to miss him or his boxes.

Jubalee considered crying, but she didn't bother. Boyfriends had vanished before. Three in college, one before David while she lived in Washington, DC. She'd have time for lovers later. Right now, at twenty-six, she needed to build her career. Work was her life. Men were simply extras she could live with or without. She barely noticed the mail piling up or the notice on the door telling her she had six weeks before she had to vacate the premises.

Then the rain came. The election was over. Her candidate had lost. She'd lost. No job would be waiting for her at dawn. No David standing in the door of their apartment this time, ready to comfort her.

Her third loss as a campaign manager. *Three strikes*, she thought, *and you're out.*

She walked through the rain alone, not caring that she was soaked. She'd given her all this time and she'd ended up with nothing. The candidate who she'd fought so hard for hadn't even bothered to phone her when it was over.

She unlocked the door to her apartment, which now looked more like a storage unit than a home. She flicked the switch and wasn't surprised the lights wouldn't come on. David had always taken care of minor things like paying the bills.

She sat down on one of the packing boxes and pulled out her phone before she realized she had no one to call. No friends. No school buddies she'd kept up with. All the numbers in her contacts were business-related except the three for her family. She scrolled down to the Hamiltons.

First number, her parents. They hadn't spoken to her since she'd missed her sister's wedding. Jubalee shrugged. Really, how important is a bridesmaid?

Destiny's wedding was beautiful anyway. Jubalee had seen the pictures on Facebook. One missing too tall, too thin sister would only have upset Destiny's perfect wedding photos.

She moved down the list. Destiny. Her sister, six years older, always prettier, always smarter, had never liked having her around.

Memories of her childhood ran through her mind like flash cards—Destiny cutting off all Jubalee's hair when she was three. Telling Jubalee she was adopted when she was five. Leaving her at the park after dark when she was seven. Slashing her bike tires when she was ten so she couldn't tag along after her big sister. *Oh, yeah,* Jubalee thought, *don't forget about telling me I was dying when I got my first period.* The whole family still laughed about her writing out her will at twelve. If big sisters were measured on a scale of one to ten, Destiny would be double digits in the negative.

No, she decided, there was no need to talk to Destiny whatever-her-last-name-was-now.

She moved down to the next Hamilton on her contact list. Levy Hamilton, her great-grandfather. She'd lived with him the summer she'd been eleven, when her parents had gone to tour college options with Destiny. They'd all waved as they'd dropped her off at Lone Heart Pass ranch with smiles as if they'd left a bothersome pet at the pound.

Two weeks later they'd called to say they couldn't make the

trip back to Texas to get her because of car trouble. A week after that there was another college to consider. Then her father wanted to wait until he had a few days off so the trip from Kansas back to Texas wouldn't be so hard on the family.

Jubalee had missed the first two weeks of school before they made it back, and she hadn't cared. She would have stayed on the ranch with Grandpa Levy forever.

Grandpa Levy was ornery and old. Even as an eleven-year-old she could tell her parents didn't like him or the worthless dry-land farm he'd lived on since birth. Levy talked with his mouth full, cussed even more than Methodists allow, bathed only once a week and complained about everything but Jubalee.

Her parents barely took the time to turn off the engine when they finally picked her up. The old man didn't hug her good-bye, but his leathered hand pressed into her shoulder as if he couldn't bear to let her go. That meant more to her than anything he could have said.

She never told anyone how wonderful Grandpa Levy had been to her. He gave her a horse, taught her to ride, and all summer she was right by his side. Collecting eggs, birthing calves, cutting hay. For the first time in her life, no one told her she was doing everything wrong.

Jubalee stared at his phone number. She hadn't talked to him since Christmas, when the moment she'd heard his raspy voice, she'd felt like the eleven-year-old again, giggling and telling him things he probably cared nothing about. Her great-grandfather had listened and answered each rant she went through with comments like, "You'll figure it out, kid. God didn't give you all those brains for nothing."

She wanted to talk to him now. She needed to say she hadn't figured anything out.

Jubalee pushed the number and listened to it ring. She could imagine the old house phone on the wall between his kitchen and living room ringing through empty bedrooms and hallways that always smelled dusty. He lived in the two rooms off the kitchen and left the other rooms to sleep, he claimed.

"Answer," she whispered, needing to know that someone was out there. Right now, tonight, she could almost believe she was the only one left alive. "Answer, Grandpa."

Finally, after twenty rings, she hung up. The old guy didn't have an answering machine and he'd probably never heard of a cell phone. Maybe he was in the barn or over at the corral where the cowhands who worked for him lived from spring to fall. Maybe he'd driven the dirt road for his once-a-month trip to town. If so, he'd be having dinner at the little café in Crossroads.

With the streetlight's glow from the window, she crossed to the fireplace and lit the logs. Strange how after more than a dozen years since that summer, she still missed him when she'd never missed anyone else.

The paper-wrapped logs caught fire, and the flames danced off the boxes and blank walls of her life. She found a half bottle of wine in the warm fridge and a bag of Halloween candy she hadn't been home to hand out. Curled up by the fire, she began to sort through the pile of mail that had collected on her kitchen counter. Most of the time she would toss an envelope in the fire without opening it. Take-out menus. Sale flyers. Catalogs filled with stuff she didn't need or want.

One by one they tumbled into the fire along with every hope and dream she'd had about a career as a campaign manager.

In the last stack of mail, a large white envelope hand-addressed to her caught her attention. The postmark was over a month ago. Surely it wasn't something important or someone would have called her.

Slowly, she opened the envelope.

Tears silently streaked down her face as she took in the lawyer's letterhead at the top of the page. She began to read Levy Hamilton's will. Word by word. Aloud. Making herself feel truth's pain.

On the last page was a note scribbled on a lawyer's office stationery.

Miss Hamilton,

We regret to inform you of Levy Hamilton's passing. As we were unable to reach his next of kin, I followed his request and had him buried on his land. When he named you his sole heir of Lone Heart Pass, he told me you'd figure out what to do with the old place. Please contact my office when you get here.

Jubalee turned over the envelope. It was postmarked two months ago and had been forwarded twice before reaching her.

She laid the will aside and cried for the one person who'd ever really loved her. The one person she'd ever loved.

After the fire burned low and shadows danced as if circling the last bit of light, she thought she felt Levy's hand resting on her shoulder. His knotted fingers didn't seem ready to let her go.

At dawn she packed the last of her clothes, called a storage company to pick up the boxes and walked away from her life in DC with one suitcase and her empty briefcase.

She'd go home over the holidays. She'd try to find the pieces of her life and see if she could glue them back together. But together or not, she'd start over where the wind never stopped blowing, and dust came as a side dish at every meal. She may have lived there only a few months, but Lone Heart Pass might be the only place where she'd feel at home.

She'd start again.

She'd rebuild from scratch.

She'd go to Texas.

CHAPTER TWO

Crossroads, Texas
February

"Set 'em up, Charley. We'll have another round." The kid on the other side of the bar was barely old enough to drink, but his laugh was loud and demanding. "It's Valentine's Day and none of us have a date. That's something to get drunk over."

Charley Collins swore under his breath. The drunks had had enough, but he'd be fired if he didn't serve the college boys, and he couldn't afford to lose their business.

"Aren't you Reid Collins's brother?" the only one of the boys who could still form a sentence without drooling asked. "You look like him. Taller, maybe a little older. Got that same reddish-brown hair he's got. Red River mud color if you ask me."

Before Charley could say anything, another drunk shook his head wildly. "No brother of Reid would be a bartender." He burped. "Collinses are rich. Deep-pocket rich. They own more land than a cowboy can ride across in a day."

Charley moved down the bar, hoping to slip out of being the topic of conversation. He hated the way they'd been talk-

ing about women all night, but that was better than listening
to a conversation about him.

The sober one continued just loud enough for Charley to hear.

"I heard Reid had a big brother a couple of years older than
him. Papa Collins disowned his oldest son. I remember Reid
saying his dad had an armed guard escort his brother off the
ranch like he was some kind of criminal. Collins told his own
son that if he ever set foot on the land again, he'd have him shot
for trespassing."

Charley picked up the box of beer bottles and headed outside.
He'd heard enough. He needed air.

It took several steps before the noise and smell of the bar
cleared, but he walked all the way to the alley. He set the bottles down by the trash and stared at the open land behind the
Two Step Bar as he took a deep breath. He needed clean air and
space and silence. He was born for open country, and he had no
idea how he'd survive working in a beer joint and living above
it in a tiny two-room apartment.

Every time he swore things couldn't get worse, they did.

Staring at the full moon, he felt like cussing or drinking his
trouble away, but neither option was open. He couldn't quit and
he couldn't run. Not without a stake to start over somewhere
else. Charley had a feeling that *somewhere else* wouldn't fit him
anyway. This part of Texas was in his blood. He belonged here
even if it did seem half the people for a hundred miles around
were trying to run him out.

Like a miner taking one last breath before climbing back down
the hole, Charley filled his lungs and turned around.

He saw a woman in the shadows near the back door. She was
tall and perfectly built, even in silhouette. Long dark hair circled around her in the breeze. For a moment he hoped she was
a ghost. Lately he'd been a lot less afraid of spirits than women.

As he got closer, he could make out her face, not that he
needed more than the outline of her body to know who she
was. "Hello, Lexie. You miss the turnoff to the ladies' room?"

Her laugh was low and sexy. She had to be several years older than him, but nothing about Lexie had changed from the beauty queen she'd been in high school. He'd seen her come in an hour ago with some guy in a business suit and fancy boots.

"I followed you, Charley." She waited like a spider waits for a fly to land on the web. "Anyone ever tell you you're one hell of a handsome man? I was trying to concentrate on my new husband, but all I could do was stare at you. You got that mixture of Prince Charming and bad boy down pat. I can tell how good a man is in bed just by the way he moves and, honey, you are walking sex appeal."

Charley thought about arguing. She must be blind. He was two months past due for a haircut, four days late on shaving, and he'd slept in the jeans and T-shirt he had on for the past two nights.

"Yeah, I've heard that line before," he answered her question. "My last stepmother told me how irresistible I was about an hour before my father disowned me."

Lexie moved closer. "Must have been one wild hour."

He wasn't about to go into detail. Half the town probably already knew the story. He'd been screwing up his life since high school. Bulls had more sense than he did when it came to sex.

"What time do you get off, Charley? We could have some fun after midnight. My sweetie has to head back to Dallas in a few minutes."

"Thanks for the offer, but I'm not interested." He unwound himself from her arm.

He almost ran through the open door, forcing himself back into the noise and the smells as if they were a lesser kind of hell than what she was offering.

A few hours later, the bar was quiet and all the drunks were gone. He washed the last of the shot glasses and headed upstairs, nodding good-night to the bar owner, Ike Perez, as he passed.

"Tell Daniela to hurry on down. I don't want to wait on her." Perez sounded gruffer than he really was. In truth he'd been one of the few in town to even give Charley a chance. He had lots of one-day part-time seasonal jobs, but he needed something regular. This job came with low pay for weekend work and a place to live.

Charley tapped on his own apartment door. Twelve-year-old Daniela Perez, rubbing her eyes, pulled the door open. "I know," she mumbled. "Papa is ready to go."

"My little princess asleep?" Charley asked. Daniela was young, but she made a good babysitter.

"Yeah. I got a new strategy." Daniela giggled. "I let her watch TV until she nods off. Otherwise she never stops talking. That kid has an imagination that won't quit."

Charley handed Daniela her backpack. "Thanks." He passed her a ten, half his tips money for the night.

"No problem. I'd rather be here than home alone." She clomped down the stairs as he closed the door. "Good night, Mr. Collins. See you next weekend."

Charley tugged off his boots and tiptoed into the bedroom. A tiny night-light lit the room just enough for him to see the bump in the bed. Carefully, he sat down beside Lillie and pulled his daughter's small body close, loving the smell of her. Loving the soft feel of her hair.

"Good night, pumpkin," he whispered. "I love you to the end of forever."

Lillie stretched sleepily as her arm circled his neck. "I love you, too, Daddy."

He rocked her small body until he knew she was fully asleep, then moved into the living room. Taking the blanket and pillow from behind the couch, he tried to make his long legs fit into the small space.

He smiled into the silence. Lillie was his only blessing in a life full of mistakes. His father had been furious when Charley had gotten his college girlfriend pregnant. Eventually, Davis Collins had gone along with them getting married and given Charley a small allowance, but he'd never invited Sharon or Lillie to the ranch. Collins had never even seen his only grandchild.

Then, a year after Lillie was born, Sharon left Charley, claiming motherhood wasn't her thing. Charley had another fight with his dad when Davis found out Charley planned to keep the baby. He refused to increase Charley's allowance to cover child care, so Charley worked thirty hours a week and carried a full course load. Sharon's parents agreed to look after Lillie on Charley's rare visits to his father's ranch. Davis wanted no part of the youngest family member to carry the Collins name.

Charley survived almost two years taking care of Lillie alone... almost to graduation, when he'd have his degree and could forget about any family but Lillie. He'd thought his father would turn over the ranch to him and move to Dallas permanently. Maybe Davis would even eventually accept Lillie.

Then Charley messed up again. Big-time. Funny, looking back he'd had no thought of sleeping with his father's very young, very attractive fourth wife until she walked into his room and his brain shut down.

At first he thought his father would cool down. After all, Davis bragged all the time about sleeping with other men's wives. Even after his dad kicked him off the ranch, Charley thought he'd go back to school and finish his last semester. But no money came in for rent or tuition. His car was repossessed. He took incompletes in his courses, planning to return to college as soon as he got on his feet. But there was Lillie to take care of and a kid couldn't live in the back of an old pickup and grow up on fast food.

He had finally given up trying to survive and stay in school. He'd borrowed enough to buy an old pickup and made it back to Crossroads. Now Lillie was five and he was no closer to finishing school. No closer to getting his life in order.

He'd sworn off women forever. He'd probably never live down what he'd done. Not in this town. Only he lived with the shame and got up every morning and did the same jobs he hated because of Lillie.

That first year after Sharon left she'd cried for her mother. Charley made up his mind that she'd never cry for him and vowed no matter what mistakes in life she made, she'd never stop being his daughter.

In the stillness of his little apartment over the bar, Charley counted the jobs he had lined up for the next week. Cowboying on two ranches for one day each, hauling for the hardware store on Wednesday, stocking at the grocery any morning he could.

His ex-wife's parents, Ted and Emily, helped when they could. They'd take Lillie to preschool on the mornings he had to leave before dawn, and pick her up on the days he didn't get off work early enough. But every night, Charley wanted to be the one to tuck her in.

Sharon's folks were kind people. She'd apparently abandoned them as well when she'd left Lillie. They hadn't heard from her in over a year and that had been only a postcard saying she was moving to LA. The old couple didn't have much, but they were good to Lillie. Some days he thought the kid was their only sunshine.

He smiled as he drifted to sleep. He had a very special standing date come morning. Saturdays he made pancakes with Lillie and then they'd saddle up her pony and his quarter horse and ride down into Ransom Canyon while the air was still cold and the day was newborn. They'd ride and talk and laugh. He'd tell her stories his grandfather had told him about the early days when longhorn cattle and wild mustangs ran across the land.

When they stopped to rest, she'd beg him for real stories. Her favorite was all about the great buffalo herds and how, when they stampeded, they'd shake the ground.

She'd giggle when she put her hand on the earth and swear she could feel the herd headed toward them.

Charley would laugh with her and, just for a moment, he'd feel like the richest man alive.